Dec 2020

D0463682

THE PERFECT DAUGHTER

Books by Joseph Souza

THE NEIGHBOR

PRAY FOR THE GIRL

THE PERFECT DAUGHTER

Published by Kensington Publishing Corporation

THE PERFECT DAUGHTER

JOSEPH SOUZA

KENSINGTON BOOKS
www.kensingtonbooks.com

KENSINGTON BOOKS are published by

Kensington Publishing Corp.
119 West 40th Street
New York, NY 10018

All Kensington titles, imprints, and distributed lines are available at special quantity discounts for bulk purchases for sales promotion, premiums, fund-raising, educational, or institutional use. Special book excerpts or cus-tomized printings can also be created to fit specific needs. For details, write or phone the office of the Kensington Special Sales Manager: Attn. Special Sales Department. Kensington Publishing Corp, 119 West 40th Street, New York, NY 10018. Phone: 1-800-221-2647.

Library of Congress Card Catalogue Number: 2019953626

Kensington and the K logo Reg. U.S. Pat. & TM Off.

ISBN-13: 978-1-4967-2638-4
ISBN-10: 1-4967-2638-3
First Kensington Hardcover Edition: May 2020

ISBN-13: 978-1-4967-2640-7 (ebook)
ISBN-10: 1-4967-2640-5 (ebook)

10 9 8 7 6 5 4 3 2 1

Printed in the United States of America

To Ciara Noelle and Teddy Bear

PART ONE

ISLA

S HE SHOT UP OFF THE MATTRESS, HER FACE BATHED IN A SHEEN OF sweat. Had she just heard something? Or had she suffered another bad dream? She'd been having a lot of them lately, ever since that rich boy from Harper's Point vanished without a trace. No, something seemed not quite right. She glanced across the bed, registering Ray's absence. It was just like him to disappear when she needed him most.

The alarm clock on her nightstand flashed 3:32 in red digits. She turned toward the large bay window, which Ray had installed last year, despite having no funds to do so. A wonder the bank had even loaned them the money. And yet it really opened the room up and provided them with a beautiful view of the bay and the ocean far below.

She remained perfectly still. Then she heard it again. A loud crashing noise downstairs. Someone appeared to be mucking about in her kitchen. A jolt of adrenaline spiked through her. She flung off the well-worn quilt, the same quilt her mother had made as a wedding present for them so many years ago. Her mother, God bless her soul, had been one of those quilt-obsessed women who the older she got, the more fanatical about quilts she became.

She walked over to the bay window and noticed that Ray's beat-up truck was not parked in its usual spot. Not like he hadn't disappeared from their bed before, often in the middle of the night. She'd gotten used to waking up and not seeing his long, wiry body next to hers.

Another loud smashing noise came from downstairs.

Terror gripped her as she quietly opened the bottom dresser drawer. Reaching down, she punched the four-digit combination into the electronic keypad on the safe and waited a few seconds. The door to the safe opened and revealed the loaded Glock. The sight of the gun scared her, but she was now glad to have it. She picked it up and let its weight settle in the palm of her hand. Then she pulled out her phone and dialed the Shepherd's Bay Police Department instead of 911, knowing that all 911 calls were directed to a regional dispatcher twenty miles away, and they didn't know their ass from their elbow about the street patterns in this town. Karl Bjornson answered. She'd known that voice since they were high school sweethearts.

"Someone's in my house, Karl," she whispered. "Hurry up and send someone over."

"You sure it's not the wind? It's been blowing pretty hard tonight, and you have all those trees around your property."

"I know what I'm hearing. The noise is coming from inside my house. Besides, I think I know the sound of wind blowing through the trees." Something else crashed downstairs and jolted her to the reality of the situation.

"Where's Swisher?" Swisher had been Ray's nickname since childhood.

"How the hell should I know? Just send someone—and fast."

"Okay, Isla. Take it easy. I'll be right over."

Holding the gun aloft, Isla tiptoed to the doorway, trying to be as quiet as possible. Her two kids lay asleep in their rooms, hopefully unaware that an intruder was rummaging through their house. She cinched her robe so as not to trip over it and made her way downstairs. Her face grimaced in agony every time one of the worn floorboards creaked underfoot, and she prayed the intruder in her kitchen wouldn't hear her approaching. She gripped the Glock in hand once she reached the landing.

Her heartbeat raced as she leaned against the kitchen doorframe. She took a few deep breaths, psyching herself up, grateful that she'd always been a light sleeper. Would she have the nerve to shoot the bastard if it came to that? Yes, she realized, she would.

Hopefully, the mere sight of her would scare the person away. Besides, her house held nothing of value.

Still gripping the gun with two hands, she held it up by her chin so that the barrel pointed toward the ceiling. Her hands trembled at the prospect of shooting another human being. From the sounds of it, the intruder seemed perfectly fine rummaging around in her kitchen. But what were they looking for? She counted down from three, took a couple of deep breaths, and then jumped out, pointing the weapon.

What she saw surprised her.

KARL

ALTHOUGH THE NIGHT SHIFT MEANT EASY MONEY, KARL BJORNSON never liked the crazy hours or the way it wreaked havoc on his body. It threw off his schedule for days to come. But since he had a daughter in college, he couldn't afford to turn down any overtime shifts offered to him. Not like he had much of a choice. The Shepherd's Bay Police Department employed only five full-time officers, one of them being the chief, and Harry rarely worked overnight unless absolutely necessary. Steve Needham had called in sick earlier with the flu, and none of the other officers could fill in on such short notice.

He was pouring his third cup of station coffee when the call came in from Isla Eaves. It had never made any sense for the station to keep a drip coffeemaker when they could have owned one of those fancy new machines where all you did was insert the plastic cup of your choice, press POWER, and voilà!

He donned his cap and headed out with coffee in hand. Normally, he would have welcomed a call at 3:33 a.m. But not this one. Not from Isla Eaves. And especially not when he'd been working to find that missing rich kid, Dakota James, by marking up all the areas on the town map that had not yet been searched. It puzzled him how a kid could practically disappear into thin air, especially a kid from such a wealthy part of town.

A warm breeze stirred as he headed out to his car. It was late June, and summer was in full swing. The older he got, the more he hated summers in Shepherd's Bay. Not the weather, per se, but how this Maine town had transformed into something completely different from what it used to be. There had always been the swell of the summer crowd, monied and boozy, but now that more rich folks had moved in, it seemed the asshole ratio had increased significantly. Many of them had come from New York and Massachusetts, had moved away from their overcrowded and overpriced state. They'd come here to enjoy small-town life and all the natural beauty the place had to offer. That demographic shift had created an entirely different set of problems, pitting the rich outsiders against the working locals.

But they had brought good things, too. Better restaurants and high-end coffee shops. A microbrewery and a fantastic gelateria. A state-of-the-art boatyard that employed a dozen locals. The effect was to put more money into the town's coffers and create much-needed jobs. All in all, he thought their presence in town had been a positive development.

He drove through the dark streets with urgency, and yet at the same time feeling highly ambivalent about seeing the woman he'd fallen hard for back in high school. Although he'd gotten married and divorced since that time and had a kid, he'd always carried a torch for Isla. Too bad she had married that loser, Swisher Eaves.

The early morning blackness flew past him. He sipped his bitter brew as he guided the cruiser down the two-lane road. The surrounding trees rustled in the wind, convincing him that this call would be a false alarm. Regardless, he had an obligation to check on the matter, despite the fact that crime in this part of town was practically nonexistent.

He turned onto the road leading to the Eaveses' home. Tall pine trees lined either side of the driveway. His thoughts wandered as he reflected on all the time and energy he'd put into searching for Dakota James. He felt his eyelids closing and his head falling ever so briefly on his chest before he snapped his head up to keep from nodding off.

What the hell had happened to that James kid? Maybe he'd run away from an abusive home. He was the scion of Massachusetts tech wealth that had fled the Boston area for a simpler life in Shepherd's Bay.

Funny how he had never viewed his hometown as anything special. The rugged ocean and nearby mountains he'd taken for granted. He had grown up poor and as a kid had worried more about surviving than having fun. Nowadays, leisure seemed to be the new norm in this town, and he had landed on the short end of that coveted American dream. But material things had never given him much pleasure, anyway.

He parked in front of the house. A light shone in the kitchen. The chirp of crickets pierced the humid air as he made his way out of the cruiser. A cursory glance around the grounds convinced him that no break-in had occurred. And yet Isla was no pushover. If she called the police for help, she really had to believe that someone had broken in.

Something seemed off to him as he walked toward the front steps. He took out his flashlight and shone the beam along the matted dirt. Instinctively, he rested his hand on his holster. In all his years as a Shepherd's Bay cop, he'd not once fired his weapon. He had taken it out a few times but thankfully had never had to use it.

He climbed the stairs. The briny tang of ocean struck him as particularly strong as a breeze blew in from the northeast. On a clear day, one could see the ocean from here, as well as all the expensive homes that had been built on Harper's Point. A new monstrosity had risen up on the north side of the peninsula, and it looked more like a castle than a home, replete with a giant rotunda. Although many of these newcomers had become year-round residents, some who lived in these McMansions stayed in them only a few weeks each summer.

His heart raced in his chest, not from fear but from the anticipation of seeing Isla. They'd spoken off and on throughout the years, whenever they bumped into each other at the post office or the supermarket. They spoke awkwardly, like exes were prone to do. Sometimes, on slow days, he'd cruise past her salon in the center of town and catch a glimpse of her cutting a client's hair. One day he had even sat in Cafe Bello across the street and had watched her work. He hadn't thought she could see him from where he sat, especially while wearing a baseball cap with the visor pulled low. Although it had pleased him to watch her, it had also filled him with guilt and made him feel like a stalker, and he'd never done that again.

Something had passed between them the day they bumped into each other at the missing boy's vigil. An understanding? The realization that there but for the grace of God go I? It just as easily could be their own child who had disappeared instead of Dakota James. The mystery of the kid's disappearance fourteen weeks ago had been driving him crazy. He had been struggling to find a clue indicating where he'd gone or who had taken him. Was there a killer in town? Had Dakota bolted from an unhappy home and settled somewhere else? Or if someone had killed him, was his body still in Shepherd's Bay?

He knocked on the door and waited a few seconds. What would he say to Isla? How would she react upon seeing him again in person? He stared down at his feet for lack of anything else to do. Finally, the door opened, and he raised his head in anticipation of old times.

ISLA

*H*ER FATHER GAZED INTO THE BARREL OF THE GLOCK, LOOKING AT her with a puzzled expression. Gray whiskers poked out of his chin and cheeks, and he had cuts from where he'd shaved. Isla froze upon seeing him. On the floor lay shards of broken glass. All the lights in the kitchen shone down upon them. Her father, bare-footed and in his boxers, turned casually away from her and began to shuffle toward the refrigerator, mindless of the fact that his daughter had a gun pointed at him.

Isla felt a tear forming. And yet before she had a chance to process her father's reaction, Scout turned the corner with a bell in his mouth and dropped it at her feet. It was the dog's way of telling her that her son's blood sugar was rapidly dropping. She turned and ran frantically up the stairs toward Raisin's room. Scout followed behind her.

After waking Raisin up, she inserted a test strip in a blood glucose meter, then used a lancet to prick Raisin's fingertip. She drew a drop of blood, and then touched and held the edge of the test strip to the drop of blood. Seventy. The reading was low but not dangerously so. But that number could change quickly if the boy didn't get sugar into his system. She cradled Raisin's sweaty head in her arm and lifted him up to a sitting position.

"What's the m-m-matter, Mom?"

"Scout alerted me, honey. You need sugar," Isla said. She grabbed the packet of Skittles on his nightstand and emptied a handful into his sweaty palm.

"But I feel fine. I just want to go back to sleep."

"You know the drill, kiddo. Now hurry up and swallow these."

"Why are you holding that gun?" Raisin asked as he wiped his eyes. He held the Skittles in his hand and stared at the Glock.

"I thought there was an intruder."

"Cool. Can I hold it?"

"You know how Mommy feels about guns."

"But you don't mind when Dad goes shooting."

"Your dad's a grown-up and can do whatever he wants. When you become a grown-up, you can do as you please, too."

"So why do you have one?"

"This gun is for defending ourselves," she said, nodding toward the Skittles in his palm.

"From what?"

"In the event someone ever tries to break in or hurt us."

"Why would anyone do that? We have nothing valuable in here."

"Please, just eat your Skittles," she said, pointing at the candy in his hand.

Isla waited until he swallowed them. Then she passed him the juice pouch and watched as he sucked all the liquid out through the straw. Her nerves on edge, she waited impatiently for the sugar to kick in while Scout sat quietly on the floor below her. After cleaning the sugar off his fingertips with a wet wipe, she tested him again fifteen minutes later, and this time his blood sugar sat comfortably in the low one hundreds. She grabbed a liver treat out of her pocket and held it out to the miracle dog who'd saved her child's life more times than she could remember.

"Good dog. Good dog. Treat. Treat," she said, watching as the Lab wolfed down the reward treat. When he swallowed it, she scratched behind his ears. She turned to see Raisin closing his eyes and slipping back into sleep, as if nothing had happened. And like that, another disaster had yet again been averted thanks to Scout.

She stood at the threshold of Raisin's bedroom and watched as Scout sat beaming by her son's bed, his chest out and his head held high. The Lab always appeared proud of himself after his life-saving actions. Smiling, Isla didn't know what she would do without Scout. The dog had cost twenty-five thousand dollars, but thanks to the generous donations from her church and the community, they had been able to buy this highly trained animal. A dog keenly attuned to the rising and falling blood sugars in her eleven-year-old son, who had suffered from this debilitating disease from the age of three, when a severe bout of strep throat compromised his immune system.

Something shattered downstairs, and she remembered that her father was still roaming around in the kitchen. It chilled her to think that just five minutes ago she had had a fully loaded Glock pointed in his face. She pulled the door shut and proceeded down the hallway until she came to Katie's room. Her daughter must have been exhausted after her softball team won the state championship yesterday. She twisted the doorknob and peeked inside the darkened room. Light from the hallway streamed inside and illuminated the empty bed. Where had her daughter gone?

Before she could answer that question, she heard a knock on the front door. The night was getting more bizarre by the minute. Could it be Katie? She suddenly remembered that Katie had gone to a party that evening to celebrate the team's championship season. She breathed a sigh of relief. Now the question was whether she'd ground Katie for breaking curfew or whether she'd cut her some slack. Rules were rules, and yet Shepherd's Bay had won the only state softball championship in its school's history. It had been over twenty years since any Shepherd's Bay team had won a title in Maine.

The Glock. She felt stupid now for taking it out of the safe. And yet its presence next to her all these years had allowed her to sleep soundly at night, especially when Ray slipped out to conduct whatever business venture he happened to be working on at the time.

She went into her bedroom to place the gun back in the safe, reengaged the lock with a push of a button on the keypad, then double-checked that she had securely locked the safe door. She went downstairs, praying that Katie hadn't drunk alcohol or got in a car with an inebriated friend.

When she returned downstairs, she saw Karl Bjornson, dressed in his police uniform, sitting at the kitchen table with her father. Her father was conversing with Karl as if they were old friends, and he laughed as he recounted old tales about fishing with the cop's father. Five minutes ago her father had been stumbling around the kitchen in a daze, breaking glasses and staring into the barrel of a gun. Now he was remembering events from thirty years ago with precision and clarity. The doctors had explained that his disease would have its ups and downs, but as she watched him now, the complexity of the human brain revealed itself in all its frailty. Good thing she'd taken her father in when she did.

Karl faced away from her and didn't see her at the kitchen doorway. For whatever reason, she'd forgotten that she'd called the station in a moment of panic. His presence both disappointed her and brought back old memories. Not because of the intimate past they had once shared, but mostly because he wasn't Katie. She wished she could tuck her girl into bed, with a kiss and a gentle hug, and let her sleep until noon. Maybe it was a good thing Katie had gone to a party and stayed past her curfew tonight. It meant her little girl wasn't so little anymore. After next year she'd be off to college and gone for good.

She stood with her arms crossed, admiring Karl from afar, impressed by the way he sat listening to her father retell his old stories, stories that she'd heard hundreds of times before. Karl looked good, although she could see only the back of his dirty-blond head. She'd seen him around town throughout the years, their lives occasionally overlapping.

Working at her salon, she overheard everything that happened in Shepherd's Bay, even when people didn't think she was listening. Unless she was in the back room, Isla knew whenever Karl cruised past the shop, and she was certain that he made detours around the block to observe her. The idea that he still liked her made her happy in a small sort of way. She remembered glancing out the window one morning and seeing him sitting in that fancy coffee shop across the street, drinking coffee and pretending to read the paper next to the floor-to-ceiling window. He'd worn a baseball cap pulled low over his forehead. She remembered thinking at the time, *Of all people, why is Karl Bjornson in the downtown area and drinking coffee at an expensive café?*

She and Karl had dated their senior year, and it had been an unlikely pairing. He'd been the quiet, shy boy who grabbed his backpack and disappeared alone in the woods. She'd been outgoing and active, and she'd had friends in every clique. She'd starred in the school's musicals and acted in the award-winning dramas. That she ended up falling for him had surprised even her. Their mutual attraction had been a slow burn, and the more time she had spent with him, the more she had appreciated his gentle nature and bone-dry humor.

But she'd had goals to accomplish and things to do before settling down. She'd forgotten how ambitious she'd been as an energetic high school senior. She'd hoped to attend college and then try her hand at acting. Maybe move to New York City and make a go of it. The men of her dad's generation had typically graduated from Shepherd's Bay High and married their high school sweetheart and then had either followed their father into lobster fishing or ended up toiling in the boatyard. The more adventurous and more ambitious male high school graduates had made the one-hour journey to the shipyard and had worked on the massive vessels being constructed for the navy. The young women had married and become wives and mothers and stayed home to take care of their children.

Somehow, she had dropped out of college and ended up with Ray, known as Swisher to everyone in town. She'd returned to Shepherd's Bay before she could accomplish all the things she'd set out to do. Before she got a chance to travel to Europe and visit all the places she hoped to see. Or act in an off-Broadway play. Despite all of Swisher's faults, and he had many, she rarely looked back on her life and regretted the decision she'd made, mostly because of the precious gifts Ray had given her: Katie and Raisin.

And yet as she watched Karl conversing with her father, she couldn't help but wonder what might have been had she stayed with him. Or whether she might have found true love with the strange boy she fell hard for back in high school. Her religion had taught her that God had a plan for everyone. For whatever reason, God had given her this life, and she couldn't complain.

She cleared her throat and made her way into the kitchen. Upon seeing her, Karl stood and smiled. She wished she had a pot of coffee brewing and some pastries to offer. It was the least she could do after he had rushed over here and had humored her old man for a few minutes, something Ray never did. Ray had little patience for anything, and she was convinced beyond a doubt that Ray suffered from some undiagnosed form of ADD.

"False alarm," she said, resting her hand on her father's shoulder. "But thanks for coming."

"I told you it was the wind."

"Oh, it definitely was not the wind," she said, laughing. He had seen the broken glass on the floor and was trying to be nice. "Hey, you want a cup of coffee?"

"I really should be returning to the station."

"Oh, come on, Karl. Sit down. It'll take only a few minutes to brew a pot. And it's not like there's tons of criminal activity going on tonight." She filled the coffeemaker's water reservoir and pulled out a bag of the expensive coffee she'd purchased from that café across from her shop. "Look, I have the good stuff, which I save for special guests. French roast." She added the coffee grounds into the filter and switched the machine on.

"It's been a slow night, and I certainly could use a good cup," he said, sitting back down.

"Can't imagine the police station splurges for good coffee."

"Not with this chief in charge. Harry counts every penny."

"Stay put. I need to put my father to bed, and I'll be right back." She guided her father to his small bedroom on the first floor, kissed him good night, and then tucked him under the covers.

"Thank you, Clara," he mumbled. Clara was her mother's name.

"It's Isla, Dad. I'm your daughter, remember?"

"Yes, of course I remember. I'm not an idiot, you know." He closed his eyes and rolled over.

"Sleep tight, Dad."

She heard the coffee machine belching as soon as she entered the kitchen. How many years had it been since she purchased a new coffeemaker? Her heartbeat ticked a little faster at the prospect of being alone with Karl Bjornson. Good thing Ray was not around to see this, because he had never liked Bjornson, dating all the way back to high school. She remembered Ray teasing him in the hallway one day, in front of the other kids, and Karl taking it with good-natured stoicism, which had impressed her even back then.

The coffee finished brewing. She grabbed two cups, spoons, a bowl of sugar, and the pint of half-and-half and placed them on the table between them. When she put one of the cups down, she noticed a thick brown stain running along the rim. She prayed he didn't see it. She quickly replaced the cup without saying anything, knowing Raisin had yet again failed to check the dishes before putting them away. She poured two cups, making a mental note to remind him to do a better job next time. Karl made no move for the cream or the sugar, which didn't surprise her. He'd always maintained spartan habits.

He sipped his brew. "Great coffee."

"Glad you like it." Isla sat down across from him.

"The coffee at the station is the absolute worst, but that's all we have on the night shift."

"How did I know you liked gourmet coffee?" She smiled.

"I don't know. How *did* you know?"

"Maybe a little bird told me." She leaned forward in her chair, two hands wrapped around her cup.

"A feathered friend I might know?"

"I saw you sitting in Café Bello one day, while I was working on a customer."

"Spying on me, huh?"

She sipped her coffee so as to hide her grin. "I'm thinking it was the other way around."

"For your information, I sometimes go over there on my days off and work on police business. It's nice and quiet in there, and the coffee's good. Expensive but good."

"Whatever you say."

"You really think I was spying on you?" The subtlest hint of a smile came over his face.

"Just saying, buster." She used to call him *buster* back in high school.

"What exactly are you saying?"

"It's like the way you used to stare at me from your locker."

"If I remember correctly, the feeling was mutual."

She sipped her brew. "Any word on that missing kid from Harper's Point?"

"Nothing. It's as if he dropped off the face of the earth."

"That's too bad. His mother used to be one of my clients. Can't even imagine what that poor thing is going through."

"Goes to show you that money can't buy everything."

"She'd been coming in before Dakota went missing, and had always been so happy and upbeat. Then that happened. You can imagine how difficult that conversation was when she finally came in."

"What did you say?"

"What could I say? I expressed my sincerest apologies and told her not to give up hope. Then I worked on her in silence."

He sipped his coffee. "I didn't know your dad moved in with you. Did he sell his place up on Evans Road?"

It impressed her that he remembered the old home she grew up in. "He moved in with us two weeks ago. They diagnosed him with Alzheimer's last year. It got to the point where it wasn't safe for him to live alone anymore."

"Sorry to hear that."

"Life happens, you know?"

"That's a tough one. My grandfather got diagnosed with Alzheimer's, and it made him angry as hell." He fiddled with his spoon. "Hey, I heard about the girls winning the softball championship yesterday. That's pretty awesome."

"So awesome that Katie never even made it home tonight."

"Kids will be kids, right? Not like we didn't do the same stupid stuff when we were younger."

"Funny, I don't remember you doing anything but climbing mountains and trudging through woods."

"Was I that much of a Goody Two-shoes?"

"Worse than you know."

He smiled and shook his head.

"Anyway, you think I want my kid doing the things I did back in high school?" She could feel the easy chemistry between them returning. She tried to shrug off the feeling, but there was no denying it.

"We sure had some fun back then. And we're still here to talk about it."

"Sometimes I wonder if that's a good thing."

He stood. "I really gotta go. Thanks for the coffee, Isla."

"Honest, I really did think someone had broken in. Dad's never gotten up and wandered around like that before, breaking glasses and making a racket."

"Call me anytime you want. The coffee alone is worth the visit."

"What about the company?"

"Most definitely worth it. Your dad's a great conversationalist."

"Wiseass." She smiled. "I hope you find that James kid."

"Me too." He stared into her eyes. "How's Raisin, by the way?"

"Fine. As long as he has Scout by his side, constantly alerting me about his blood sugar levels."

"That dog is amazing."

"And worth every penny. Not sure Raisin could have a normal life without him. He's our wonder dog."

She walked him to the door, stepping over the broken glass, remembering how they had kissed all those years ago, as high school seniors. Karl exited and made his way down the steps. Off in the distance, she could see the barest hint of light creeping up over the horizon. He slipped into his cruiser and disappeared down the narrow driveway. A cool ocean breeze ruffled her hair as she stood in the doorway, admiring the first brilliant moments of sunrise. She loved the clammy smell of ocean. It was as much a part of her as anything else in this town.

She shut the door and returned to the kitchen table. It felt nice being in here with all the lights off and the house quiet. Raisin slept soundly upstairs, with Scout by his side, ready to pounce at any significant change in the boy's blood sugar. Her father lay tucked away in his room, hopefully dreaming pleasant dreams. If only Katie were home, she'd feel more relaxed. With Katie entering her senior year in the fall, she knew she better get used to her daughter being away for long periods of time. In many ways, Katie had gotten lost in the shuffle of their crazy family dynamics, and Isla had to remind herself to spend more time with her before she was gone for good.

Dakota James had disappeared three and a half months ago, and it was all anyone in town could talk about. Isla couldn't imagine the pain his mother must be going through. She didn't know if she could bear such suffering if one of her own kids went missing like that.

After drinking her cup of coffee and sweeping up the broken glass, she decided that returning to bed was no longer an option. She poured herself another cup and sat quietly, thinking about all that had happened in the past year. Despite Raisin's illness, her father's recent diagnosis, and Ray's irresponsible ways, she felt herself a lucky woman. At least she hadn't lost a child like the James family had.

ISLA

SHE HAD ALREADY BEEN UP FOR EIGHT HOURS AND HAD DEALT WITH so much, and now this. The minivan's engine light flashed on as she drove Raisin to his soccer game. It had been doing this for the past two weeks now, and this malfunction had been accompanied by a weird pinging noise coming from the engine. With over a hundred thousand miles on the odometer, Isla prayed the minivan wouldn't break down on her now. Ray had sworn he'd look at it at some point, but so far he hadn't. As far as the engine light being on, Ray had mansplained that car manufacturers designed them like that in order to get more service calls. "A complete scam," he'd claimed.

She looked in the rearview mirror and saw Raisin sitting quietly in his white soccer uniform. Next to him sat Scout, staring out the window, his medical vest outfitted with two pockets. One pocket contained Scout's liver treats, potty bags, and water bowl. The other pocket held everything Raisin needed in the event his blood sugar levels dangerously spiked. They had perfected the system over a number of years now and had crisis avoidance down pat.

The sun shone with an unusual intensity this morning, foreshadowing a wonderful Maine summer. It seemed that as of late she'd been attending one sporting event after another. Just the other day she'd watched her daughter's high school team win the state softball championship. It had been one of their family's finest moments and worth every mile logged on her shitty minivan. To see her daughter so happy had made all the sacrifices worth it. The only thing that would have been better was if Ray could have been there to witness the victory. If not for herself, then for poor Katie, who had been searching for her father the entire game.

Of course there never would have been a championship without Katie's best friend, Willow. She'd transferred from exclusive Chance Academy, ten miles up the coast, after her sophomore year. An amazing pitcher, she had struck out fifteen batters and had pitched a no-hitter in the championship game. Her talent had been on full display months before, when she starred in *Grease*, the school's winter musical. If that wasn't enough, she was drop-dead gorgeous.

Her parents, Gil and Felicia Briggs, had moved the family to Shepherd's Bay two years ago and had built a massive postmodern home along the waterfront. Isla had driven past it a few times as it was being built and had marveled at the design and the landscaping. It always amazed her that these newcomers were so wealthy. While she was growing up, this town had been blue collar and gritty. The Briggses' sleek home both awed her and made her slightly jealous. It shamed her to feel this way, because she'd always been raised not to envy her neighbors for what they had.

She'd heard rumors that Gil Briggs had been a big shot out in LA. Other than that, she didn't know Willow's parents very well and merely said hello to them from time to time. They kept mostly to themselves, especially Felicia, who never spoke to any of the other parents. For whatever reason, Felicia mystified her, and she typically spent a good portion of the game studying the exotic-looking woman. Felicia always wore dark sunglasses to complement her perfectly colored mane of jet-black hair. And sported long lacquered nails, thumb rings, and dangling earrings that sparkled in the sun. And yet for whatever reason, the woman seemed lonely. Isla had many times wanted to go over there and introduce herself, ask if Felicia wanted to go get coffee sometime, but somehow she had never gotten up the nerve.

Felicia always stood by herself, because Gil had taken to filming the girls. He'd started in the fall, after getting all the kids and their parents to sign waivers. His goal was to try to sell the film footage to one of the cable networks, marketing it as a reality show based in Maine. All the girls who had signed on to the project seemed excited about the prospect of becoming reality stars and appearing on TV. Isla wasn't thrilled by the idea, but she couldn't deny Katie the opportunity it might one day provide her. And if the show took off, and Katie made a few dollars, it could help defray some of her college costs.

The entrance to the soccer field appeared up ahead. To her left she saw Ridley's farm. Dairy cows grazed languidly in pasture, their oversized mouths gently chewing on sprouting grass. Years ago, they'd opened an ice cream shop in the front parking lot, and it had become quite popular during the summer months.

She pulled out her phone and called Katie. For the third time this morning, her daughter's phone went directly to message. *What's wrong with that girl?* She tried Ray. Nothing on his end, either. She couldn't believe harvesting seaweed could occupy so much of his time. Another example of Ray being Ray. She'd never known him to be anything but irresponsible, even when she'd fallen head over heels for him after returning from college. Never a day went by when Ray, always looking to earn an easy buck, didn't talk about one of his new business ventures. His faults had seemed lovable when she was first getting to know him. Now they were glaring.

"Mom?"

"Yes, Raisin?"

"Do I have to play today?"

"What's up, kiddo? You not feeling well?"

"I feel fine. I just don't feel like playing this morning."

"Then what is it? Because you usually love to play soccer."

"I don't know. I get tired of it."

"But you're the best player on the team."

"Sometimes the kids on the other team can be real jerks. They say a lot of mean stuff about Scout, ask if he's my Seeing Eye dog or something."

"I know it's hard for you, buddy, but we talked about this. You can't control what other kids say. Just ignore them and do your thing."

"At least the kids on my team understand why Scout needs to be near me."

"Those are your real friends, Raisin. And remember, what doesn't kill you makes you stronger," she said, staring at him in the rearview mirror. "You made a commitment to your team, and so you're going to honor that commitment. Understand?"

"Fine," he said, looking out the window. "Is Katie or Dad going to be at my game?"

"Katie slept over a friend's house last night, and your dad's working."

"Okay," he said, disappointment in his voice.

Isla turned onto the road leading to the field. A lot of cars had already gathered in the lot. She parked and guided Scout out of the backseat, then made sure to grab his blanket—or place—off the van's floor. Scout was at work now and understood never to leave his place once she spread it over the grass on the sidelines. He would sit perfectly still on his place throughout the game, ready to pounce if he alerted on his boy.

Members of both teams ran around the field and kicked the ball around. Scout gave Raisin a perfunctory sniff before the boy ran out to join them. Then the referee arrived and blew his whistle, signaling the start of the game.

Isla stood next to the other parents, making sure Scout had enough room to see the field. She spread the place out over the grass, and the dog went into a downstay position, understanding that he was never to move from that position unless he alerted. Over his body rested the medical vest. Every parent on the team understood and valued Scout as a service dog—and knew never to scratch his ears or treat him like a family pet.

Something passed over Isla as the game started. Fear? Worry? She glanced down and noticed that Scout was staring up at her, as if worried about something. Sometimes she believed that he could actually read her mind. Two years ago Scout had detected a low sugar level in one of Raisin's teammates, and Isla had given the kid the candy bar she kept in her pocket.

She tried calling Katie and Ray again. Still no answer from either of them. Ray's failure to reply didn't concern her; he ignored her all the time. But Katie always called back in a timely manner. She glanced at her watch. Ten past noon. Could something have happened to her? Like it had to Dakota James? *No*, she told herself. *Stop being such a worrywart.*

She'd noticed a slight change in her daughter's behavior since Katie had become friends with Willow. Katie seemed more detached and moody after meeting Willow, less exuberant than her usual self. Prior to that, Katie earned straight As, attended church with the family every Sunday, volunteered at the senior center, and never gave her any problems. She was not a star on the softball team or in the school's musicals, like Willow was, but Katie was a consummate team player.

Raisin scored an easy goal two minutes into the game. Isla would have clapped had she not been calling the parents of Katie's friends. Every one of them said that Katie hadn't slept over at their house last night. Isla paced the sideline, one eye on Scout and one eye on the game. Scout sat perched on his mat, watching Raisin, his nostrils flaring as he scented the air. After Raisin scored his second goal, an amazing kick from twenty feet out, he ran over to where Scout sat and let the dog check him over. When Scout didn't react, he ran back onto the field.

Finally, she called the Briggses. She probably should have called the Briggses first, owing to Katie's recent friendship with Willow, but something had prevented her from doing so. Her own vanity? Yes. Felicia intimidated her, and she felt ashamed that she'd put her own insecurities over her daughter's safety. After two rings she heard a woman's voice.

"I'm sorry to call you like this, Felicia, but did Katie happen to sleep over at your house last night?"

"No, she's not here. Neither is Willow. We assumed the girls slept over at your house."

"Well, they didn't. Do you know any other parent that might have hosted them?"

"I don't. They spent some time here last night but then left. Willow's very particular about where she sleeps. I doubt she'd choose to sleep anywhere else, with the exception of your house."

"It's past noon, and I haven't heard from Katie. That's not like her."

"Willow hasn't checked in with us, either, unless she called my husband."

"I'm starting to worry," Isla said.

"Maybe we should call the police, although I'm sure the girls are just fine."

"All the same, I'll call them after I get off the line with you." But the phone had already gone dead.

As she was about to dial the police, Isla saw Raisin dribble past three defenders and score an easy goal. Enthusiastic applause went up from the parents around her. Across the way, however, she heard some angry parents taunting Raisin and making fun of him. The expression on Raisin's face looked anything but joyful, and he sprinted over to Scout as if he hadn't seen him for weeks. He knelt down and stared at Scout, allowing the dog to fully vet him. When Scout failed to detect any significant change in his blood sugars, the dog rested his chin on his paws and stared straight ahead. Isla glared across the field at the two parents who had jeered at her son. She had half a mind to go over there and confront them, but then she remembered the advice she'd given Raisin earlier.

"I don't want to go back in the game, Mom."

"You can't let those jerks get to you."

"It's not that. It's just that it's too easy to score against this team. I feel bad for those kids out there."

Sometimes she wanted to cry because of Raisin's decency.

"I could probably score ten goals if I wanted. What fun would that be?"

"Not much," she said. "Talk to your coach and see what he thinks."

"He'll want me to stay in the game until halftime. I don't want to look like a baby in front of the other kids."

"You want me to talk to him?"

"Heck no, Mom. Don't do that. I'll look like a wuss if you start complaining in front of everyone. I can deal with Coach."

She called the police, watching Raisin walk over to where his team huddled around the kneeling coach. A voice she didn't recognize answered, and he sounded like a young kid. She didn't know any of the officers on the force, except for Karl Bjornson. Isla reported her daughter missing, and the officer told her not to worry, that she was probably just sleeping over at a friend's house.

His patronizing tone made her want to explode with anger. But then he informed her that there was not much he could do at the moment. Today was Sunday, and the chief was out of town on business.

"Call back later if you still haven't heard from her," the cop instructed.

A stab of panic shot through her as Raisin dribbled past the defenders and headed toward the goal. He stopped in front of the net, poised for an easy score. But then he swiveled around and passed the ball to a less talented teammate off in the corner. His coach barked at him to be aggressive, but Raisin ignored him and did the exact same thing when the ball came to him again.

Isla stared down at her phone, as if waiting for a call to come in. Where the hell was Katie?

KARL

AFTER HE GOT OFF THE NIGHT SHIFT, HE WENT INTO CAFÉ BELLO and sat down to work on the James case. If he went home now, he knew he'd fall asleep on the couch and get only a few useless hours of toss and turn. Seeing Isla last night had caused much of his unrest. He couldn't stop thinking about the quiet hours they'd spent together in her kitchen. It reminded him of older times, when they would sit after hiking and talk about times past. Of course he had no hopes of getting back together with her. His visit had been strictly professional. But after he was up all night, drinking shitty coffee and roaming the empty streets, his mind tended to play tricks on him, convincing him of possibilities that just didn't exist.

Isla had looked beautiful last night, bathed in the soft glow of kitchen light. Sure, she'd aged some and put on a few extra pounds around the middle. But what an amazing woman, taking care of a sick child and a father suffering from Alzheimer's. How he would have loved to wrap his arms around her, bathrobe and all, and kiss her.

He opened his computer. Why was he torturing himself like this?

She'd chosen college over him all those years ago, and it hadn't come as a surprise. He hadn't necessarily fought hard to keep her. He had believed Shepherd's Bay to be a dead end for ambitious kids like themselves. Until he had realized that ambition was as overrated as it was misleading. He'd considered moving closer to her college so they could be together. They had fully planned on being a couple while they figured things out, whether that be long distance or not. It was a vague notion they had once shared, as sincere as it had been unlikely. But at the time they had truly believed it could work. They'd been too young to know the realities of life and the whims of fate. And then Isla had decided that she'd rather be free to explore other options during her college years and that they could then reassess their relationship after she graduated.

It was a blow to his plans at the time, but he knew he had to give her the space she needed, and he figured that a four-year hitch in the Coast Guard would sync perfectly with her college years. It would get him out of Shepherd's Bay and keep him from constantly thinking about her. College was not in his future. Not initially, anyway. Not until he discovered what he wanted out of life and where his interests lay. Then, by that point, he decided that college was not for him.

Somewhere between boot camp and her first year of college, they lost contact. It happened naturally, as their relationship dissipated. His Coast Guard time passed in unremarkable fashion, and by the end of it, he assumed that Isla had moved on from him and met someone else. He met Sofia in San Diego during his last stint, and they married after six months of dating, a move completely out of character for someone like himself, a person who typically proceeded with caution on all things. Nine months later they had a daughter. After he was discharged, he managed to convince his new wife, after much persuading, to return home to Maine with him.

He ran into Isla at the drugstore one day and discovered that she had married Ray "Swisher" Eaves and had a two-year-old daughter. Of all the people to marry, Swisher Eaves was the last guy he had expected her to end up with. Despite the fact that he was married himself, the news sank him into a months-long depression. It reminded him that life never turned out the way one expected. Seeing her around town had been like sticking a needle into his heart and only reminded him how tenuous his own marriage was.

He dropped the James file onto the burnished oak table, feeling his blood pressure spike. Why? He knew why. Because Swisher didn't know how good he had it. Because he knew for a fact that Swisher took Isla and his kids for granted. He had been that way since high school and hadn't changed, like most boys from Shepherd's Bay.

And the saddest part was that Swisher was an incredibly talented guy. Always had been. Great at everything he did. A natural athlete, with charisma and charm. Young kids back in high school used to ask for his autograph after high school basketball games. Ridiculously handsome in a town filled with wrinkled mechanics and portly fishermen, he stood out like a prince among peasants. He could fix nearly any kind of engine or machinery and had a gift as a painter of landscapes. Self-taught, of course. But Swisher had one fault that prevented him from succeeding in life: a debilitating lack of focus, which kept him from sticking to one thing for any length of time. The more he thought about it, the more he could understand how Isla had fallen for a guy like Swisher. In contrast, he could also understand how she might grow weary of his many schemes and crazy business ventures, as well as his inability to provide a stable life for his family.

The coffee shop's lights dimmed. His papers lay strewn over the table, lit by the screen of his glowing laptop. He sipped his coffee, hoping that the caffeine might make him more alert. Only the caffeine was now having the opposite effect, and soon after the first sip, he felt an overwhelming wave of exhaustion sweep over him. He swore he would not take any more night shifts if he could help it, no matter how many bills needed paying. If only his daughter had gone to UMaine instead of pricey Colby College, his finances might be less disastrous.

His eyelids began to close. He took another sip of his Costa Rican estate. At three dollars a cup, he hoped it might jolt him awake. No such luck. Best to drag his ass to bed and try to get some shut-eye. On a gorgeous day like this, when the sun shone brightly on their little town, he knew sleep would be hard to come by. No sense sitting in this café with all the hipsters and well-to-do reading newspapers and killing time.

Miles Davis trumpeted over the speakers. He glanced over at the barrister, with his numerous tattoos, earrings, and requisite man bun. Probably used his daddy's money to buy this coffee shop. There'd been no decent coffee in town until Cafe Bello opened its doors. He actually enjoyed the ambience and decor of the place. Abstract art and edgy photographs hung on the walls. Jazz played low in the background. In the corner sat a coffee table formed out of an old lobster trap, covered with picture books, and surrounded by beaded leather sofas.

He closed the James file and shut down the laptop. The case would have to wait. His phone rang just as he stood to leave. It better not be the station. No way could he work another overnight shift. He answered it and discovered that two girls from Shepherd's Bay High had not returned home after the celebration last night. One was Willow Briggs. The other, Katie Eaves.

ISLA

A MILLION THOUGHTS RAN THROUGH ISLA'S MIND, AND NOT A ONE of them was good. Karl sat across from her at the kitchen table, cement bags hanging under his eyes. He jotted something in his notebook whenever a relevant fact came to light. In the other room she could hear the whiz-bang action coming from the television. Raisin sat transfixed in front of the flat-screen, watching one of those *Transformers* movies with two of his friends.

She glanced up at the clock and saw that it was just past five. Where in the world could Katie be? Privately, she blamed Willow Briggs for whatever had happened to her daughter. Aside from Willow's many talents, everyone knew her to be a wild child and a headstrong girl. Worse, she was absolutely gorgeous and knew it. Willow had a subtle way of flirting with the opposite sex that struck Isla as wholly inappropriate. In fact, the few times she had visited, and Ray had happened to be home, he had gone out of his way to accommodate her. Isla had thought Ray pathetic for doing this and had told him so, and he had acted as if she'd lost her mind. Katie had noticed this behavior, as well, and had rolled her eyes whenever her father doted on Willow, but she had never said anything. Because Willow struck her as needy and seemed to enjoy being the center of attention.

She got up and made a pot of coffee to keep herself busy. While filling the coffeemaker's water reservoir, she gazed out at the bay and, beyond that, the ocean. Sunlight glinted off the smooth surface of the water. From this vantage, she could make out the majestic suspension bridge leading to Harper's Point, the peninsula where the Briggses and all the other affluent families lived. She wondered if Willow's parents were as concerned about the missing girls as she was right now.

"So what happened after the game?"

"I already told you what happened, Karl. Shouldn't we be out searching for the girls?"

"We've got every officer on patrol looking for them. We've even put a call into the state police for some backup help."

"That's all good and fine, but shouldn't we be doing something other than sitting here?"

"What you should be doing now is answering my questions."

"There was a big celebration after the game. We all stood around the field and watched the girls get their trophies. Lots of hugs and pictures. After about thirty minutes passed, I asked Katie if she wanted to go home with us. She said no, that she wanted to stay back with some of her teammates. Supposedly, one of them was going to have a cookout for all the kids."

"Does Katie drink or do drugs?" Karl asked, his head bent over the notebook.

"How could you even ask me that? She is a straight A student and attends church every Sunday."

He looked up from his notebook. "You understand I have to ask you these questions, right?"

She crossed her arms and sighed. "No, I'm fairly certain Katie doesn't drink or do drugs."

"That you know of?"

"Yes, that I know of."

"I asked the Briggses the same question, and they said that Willow occasionally has a glass of wine with dinner. They are okay with it as long as she drinks in moderation, but I have a hunch that maybe she likes it a little too much."

"My kids know that drinking's unacceptable in our household— except for Ray." She looked away from him. "I should have never let her hang out with that girl."

"So you believe that Willow is somehow responsible for this?"

"I could tell something is not quite right with her. Call it mother's intuition," she said. "Of course Willow is always nice when we have her over. Despite the big house she lives in, she is always complimenting us on what a nice home we live in." She wanted to explain how Willow had eventually managed to win her over, despite the warning alarms going off in her head.

"We're checking with their friends. Maybe they all piled into a car and took off on a road trip down to Portland and decided not to tell anyone."

"Katie would have definitely called me if she did something impulsive like that."

"Kids change as they get older. Peer pressure and all."

"Katie isn't like that."

The sound of a truck rumbling up the driveway filled the kitchen. Isla moved to the window to see who had arrived. For a second she thought it might be Ray coming home to check on her, but on closer inspection, she saw that it was Drew, Katie's boyfriend. She prayed Katie was with him, only to realize a few seconds later that the passenger seat was empty. Drew jumped out of his truck and bounded up the stairs to the kitchen door.

His aggressive knock on the door rattled her. Isla did not have the patience to deal with Drew right now, but she decided to deal with him, anyway. She opened the door and took him in with her eyes. With his sandy blond hair, square face, and blue eyes, he resembled someone who had just walked out of a nineteenth-century Iowan cornfield. He was a year ahead of Katie, and his main goal in life was to one day own and operate his own lobster boat, like his father. And his father before him. Isla didn't necessarily look down upon this lifestyle, but she wanted more for Katie, the same way she had wanted more for herself those many years ago, when she had dreamed all those big dreams. And with the Gulf of Maine warming because of climate change, and with the lobster catch dropping year after year, she wondered what the future would hold for men like Drew. There weren't many other good jobs in town for high school graduates.

"Where the hell is Katie?" Drew said, walking past her and into the kitchen.

"We don't know. That's why the police are here. We're trying to find out what happened to her."

His eyes drifted with suspicion to Karl. "Is it bad enough that you had to get the cops involved?"

"No sense taking any chances."

"I told you this would happen. I warned Katie to stay away from that bitch. She's nothing but bad news."

"Watch your language, Drew," Isla said.

"Those rich newcomers suck. Why'd they have to come here and ruin our town like that? Even my dad says we were much better off without them."

"Go home, Drew." She refused to let him in. "I said, go home."

"I'm gonna call some friends and go look for her. Shouldn't you be doing the same?"

"As you can see, I'm talking to the police right now."

"Where's Swisher?"

"Mr. Eaves to you."

"He tells me to call him Swisher."

"I can't get ahold of him. I assume he's out on business."

Drew laughed, but it was not a happy laugh. "Right, that seaweed business of his."

Karl walked over and stared at the kid.

"Where were you yesterday?" he said.

"I was at the game yesterday afternoon, and then I went straight home and didn't leave the house again. I asked Katie to meet up with me that evening, but she said she was going to a party with some of her teammates. It pissed me off because I had a feeling she'd be hanging out with *her*."

"What do you have against Willow Briggs?"

"Katie changed when she became friends with her. I warned Swisher that Katie was gonna get in trouble by hanging out with that girl, but he didn't listen to me. Now look what's happened. Katie's gone, and the cops are involved. I wouldn't be surprised if that missing rich kid also got tangled up with her."

"Don't be ridiculous," Isla said, secretly fearing the same thing.

"What did you do when you got home after the game?" Karl asked.

"Me, Jeff, and Jason hung out in my garage, drinking beer and working on Jason's pickup. I was helping Jason put in a new transmission."

"You guys are too young to be drinking."

"Whatever."

"You have their phone numbers?"

"Sure." He gave them to Karl.

"You can expect a call from me, Drew. I might have some other questions I want to ask you."

"Whatever. Just hurry up and find Katie," Drew said before heading back out the front door.

Isla walked over and slammed the door shut, her nerves on edge.

She stared out the window over the kitchen sink and watched as his pickup sped down the hill, kicking up dirt and debris in the process. She grudgingly appreciated his concern for Katie, as belligerent as he could sometimes be. Drew was a simple boy who should have been born in an earlier era. His view of Katie seemed antiquated and she could understand why Katie had started to drift away from him—and this gritty town that had nurtured her.

And yet who was she to talk? She'd married Ray, the poster boy for Shepherd's Bay masculinity. Then, after dropping out of college and returning home, she'd attended beauty school and learned to cut hair and taken over her grandfather's barbershop in the downtown area.

She remembered her grandfather and how he had worked as a barber for over fifty years. He had cut the hair of generations of Shepherd's Bay families and had known more about this town than just about anyone. When he had decided to retire and pass the barbershop on to her at no cost, she hadn't been able to believe her good fortune. She'd agreed to assume the lease after she finished beauty school. Her grandfather's only stipulation was that she work with him as an apprentice for a year and learn the art of barbering, which would give her additional skills as well as enable her to carry on the shop's tradition. The more skills she had, the better to survive in this hardscrabble town. She happily agreed to this, and in that year she grew closer to him than ever.

He taught her how to cut men's hair and do tight tapers and fades and military flattops, which were the most difficult cuts to master and were prevalent among old-timers and the few Coasties stationed here. He demonstrated how to shave around the ears and along the neck, and how to give full-on shaves using strop, stone, and a straight-edge razor. Beard trims were tricky, with so many styles that she often took notes afterward just to keep track. But what he didn't overtly teach her, what he modeled instead, was how to deal with customers. She saw an easygoing and laid-back man, more a listener than a talker, and was shocked at what some of his customers discussed with him as he trimmed their hair: infidelity, sex, disease, death, politics, financial crises, among the many topics.

Cutting men's hair proved much harder than she had initially thought, and she struggled with her technique those first few months. But her grandfather showed lots of patience with her, as did many of his customers, who generously allowed her to experiment on them. They laughed when she screwed up, and gave her a big tip regardless of how they looked afterward, happy just to have an attractive and friendly woman working on them. She learned to follow the Boston sports teams and to speak the language, so much so that she could discuss batting averages, nickel defenses, and power plays. She discovered that men were much easier to please than women, especially when cutting their bangs, and that knowing the score of a Red Sox or Bruins game was often far more important than making sure their sideburns—or sideboards, as many of the locals called them—were even. Little did she know, but all that time he was training her, her grandfather was quietly transitioning all his old customers over to her.

Barbering had been such an important part of his life that he died a little over a year after retiring. He had no other hobbies or passions. It was the social aspect of his profession that had kept him going. She missed him dearly. Not a day went by in her shop that she didn't think about him.

They returned to the kitchen table. Karl parked in front of his computer as loud explosions burst forth from the TV. A door opened in the hallway, and before she could get up, she saw her father shuffle into the kitchen. He was dressed neatly in brown trousers and a white button-down shirt, and he smiled brightly upon seeing Karl.

"Well, look who's here," he said, walking over and putting a hand on the cop's shoulder. "You taking my daughter out on the town tonight?"

Karl's face blushed, and he looked over at her, as if asking for help.

"We're not going anywhere, Dad," Isla said, averting her eyes from Karl's embarrassed gaze.

"Good. Maybe he can stay for supper tonight and we can play Crazy Eights."

"Dad, why don't you go sit out on the deck for a little while? The weather's nice. I'll bring you out a sandwich."

"A sandwich sounds great." He leaned into Karl's ear and said, "Make sure you bring her home before eleven."

"Will do, Mr. Lee."

Embarrassed by her father's words, Isla guided him out to the deck and waited until he sat down. He could sit there for hours, staring out at the ocean. She wondered what went through his mind. Did he think about his past? His wife and family? Or did random memories pass haphazardly through his diseased brain? Was he happy to live in the moment, his memories coming and going at will? He was a good man, and she missed the easy way he had about him when he was healthy. She kissed his head and headed back inside.

"I'm so sorry about that. It's the Alzheimer's making him act that way."

"Don't be silly. There's nothing to be ashamed of."

"No, I suppose not. It's just that what he remembers is so random."

"Maybe he's remembering some good memories."

"Maybe," she said. "You always did bring me home by curfew."

"That doesn't mean I wanted to." He stared down at the table. "I'm just sorry to see your father like that. He was always such a good guy."

"Thank you."

Karl picked up his computer and stood. "I think I have all the information I need for now."

"You look tired. Have you gotten any sleep since you went off shift?"

"No, but then again, I don't need much to begin with."

She could tell he'd just lied.

"Don't worry, Isla. We're going to find her."

"I know." Tears bubbled in her eyes.

"I swear I won't rest until she's back home with you."

She nodded, unable to speak, and watched as he left.

What to do? A vague feeling of dread came over her as she rinsed out the cups and emptied the coffee filter. She desperately needed to find Katie. She checked on her dad and found him staring blissfully out at the ocean, his calloused hands intertwined over his chest, the sandwich still untouched on his plate. In the living room, the boys had switched to playing video games. Scout looked up at her and yawned, a good sign. Calmness prevailed inside Raisin's mercurial body.

Once again, she called Ray on her cell phone, and again, the call went directly to message. Had he shut his phone off? Lost it? Goddamned Ray. She wanted to throw her phone against the wall and never see that asshole again. If not for all the medical bills, she would have left him years ago. But the kids still loved him. And she knew that Katie would take it hard if the day ever came when she had to kick him out of the house. The effect it might have on Raisin's health also concerned her. Best to keep the status quo for the time being.

She paced the kitchen, adrenaline fueling her worry. Something had to be done. If tomorrow came and Katie had still not returned home, she'd form a search group and look for her. The members of her church, Our Lady of Lourdes, would gladly help her look for Katie. She bit her thumbnail and began to strategize, in the event that happened. No time for tears, because she knew she had to stay strong if she was to bring Katie home safe and sound.

The salon. She'd need to go downtown and hang a CLOSED sign on the window. Her clients would understand—she hoped. Many of them came from the wealthy part of town, and her prices reflected the new demographics. Secretly, she gave her grandfather's old clients a deep discount. But they seemed to be dwindling down lately because of their age and the changing socioeconomic conditions of the downtown area.

Her mind returned to Ray, mainly because she didn't want to consider the worst-case scenario, like that James kid, who had disappeared over three months ago. She stomped out to where Ray's art studio sat along the edge of their property. He'd built it himself. His man cave, he called it, as if being away from home all the time wasn't enough privacy. It was off limits to everyone—unless Ray invited you in, and he rarely, if ever, invited anyone inside. It was where he worked on his schemes, patents, and harebrained ideas. It was also where he brushed his oils and acrylic onto canvas. He created stunning paintings of Shepherd's Bay, filled with tugboats, lighthouses, and lobster boats cruising through the water. She had to admit that he could make a decent living were he to persevere in his art and take it more seriously. It frustrated her that the man she married had so much talent and let it all go to waste.

He'd put a cheap lock on the door. She tugged at in frustration, having no reason to invade his space. But now she wanted to hurt him like he'd hurt her all these years. Violating his space would help her vent, though she knew that nothing she did now would bring Katie home. Angry, she returned to the basement of the house, found the rusty spare key on the nail, and made her way to his art studio

She undid the lock and went inside, flicking on the switch. Dust floated through the light. Clutter was piled high everywhere she looked. Gadgets and tools of every shape and size lay in various places. Over in the corner she saw copper tubing and knotted two-by-fours that he'd pilfered from various job sites. At the far end of the studio stood an easel with a half-finished painting on it: a harbor with two sailboats. Below it, stacked up against the wall, she noticed a collection of paintings. After walking over, she began to flip through them. She saw scenes depicting the water, mountains, and open fields. But about halfway through, she saw one canvas that shocked her. She pulled it out. It was a graphic painting of a nude woman lying on her back—a woman she knew.

The painting shocked her. Had Ray slept with the woman in this picture? Of course he'd deny it if asked, claiming artistic license. But she knew of no portrait models in Shepherd's Bay who would choose to pose in such a lewd fashion.

Ray's portrait paintings, while skillfully done, veered toward the pedestrian: sports stars, celebrities, actors and actresses. Every once in a while a wealthy banker or lawyer would commission him to paint their portrait. One local judge had even hired him for his services, and the painting now hung in his chambers. She remembered seeing it and feeling slightly put off by the judge's weird dimensions.

She wondered if the woman's husband knew that she'd posed naked for Ray, not that it mattered now.

It made her want to cry. She so badly wanted to love Ray and have him love her in return. People wanted a reason to love him, and then if they failed to find one, they made one up and loved him, anyway. He had that strange effect on people. He was generous to friends and strangers alike, almost to a fault, unless you pissed him off. Then he was your worst enemy. People always claimed that Ray would give you the shirt off his back. And she knew he would. But it seemed the only people who didn't benefit from that shirt were his own family.

KARL

WITHOUT QUESTION, THE BRIGGSES OWNED THE NICEST HOME ON all of Harper's Point. He could hear the rhythmic sound of waves off in the distance and rolling onto the beach. He'd waited less than thirty seconds before a man's voice answered over the speaker. He gave his name and, as instructed, held his police badge up to the security camera for the occupant to see. After a few seconds the man buzzed him in.

His eyes widened at the sight of the place. An all-white interior with massive floor-to-ceiling windows offered him a 180-degree view of the ocean. The floor consisted of huge gray tiles neatly laid out in a grid. The kitchen was an open-concept design with a massive island, speckled marble countertops throughout, and a gigantic stainless-steel sink. But the defining feature of the entire space had to be the antigravity-looking stairway leading up to the second floor. It was an architectural gem, and he couldn't stop staring at it.

He stood alone in the house, not knowing where to go or what to do next. The sleek white sofas in the living room looked as if they'd never been sat on. A series of tan spheres hung down from the ceiling, and he assumed they were lights. He stared up in awe as he waited for someone to appear and address him. For some reason, he had an overwhelming desire to shout something out in this cavernous structure and hear the echo of his voice.

A few minutes passed before he heard the tap of footsteps. He looked up and saw a man with gray hair and silver-studded, black-framed glasses walking down those futuristic stairs, stairs that seemed to grow magically out of the wall. He held out his hand as the man approached.

"Gil Briggs."

"Detective Bjornson." He clasped the man's hand. "I just want to let you know that we're doing everything in our power to find your daughter."

"Thank you. My wife and I are worried sick about her. Willow means the world to me."

Me? "Where's your wife?"

"She's up in her room. Willow's disappearance has taken a lot out of her. I tried to tell her that Willow will be located and returned to us safe and sound, but she's not optimistic."

"Why's that?"

"It's in her nature, I suppose. Living all those years out in Los Angeles tends to kill a bit of your soul."

"Can you tell me about your daughter?"

"Willow's an extremely talented girl, as you probably already know. She pitched a no-hitter in the championship game the other day, but she's also an amazing singer and dancer. If I can manage to sell this reality pilot I'm filming, her opportunities will be endless. But, like most kids her age, she does have a rebellious side."

"Oh?"

"She's strong willed and stubborn. I know she smokes a little pot every once in a while, but that doesn't worry me too much."

"She told you this?"

"No, but her mother saw her smoking weed on one of those social media sites. Willow didn't know we had her password. We never confronted her about it, because we want to respect her privacy as much as possible. We figured it's only marijuana, and we all smoked a little weed back in high school, so it's not really that big of a deal."

"What about her friend Katie?"

"Seems like a nice girl. Not the usual type of kid Willow makes friends with, but for whatever reason, those two hit it off last year, when Willow transferred to Shepherd's Bay High."

"Why did she transfer?"

"She was getting into some trouble at her previous school. Nothing major, mind you, but enough to warrant our attention. Finally, she came to us, begging for a more authentic educational experience. She was tired of dealing with all these rich kids, especially after we moved here from LA. So we did what was best for her."

Karl couldn't help checking out his surroundings some more, and he felt guilty about enjoying this house when two girls had gone missing. He wondered what it would be like to live in such a home. Hell, he couldn't even afford the taxes on a house like this, never mind paying for the heat and utilities.

"She's our only child, Detective," Briggs said. Tears streamed down his cheeks. "You need to find her as soon as possible. I'm begging you."

"We're doing our best, Mr. Briggs."

"My wife and I are worried sick over this. Felicia's heavily medicated and barely able to function."

"Please give her my regards."

"Yes, of course." Briggs paused for a moment. "Willow has such a promising future ahead of her. Please bring her home before anything bad happens."

"Is this promising future your plan or hers?"

"Oh, definitely hers. No question about it. I started her in acting classes when she was a young girl, but since then, all of Willow's interest in performing has come from her. She fell in love with the stage and hasn't looked back."

"Nice to have goals in life."

"You have to have a lot of drive to succeed in this cutthroat business," he said, wiping his eyes on his sleeve. "Besides, she comes from good genes."

"Oh?"

"Martin Scorsese's my second cousin."

"Loved *Taxi Driver*."

"I'm a *Goodfellas* guy myself, but *Taxi Driver*'s a classic."

"Briggs doesn't sound Italian."

"My great-grandfather's name was Briggliotta when he first arrived at Ellis Island. I'm sure you can figure out the rest."

"Shortened for convenience."

"You got it," Briggs said, pointing at Karl's name tag. "Bjornson. Is that Swedish?"

"It is, even though it has only one s, like the Norwegian version of the name. Somehow my family lost the extra s."

"I love Ingmar Bergman."

"Never heard of him."

"He's a Swedish film director. *The Seventh Seal* is one of my favorite films of all time."

"Don't think I've seen any of his movies."

"Then you really should, because he's a genius," he said. "Were you born in Sweden?"

"No, my ancestors emigrated from there in eighteen seventy and settled in New Sweden, Maine."

A woman's voice called for Briggs.

"Excuse me, but I have to take care of my wife now. Please do whatever you can to find my daughter."

Karl shook his hand and thanked him for his time. That was a strange way to end the conversation. Karl made his way to the door. Before closing it, he took one last look at the inside of the house and saw Gil Briggs sprinting back up those crazy stairs, seemingly suspended in midair.

ISLA

SEEING THAT RAISIN'S NUMBERS WERE FINE, SHE PUT THE TEST KIT away and sat next to him on the couch. The normal routine consisted of testing Raisin at least twenty times throughout the day. Keeping track of Raisin's glucose levels was a life-and-death ritual, something that had become second nature to her. In the event she went outside or got stuck on the phone, Raisin had been taught to take and analyze his own numbers. When at school, he made frequent trips to the nurse so she could check him out. The worst and scariest moments were when he suffered a blackout or seizure.

She sat with Raisin and watched TV, trying to control her growing anxiety over her daughter's whereabouts. Thank God Raisin had a calm and gentle nature and never seemed to get too rattled about anything. It worried her that he hadn't asked about Katie yet. Was he in denial? Or maybe he just didn't want to talk about her disappearance. Scout stood up and looked at her with his big brown eyes before settling down, in what she liked to call his seal posture.

Her phone buzzed. She knew it was a fellow parishioner responding to her request for help. Tomorrow morning they planned to meet and begin a search for the girls. The cops had begun their own search, but with a force of five, they could hardly be expected to cover much ground. All the officers on the force had volunteered their time to look for the two girls, as had officers from some of the surrounding communities.

Canned laughter came from the TV, and Raisin let out a series of giggles. Along the floor were Scout's bringsels. Scout had been trained to pick up common, everyday objects with his mouth—bringsels—and bring them to her in the event Raisin's blood sugar spiked. There were also bells on hooks scattered throughout the rooms, which Scout could gather in his mouth and ring if alerted.

The missing James boy flashed through her mind. No, she didn't want to go there and allow negative thoughts to dominate her thinking. She remembered seeing his distraught mother weeks afterward and wrapping the styling cape around her fragile shoulders. Her face had looked as pale as the neck strip she'd looped around her. And the poor woman had lost a lot of weight. Even her hair had seemed to lose its natural luster and turn prematurely gray. Isla enjoyed cutting hair and talking to her clients, but some days it proved difficult. Like when a client suffered some sort of tragedy and broke down sobbing in her chair. No way she could be cheerful and upbeat when that happened, and the gloom usually stayed with her the rest of the day.

The TV show ended, and Raisin yawned. Isla wanted to get him to bed as soon as possible so he wouldn't see her fretting. With Katie still missing, she knew she'd not get any sleep tonight.

"Time for bed, buddy."

"I know you're scared, Mom, but don't worry. Katie will be home soon."

"I know."

"Can I go help you look for her tomorrow?"

"How do you know about that?"

"It's why you've been looking at your phone all night, isn't it?"

"Yes, but I need you to stay in school tomorrow. You've got only a few days left, and you've already missed too many this year."

"But I don't care about school. I want to help find Katie."

"Like you said, we'll find her and bring her home. Half the congregation will be out helping me look for her. And the police are searching, too."

"Scout can help. Maybe he can follow her scent."

"Scout's a lifesaver, for sure, but he's been trained to do one job in life, and that's care for you. You two need to keep as normal a routine as possible for the sake of your health."

"Jeez, Mom, I'm not Humpty Dumpty sitting on some stupid wall."

"Humpty Dumpty?" She laughed. "What made you think of him?"

"'All the king's horses and all the king's men couldn't put Humpty together again,' but he didn't have a dog like Scout watching over him."

Isla's father had been asleep for a while now. He slept at least ten hours a day, every day of the week. After Raisin went to bed, she paced the dark house, unable to keep her emotions in check. For the hundredth time, she called Ray and got the same response. She knew she'd need to nap at some point this evening, so she threw a blanket and pillow on the couch and closed her eyes.

A thought came to her as she stared up at the ceiling. She went into Katie's room and clicked on the light. Breaking the norm for most teens, Katie kept her room in spotless condition. Not a thing appeared out of place. Isla never had to tell her to clean up or make her bed. Katie even vacuumed the carpet once a week. Isla glanced at the desk Katie did her homework on. Over the past year, she hadn't been using it as much, choosing instead to study over at Willow's house. Or to finish her homework in study hall. The sight of this empty room caused a pit to form in Isla's stomach. She knew Katie's days in this household were numbered, and she'd soon be off to college, but she'd not expected to see the room so empty so soon.

Isla sat on the bed and stared at Katie's laptop. In September Katie would be starting her senior year and would be filling out the first of her college applications. They planned on making campus trips later in the summer and doing some mother-daughter bonding, bonding that she'd recently neglected because of Raisin's and her father's medical conditions. Part of her was eager to help Katie make that exciting life transition. The other part of her felt depressed that her daughter would soon be leaving.

Choosing a college had been all Isla could think about when she was a high school senior. She remembered how excited she'd been when she got accepted and when her parents dropped her off at the university. The prospect of meeting new friends, the parties and football games, the intellectual rigor of the high-level classes she would be taking had been exhilarating.

However, one of her professors had spoken to her that first day in class, and everything had changed. She had felt excited that a handsome, intelligent man like him would take notice of her. He cut quite a figure on campus, with his longish black hair and tweed jackets. Wearing boat shoes and jeans, he stood over six feet tall and seemed never to arrive to class without his signature plaid scarf entwined around his neck. He'd written three novels, none of which she'd ever heard of, but supposedly, they'd received great critical praise. She tried reading his dense, difficult prose, but when she couldn't understand it, she felt stupid. During office hours, he smiled with delight when she praised his work and asked what she thought was a series of interesting questions. He explained that there was no clear meaning to his prose and that readers were free to come to their own conclusions. Bullshit meters went off in her head after he lectured her about his work, but she pushed them back down, chalking it up to her lack of sophistication.

But then, when she seemed happiest, he would criticize one of her essays in front of the class, often in a cold and callous manner. Later he would apologize during office hours, telling her that he was only trying not to show favoritism. He was good, because the more he criticized her, the harder she worked to win his approval.

This went on until the end of her freshman year. His behavior confused and inspired her, as irritating and humiliating as it seemed to be. Yes, she was attracted to him, and it was an attraction unlike anything she'd experienced with the boys she'd fallen for in the past. He was sophisticated and had flair. But she never thought to follow through on her feelings for him; she really didn't think an esteemed professor like him would want anything to do with a dumb girl from the sticks of Maine.

He convinced her to stay the summer instead of returning home. He got her a job in the English Department, filing and doing data input. Oddly, he chose instead to travel throughout Europe that summer and do research for his new novel. But he emailed her every few days, telling her how much he looked forward to seeing her in his class come fall. She remembered how the tone of their exchanges changed that summer, despite the fact that they barely saw each other. It thrilled her to see him when school started up in September, although it also made her slightly uncomfortable.

He encouraged her to take his Advanced Fiction seminar and looked magnificent when he showed up to that first class. Five other students sat around the conference table, all of them seniors, and it was obvious she was way out of her league. Besides, her major was theater arts, not creative writing. Tanned and relaxed, the professor smiled warmly at her when she took a seat across from him.

He asked her out for coffee afterward, and she felt thrilled by the invitation. They ate fancy French pastries, sipped espressos, and she mostly listened to him talk about his adventures in Europe. He lived nearby and wanted to show her some of the things he'd purchased while traveling. She thought it a bit odd at the time, but the way he looked at her made her feel like the most important girl in the world.

Back at his apartment, he gave her a gift, a brown leather jacket purchased in Florence. She protested, claiming that the jacket was way too expensive and that she could not possibly accept such a beautiful gift. But he insisted. Then he asked if she'd try it on for him. He spun her around so that she faced the mirror hanging on his closet door. She had to admit that the jacket looked amazing on her. Suddenly she felt his arms wrapping around her waist.

Isla snapped out of the memory and returned to reality. Why had she just been thinking about that pretentious jerk? She stood and walked over to the desk. Turned on the laptop and punched in Katie's password. She had put it to memory one night when she had to borrow Katie's laptop to print out some emergency medical instructions for Raisin. Thankfully, Katie had never thought to reset it.

Whether this would help her or not, she didn't know. She clicked on an icon, and photographs filled the screen. She started at the beginning of last year and began scrolling through them. Many of the photographs consisted of Katie and Drew, and Katie and Raisin. But then the nearer to the present she scrolled, the more photos she saw of Katie and Willow. At theater practice. The two of them posing after rehearsal, their legs kicked out like those of the Rockettes. The two of them relaxing together backstage. Katie was a pretty girl, but what struck Isla was how beautiful Willow photographed. She could be a fashion model for *Vogue*. She envisioned Willow posing some day for a Gap commercial or for a Victoria's Secret ad. Or possibly being on a big screen high up on a building in Times Square.

She scrolled through more of the photos, until she came upon one with Katie and a boy. He stood much taller than her and was very good looking, with strong white teeth and a scruffy beard. His blond hair was swept back until it swirled into a man bun over his crown. He was dressed in casual hipster garb, the kind of fashion one might see young men wearing in LA or Brooklyn. In another photo, he wore a mustard-colored knitted beanie cap. One photo was of all three of them standing arm in arm. In another the boy had his long arms wrapped around the girls' shoulders. In the next photo he could be seen kissing Willow's cheek while looking into the camera. In the next he posed while kissing Katie—again looking into the camera.

Katie looked different to her in these most recent photos. It took her a few seconds to realize why. It was because she wore a good deal of makeup in them. And not just makeup that most girls her age wore. It was as if someone with advanced cosmetic knowledge had done her up for a glamorous photo shoot. Dramatic lashes. Heavy pink shade over the eyelids. Rouged cheeks and vampiric lips. In the wrong hands, this makeup would have made her look terrible. But Isla had to admit that Katie looked amazing. Looking as she did in these photos, she, too, could pose for *Allure* or *Seventeen*. Of course, since she was five-three, modeling appeared out of the question for Katie.

It became obvious to Isla that Willow Briggs had a powerful hold over her daughter. Possibly more so than she even realized. Willow had changed her daughter from an innocent town girl into someone more cosmopolitan and worldly. It wouldn't be so unnerving if this transition had happened later in life, but she didn't want her sweet young daughter corrupted in high school. There'd be plenty of time for that later. She cursed herself for not being a more attentive mother. Maybe she should have put her foot down when it came to Katie hanging out with Willow Briggs.

Something else came to her, and it filled her with dread. Had Katie been dating that boy in the photos? And yet Katie had a long-time boyfriend. As she looked back on things, it seemed easy to imagine Willow being sexually active. She tried to give Willow the benefit of the doubt and not to judge, but the thought of these girls having sex so young haunted her.

Her father, Gil Briggs, had been filming them for his reality pilot, *Shepherd's Bay*, and Willow would no doubt be the star of the show. The camera would love her, and she'd love it back. Isla remembered a show called *Laguna Beach* a few years back, about a clique of beautiful, rich teens fighting with one another, behaving badly, and sleeping around. The show had been a huge ratings success. Could *Shepherd's Bay* have that same potential? Would it be trashy and addictive, and set in a coastal Maine town?

Then another thought came to her, and it momentarily lifted her spirits. Maybe this entire ordeal—the two girls having gone missing—had been staged to create drama for the show. And maybe this drama would help it get picked up by a major network. Yes, that was probably what had happened, and Katie had to be in on the plan. It had to be the reason why the girls had not yet contacted anyone.

Isla turned on her daughter's printer, prayed that there was some ink left in it—she could hardly afford a new ink cartridge right now, and the nearest office supply store was thirty miles from town—and printed out two pictures of the boy. Then she waited for the sheets to inch their way out. She had to discover the identity of the boy in these photos. Maybe he was the key to finding the girls.

KARL

*T*HE CHIEF ORDERED HIM TO GO HOME AND SLEEP, AND HE DIDN'T argue. All the caffeine in his system had been making him more tired than he actually was, if that was possible. So he surrendered to exhaustion and went back to his small apartment.

Where he collapsed in his bed and tossed.

And turned.

And thought about the missing James boy and now the two missing girls.

Then he turned and thought about Sofia and their years together, before she returned to her hometown of San Diego. She had never found comfort in the cold climes of Maine. And truthfully, they had married too early and had never been right for one another. Sofia had blamed him when their daughter chose to attend a small private college in Maine instead of one of the state universities in California. By that time their divorce had been finalized and she'd moved back to San Diego. But Amber's decision to go to Colby had had nothing to do with being closer to him. She'd traveled the farthest distance possible from San Diego and her mother, but in the process, she'd gotten farther away from both of her parents than ever. Since Sofia had no money, except for the pittance alimony she received from him each month, he ended up paying Colby what he could, which wasn't much. The remainder Amber had to make up with financial aid and school loans, and because of this, and his financial shortcomings, she seemed to resent him.

He tossed. Why did exhaustion preclude sleep? He thought sleep more indicative of boredom—and he was anything but bored. Sleep required shutting down the inquisitive mind, and a police officer's mind seemed to race nonstop. Always questioning. Always thinking. That was why cops drank a lot—even cops from small towns such as Shepherd's Bay. To drown out the many voices in their brain that were competing for attention.

That evening alone with Isla had made his overnight shift more manageable. He couldn't stop thinking about her. He wanted to find Katie alive and well and become Isla's white knight. Feel her embrace when she thanked him profusely for returning Katie home to her. How nice it would be to wrap his arms around her and feel her lips pressed against his like when they'd been teenagers.

Fat chance.

What if he could do something about her shitty marriage to Swisher? Like set him up by putting drugs in the cab of his pickup truck. Bad thoughts filled his mind. Swisher didn't deserve a woman like Isla. The guy couldn't even take care of his own sick son. Karl had seen him stumbling out of a fishermen's bar one evening with a woman hanging on his arm, the two of them laughing drunkenly as they staggered along the sidewalk. He'd debated pulling him over for a DUI, but then they had disappeared into another bar, and he had decided to put it out of mind. Forget it had ever happened.

Before he did something he might regret.

Like Taser him and kick the shit out of him. Only problem was that Swisher was an ornery bastard when wronged and was tough as nails. But Karl knew he'd had righteous indignation on his side—and a wood baton.

His alarm went off, and he realized he'd fallen asleep. The sun shone through the gauzy white curtains, momentarily irritating his eyes. He needed sustenance before he resumed his search for those two missing girls and the James boy. He showered and dressed and then headed out. On his way to the station, he stopped at a nearby convenience store for his first shitty coffee of the day.

Live to fight another day, he thought as he took the first sip.

ISLA

Six in the morning and the temperature had not yet hit fifty: that was Maine in a nutshell. By noon it could hit eighty degrees, with high humidity. Or it could be raining, with thunder and streaks of lightning. Old-timers frequently talked about the snowstorm that had hit in June one year. Isla pulled up to the designated spot near the coast and noticed that she was the first person to arrive. With what little money she had, she'd gone into Baker's Donuts and tried to purchase two dozen assorted for the volunteers. But then Ed Baker had come out of the fry room, covered head to toe in flour, and had refused to take her money.

A steaming cup of coffee sat in the cup holder between the seats. She let the engine idle a few seconds so she could bask in the heated cab for a bit longer.

Her sister-in-law had come over earlier in the morning to keep an eye on Raisin. She could trust Deb with her son's life, as Deb knew what to do in the event of an emergency. Although she was Ray's older sibling, Deb felt more like a sister to Isla than anything else, and she felt fortunate to have her in her life. Deb had also agreed to watch Isla's father. Up until the other night, her father had been able to stay home alone, but now the disease seemed to be progressing so rapidly that she wondered if she could adequately care for him.

The ocean glistened a thousand feet from her car. Whitecaps rolled in along the seaweed-encrusted beach. A little ways up the shore, it turned rocky and rugged. Developers had for the past few years been trying to decide how to build more homes atop these rocky outposts.

Hunger gnawed at her, and she realized she hadn't eaten since supper last night. She sipped her hot coffee and stared out at the ocean. An oil tanker cruised off in the distance. The sugary, yeasty scent of fried dough filled her nostrils, and she found her hand digging into one of the pink boxes, which had been secured with pastry string tied up into a bow. At random, she pulled out a powdered molasses doughnut and bit into it, then followed it up with a sip of coffee. The pillowy mix of sugar and dough practically dissolved on her tongue once the hot coffee washed over it. Ed Baker made one helluva doughnut.

What's taking everyone so long to get here? We need to start searching for the girls.

Staring out at the ocean, she remembered a time when these monstrous mansions didn't exist. When this strip of land accommodated modest homes inhabited by lobstermen and their families, before ocean views became a valued real estate feature. When that happened, the swift rise in property values and real estate taxes pushed all these old families out, making the area affordable only to affluent out-of-staters looking for a bargain.

The changing nature of Shepherd's Bay had been a sore topic around town. Isla had concluded that change was inevitable. On one hand, it made her sad to realize that Shepherd's Bay was not the same town she grew up in. And yet many of her new clients happily paid top dollar for one of her cuts. And cutting men's hair was so easy, it felt like stealing money. Most of the older men had receding hairlines and little to no hair to cut, and they never fussed or complained afterward. More clients kept coming to her as the word spread in town, and the fact that the nearest barbershop to hers in Shepherd's Bay was twenty miles away helped, too.

She remembered walking along that same beach with her parents when she'd been a little girl, her mother cradling her baby brother in her arms. They had set up blankets and chairs and then had swum for hours. Her father had taken her by the wrists and towed her through the churning waves. He'd been a handsome guy back then; many said he'd resembled that actor who appeared in all those old black-and-white *Twilight Zone* episodes.

Now there were lawsuits and questions about who controlled the beach access behind these mansions. The owners of these homes didn't want the public mucking about on what they believed was their private property, obstructing their spectacular view and invading their privacy. It disgusted her that people from out of state would have the audacity to take what had been a natural right to citizens for as long as anyone could remember.

Before she knew it, cars started to turn into the parking lot. *Finally!* She got out of the car with boxes in hand and offered doughnuts up to the volunteers, desperate to start searching for Katie . . . and Willow. She prayed that all this had been staged for Gil's stupid reality show.

Drew pulled up in his truck. Then he and his three husky friends piled out, carrying energy drinks. They made a beeline for the doughnuts and wolfed down half a dozen before Isla shooed them away and offered doughnuts to the other volunteers.

Drew seemed anxious and pissed off about the whole ordeal. He missed Katie, but Isla also knew how much he despised all these wealthy newcomers.

A Mercedes SUV pulled up, and Gil Briggs emerged from it with his fragile wife. She looked sickly and frail and wore a blue scarf over her head. Her thin hands were buried deep in the pockets of the designer jacket she had on, and her mysterious eyes hid behind designer sunglasses. Had she ever seen the woman's eyes? Isla wondered. Drew glanced at the couple and scoffed, grumbling something rude under his breath, but he knew better than to confront grieving parents.

Isla approached Gil with the boxes of doughnuts. Only a few remained. Gil's eyes appeared red from crying. As she approached, he reached out and embraced her, sobbing violently. It occurred to her that maybe he hadn't set all this up in order to spice up his reality show. She shared his pain but wanted to stay strong for Katie's sake. Because she knew in her heart that Katie was out there, alive and well, and waiting to be found. And if Katie was alive, she was the type of kid who would make sure her friend was alive, too.

Gil released her but continued to sob. People came over and said kind words to him. They listened sympathetically while he told everyone how much he loved and missed his precious daughter, as if she was the only girl who'd gone missing. It irked Isla. She wanted to remind him that her daughter had gone missing, as well. But she held her tongue, her eyes alternating between Gil and his aloof wife.

Felicia stood like a statue, neither speaking nor showing any emotion. Isla assumed from Felicia's movements that she was on some kind of medication. She couldn't blame her. It wouldn't be the way she'd want to face this crisis, but everyone reacted differently. And yet the sight of this statuesque woman mesmerized her. If she didn't know her identity, she might have mistaken Felicia for a reclusive Hollywood starlet.

"I couldn't live with myself if something happened to my baby," Gil said. "I'd move heaven and earth to bring her home."

"They're okay, Gil. Our girls are resilient kids," Isla said.

"Willow is all I have. You at least have another child."

Isla wanted to slap him for that inappropriate remark. Lucky for him, something caught her attention just then. Over his shoulder, she saw a Porsche SUV pull up next to the Mercedes. Out of it stepped Samantha and Beckett McCallister. Beckett looked exceedingly handsome, like one of those soap opera actors her mother used to watch back in the day. Like that Mitt guy who ran for president years ago. He exuded equal parts privilege and restraint, maintaining a stiff upper lip in the face of tragedy. The two of them were dressed casually in crisp jeans and Ivy League–themed sweatshirts.

Samantha was her best and biggest cheerleader at the salon, recommending Isla to all her friends and neighbors. She gushed over the way Isla styled her hair, and Samantha's words of praise filled a void in Isla's ego that Ray couldn't even begin to meet. When Samantha's wealthy friends began to patronize the salon, for the first time since opening her door for business, Isla started to make a profit.

She was moving over to greet Samantha when she saw the back

door to the SUV open. Out stepped a young man wearing a knitted beanie cap. A swath of fine hairs dotted his jawline. Isla couldn't believe his outfit. Was he going to a rave party or planning to search for the two missing girls? He had on a green bomber jacket with a bizarre coat of arms on the breast. Beneath that he had on a ribbed T-shirt and tapered black jeans with hideous designer rips over the knees. Isla imagined prepubescent and underpaid Vietnamese kids ripping the jeans in sweatshops in order that entitled scions like him could wear them to search parties.

She suddenly realized that she recognized him.

Isla had barely had time to take him in when Drew started shouting. The kid looked up from his phone and staggered sideways as Drew bull-rushed him, but then Beckett and a few of the other volunteers came between them.

"Get away from us," Beckett ordered Drew. "Julian, get back in the car."

Julian!

"Screw him, Dad. I'm not letting this chump keep me from looking for my friend," Julian said.

"You're lucky there's people here, Julian, or I'd kick your ass," Drew said.

"Anytime, dude. You know where to find me."

Isla stuck her fingers in her mouth and let out a shrill whistle, and everyone turned toward her. She stared at Julian, the boy in her daughter's photos. Why hadn't she made that connection sooner? This added a new wrinkle to the mix. Not only was Samantha her most prized and valued customer at the salon, but Julian was her *son.*

"Drew, go home. And don't come back until you can show some respect for the other volunteers," she said.

"That scumbag doesn't give a crap about finding Katie. He's probably the one responsible for the two of them missing," Drew muttered.

"Screw you, dude. You're tripping if you think that," Julian said.

"Stop this right now. Both of you," a man's voice shouted.

Chip Hicks stood in front of Drew now, his hand on the kid's chest. Chip Hicks, the beloved social studies teacher and girls' softball coach. The baseball player from Shepherd's Bay who starred at UMaine before playing two years in the minors.

He went on. "This is not about the two of you. We came here to find two beloved girls in our community. So show some respect for the parents of these kids, you hear?"

"Dude started in on me as soon as I got out of the car," Julian complained, pointing at Drew. At least a dozen stacked bangles hung from his wrist.

"I don't care who's to blame. Let's work together and put all our energies into finding Willow and Katie. That's what's most important here," Chip Hicks responded.

Why did it bother Isla that he chose to say Willow's name first? Her reaction felt stupid and petty, although now she missed her daughter so much that it physically hurt to hear her name. Like being in the midst of a bad flu, when every single inch of one's body ached. She had to find her daughter. It didn't matter who got top billing. Willow would most likely gain her fair share of attention throughout the course of her life.

The presence of Chip Hicks in this search party made her feel better. As a teacher and coach, he had plenty of experience taking charge in tense situations. Revered by the locals for his storied athletic past and his deep connection to Shepherd's Bay, Hicks commanded a certain amount of respect in town. His father had been a high school principal, and the middle school had been named after his grandfather. Chip Hicks was the walking embodiment of Shepherd's Bay and a great source of pride to the locals. So why in the world was he still single?

"How you holding out, Isla?" Chip asked her after he had diffused the tension between the boys, and he and Isla were out of earshot of the others.

"I'm barely holding it together, to tell you the truth."

"Well, hang tough. We'll find them."

"Thanks for all you've done for the girls, Chip."

"Hey, these kids are my life. I love them like they're my own." He hugged her. "Now let's get cooking."

Dense woods rolled across the landscape in front of her. Off in the distance, she could see the mountain that put Shepherd's Bay in its shadow. It wasn't much more than a hill, really, at twenty-five hundred feet, and Isla had hiked it so many times, she knew just about every inch of it.

Chip took charge and began directing people where to go. He assigned everyone in the parking lot to one of several groups and exchanged phone numbers with the group leaders in case they came across something in the woods. He had made sure that the Briggses and McCallisters were in separate groups.

Before her own group entered the woods, Isla glanced over and saw Felicia shuffling forward, her arms wrapped around her thin frame. Past Felicia, she saw Julian, who was staring at his phone as he trudged ahead, as if this was all a major inconvenience for him. Why had Katie been taking pictures with Julian when she'd been dating Drew since her freshman year? It didn't look good. Besides, Julian acted like a privileged and spoiled kid. She guessed he must have been a handful to raise. Was he involved in the girls' disappearance, like Drew had claimed? She needed to know more about Julian, although she needed to come by this information in a way that it never got back to his mother. She couldn't afford to lose business over rumors and innuendo.

But first she needed to find Katie. It was all she could do to keep her emotions in check. Everything else came secondary to finding her. And Isla knew in her heart that Katie was alive. The strongest attachment a mother could experience was to her child.

The ocean's roar receded behind her as she walked farther into the woods. She looked back one last time, hoping to see Ray pull up in his truck, before disappearing into the dense growth of trees.

KARL

*T*HE PROBLEM WITH SHEPHERD'S BAY, HE KNEW, WAS THAT IT WAS vast and sprawling in size, composed of dense woods, hilly terrain, a coastal peninsula, and miles of rocky shoreline. Searching for three missing kids was time-consuming and difficult work. If it was true that Dakota James's spirit was still trapped inside his body, then it was out there and calling for release.

Karl gripped his machete and hacked his way through the thick vegetation that crossed his path. The trail he followed led to the top of Mount Bloom, and the only reason he was taking it was that he knew the summit was a popular spot for kids to party, away from adults. At just under a thousand feet, the mountain lent itself to a quick hike.

How many times had he made it up this mountain? Too many to count. Hiking had been his personal therapy. There was nothing better than reaching the top and then gazing out over the town and the coast. The sun's light fought hard to permeate the canopy of leaves above him, making the air feel crisper and cleaner the higher he climbed. He thought about what he might find and tried not to dwell on it. Or *whom* he might find. The increasing heat of summer would speed up the decaying process. And then he thought, *They're not paying me anywhere near enough to do this job.*

He swung the machete, cutting shrubbery. Nature looked different when one was searching for bodies, as opposed to hiking for pleasure and enjoying the view. He tried his best not to think in such negative terms. Searching implied death, and that was why the woods had taken on such an ominous hue today.

And yet what did he know about searching for missing persons? He'd rarely done it in his time as a Shepherd's Bay police officer. He knew as much as the next guy who read newspapers or watched those silly crime shows on television. Maybe less. Because of that, he scolded himself for being so negative. He had to continually tell himself to be more positive. To believe that the glass was half full rather than half empty.

Sixteen years now as a cop and he'd fallen into the job by accident. He had had a wife and daughter when he'd moved back to Shepherd's Bay and needed to find work. The hard part had been convincing his wife to move cross-country to the East Coast. San Diego was too expensive, and they would have never been able to buy a home there. He had explained to her that in Shepherd's Bay they could afford to buy something nice and raise a family, and that she could stay home and take care of their daughter. He'd finally convinced Sofia to uproot herself, knowing that she had no idea what she was in store for come winter.

He had tried his hand at fishing for a while but hadn't been able to overcome the seasickness and the loneliness of being out at sea for days on end. Shepherd's Bay didn't offer many well-paying jobs for a man trying to support his family, so when an opening came up in the small police department, he jumped at it. His status as a Coast Guard veteran helped him, as well as the fact that there weren't too many interested or qualified candidates in town. So he interviewed, got himself hired, went to the academy, and started working the night shift as the lowest cop on the totem pole.

The first citation he handed out in Shepherd's Bay happened to be to Swisher Eaves. First night on the job. What were the odds? Swisher had been traveling eighty in a forty-miles-per-hour zone. Criminal speeding. Swisher used all his considerable charm to try to persuade him not to issue him a ticket. Then he tried flattering him, saying how surprised Isla would be when he told her whom he'd run into today. Did he know the two of them had been a couple back in high school? He remembered Swisher slipping that tidbit into the conversation before mentioning that he and Isla had a young daughter and planned on having more kids. He invited Karl to come over for dinner some night. Relenting to Swisher's persistent charm, he ended up issuing him a warning.

The hill steepened. This was the part of the trail that he liked best. Sweat bubbled on his brow as he pushed himself forward. He felt the burn in his calves and thighs. He took in everything around him and examined the flora for broken branches, crushed leaves, or anything that might indicate human intervention. He swung the machete in anger and chopped and cut, and then cut and chopped. He thought of Isla sleeping with that jerk. Then about the time they'd kissed back in high school. He thought about how stupid he'd been to let Isla go and thus find her way eventually into the arms of that asshole. It had been his own fault. All his troubles in life he'd brought on himself. He should have fought harder to keep her, but it was too late now for regrets.

As he was lost in thought, the peak of Mount Bloom arrived with a sudden clarity. Blue sky filled the void near the top. Large boulders and trees took up space wherever he looked. He practically sprinted the last hundred yards, his lungs filling with air. Sweat dripped from his crinkled brow as a strong breeze rustled some dirt atop one of the lookout boulders. It swirled and formed into an eddy. He climbed atop the boulder and stared down at the tiny kingdom below, noticing it unequally divided between the haves and the have-nots. Unequal in that the have-nots resided in the vast interior part of the land. Unequal because the monied possessed the tiniest and most desirable real estate holdings along the coast.

His body felt tired in a good way. He was exhausted from his extensive search but was relieved that he had not turned up anything ghastly. Like two dead girls.

He stared down at the town and the dense woods surrounding it. The ocean roiled, and waves smashed against the rocks along the shore. The bay, however, appeared calm and glassy. Connecting the mainland to Harper's Point was the majestic suspension bridge, which had been built a few years ago to replace its worn and run-down predecessor. Somewhere in that vast expanse of vegetation below lay the decomposing body of the James boy, assuming that he hadn't run away from home, which Karl had never believed was a plausible theory. He felt a stirring in his gut that told him these missing-child cases were intimately connected. Were the girls victimized by the same person who harmed Dakota James? Was one of the wealthy newcomers responsible for all this tragedy? Or was the malefactor a bitter townie hell-bent on getting revenge for the way the town had changed? Too early to know, but every hour that passed made it less likely that they'd find the girls alive.

He swung his machete through the air and headed back down an alternate trail, praying for the best. Keeping his eyes open. His ears, too. He couldn't bear to see the grief on Isla's face if Katie turned up dead. She'd been putting on a brave face for the past few days, but that would all fall away if his worst fears came true.

ISLA

THE REALITY OF THIS SEARCH PARTY STRUCK HER AS PROFOUND WHEN she found herself deep in the woods. She thought of *Grimms' Fairy Tales* and all the negative connotations related to forests.

The crunch of decomposing leaves underfoot constantly reminded her of the grim task at hand. Every step taken brought her closer to Katie. Every time she looked through the woods and didn't see her daughter, she was reminded that Katie's body hadn't been found. That she was still alive and breathing.

She wanted to call Ray but didn't. There came a defining moment in every marriage, a moment when one spouse made a move that determined the outcome. Whether or not Ray meant to screw up, whether it was by accident or intentional, it didn't really matter to her now. She'd never forget what he'd done—or what he hadn't done—in her family's greatest time of need.

She picked up a stick and poked the ground. Dead leaves gave way under the stick. If only that crunching sound would go away. It was a constant reminder that her daughter was missing. She prayed for God to deliver her daughter safely back to her. Many of these people searching were members of her church. She adored them all and felt lucky for their presence in her life. But religion seemed entirely different than her belief in God. Would God be so callous as to allow her only daughter to be snatched from her arms? If so, then why pray so hard for God to help find her? Would a loving God have created the sweetest boy in the world, only to give him such a devastating illness? She had a love-hate relationship with

God. Still, she prayed every day that Scout would watch over Raisin and keep him safe. She did believe that God had a plan for everything in life, and that maybe Raisin's health had been designed to bring Scout into their lives. Or maybe God had given her this life in order to test her faith.

Someone off in the distance shouted. Had they found something? Isla's heart raced, and she turned in anticipation of the worst. But just as quickly, another person relayed that it was a false alarm. Merely a log covered in moss.

She remembered carrying Katie in her arms when she was a little girl and pushing her in the stroller. Those were the early days, when Ray had his act together somewhat. As a couple, they had once resembled the First Family. Or a family in a commercial. Why he'd chosen her out of all the girls in town was a mystery, although she better understood how it had happened in hindsight. After that bitter college experience, she knew she had had a lot of work to do picking up the pieces and rebuilding her self-esteem. She had been low-hanging fruit, and Ray had determined that she was ripe for the picking.

Ray had come along almost by accident and had taken her breath away. They had run into each other at the summer fair one day, and right away he had bought her a giant blueberry cotton candy. They had walked around, talking about the town and the people they both knew, until they reached the stand with the basketball hoops. After three successful shots, an almost impossible feat at the annual country fair, Ray had been awarded a giant stuffed teddy bear, which he'd proudly handed over to her. She remembered lugging that bear around the fair grounds for the rest of the night, all eyes on the two of them. Near the end of the evening, he had reached out and held her hand, and she hadn't resisted, because it had felt good to be desired.

Beautiful to behold, Ray had carried himself with a confidence not much seen in these parts. With his shirt off, he sported tanned, wiry muscles. He'd done crazy things back then, too, all designed to impress her. Doing backflips off the local quarries. Standing on the seat of his motorcycle while riding at a good clip. Driving backward through the fast-food lane and then imitating a pompous

French dude. After she had dealt with pretentious academics for the past few years, it had felt good to be pursued by an old-fashioned guy.

She had fallen for him right away, blind to his obvious shortcomings, ignoring what friends and family whispered about him, laughing at every silly joke he made. Love had blinded her, and like a dumb ass she'd fallen for it, staunchly defending him to others. She could have sat with him on the beach for hours, drinking wine and listening to him lecture on the art of da Vinci. Or talk about great movies or economic policy or the effects of prescription meds on the youth of America, even though half the time she'd been convinced that he knew nothing about the subject he was lecturing her on. She had liked watching how animated he got when he spewed his bullshit, the flames from the bonfire illuminating his handsome face, the wine warping her perception of Ray "Swisher" Eaves. And in that way she had let herself fall in love. When he'd told her how much he loved her, it was as if God Himself was speaking.

She had fallen for every stupid and predictable line of his, ignoring the voice in her head telling her to run like hell. She realized only now that she had fallen in love with a romantic notion of Ray Eaves, and all the negative stuff fell away. He had filled the void left by that lecherous professor who had played her like a fool. Who had used and abused her, and then had tossed her to the curb, another unintended victim of academia. Then there was the sting of returning home and finding a life for herself, discovering an identity that she could slip into and call her own.

And before she knew it, she got pregnant with Katie—and engaged to Ray.

But he had delivered to her the most precious gifts she could ever be given: Katie and Raisin. No matter what he'd done, she couldn't deny this fact or be more grateful to him for those two kids. They were her greatest accomplishments, and from a man who let her down on a regular basis, that was saying a lot. Her love for him lessened with each day she stay married to him, while her love for Katie and Raisin continued to grow. And yet he would come home some nights and act like the old Ray, pull her into his loving embrace, his unshaven cheek tickling her skin, his lips showering her neck and face with kisses. Sometimes, he'd even give her a wad of cash, as if it were a precious gift, when he should have been providing for his family on a regular basis. It made her sad that he squandered away his God-given talents, and even sadder that he failed to fulfill his obligations as husband and father.

She couldn't deny that Katie had adored him as a young girl. What had there been not to love? He'd been the sun and the stars in her eyes. Then Raisin had come along, and he'd adored his father for a while. Ray had decided to name him Raymond Jr., but the little boy hadn't been able to pronounce his name properly; it had come out as Raisin. Time and time again. So that was what everyone had started calling him. And as she'd grown older, poor Katie had never stopped looking for her father at her ball games, concerts, and recitals. Raisin had given up on his father sooner than his sister, understanding him for who he was. He didn't love Ray any less. He'd just come to understand and accept his dad's limitations.

Three hours of arduous hiking and thinking about the past had made Isla's feet hurt. A cell phone rang off in the distance. The leader of her group answered the call, then announced that it was time to turn back. The forecast called for rain, and not everyone had dressed for inclement weather. They'd done all they could for the time being. She headed back with the group. If it was possible to be sad and happy at the same time, she accomplished it. Not finding her daughter in these woods gave her hope that Katie was still alive.

People huddled in the parking lot and hugged her, expressed confidence that the girls would soon be found, although she could tell from their expressions that their words betrayed their true feelings. At one point, she looked across the parking lot and saw Samantha McCallister hugging Gil Briggs. The parking lot now resembled a high school cafeteria: the cool kids at one end and the regular kids at the other.

Felicia caught her eye. She stood tall, chin high, her sunglasses temporarily removed from the bridge of her nose. Those smoky eyes! Where had Isla seen them before? She thought Felicia looked quite beautiful—and vaguely familiar. As she stood staring at the mysterious woman, someone tapped her shoulder. She turned around.

"I'm so sorry for all that's happened, Isla," Father Delaney said, looking more like an altar boy than a priest.

"Thank you."

"You and your family will be in my prayers tonight."

"No offense, but it's not me I want you to pray for."

"God's watching out for Katie. I just know it. One way or another, He'll bring her home."

"That's what I'm worried about, Father. God's home can wait a little longer, as far as I'm concerned."

"Amen to that. Take good care, Isla."

Suddenly rain fell. First in drops and then in sheets akin to plastic wrap. They hid her tears and allowed her to escape the well-meaning volunteers offering up words of hope and optimism. She ran back to her car, covering her head with her coat, climbed behind the wheel, and sped out of the parking lot, past the fleet of expensive cars idling at the far end.

Streams of white water cascaded down her windshield as she drove home. As she turned into her driveway and then steered her vehicle up it, rainwater sluiced down either side of the dirt road. She couldn't help dwelling on the fact that the roof to her house leaked in various places. This was just one of the many repairs that needed to be done on the house. She parked, jumped out of the minivan, sprinted up the steps, and barged inside, then collapsed in tears on the couch. Raisin looked up at her from where he sat on the floor, his hands wrestling with the controller to his video game. Scout sat on his haunches and seemed to study her. Raisin paused the game, stood up, and walked over to hug her. She felt his hands squeeze her waist. She glanced over his thick mop of hair and saw her dad sitting in his recliner. A few seconds later her sister-in-law walked into the room.

"Don't worry, Mom. They'll find her," Raisin said.

"I know they will, sweetheart."

"And she'll be as good as new when she comes home," her father added.

Did her father understand what he'd just said? Did her father have any idea that his granddaughter had gone missing? Or was he merely aping Raisin's sentiments? She let Raisin hold on to her, despite feeling unworthy of his love. It was what she needed most right now. And yet for some reason, she felt like the worst mother in the world.

She wanted to sleep and not wake up, although, oddly, she didn't want to die. Was there a name for that gray state between the two realms of consciousness? Between sleep and death? When reality became too painful to endure?

But life carried on, regardless of one's feelings. She had to drag herself up off the couch and make dinner. Fill Scout's bowls with water and food. Do laundry. Unload and load the dishwasher. Clean the house. She wanted to cry at the prospect of performing such mundane duties in the face of tragedy. But they had to be done. Life failed to stop just because her daughter had gone missing.

Her sister-in-law kissed her good-bye and let herself out.

She lifted her head from the couch pillow and saw Raisin sitting on the floor and reading a book. Her father was still sitting in the recliner across from her, staring at the wall in front of him.

"I'm hungry, Mom," Raisin said.

"Me too," her father added.

"Okay, guys, I'll start dinner in a jiffy," she said. "Give me a minute."

"Where's that daughter of yours?" her father asked.

Raisin turned and grimaced. "She's still missing, Grampa."

"Well, she should probably come home and wash up for dinner," he said. "Those hands won't wash themselves, you know."

"Stop it, Grampa!"

"Take it easy, Raisin. Your grandfather doesn't understand what's happening," she whispered.

"How can he not?"

"His brain's getting worse." She stood and walked over to her father, then rested a hand on his shoulder. "How you doing, Dad?"

"I'm a lot better than you know, lady. You can't put anything past me. You think you can move into my home and try to steal all my stuff? Think I don't notice that there's no money in my wallet?"

"That's not true, Dad. We love you. We would never take what's yours." She leaned over and kissed his cheek. "You can stay here for as long as you like."

"I don't trust you. I'll go and stay with your husband if I have to. He'll take me to the police and tell them what all of you have been doing. How you've been stealing all my money."

"Except that Ray lives in this house with us."

"Is that so? Then where is he?"

"I need to make dinner, Dad." She sighed.

"Please hurry and make dinner, sweetie, because I'm starving."

Making dinner now felt like running in mud. Everything slowed down and gained mass. The Teflon pan in her hand felt like an anvil formed out of uranium. She pressed the patties into shape and laid them down in the butter-greased skillet. Put some frozen vegetables in boiling water and tots in the oven. Then she mixed some pudding in a bowl and stuck it in the refrigerator to chill.

She couldn't erase the image of that racy painting from her head. Wouldn't Ray be surprised to learn that she'd lifted it out of his collection in the art studio and hid it in the cellar? She had once known the woman in that painting. She couldn't be sure when Ray had painted it, but she was certain he had done it while the woman was still married. Had that bastard slept with her? She didn't doubt it, Ray's wandering eye having been a lifelong habit. She'd nearly crushed the canvas on one of the tree stumps in the yard before deciding to keep it. Maybe she'd confront him with it. Or better yet, maybe she'd show the woman's ex the painting and see what he had to say.

But what would that do except extend the hurt and suffering to others? No, she wouldn't do that. She'd been brought up better than to hurt people's feelings. She would replace the painting in the art studio and say nothing. Forget she ever saw it.

Why was she thinking about Ray's painting while Katie was still out there, begging to be rescued from whatever situation she'd gotten herself into? She peeked out the small window over the kitchen sink and watched as the rain bucketed down. A heavy mist lingered over the coast, hiding the ocean but not the bay. The Northern Lighthouse swung an amorphous beam of light through the pea soup. She fought back the tears, thinking about Katie. Hopefully, her daughter was at least warm and sheltered.

She got jarred out of her thoughts by the sound of Scout's bells. From the kitchen she could see into the living room and saw Scout staring at Raisin and then at her, and bowing his head to alert her that something was happening. Moving into action, she grabbed the test kit on the counter and ran straight to her son. She drew a drop of blood, and then touched and held the edge of the test strip to the drop of blood. Low eighties, not terribly low, but that number could dip further, and fast, if not addressed. She took a few gummy bears out of the package sitting on the coffee table, and handed them to Raisin. He cupped them to his mouth and began chewing. She suddenly became aware of the sound of meat sizzling in the skillet. Dinner would have to wait fifteen minutes or so until his numbers had adjusted. After fifteen minutes had passed, and Raisin's number stabilized, she removed a liver treat from her pocket and held it out to Scout. "Good dog. Good dog. Treat. Treat," she said to him, watching as the Lab happily snatched the liver treat out of her hand. The treat was Scout's incentive to continue doing the job he was put on earth to do, and also because she deeply appreciated this unique animal that God had gifted them.

The dog strutted proudly past her father, his head held high. "You should let that dog run outside and get some fresh air. It's not normal for a mutt to stay cooped up like that all day."

"He's Raisin's service dog, Dad."

"What the hell's a service dog? I've never heard of such a ridiculous thing in all my life. And who's this damn Raisin you keep talking about?"

Isla shot her son a look, as if to say, "Be nice."

"I'm right here, Grampa."

"I'm not an idiot, you know. I know damn well who you are. You're with her. The two of you are trying to steal all my money and get rid of me."

"How about we eat supper now?" Isla said, trying to defuse the situation and keep her emotions in check.

"Supper! Now, you're talking."

The three of them walked into the kitchen, and Isla put the food on the table. Then they sat down at the table, and Isla asked Raisin to say grace. Her father made the sign of the cross, a ritual every Catholic child of a certain age could do from memory. It was these same Catholic rituals, of which there were many, that she fell back on for comfort and support. Raisin recited a common prayer without emotion and finished with a pronounced *amen*, as if to say, "Roger and out, God." Then the three of them ate in silence.

But her mind rebelled against this artificial stillness. She couldn't stop thinking about Katie. "Pass the tots," and she thought of Katie. "More juice?" and Katie. The pudding reminded her of Katie. It didn't help that she kept glancing at Katie's empty chair throughout the meal. So much so that she gave no thought to the fact that Ray's chair also sat empty.

After Raisin and her father went to bed, Isla sat on the couch in the dark and logged on to the computer. Instagram. Facebook. Finstagram. Twitter. Google. Anywhere she could search for any information about Julian McCallister. Something about that boy troubled her. She'd seen trust funders like him when she was at college. She understood their lack of awareness in regard to wealth and privilege. Kids like Julian seemed to think that the rules didn't apply to them. Or that their daddy's money allowed them to skirt all and any authority. Girls existed to serve as their toys, and they never took no for an answer—even when the girl explicitly told them no. It occurred to her that her abusive professor may have been brought up in that same kind of environment.

Isla found photos online of Julian with his rock band. He was the lead guitarist, of course. And photos of him and his rich, privileged friends dressed in designer clothes and drinking, vaping, smoking weed. In every photo he smiled in a stoned manner, wore that knitted hipster cap, and sported that fuzzy beard. Isla registered the long, flowing hair, the kind certain girls preferred. In some photos, he'd tugged it up into a man bun on the crown of his head. Lots of Instagram and Facebook entries, all open to public viewing. There were hundreds of them. Knowing she wasn't going to get much sleep tonight, she began to scroll through the remaining pictures she'd uncovered.

She stopped when she saw the photo of Julian sandwiched between Katie and Willow, his long arms over their shoulders. All three of them were smiling. Willow was almost as tall as him. It was the same photo she'd discovered on Katie's computer.

Isla sensed that she was onto something. What if he had something to do with the girls' disappearance? He hadn't looked very excited to be part of that search party today. She needed to mention Julian to Karl and see if he would look into the kid's history. *Leave no stone unturned.* Maybe she'd start asking around town herself, at the risk of offending her best client, Samantha. But Katie came first and foremost. The hell with her salon. Katie needed her right now, and she would do anything in her power to bring her back.

KARL

*T*HE HEAVY RAIN HAD SUBSIDED BY THE TIME HE ROUSED HIMSELF OUT of bed. He hadn't slept well. Events had conspired to deprive him of what he typically took for granted. He made his way into the kitchen and started some coffee. While it brewed, he showered and shaved. The search would continue this morning, although the odds of finding the two girls alive lessened with each passing hour. Today the state police would be bringing in dogs and a helicopter.

When the coffee finished brewing, he poured himself a cup and sat in front of the television. He couldn't remember the last time he'd watched the stupid thing. The light from the screen filled his tiny living room and endowed the space with an otherworldly glow. It had taken only a few minutes for the crisis in Shepherd's Bay to make the national news. The story of the two missing girls appeared to be a ratings boon. Reporters had interviewed the police chief and a few other volunteers, all of whom he knew in one way or another. Optimism prevailed, as it usually did so early in a search. People were optimistic by nature, until they weren't. Of course he'd not done many missing-person searches in his capacity as a police officer. Sure, he'd helped look for a few old people with dementia who'd wandered off, but they had been quickly located by fellow officers or loved ones. The only dead person he'd ever seen was the bloated body of an old lobsterman who'd gone overboard in a storm and washed ashore.

He wondered about Isla. If he hadn't been able to sleep, he doubted that she'd managed to get any slumber. He envisioned himself finding the two girls in a cabin somewhere deep in the woods, hiding out from the world, as if this was all some kind of crazy scheme to become famous reality stars, the two girls having no way of knowing how frantic their parents or the community at large was. Nor would they have any idea how much time, effort, and money had been expended to find them. He wouldn't put it past Gil to be in on the plan. If this was true, criminal charges would certainly be filed.

Bitter thoughts of his failed marriage came back to him. The last year had been the worst. They had barely spoken to one another, as the marriage had appeared all but over. Much of it was his own fault. He had never denied his role in bringing his wife and daughter here or the fact that he worked crazy long shifts. Although she had agreed to come to Maine, Sofia had never really wanted to live in this small, frigid town three thousand miles from home. Their inability to communicate had only intensified the gulf between them, making matters worse. The root of many arguments had been money, but money had merely been a proxy for the many other problems that lay beneath the foundation of their crumbling marriage. Because of that, he had worked extra shifts, which had only deepened their rift, compounding their feelings of loneliness and despair.

That last year, during a particularly heated argument, she blurted out that she didn't love him. She stated what they had both known for a long time. Although he knew it to be true, her words still jarred him. Something in the way she said this, so defiantly and without remorse, made him suspect that she was seeing someone else. Was he imagining such an affair? But then the more he thought about it, the more he convinced himself that she was being unfaithful to him. While he patrolled the streets, keeping citizens safe, he kept thinking that she was out screwing around on him.

He took a week off from work and rented a car. Then he proceeded to stalk his own wife. This foreshadowed their demise as a married couple, but he didn't care at that point. It didn't take long before he learned the truth. She was cheating on him, and in his own home—in his own goddamned bed! How stupid he'd been.

A loud commercial on the TV jolted him from his reverie. He noticed that the sun had started to rise. He loved this time of morning. So filled with optimism and hope. When he was fueled with hot coffee, his insulated life seemed far better than how it looked to others.

He felt that something might break today as he left the house and headed toward his cruiser. He didn't want to admit it, but he felt certain he would find Katie alive. If he was honest with himself, looking back on his relationship with Sofia, he'd even venture to say that the breakdown of his marriage had been mostly his fault. He was a loner by nature who had trouble expressing his feelings. His wife must have suspected that his heart lay elsewhere. She must have known that the man whom she married, and who had moved her three thousand miles away to Maine, was in love with someone else.

That obviously had to be the reason why she'd slept with Ray "Swisher" Eaves.

ISLA

On the second day of searching, Isla was surprised to learn that additional citizens had volunteered to help look for the girls. The parking lot today was jammed with news vans adorned with satellite dishes and lettered with the logos of their news stations. Most hailed from Portland, but a few came from the cable news networks. Reporters stood everywhere, gripping microphones and speaking to cameras. Some interviewed volunteers, rotating them in and out of the queue. She saw the old police chief answering questions. Chip Hicks stood in front of another mic.

Such a circus, she thought. She tried to control her growing frustration at this nonsense. All of this made it more difficult to get started searching for the girls. She wanted to scream at these disgusting media people, who were intent on exploiting her daughter's disappearance.

A helicopter buzzed overhead. Dogs barked off in the distance. She glanced over and saw the McCallisters standing next to their neighbors from Harper's Point, all of whom had volunteered to search for Katie and Willow. For whatever reason, she couldn't find Julian in the crowd today. Had he already tired of searching?

As grateful as she was for everyone's assistance, she still couldn't get over the fact that the town's citizens had segregated themselves by wealth in the parking lot. If anything, this crisis should have brought people together, not pushed them apart. But that didn't concern her right now. Only finding Katie did. It occupied her every waking thought.

Why hadn't Chip Hicks given everyone their marching orders yet? She saw Gil Briggs speaking to a reporter. Felicia stood silently next to him, her thin arm looped through his. Tears flowed from Gil's eyes as he kept repeating over and over how badly he wanted his little girl back. Overcome by emotion, he waved off the camera and broke down into violent sobs. Maybe her stoic New England upbringing was to blame, but she found his behavior off putting. Then it made her wonder if she'd been grieving enough. Who knew in these situations how anyone would react? It sounded odd to think that way, but she understood that she needed to keep her head clear in order to do what she had come here to do. Grieving was reserved for the dead, and she had to keep reminding herself that Katie was not dead, but was alive somewhere and waiting to be found.

People came over and consoled her as a whistle blew, signaling that the volunteers should break up into their groups. She hastily thanked everyone, then made her way toward her group. She had no need to stand around and chitchat when there was so much ground to cover.

Everyone spread out and started walking into the woods. She opened her eyes and ears and looked for any sign of Katie and Willow. She couldn't wait to bring her girl home. Then she'd never let her out of her sight.

Three hours later and still nothing. Her legs hurt and her stomach growled, but nothing would keep her from pushing forward. She stopped and pulled out her water bottle. On either side of her, she could see the other volunteers keeping pace. She couldn't rest too long, but she needed a quick break in order to keep up her strength. She took a swig of water and stared up at the treetops and watched as a helicopter zipped by overhead. Then she stashed the water bottle back in her pack and resumed searching.

Ten minutes later she heard someone shouting. Her heart raced, and she froze, hoping it was a false alarm. But the shouting continued, and so she ran in the direction of the woman's voice. A small crowd had gathered. Expecting the worst, Isla pushed her way through, only to realize that the woman was talking on her phone. She recognized Etta Perceval. Their eyes met, and Isla sensed something big was happening. Nervous, she put her hands to her mouth and prayed to God for a miracle.

"They found her, Isla. Your Katie's alive."

ISLA

"**W**HERE IS SHE?" HER HEART GALLOPED IN HER CHEST.

"Thatcher Road. By the bridge."

What is she doing there?

She knew the exact location of that bridge. As kids, she and her friends used to jump off it and into the river on hot summer days. She took off running, dodging roots and rocks, leaves crackling underfoot. Her lungs burned, but she didn't care. Katie had been found alive; she had known all along she would be. She couldn't believe how fortunate she was to have her daughter back. But what about Willow? Had they found her, as well?

She ran out of the woods and sprinted toward her car. Reporters stood around their vans, drinking coffee and trading small talk. As soon as they saw her, they rushed forward, understanding that something big had happened. She reached her minivan, jumped in, and prayed it would start. She turned the key and heard the engine whimper. After she pumped the gas pedal, it roared to life. She sped past the vans and headed toward Thatcher Road.

The roads were empty as she sped along them. The speedometer read eighty, though she was driving in a forty-miles-per-hour zone. In the rearview mirror, she saw the caravan of news vans trying to keep up with her. Her pulse raced, and she struggled to breathe, as well as to keep the minivan from swerving over the yellow line.

She turned down Thatcher Road and accelerated under the

canopy of trees until she saw Turner Bridge up ahead. A police car sat parked on the shoulder right before the bridge. She pulled up to the bridge and saw a young cop blocking her path. She jumped out of the minivan with the motor running and sprinted toward him. She was about to ask the whereabouts of her daughter when she saw Swisher standing on the other side of the bridge and holding Katie in his arms. Where the hell had he come from?

She stood there in shock, staring at the two of them and trying not to feel jealous. Katie sobbed uncontrollably against her father's chest. The sweatshirt she had on was ripped, as if she she'd been savagely attacked, and her face looked so bloodied that she appeared almost unidentifiable. Isla didn't know whether to be happy that Katie had been found or pissed off that Swisher had been the one to arrive at Katie's side first.

None of that matters now. What matters is that Katie's alive.

Before she could move, a slew of reporters and camera crews pushed past her. They set up at spots along the bridge and began to film the father-daughter reunion. The reporters seemed momentarily speechless at the sight of Katie sobbing. Isla knew this dramatic reunion made for great TV. Their sympathies didn't last long, however. As soon as the first reporter started shouting out questions, the others followed suit, running up to the two of them with the urgency of a pack of jackals.

A siren blasted behind her. Isla turned and saw an ambulance racing toward the bridge. The cop ordered her out of the way so that it could get through. Numb, she tried to locate her daughter in the crowd. She called out her name, but her voice got drowned out by the chaotic questions being shouted.

The paramedics jumped onto the pavement and pushed a stretcher past her. Her head spinning, Isla felt powerless to do anything. She saw Ray violently shoving the horde of reporters out of the way, ordering them in no uncertain terms to back the hell off. The medics pushed through the reporters and helped Katie onto the stretcher. Isla was shocked to hear Katie shriek in agony at the prospect of being separated from her father. She threw her arms up and reached for him, but he drifted back as the paramedics whisked her into the ambulance. Isla searched for Ray, only to see him running toward his pickup truck, parked on the other side of the bridge.

"Ray," she shouted. "Ray!" But he jumped in and sped off.

By the time she turned back to the ambulance, it had traveled halfway down Thatcher Road, siren blaring and lights flashing. She returned to her minivan and followed it to the hospital.

PART TWO

KATIE

*T*HE MAN STANDING OVER ME WANTS TO KNOW MY NAME, BUT I'M unable to speak. I'm under heavy medication, which has taken the creepy out of all this and put me at ease. He is wearing a stethoscope and is very good looking, with longish black hair. He only slightly resembles that TV doctor, Patrick Dempsey, on my favorite show. Of course that was before they killed him off in that spectacular car crash. That was one tearjerker of an episode. I remember crying like a baby after they pulled the plug keeping him alive, and looking over at my mother, only to see that she was crying, too.

My name is Katherine Denise Eaves, but the words don't seem to come out. They refuse to leave these bloodied, cursed lips of mine.

So what happened to me? How did I end up here?

My head feels like someone drilled a hole in my skull and poured molten hot lava in it. My thinking is fuzzy and dreamlike. The drugs they've given me numb the pain and make me feel warm inside, although warm is the last thing I should be feeling right now.

Where's my phone? I feel naked without it. Apple: the crutch of my generation.

Something bad happened to me, but I can't quite remember what. Maybe I don't want to remember. Maybe it's best I *don't* remember.

But there are certain things that I *do* remember. I'm almost seventeen. I go to Shepherd's Bay High. My little brother's name is Raisin, and he suffers from a severe form of diabetes that requires him to have a medical dog around him at all times. My father's nickname is Swisher, and my mother owns a hair salon in the center of town that used to belong to my great-grandfather.

For some reason, I can't talk. Is it the medication or the injuries to my head? And why is it I can't recall certain things?

Then I remember my friend Willow, and the tears begin to flow down my bruised cheeks. What happened to her? Did I cause her any harm by something I did?

The doctor puts the stethoscope to my chest, and I freak out for no apparent reason. I scream, twisting and turning in the sheets, until one of the nurses plunges a needle in my arm and I go all sleepy.

I wake up sometime later. The room is dark. I'm not sure I like being alone, but I'm not sure I want to be around people, either. It feels safe in this room, safer than wherever I'd been. Honestly, I have no recollection of that place. My face hurts from the slightest of movements. I reach up and touch the assortment of fresh scabs and bruises around my eyes. It feels numb, if a little tender to the touch. When I get up to use the bathroom is when it really hurts. I see a pale, bruised face staring back at me in the mirror. I barely recognize the girl. Not because I don't know who I am, but because the girl in the mirror is such a complete contrast to the girl in my mind's eye.

I return to bed and stare up at the dark ceiling—and try to remember what happened. Nothing comes to mind. Maybe it's best if I start from the beginning, when I first met Willow Briggs. I close my eyes and think back to that day.

It happened during my junior year, on my first day back from Christmas vacation. I can remember it so vividly that it feels like it happened yesterday. The morning started out chaotic. My mother busied herself downstairs, cooking bacon and eggs and arguing with my father about his whereabouts the previous two days. My father, who advertised himself as a jack-of-all-trades, claimed to have been working a job way up in Jonesport, although he didn't say what kind of job he'd been doing. It seemed that every few weeks he had a new business venture.

I remember walking downstairs and feeling the frigid air, as the wood stove had yet to completely warm the first floor. Outside, a blanket of fresh snow covered the landscape, except for the driveway, which my father had plowed and cleaned upon arriving home.

I set my book bag down on the floor and glanced up at the clock. Twenty minutes until the school bus arrived at the end of our driveway. After two weeks of vacation, I couldn't wait to get out of this crazy household.

My parents stopped bickering at the sight of me, but I could sense my mom's anger. My father, on the other hand, always seemed unflappable and happy. Nothing seemed to faze him. He smiled and greeted me with a singsong *good morning*. It pissed me off that I could never get mad at him. It pissed me off because I knew that he treated my mom like crap.

"Morning, sweetheart."

"Hi, Dad."

"Excited to be returning to school today?"

"Not really. School's pretty boring." I sat down at the kitchen table.

"I know what you mean. I hated school when I was your age."

"Way to encourage her, Ray," my mother said.

"Hey, I'm just telling her like it is. School's not for everyone, you know." He snatched a strip of bacon off the paper towel and bit off the crispy end. Bacon, the official food of the Eaves family.

"Katie's different than you, Ray. She's going off to college to make something of herself."

"No, she's going to *Harvard*. That's a university, Isla, not a college."

"How would you know?"

"Just because I didn't go to college doesn't mean I don't know things."

My mother placed a plate of scrambled eggs, bacon, and toast in front of me. I could tell she was annoyed at me, as if talking to my father had made me a traitor to her cause. Betraying her was the furthest thing from my mind. I loved my mother and felt sorry for the burden placed on her shoulders. But their marital troubles had nothing to do with me. I needed him in my life, no matter how much he let us down.

My father sat down, sipped his coffee, and read the paper. I gobbled down half my breakfast and grabbed my coat, eager to get off to school. It seemed like a welcome relief after the drama of this morning.

As I grabbed my book bag, I heard that familiar sound of bells going off. My mother turned, and I saw fear come over her face. I looked to my father, but he'd already sprinted upstairs to attend to Raisin. Thank God for Scout. Although Scout was not the dog I had envisioned when my parents said we were getting a dog, he was gentle and loyal, and his presence in our household had proved crucial to our well-being.

Raisin.

Undoubtably, the cutest boy ever. He was nearly six years younger than me. I remember how hard my parents tried to get him to say his birth name, Raymond. But it always came out Raisin. Week after week, month after month, until we all just gave up and started calling him Raisin. The name fit, and after that last attempt, no one could ever consider calling him anything else. Even when he started school, the teachers called him Raisin. Shepherd's Bay was a tight-knit community, and his kindergarten teacher, Mrs. Gagne, attended the same church as us and had known him from the day he was born.

I couldn't leave for school knowing Raisin was in crisis. He came down with diabetes at the age of three, which meant that his blood sugar levels could range from normal to dangerous before anyone knew it. When I was a little girl, the sound of Scout ringing his bringsel bell would terrify me, and I began to associate that ringing sound with the thought of him dying.

When Scout first came to us, my mother would organize these, what she called, Go Find training sessions. The purpose of these sessions was to introduce Scout to us, in the event he ever needed to grab someone and alert them to Raisin's high or low blood sugar. More importantly, these sessions helped Scout locate Raisin if, for whatever reason, the two of them ever got separated.

We would all stand in a circle and then my mother would direct Scout to go find a certain family member. In his mouth would be a bringsel: a designated item of some sort that Scout would deliver to the person she directed him to find. Then my mother would hide Raisin somewhere around our house and Scout would have to find him. Each time she hid him, Raisin would be further and further away, until one day my mother hid him in the woods a hundred yards away. Scout was amazing during these sessions. Somehow, he would always manage to find my brother. Then he would get his treat and strut around proudly, showing off his stuff. I remember this one time, when my mother wanted to really challenge him, when Scout tracked down Raisin a half a mile from our home. We all jumped up and down and celebrated what our miraculous dog had accomplished.

I looked over at my mother. She stood paralyzed like a statue, frozen and waiting in anticipation for my dad to come down. She was the one who usually handled Raisin's emergencies. But my father, despite his many faults, knew as well as anyone how to deal with Raisin's ever-changing blood sugar. No one ever questioned Ray "Swisher" Eaves's competence when it came to most matters. They may have questioned other things about him, but certainly never his competence. I knew this because I heard it said all the time.

Just about every day at school, I was reminded of Ray "Swisher" Eaves's competence. His name adorned the banner hanging from the gym's rafters. Not only was he the number one hoops scorer in our school's history, but he had also captained the team that won the only two state championships in Shepherd Bay's history. He scored twenty-seven points a game his senior year, and his team photograph hung in the trophy case, along with the two giant trophies in the shape of basketballs.

"He's fine now," my father said as he swaggered down the stairs. "A little low is all."

"Thanks for handling that," my mother said, all the bitterness now gone from her voice.

"Piece of cake," he said, returning to his paper. "He's going to be a little late for school, though. I'll drive him over when he's ready to roll."

"I'll go upstairs and help him along," my mother said. She turned and kissed me on the cheek. "You can run along to school, honey. I hope you have a good first day back."

I left the house and trudged down the driveway in the new L.L. Bean boots I got for Christmas. The fresh white snow crunched underfoot. As I waited for the bus, I realized that this morning's chaos had put me in a bad mood. I had no desire to be the nice Katie Eaves and say hi to everyone as I walked to the rear of the bus. Or ask them how they had spent their school vacation. From where I stood on the shoulder of the road, feeling the chill of winter penetrate my bones, I could see all the chimneys in the valley below spewing smoke, the result of the wood and pellet stoves working overtime to keep houses warm. A blanket of mist hovered just above the ocean. Were I not so out of sorts, I might have better appreciated the beauty of this scene.

The bus pulled up along the shoulder, heaved a wary sigh, and swallowed me whole. I politely said hello to Mr. Jones behind the wheel. He didn't appear to be a day under eighty, but he was always kind and friendly. I nodded to all the kids as I made my way down the aisle, trying to maintain my equilibrium as the bus lurched forward. I sat in an empty seat near the back and watched the winter wonderland pass me by, contemplating my tedious existence in this tedious town.

Despite my stellar grades, school bored me. So did most of the kids, all as eager as I was to escape the monotony of our educational system. And it wasn't just school, but everything in this town. I felt stuck in a cycle of exceeding expectations, trapped and sinking deeper. What I would have given just to earn a B and take all the pressure off my shoulders. But I couldn't let my guard down. I saw the life my parents lived and realized that I couldn't ever let myself get that way. I wasn't immune to their struggles, struggles that I swore not to repeat. My mother had dropped out of college and had never explained why. And I wanted to know why. Why had she quit college and moved back to *this*? Why had she married my father if they fought constantly? She was always warning me not to make the same mistakes she made. To stay in school and be a strong and independent woman and earn my degree. No way I wanted to end up being a hairdresser like her.

Honestly, I yearned for something more exciting than life in Shepherd's Bay. I couldn't wait to get away from here and start my college career. It would be a new experience meeting interesting and intelligent people. Although I was a good softball player, I knew softball wouldn't earn me scholarship money. Same with my involvement in the school's theater group. If I was to have any hope of escaping from Shepherd's Bay, it would have to be using my brains. And because of that, I studied constantly, deathly afraid of lowering my standards and settling for anything less than an A.

The bus ride calmed me. The movement and the powerful engine shook the skittishness out of my nerves. The school bus passed through town and picked up all the bleary-eyed students returning from Christmas break. The fresh snow put this town in a better light, although the virgin whiteness would soon be crusted over with dirt.

The bus pulled up in front of our dilapidated brick high school. I waited my turn before filing down the aisle and making my way out the front door of the bus.

The bus lurched a few times before pulling away. Grasping my book bag, I made my way up the steps leading to the front doors of the school. But before I entered, I noticed a shiny black Mercedes pull up to the curb. No one ever drove a car like that to our high school. Most kids took the bus, and those that did get rides usually jumped out of a tattered old pickup truck.

For some reason, I stopped and stared at this exotic car. The two people in the front seat appeared to be arguing, with the driver gesticulating wildly. I didn't exactly crane my neck to see, but I might have tilted my head some to catch a glimpse of what they were going on about. The driver, a middle-aged man wearing black designer eyeglasses, leaned over and kissed the girl on the cheek. She didn't budge, unmoved by his affection, her long arms crossed over her body. Kids passed me on either side, and I could hear their footsteps on the crystals of rock salt spread out over the sidewalk. *Crunch! Crunch! Crunch!*

The girl who emerged from that car was a creature the likes of which I'd never before seen. She was tall, with blond hair and striking blue eyes. I was so caught up in their drama that I didn't even realize I'd been staring at her. She wore black leather boots with three-inch heels, designer jeans, a gray cashmere sweater, and a belted wool coat, with two different-colored knitted scarves wrapped around her neck.

"What the hell are you staring at?" she snapped when she caught up with me at the doors.

I was so stunned by her words that I didn't know how to respond. People rarely, if ever, spoke to me in such a forceful and rude manner. The folks in Shepherd's Bay were, for the most part, polite people. Everyone in this town was so used to seeing the same people day after day that no one could afford to be pissed off with anyone for too long.

"Yeah, you. Why are you standing there like a lost puppy?"

"I'm—I'm—I'm so sorry. I was just . . ."

"You were just what? Spying on me and my daddy?"

"No, not at all. It's just that I don't usually see a car that nice."

She turned and watched it drive away. "So you like the Benz?"

"I do. It's gorgeous." I couldn't take my eyes off her. "I'm sorry if you thought I was staring at you."

She took a few steps toward me, so that she practically stood on my toes. I looked up at her, scared and yet excited at the same time. She didn't say anything, which made this encounter more awkward than it should have been. She chewed a wad of gum, the only flaw in her character that I could detect.

"I should really go to class now," I said.

"Willow Briggs." She held out her hand.

I shook it; her grip was strong. "Katie Eaves."

"I'm new here at this school. First day."

"Oh wow," I said cheerfully. "I can show you around if you like. I've lived here my entire life."

She laughed. "Lucky you."

"I know, right?" I joined her in laughing. "Where did you move from, Willow? Portland?"

"Portland, Oregon? Hell no." She looked up at the brick building that passed for our high school, blowing a bubble through her perfectly formed teeth. "What a shithole."

"It's really not that bad." It really was.

"Maybe not, but it's ten times better than my old school."

"See? There's a silver lining to everything."

"Damn, girl. Are you always this annoyingly cheerful?"

I shrugged, wondering how that was a bad thing.

"Will you walk me inside, Katie Eaves? That way I can start my day having at least one bestie."

"So we're besties now?" I looked up at her with a welcoming smile.

"My father's always saying that friends are like assholes. Everyone should have at least one."

"So am I the first asshole you've met today?" It felt deliciously naughty to speak this way.

"Girl, I kid you not. You're, like, a one-of-kind asshole."

"So, is that a yes?"

"Most definitely, it's a yes."

Willow and I walked through the doors together, and I could feel all eyes on us. I knew then that everything was about to change in my life. It excited me. It gave me hope that I could make it through the rest of my high school years without dying of boredom.

If I had only known then how much my life would change, I might have reconsidered becoming friends with Willow Briggs that day.

ISLA

*I*SLA PACED THE HALLWAY OUTSIDE OF KATIE'S ROOM. SHE HAD BEEN AT the hospital over twelve hours and had seen Katie only once in that time. Ray had come and gone after the doctor told him it might be a while before Katie came to.

Her daughter had been sedated when she had finally gotten to sit with her, and Katie's face appeared so battered and bruised that it had shocked her. She seemed to have suffered significant memory loss, as well. She'd been violently attacked, that much was clear, but because of her head injuries, she couldn't yet tell them who had done this to her.

She checked on Drew and found him asleep on the sofa in the waiting room. Earlier she'd insisted that everyone else go home and get some rest. They'd reluctantly acquiesced. It had been a long two days of searching, and the well-meaning volunteers hadn't helped any by hanging out in the waiting room. In fact, it had made her feel guilty that they weren't home, in their own beds. She went to the cafeteria and helped herself to a cup of coffee. Despite her own lack of sleep, she felt not the least bit tired. The discovery of her daughter was enough to keep her pistons knocking for days. God had listened to her prayers and come through big-time. She couldn't wait for the moment when Katie woke up and could tell them what had happened to her and Willow.

She reminded herself to have a talk with Ray once he came back to the hospital. Like, why hadn't he returned her calls? And what had he been doing all that time?

What worried her most was the psychological damage Katie may have suffered. Learning the nature of the attack would answer some of her questions, as would finding Willow Briggs. The doctors had said they would have a better handle on her condition once she came to and they could better assess her mental state.

She sat outside Katie's room, sipping coffee and trying to deal with the facets of this crisis. The hard work would soon begin: helping her daughter cope with whatever horrors had beset her. She tried not to dwell on what had happened, or on the severity and nature of the crime, choosing instead to be thankful that her daughter had been found alive.

She couldn't help thinking about Willow. What had happened to her? Was she still alive? If Willow's father had been upset before the discovery of Katie, she couldn't imagine what he was feeling now. She thought about how she would feel if the roles were reversed and it was her daughter who was the one still missing.

Her mind churned, and she couldn't sleep even if she tried. Nurses and doctors walked past her, trying to give her enough space to breathe. They'd been so exceedingly kind to her and her family that it made her feel guilty that she wasn't able to reciprocate such kindness.

She discovered how lost in thought she was when someone sat next to her. The person's shoulder brushed up against hers in a strangely intimate way. She turned and saw Karl's familiar profile. He was dressed in civilian clothes and wore a baseball hat that covered his gray-blond hair. His thin, arched nose unevenly separated his cheekbones. He looked thinner than she remembered. Why hadn't she noticed this before, when he'd sat in her kitchen while conversing with her father? Was it because of the baseball cap and the civilian clothes he was wearing?

Why had he come here? Was he here in an official capacity or as a friend—a special friend from a long time ago that she'd all but put out of mind? She looked away from him and stared at the green wall across the hallway and didn't talk for a few minutes.

"Thank you for coming," she finally said.

"How's she doing?"

"The doctors don't really know at this point."

"I'm sorry."

"Why are you sorry?"

He shrugged.

"Same old buster," she said.

"Seems the more things change, the more I stay the same."

"Sometimes change is a good thing. It can mean growth and maturity."

"I guess."

"Have the police made any inroads on the case yet?"

"The state police bagged Katie's clothes and took them down to the lab. We'll find out later what they've discovered . . . fibers, DNA, the usual stuff."

"What about Katie's friend?"

"There's been no sign of her. As you might expect, her father is quite distraught."

"I assume they're resuming the search for her tomorrow?"

He nodded.

"I wish I could be there and help them look for Willow, but Katie needs me."

"People will understand why you can't be there."

She snatched a quick glance at his profile, not quite believing that as a teenager, she had fallen for him so many years ago.

"How's Raisin taking the news?" he asked.

"Poor kid has been through so much lately, he rarely shows any emotions, especially the way Ray and I have been getting on as of late." Did she really say that? Her mind felt so jumbled now that she could barely control what passed from her brain through her lips. Fortunately, he let the comment pass.

"We'll be investigating Katie's disappearance and trying to determine who did this to her and why."

"Do you think any of this has to do with the missing James kid?"

"Can't know for sure, but it's entirely possible. Two rich kids missing in this small town seems a bit too coincidental for me. Katie might have just been in the wrong place at the wrong time, which is why she's still alive."

"What's happening here, Karl?"

"I don't know." He shrugged. "Just don't tell me how wonderful this town used to be, when we both know that most people here could barely make ends meet."

"I wasn't going to say that."

"It seems that all I hear lately is misplaced nostalgia about how wonderful Shepherd's Bay once was."

"We both know that there's been a lot of animosity here since these newcomers arrived."

"There's also been a lot of good things happening, too."

"The only reason my shop survives is that this new money has been coming into town. My grandfather would be shocked to know I could charge twenty-five bucks for a men's haircut."

"Your grandfather gave me my first haircut when I was a kid. I think my mother paid five bucks."

Thinking about her grandfather made her sad. "So you think one of the locals committed this crime?"

"I don't know what to believe anymore, or who to believe. The only thing I want to do is keep an open mind throughout this investigation."

"Of course." She sipped her coffee.

"Where was Ray when all this happened?"

"I don't know. You'll have to ask him yourself."

"I plan to."

She turned to him. "You don't seriously think Ray has anything to do with this, do you? Because he loves Katie and would never do anything to hurt her."

"No, but I still need to be thorough and check everyone out."

"You should probably be looking at one of those townies hell-bent on sticking it to the rich folks on Harper's Point."

"Wait until they enact this new property tax on residences worth over a half a million bucks. Now, that will really piss those people off."

"Assuming the town council passes it."

"If it's passed, that tax could completely change the character of the downtown waterfront."

"And put me in the poorhouse again."

"Who owns your building?"

"The McCallisters," she said. "Which brings me to another matter.

Have you looked into the background of their son, Julian McCallister?"

"Is there any reason to?"

"I found a few photographs of him mugging with Katie and Willow. Something seems off about that kid, if you ask me."

"Based on what?"

"Based on a mother's intuition."

"A mother's intuition is strong, but I'm not sure that's enough proof to dig into this kid's past." Karl took out his pen and pad and wrote down Julian's name. "Then again, it never hurts to check everything out."

"I would think as a detective, it's your duty to leave no stone unturned."

"That's true, but I'm not really a detective. We're too small of a department for that."

The sound of a door opening and closing jarred Isla out of the flow of conversation. She looked past the sad-looking cop and saw Drew walking toward them. She knew him to be mostly cheerful, but when angry, he took on a more sinister appearance. And she had rarely seen him this angry.

"Where's Katie?"

"Relax, Drew. They're not allowing anyone to see her just yet. And when they do, it's family members only," Isla said.

"That's bullshit. I'm her boyfriend."

"Go home, Drew. Get some rest."

"I'm not going anywhere until I see her and make sure she's all right." He glared at Karl. "What the hell are you doing here? Shouldn't you be out looking for the sick bastards who did this?"

"Do you have anything you want to tell me, Drew? Something that might shed light on this case? Otherwise, I suggest you mind your manners."

"I already told you, Katie changed after she met Willow Briggs. She wasn't the same." He looked close to tears. "Tell him I'm wrong, Mrs. Eaves."

"You're just being emotional, Drew. Willow is a good friend to Katie. Yes, she has some issues, but who among us doesn't?"

"That's not true, and you know it. Katie used to be sweet and kind. She wasn't the same after she met that rich bitch and her hipster friend, Julian. I'm telling you, she changed for the worse."

"It's natural for people to change as they get older. Neither you nor I can stop Katie from maturing, just as you can't keep her from going away to college. It's a fact of life," Isla said.

"I don't have a problem with Katie going away to school, if that's what she really wants. We talked about her attending Coastal Community College, so we could be together, and she liked the idea. Then she met Willow, and now she refuses to talk to me about her future plans."

"Can't you see, Drew? She is trying to develop her own identity."

"You're wrong about that. Katie loves me. Ask Swisher."

"You can't accept the fact that she is eventually going to leave here and go away to college."

"You don't know what the hell you're talking about. I'm going inside to see her." Tears streaked down his cheeks.

"Oh no you're not," Isla said.

Drew headed toward Katie's room, and Isla moved to try to stop him. She grabbed hold of his arm, but he shrugged off her grasp. The sour scent of alcohol emanated from his breath. He opened the door to Katie's room and burst inside, calling out her name in exaggerated sobs. Isla stopped in the doorway and watched with dismay as he fell to his knees and cupped Katie's hands in his own. Karl pulled up beside her and stood watching this sad scene. Isla felt for the poor boy. He was an unsophisticated townie with simple needs who wanted to marry and have kids, and he knew that Katie had been slowly slipping away from him.

A nurse rushed in and saw what was happening, saw the size and temperament of Drew, and called security. Less than a minute later, two uniformed officers stormed inside Katie's room. They stopped for a second when they saw Drew kneeling at her side and sobbing, telling Katie how much he loved her. Then, gently, each officer secured him by an arm and escorted him out of the room.

"Please go easy on him," Isla said to the two security officers. "He's my daughter's boyfriend and is quite shaken up about all this."

"Okay, but he needs to leave the hospital immediately," the one wearing the stripes said.

"I'm a cop. I'll drive him home," Karl offered.

"I can drive home myself," Drew said.

"I can smell the booze on your breath, Drew. You're in no condition to be behind the wheel. You can have one of your friends drive you back in the morning to pick up your truck," Karl said.

Katie's eyelids fluttered and then opened. She looked around the room, as if seeing it for the first time. Isla couldn't resist going over and taking her daughter's hand. Despite the black eyes and bruises, the proliferation of raw cuts and angry scrapes, Katie looked beautiful in the soft glow of the light. The nurse stood just behind Isla, allowing her a few precious moments with her daughter.

"Hi, Katie. It's Mom."

Tears formed in her daughter's eyes. "I'm so sorry."

"Don't you worry, honey. Everything will be okay now that you're back with us, safe and sound."

"Where's Willow? How's she doing?"

Isla stared at her, not wanting to upset Katie. But she didn't want to lie, either.

"Mom, please tell me that Willow's okay."

"Honey, they haven't found Willow yet."

"You mean she's still out there?" She squeezed her eyelids together.

"Yes, but we have a lot of volunteers out searching for her. We'll find her one way or another. Don't you worry."

"I'm afraid."

"Afraid of what?"

She opened her eyes and wiped the tears away with her fingers. "I don't know. I just am."

"Katie, can you remember anything about what happened to you?"

"I've tried real hard since I got here, but I can't remember anything. My memory's blocked or something."

"It'll come back to you. Keep trying, if you're able."

"Can you at least tell me who won?"

Isla was puzzled by this question. "Who won what?"

"The softball game. Did we win the championship?"

"You mean, you can't remember?"

Katie shook her head.

"Shepherd's Bay won the game, honey. Willow pitched a no-hitter and drove in the only two runs."

KARL

*D*REW SAT SLUMPED AGAINST THE DOOR IN KARL'S PICKUP TRUCK, HIS arms folded across his powerful chest. The smell of stale alcohol filled the cabin. The streets were dark and quiet at this early morning hour. Karl loved Shepherd's Bay when it was like this. He passed a police cruiser, saw Dave Jansen behind the wheel, and waved. It felt much better being a civilian right now than working that long overnight shift. From working the graveyard, his sleep pattern had been thrown off-kilter, and he knew it would be a few days before he settled back into a normal rhythm.

He recalled sitting next to Isla at that hospital, in the dim light, their shoulders lightly touching. No one knew what had happened to Katie or what the future might hold for the poor girl. What if she'd been sexually violated or worse? It might take years for her to recover from such trauma, if she recovered at all.

He considered the Willow Briggs situation. It didn't bode well for her that Katie had been found alive with no sign of her friend. The theory that they had run away together could now be thrown out, leaving him with only a few alternative theories, all of them bad.

Drew sat in silence next to him as he weaved through the streets. Finally, he came to the Nelsons' residence. They lived in a sprawling, weathered home that had been added on to many times in a slapdash manner. Rusty cars and pickup trucks littered the property. In the back sat a battered old lobster boat resting on concrete blocks. Green steel lobster traps were piled up everywhere, in various states of disrepair. He stopped in the dirt driveway and looked over at Drew. The kid returned his gaze with an angry scowl before opening the door and stumbling out. Karl leaned over the seat and rolled down the passenger-side window.

"Call me if you need a ride back to your truck."

Drew reached back, without looking, and waved him away. Then he staggered up the stairs and disappeared inside the house.

Karl turned around in the driveway and headed toward Harper's Point. No sense going home when he couldn't sleep. Unlike most of the other locals in town, he didn't loathe or envy these newcomers. In fact, he found their presence here, on balance, somewhat of a positive development. They added to the crumbling tax base and brought a sophistication to Shepherd's Bay, which had helped put it on the map. These people had escaped crowded, crime-ridden, and overpriced cities, which had begun to sink under the weight of their own burdens, and had arrived on the shores of Shepherd's Bay like wide-eyed refugees from a hostile land and found tranquility, natural beauty, and honest, hardworking people, not to mention a cheap cost of living. They had only to survive the brutal winters.

He loved everything about harsh Maine winters. He loved when a nor'easter dumped three feet of snow on the landscape, amid howling winds, and everything in town shut down. On his days off, he would often put on his snowshoes and walk for miles across the rugged terrain. Or else cross-country ski along one of the many trails that cut across the beach and into the thick woods.

He cruised through the deserted downtown area, past Isla's shop, and made his way toward the new homes snaking along the water. The lights were off in every house. He slowed down to admire them. They started at around a half a million dollars and went up considerably from there, especially the homes along the shore. The neighborhood stretched back a few blocks toward the bay side. Of course, the ones on the Atlantic were far grander and more luxurious, with beach access and amazing ocean views.

He stopped momentarily at the house where the James boy had once lived. Modest for Harper's Point, it sat a few streets away from the shore and within walking distance of the lone public beach. He remembered a few months ago sitting at the Jameses' large dining-room table and interviewing the kid's distraught mother, stopping every few moments to allow her to cry.

Circling around Harper's Point, he noticed that the farther away from the neighborhood he drove, the greater the number of older houses he passed. Most of the longtime citizens here had been forced out on account of the taxes, which had been steadily increasing, thanks to the steep rise in land prices. Their houses would eventually get bulldozed and replaced by much larger ones.

He reached the end of the block and headed back toward the Point. Once he reached the end of the street, he saw the Briggses' mansion in all its glory. It was by far the most impressive home in the development and featured a large spiral turret. How badly he wanted to receive a full tour and see how the other half lived. Just being inside the Briggses' home that one time had taken his breath away.

He stopped in front of it and let the engine idle. What were the odds that two kids from Harper's Point would go missing? Was there a serial killer in town targeting rich kids? It seemed ludicrous on the face of it. Had Katie's life been spared because she'd grown up here? He remembered how angry Drew had gotten, and for a brief second considered him a suspect. But the thought of that kid kidnapping his girlfriend and two rich kids seemed silly. Same with Ray, although he still needed to find out where Ray had been the past three days. The person who had done this was far more calculating and cunning and had to be filled with rage as much as restraint. Someone who resented the way this town had changed, and wanted to make sure the rich paid with their most precious currency: their kids.

An activated light turned on, on the house next door. A tall, handsome man stepped out onto the walkway, dressed in a silk robe and slippers. The man glanced in his direction. Karl recognized him as Beckett McCallister, owner of a number of commercial properties in town and one of the leading opponents of the new real estate tax being proposed. When Councillor Elmer Stowbridge passed away in February, at the age of eighty-six, the town council became gridlocked on the issue, at four to four. The next elected councillor would cast the swing vote.

The proponents of the tax claimed that it was for the good of the children. The money would go toward rebuilding the schools' crumbling infrastructure. The wealthy citizens along the water complained that they'd been targeted on account of their excessive wealth and the fact that they sent their kids to prestigious Chance Academy up the road. Everyone knew that to be true, and yet the tax hike still resonated with the locals, who were envious of the wealthy newcomers' status. Chance Academy sat on an impressive bluff overlooking the ocean and cost forty-four thousand dollars a year per child to attend—and it wasn't even located in Shepherd's Bay.

So why had Willow chosen to attend Shepherd's Bay High instead of Chance? Had something bad happened to her at that priccy school? And why had Drew and Isla been so insistent that Julian was involved with the girls' disappearance? Julian attended Chance and lived next door to Willow. The missing boy, Dakota James, had also attended Chance.

Beckett appraised his surroundings before disappearing through the front door. Karl sighed in relief. A light was extinguished inside the house as Beckett wormed his way through it. He wondered if Julian was asleep upstairs, in one of the bedrooms. Something told him it wouldn't hurt to talk to Julian at some point and see what he knew.

KATIE

I LIE HERE IN A SUSPENDED STATE THAT'S PART DREAM AND PART MEMory. My soul feels diseased and rotten, as if it's teeming with maggots. Maybe it's the heavy drugs those nurses gave me. Or maybe it's the hard reality of what's happened that prevents me from remembering.

They want to stick needles in me and poke me and take my blood, but for some reason, I refuse to let them. I've hated needles my entire life, thanks to Raisin's illness. I scream whenever they approach, so now they mostly leave me alone.

There certainly can't be any worse place for me right now than this uncomfortable hospital bed. People come and go and smile at me, as if I'm some kind of porcelain doll. Or maybe they see me as a victim. It's entirely possible I *am* a victim, but their shallow sympathy irks me all the same. Maybe I'm not really a victim, but something else. Something worse. Then their sympathies will seem stupid.

It's weird. I feel like throwing up a lot of the time. One moment I'm starving, and then a few minutes later, the sight of food repulses me.

My mother, to my dismay, dotes on me constantly. My dad, if he were here, would stand behind her and smile innocently. Coach Hicks came in and sat with me for a few minutes, all positive energy and chirpy blabbing about something or another. Drew balled like a baby when he first saw me. Then his face turned angry after I refused to respond to his pathetic pleas, and the security guards had to come in and escort him out. The tears that flowed from my eyes were not for him, and never would be, although he probably thought they were.

Truth was, I didn't want to see him. Or anyone else, for that matter. I would have told him as much, but I couldn't form the words in my mouth. I want only my mother with me. And Raisin, too, if Raisin ever bothers to show up. But for whatever reason, he hasn't. More than anything, I want to see Willow's smiling face.

I lose track of time, apart from the obvious separation between night and day. My sleep rhythm has become disrupted by whatever ails me. Even trying to remember what happened that night leaves me fatigued. That, combined with the heavy meds, makes me feel like a zombie.

All the lightness has drained out of me.

Forgive me if I don't remember events in chronological order, but before Drew was escorted out by security, he told me that I should have listened to him. He gave me an emphatic "I told you so." He took my hand in his own and squeezed harder than I would have liked. It made me wary of him, and I pretended to be asleep. He told me he loved me, and said that once I was feeling better, he would take care of me. Then he would rescue me from Willow and all the spoiled rich kids who had played a role in messing me up.

I still can't remember much about what happened that night, but I did an inventory of myself and concluded a few things.

I am Katie Denise Eaves, and I am a good person. Mostly.

There's nothing I want more right now than to leave this hospital.

It's dark outside, so it must be night. Or early morning.

Good people can do terrible things, just as bad people can do good things. (Why did that thought just come into my head?)

What happened to my best friend sickens me, despite the fact that I can't remember a thing about it.

Is she still alive? I pray to God she is.

Let's just say that I was never one of the cool girls at Shepherd's Bay High. When Willow befriended me that day, something changed inside me, as much as it changed the way others looked at me. I felt like a new girl. The other kids perceived me in a different light when I walked through the halls with her by my side—and I liked the powerful feeling this gave me. She had style and grace and oozed charisma, and I was quite surprised when we ended up sitting next to each other in many of the same classes. She had smarts, too, although one would have never known it by looking at her.

I wondered what she saw in me. In many ways, we were at complete opposite ends of the spectrum. She stood around five-ten and had long blond hair, smoky blue eyes, and an exaggerated gait, which caught the eye of every male she passed. I had maxed out at five-three, dressed conservatively, and had brown hair pinned back with hairpins. We couldn't have been more different. I was the old soul, as my mother jokingly referred to me, and she was the wild young thing.

When the cool girls asked to hang out with her, Willow informed them that she had more important things to do. From that point on, she became public enemy number one to those girls. By association, I became enemy number two, despite having grown up with many of them. They bared their fangs whenever we passed.

As much as they gossiped about her in the hallways and in the school cafeteria, it didn't seem to faze Willow. She'd simply extend her arm and flip them off and then walk away without a care in the world. Nothing seemed to faze her. It was only when they started taunting me that she became upset.

It happened one day after school, as we headed out the back door. Two weeks had passed since I watched her step out of that Mercedes. I remember how we stopped to look at the poster advertising the new musical the school was to put on that winter.

"*Grease*," she said in an approving tone. "I love that old movie."

"Me too."

"Did I ever tell you that my father knows John Travolta?" she said matter-of-factly.

"Really? That's so cool."

She glanced at her almond-shaped nails. "He used to be so hot back in his *Saturday Night Fever* days."

"I never saw that movie."

"Then you definitely should," she said, touching my arm. "Did you know that John has a house in Maine? He told my dad that he'd invite us up there this summer. Maybe even give us a ride in his plane."

"He has his own plane?"

"Totally. And John's a pilot, too."

"That's so cool."

"I know, right?"

"I can't believe you know John Travolta," I sighed dreamily, recalling him in his *Grease* days.

"Actually, it's my dad who knows him."

"Still, it's practically like it's you."

"I suppose," she said. "Would you like to come with us when we go see him?" She flipped her hair back and stared at me with those icy blue eyes.

"Would I ever, assuming your parents will let me."

"My parents will do whatever I tell them." She looked back up at the poster, hand on hip, as if to pose. "Is this your thing, Katie? Musical theater?"

"One of my many hidden talents." I laughed.

"Really?"

"If you're asking me if I'm in the theater group, the answer is yes, although I'm hardly one of the stars. Mostly, I'm in the background, lip-synching."

"I see they're holding auditions next week."

"Are you thinking about trying out for one of the supporting roles?" I asked.

"Supporting roles? Hell no. I plan on winning the part of Sandy Olsson."

I covered my mouth and laughed, trying not to hurt her feelings.

"What's so funny?"

"I'm sorry for laughing. It's just that Mrs. Carlson always picks seniors for the top roles, and this year Debbie Lowe has the best chance of winning the part of Sandy Olsson."

"Are you saying that the auditions are rigged?"

"No. It's just that there's a lot of really talented girls trying out this year, so Mrs. Carlson tries to give it to a deserving senior whenever possible. And not only has Debbie Lowe been waiting her turn, but she has an amazing voice, too."

"But will she judge these auditions with an open mind?"

"Of course she will. Mrs. Carlson is very fair," I said. "Geoff Coventry won the lead role of Shrek two years ago, when he was a junior, and it caused quite a stir even then. Still, none of the senior boys could sing quite like Geoff."

"Then it's settled. I'm going to win the role of Sandy Olsson."

I burst out laughing. This time I laughed because I was complicit in her plans to sabotage the school's tradition. Of course, in the back of my mind, I didn't think Willow stood a chance of winning that role. Mrs. Carlson was a tough cookie when it came to assigning roles, and Debbie Lowe had an angelic voice. More importantly, she was next in line for the lead part. Honestly, I had no idea whether Willow could sing or dance, but it would be fun to watch her try to overturn the apple cart. On appearances alone, she might warrant a second look. And in the event she somehow beat the long odds and won the coveted role of Sandy Olsson, I could imagine the outcry from kids and parents alike.

Three jackals were waiting for us as soon as we exited the doors. Despite regulations, two of them stood smoking on school grounds. They laughed upon seeing us. I nodded for Willow to ignore them, but she gave the trio a sideways glance before moving down the steps to our right.

"If it isn't Miss Perfect, hanging out with the new rich bitch," one of the jackals called.

We continued to walk, book bags slung over our shoulders. I whispered to Willow not to pay any attention to those girls. When I glanced back, I noticed them following us.

"Hey, Katie. Why's your weird little brother's name Raisin? And what's with that filthy mutt who follows him around?" Tiffany said.

I kept my mouth shut, despite the insult.

"Oh, and your mother totally messed up my friend's hair the other day. She tells me she wants her money back," Tiffany said, running over and standing in front of me. "I heard your grandfather's lost his marbles and can't even remember his own name."

"Shut up, Tiffany," I snapped.

"You gonna make me?" She turned to Willow. "Or maybe this skinny rich bitch will protect you, although looking at her skanky ass, I seriously doubt she could squash a fly."

"Leave Willow out of this. She didn't do anything to you."

Tiffany shoved me so hard that I fell back onto the pavement. The humiliation of falling hurt more than the actual fall, especially since it happened in front of Willow. The girls laughed as I pushed myself up. I brushed off the front of my dress and wiped the dirt off my behind. When I looked over, I saw Willow snatch the cigarette out of Tiffany's mouth and snub it out on her forehead. Tiffany shrieked in pain and stepped back, glaring at Willow with horror in her eyes. A red circle formed on the skin above her eyes.

"Crazy bitch. You're gonna wish you didn't do that," Tiffany said, her hands balling into fists.

Willow did something that confused me. She dropped her book bag and pulled off her boots and stood there in stockinged feet. Tiffany took a step forward, and Willow spun effortlessly like a ballerina and performed a perfect kick to the girl's head. Tiffany's eyes rolled back, and she froze temporarily in midair before toppling like a felled tree. I stood there in shock, my hands over my gaping mouth.

"Any of you other bee-yotches want a piece of me?"

The girls ran over to Tiffany, who lay on the pavement, with drool dribbling down her chin. She tried to sit up but couldn't. Her eyes were glazed over, and I knew it would be a while before she recovered from that vicious blow.

"Let's get out of here, Katie. These friends of yours are *sooo* boring," Willow said. She picked up her book bag, stepped into her boots, and strode briskly down the walkway. Stunned, I jogged to keep up with her.

"Where did you learn to do that?" I asked.

"I've been taking martial arts classes since I was three." She smiled. "There's a lot of things you don't know about me."

"That's an understatement."

"We're like blood sisters now, girl."

"We are?"

"Of course," she said, smiling as I jogged next to her. "You're Katie Eaves, and I'm Bruce Lee, slayer of all bee-yotches."

"Who's Bruce Lee?"

She stopped and stared at me, in shock. "You really don't know who Bruce Lee is?"

I shook my head.

"You've lived a sheltered life," she said. "Bruce Lee is only the greatest martial arts fighter ever. My dad and I used to watch his movies all the time."

"Okay."

"Hey, I've got a great idea. Why don't you come over for dinner tonight?"

"I'm not sure I can," I said, although I badly wanted to go over to her house.

"Come on. It'll be fun. And you can help me learn all those Sandy Olsson songs."

"Something tells me you already know them."

"Then I'll help *you* learn them, and we can sing the part together. You can be my understudy."

I felt happy for once, not having to take a friend back to my own crappy home and let them see the chaos I lived in. But it was a school night, and I knew my mother would not let me go.

I'm talking. I say things out loud in my room when no one is around. I must look insane. Certain truths are coming back to me. Something tells me I must be careful what I say, even though I'm not sure what I'm going to say from one moment to the next.

The clock tells me it's nearly nine. Since it's light outside, it's safe to assume that it's morning. If memory serves me correctly, which has been really hard to determine lately, two periods of darkness have passed. Does that translate to a three-day stay in this hospital? Does it matter?

In five minutes they'll be coming in: my mother, the doctors and nurses, friends and family. I hope I get to see Raisin. I plan on asking about Willow and seeing how she's doing. I'm definitely going to ask someone to fetch me a cheeseburger from Bay Burgers, with extra pickles. I'm famished. No, I'm beyond hungry. Is that a good sign?

Why do I need to be careful what I say? Because it will shock people? *I'm a good person*, I keep telling myself. Willow was my BFF. She still *is* my BFF. They just need to find her, so we can get on with our lives.

ISLA

*I*T AMAZED HER HOW MANY PEOPLE HAD EXPRESSED CONCERN FOR Katie. Friends and family had come to the hospital, bearing treats, casseroles, and frozen dinners, offering to lend a hand in any way possible. Many hailed from her church, older women who had plenty of time on their hands and didn't need to trudge to work each day. But there had been others, too. Drew, for example. She wondered if the boy actually loved her daughter or whether something else kept him tethered to Katie: loneliness, fear, the trajectory of what was accepted from young men in this town.

She felt happy because of Katie's return. And scared at the same time, especially when Karl walked into the waiting room. He nodded as he sat across from her, this time, unlike the last, in full uniform. Today he had come for a specific reason: to cull information from Katie. Yesterday she had spoken, although she hadn't been able to remember much about that fateful night she went missing. But speaking at least proved to be a positive sign.

Four days had passed, and Willow still hadn't been found. Where was she? Isla prayed that Katie's friend was still alive. She'd hate to break the news to Katie if the worst came to bear. To see her relive that horrific ordeal—whatever had happened to the two of them.

She nodded to Karl and stood. He held a coffee in hand and looked as if he hadn't slept in days. Drew sat in the corner, biting his greasy thumbnail and bouncing his knee in rapid succession. He looked tense and on edge as he scanned the room. She went over and explained that he didn't need to be here, but he told her that he wouldn't want to be anywhere else.

Two minutes until visiting hour. While consulting with the doctor yesterday, she'd been happy to hear that she could take Katie home soon, depending on how her daughter felt. There was nothing she wanted more right now, and for a number of reasons.

How she'd managed to keep her composure, she didn't know. Maybe after this ordeal ran its course, she'd finally crash and burn. Only she didn't have the luxury of caring for herself or her own well-being. She had Raisin to worry about. And her father. Now Katie, too. Not to mention their sorry financial situation, which seemed more dire with each passing day, despite her growing business. She had been forced to close all week and couldn't afford to shut down for two. Not only would she lose additional revenue, but also her wealthy clientele might decide to go elsewhere, never to return. No, she needed to go back to work.

She stepped into the corridor so that the others might not see her look of concern. Just thinking about Katie's medical costs caused her to experience pangs of guilt, despite knowing that she'd go deep into debt to save her kids' lives.

The sight of Ray walking down the corridor caused her adrenaline to spike. She told herself to stay calm and not lash out at him, especially when he had two cups of coffee in hand. The hospital was not the place to make a scene. She always knew when Ray was trying to suck up to her. So what had he done this time, aside from not contacting her for two whole days, then magically appearing on that bridge and showing her up?

"For you, babe," he said, kissing her cheek.

She took the cup from him, trying not to meet his gaze and fall prey to his charms.

"This is also for you." He handed her a wad of bills wrapped in a red elastic band.

"What's this?"

"What's it look like?"

"I mean, where did you get it?"

"I earned it. Profits from the business."

"Selling seaweed? Is that where you've been these past few days?"

"Processed kelp and seaweed, actually. It's all the rage these days. Supposed to have amazing health benefits."

"Why didn't you at least return my call?"

"There's no cell service on some of those isolated flats. Think I wouldn't have rushed right home had I known what happened to Katie?"

The nurse walked over as Isla slipped the wad into her pocket-book. Despite her many complaints about Ray, every once in a while he did come through—and he made sure she knew it. With the bills piling up, this would definitely help.

"You two can see your daughter now," the nurse said.

"Would I be able to talk to her for a few minutes?" Karl stepped into the corridor just then and approached them.

"She's pretty shaken up, but I suppose it's up to her parents," the nurse replied.

"Would you mind?" Karl asked, turning to Isla.

"Relax, Bjorny. My daughter's in no condition to talk to you just yet," Ray said.

Isla looked at Karl's fine-boned face and wondered if he knew that his ex-wife had once posed for Ray, and possibly done more.

"I appreciate your concern, Ray, but her best friend is still missing, and time's running out," Karl said.

"Yes, Karl, you can talk to Katie. Just give me a minute with her first," Isla said, noticing Drew walking into the corridor.

She was about to head to Katie's room when she heard someone shouting behind her. She pivoted and saw Drew and another boy wrestling each other to the floor. Drew positioned himself on top of the other kid and started throwing punches before Karl and Ray broke them up.

"You're a dead man, Julian. I can't believe you have the balls to show your face in here after what you've done," Drew barked.

"Dude, you seriously need to chill," Julian said, picking himself up. "You're not the boss man of this hospital."

"You better get him out of here before I beat the shit out of him," Drew said.

"No one's beating anyone," Karl said. He turned to Drew. "Get in the waiting room and stay there. Because if you cause any more problems, I'll ban you from this hospital for good, even if you're dying."

"What about him?"

"You attacked first. Besides, he has every right to be here just as much as you."

Drew headed back inside the waiting room after turning to snarl at Julian. To her mind, Julian didn't seem the least bit fazed by the assault. He adjusted his wool cap and stared goofily at the cop, as if asking what he should do next.

"Julian, I take it," Karl said.

"You witnessed him attack me, Officer. You going to do anything about it?"

"It's the girl's boyfriend, so let's not be so dramatic."

"Katie has a boyfriend?" Julian looked genuinely surprised.

"They've been going together since Katie was a freshman."

"Had no idea. She just doesn't seem like a girl who has a boy-friend."

"How well do you know her?"

"She is a friend of Willow's."

"And you're friends with Willow?"

"What do you think, bruh?"

"It's Officer Bjornson to you."

"Sure. Whatever, *Officer Bjornson.*" Julian snorted sarcastically. "Willow and I went to the same school, Chance Academy, before she transferred out. She also happens to live next door to me."

"Do you know what happened to Willow that night?"

"No, I do not, Officer."

"Look, Julian, it's not good for you to be here right now. I think you should go home."

"To Beckett and Samantha McCallister? No thanks."

"Okay, but you can't stay here."

"Why not? Because I don't belong? Because I didn't grow up in Shepherd's Bay, like the rest of you? That sounds like discrimina-tion where I come from."

"Boo-fricking-hoo, rich boy," Ray said.

"Stay out of this, Ray," Karl snapped. "Look, kid, I don't really care where you came from. I'm telling you to leave this hospital."

"It's a free country, last time I checked," Julian retorted.

"Then, I'll be forced to call security and have them drag you out."

"Want me to do it for you, Bjorny?" Ray said.

"Thought I told you to butt out, Ray?"

"Forget you, man. I know when I'm not wanted," Julian said. "I was only here for Katie, anyway. Check up on her. See how she's doing." He threw his arms up in resignation and took off down the corridor.

Isla saw Karl looking at her, as if asking whether he had done the right thing. Personally, she thought he should have kicked Drew out first and then taken care of Julian. Did he suspect that the Mc-Callister boy had lied to him? She had no idea what to believe anymore. She just knew that she needed to get to Katie's room and speak to her daughter before anyone else got to her first.

She dimmed the light before she closed the door behind her. She edged slowly toward the bed and saw that Katie was lying on her back and gazing up at the ceiling. Her hands were folded neatly over her midsection. Aside from the bruises and cuts on her face, Isla thought she looked angelic. She wondered what Katie was thinking or if she had any recollection of the horrific event she'd experienced. She pulled up a chair and sat next to her, and for a brief second, she thought her daughter might be in some kind of a trance.

"Katie?"

Her daughter didn't move.

"It's going to be okay, honey. I'm here for you."

Katie turned to look at her mother.

"Don't worry. We're going to get you the help you need."

"Where's Willow? I just want to know what happened to her." She closed her eyes.

"We don't know yet, sweetie. The police are still searching for her."

"How can I ever be right again when Willow's not here?" She snapped open her eyes and resumed staring at the ceiling.

"I know it's still early in your recovery, but Officer Bjornson wants to come in and talk to you about the night you two went missing."

"I can't tell him what I don't know."

"Weren't you with Willow that night?"

"That's what I'm trying to tell you. I don't remember anything that happened."

Isla heard footsteps behind her. When she looked up, she saw a doctor standing above her, with a stethoscope around his neck. He was wearing round tortoiseshell glasses. He held out his hand, and Isla thought he looked more like a college freshman than a doctor.

"Dr. Rosen," he said. "I'm the resident neurologist on staff here." She shook his slender hand.

"After examining your daughter, it appears that she's suffering from a traumatic head injury. It's best we take some brain scans, just to be on the safe side, but my best guess right now is a severe concussion. Possibly grade three."

"She's also suffering memory loss, Doctor."

"Retrograde amnesia is normal for an injury of this magnitude. I would imagine that as her brain heals, her memory will return in full. Whether this happens in days or weeks, I can't really tell you right now. It might be best for her to talk to a therapist."

"Of course. We'll set that up right away."

"Just to let you know, she's not letting us draw her blood."

"No needles," Katie interjected.

"I suppose that's something we can do later, when she's feeling better," the doctor said. "Your daughter may also be experiencing some emotional trauma, caused by whatever happened to her while she was missing. That's why talking to a therapist might help her unlock those painful memories and then deal with the pain she suffered from that incident."

"What are you implying? That this memory loss is all in her head?"

"I wouldn't say all of it, but she may be experiencing what's known as selective memory loss. Whatever happened to her may be too painful to recall, so her brain, for all intents and purposes, is blocking out everything until she's better equipped to handle the truth."

"There's another missing girl, a good friend of hers. We need Katie to remember what happened in order to help the police find her. That's why that police officer out in the hallway wants to question her."

"That's fine. I'm only suggesting that he should proceed with caution. And you better stay in the room, just in case the questioning upsets her. Sometimes, if you force the issue, it can cause a violent reaction."

"Don't worry, Doctor. I'm not going anywhere."

"Good. I'll make sure there's a nurse on standby, just in case it's too much for her to handle."

The doctor smiled at Katie before leaving the room. Isla grabbed her daughter's hand and squeezed. Then Katie nodded bravely, indicating that she was ready to answer his questions, and exactly what she could remember, Isla desperately wanted to know.

KARL

*T*HE GIRL HAD NOTHING OF ANY CONSEQUENCE TO SAY, AND THIS DIS-appointed him. It was not that he'd asked the wrong questions or somehow made a bad impression on her. Katie had honestly seemed to have no memory of the event that traumatized her. Isla had explained to him what the doctor had said and how Katie might be repressing memories from the ordeal. It seemed plausible. He'd tried every trick in his limited interviewing repertoire, even providing clues that might trigger her memory, but nothing had worked.

Isla's presence next to Katie hadn't helped. It had thrown him off his game, and he realized he couldn't concentrate with her nearby. She had looked so lovely in the soft light that it had made his Nordic skin blush, although he didn't think she had seen it in the dimly lit room.

He left the hospital, frustrated and wanting answers, but not without having gained at least some insight. For example, he'd seen the wad of cash that passed between Ray's hands and his wife's. What was that all about? He'd overheard the rumors in town about Ray starting a seaweed business. What that seaweed business entailed, he had no idea, but he would find out.

Personally, he'd never had the entrepreneurial knack that many men in this town seemed to possess, even if they'd gotten it by necessity. And everywhere he turned these days, seaweed seemed to be popping up as the healthy alternative to conventional snack foods. He'd even seen noodles made from seaweed at the Whole

Foods salad bar when he went down to Portland to visit his sister. And in colorful packages, sold as flavored chips. As for him, he'd never in his life eaten seaweed, apart from the mushy stuff that sometimes floated into his mouth during a long swim in the ocean.

A heavy rain fell on the streets as he exited the hospital. He knew this would put a damper on the search for Willow Briggs. He thought of Julian and wondered why the boy had shown up at the hospital. Was he really friends with Katie? Was he really that concerned about her health? Something told him that the kid was not telling the whole truth. Something didn't feel right to him about how everything seemed to be playing out.

He drove mindlessly through the streets, asking himself questions about all the children involved, so engrossed in his thoughts he didn't hear the constant swoosh of wet tires. Was it a coincidence that Dakota James, the other missing rich kid, came from the same side of town? Or that he'd been in the same grade as Julian at Chance Academy? Might be a good idea to see how close the two were, or if they had been friends at all. Could both boys have been interested in Willow?

Then where did Katie fit into all this? Collateral damage in a deadly teen love triangle? He'd seen only photographs of Willow Briggs, and it had taken only a quick glance for him to appreciate the girl's physical beauty. He remembered staring a little too long at one photograph of her in a string bikini and then, seconds later, feeling tremendous guilt for having gawked at a half-naked teenage girl.

Many people in town thought Dakota James had run away from home. Rumors had spread that he had quarreled often with his mother and had had issues with authority at his previous schools. Like Willow and Julian, Dakota James came from wealth, had been blessed with good genes and a financial portfolio that Karl would never even begin to know.

Only the hard-core volunteers would search in this torrential downpour. Every officer on the force was now mucking about in the woods. A number of state troopers had joined the search, as well, as had a few cops from the nearby towns. He planned to join them shortly, knowing it would be a miserable slog. But then he heard a deafening boom. A few seconds later the sky lit up, and he knew the search would be called off for safety reasons.

Goddamned Ray. It had taken all his might not to say something to that asshole. Like why did he treat his wife so poorly? Or why, of all the women in Shepherd's Bay, had he chosen Sofia to sleep with? He didn't want to consider the possibility that Sofia had chosen Ray. Did Isla know about this? He certainly hoped not. It would be quite uncomfortable for both of them if she did. It was not like his wife was the first married woman Swisher had ever slept with. Likely not the last, either. The bigger question, which he thought he knew the answer to, was, Why had Isla stayed with him for so long?

By the time he returned to the station, he received word that the search had been called off until further notice. Without wasting time, he logged on to one of the computers and began to work.

KATIE

MY MOTHER HELD MY HAND WHILE THAT POLICE OFFICER QUES-tioned me. He seemed like an odd-looking guy. I don't mean to say that he was hideous or deformed. He had this long, pale face with the word *intense* written all over it. And beady blue-gray eyes that sank deep into his skull. His nose hooked over thin, pale lips. Honestly, I couldn't take my eyes off him. Unfortunately, I couldn't provide any answers to his questions. He had to know that I wanted to discover the truth as much as he did. Or at least I think I did. Maybe a part of me didn't want to answer his questions. Or maybe I wasn't in any mood to remember the events of that night.

But I do want Willow to be found. Very much so. So in that respect, I'm fairly certain that I tried my best. Five minutes of questioning, however, left me fatigued and ready to collapse in exhaustion. At the end of our short session, he eyed me longer than I liked, as if trying to determine whether or not I'd been telling him the truth.

Maybe a brief nap will help me remember. Then again, it's probably best for me to start recalling events where I left off, which was when Willow knocked Tiffany out with that crazy kick. In all my life, it was probably the most impressive thing I'd ever seen. I developed a newfound respect for Willow after that day.

My mother tells me that there are people waiting to see me. Like church people. And my father and Drew. But I don't want to see any of them right now, especially my father, and double especially for Drew. I'm way too tired to act all sweet and polite with this darkness living inside me. I'm afraid I might say something I'll regret and prove to everyone that I'm really not the nice girl that everyone thinks I am. Because the truth is, I want to scream at the world for everything that's happened to us, mostly because I'm here and Willow's not. A movie I once watched called it survivor's guilt.

My mother makes one of her faces when I tell her I don't want to see anyone. She says that it will be good for me to be with other people and that it might make me feel better. It takes much begging and pleading before she gives in to my demands and agrees not to let anyone inside my room. Then she says something that makes me happy. Or less sad. She tells me that I'll be going home soon. But first, they have to run some tests and do a brain scan. "Anything," I beg her, as long as there's no needles involved and they get me out of this hellhole.

I close my eyes and try to remember. But the harder I try, the more my mind resists, informing me that it will do so on its own timeline.

We stood onstage, our hands locked in a human chain. Thunderous applause cascaded around us. Demand for tickets to our school's production of *Grease* had been so overwhelming that they moved it to the old Ford Theater in town. Everyone in the audience stood cheering, and not a seat in the theater sat empty—and it held nearly five hundred bodies. They had come from far and wide to see our production. We bowed in unison and then stood waiting for the applause to die down.

I saw my parents sitting in the middle row. It was my mother's fourth show and my father's first. Willow's father stood in the wings of the theater, his face hidden in the shadows and behind that stupid camera, as he filmed our musical for his reality show. "Bring Maine to Hollywood," he kept saying. "Make it appear that living in Shepherd's Bay is glamorous and exciting." Every kid and their parent had to sign a waiver form if they wanted to be a part of the show, which, as we'd been told from the beginning, faced long odds of ever getting picked up. Those that didn't want to be involved would have their face blurred if the show ever made it that far.

The applause seemed like it would never stop. I looked down the line and saw all the cast members holding hands and smiling profusely. Standing front and center was Willow, wearing the biggest grin of them all. And yet I knew those smiles would vanish once we went backstage. Then the bitterness and backstabbing of rehearsals would rear their ugly heads. Despite our friendship, I knew she was not entirely without blame.

This smiling chain of performers bowed again to the crowd. Willow's talent as a singer and dancer blew me away. She was far more gifted than anyone could have imagined, and the senior girls in our theater group might have begrudgingly accepted her into their clique had it not been for her diva-like attitude throughout the production. But Willow didn't care. She didn't want any part of their clique. She had already made up her mind about her classmates after that first day at school, had decided that she would have nothing to do with them. News of her whupping of Tiffany had spread like wildfire throughout the school and had given her somewhat of a reputation. Unwillingly, or maybe not so unwillingly, I'd cast my lot with Willow, and it was now too late to turn back.

Once backstage, my classmates segregated themselves in their various corners. Willow's father—he insisted that everyone call him Gil—strolled around the room, filming everyone's reactions. All the bitter feuds during rehearsals didn't damper our enthusiasm for a job well done, especially after that thunderous reception we received, the likes of which none of us had ever experienced. No one in town could ever remember a high school production being moved to Ford Theater. Or selling out every show. It was unheard of.

I sat with Willow as she removed her makeup, the two of us an island among a sea of exhausted performers. It felt awkward sitting next to the show's star and not basking in her glory. Looking at her, one would have thought that she'd bombed on the biggest stage of her life. But quite the opposite had happened, and now she was the biggest star ever to come out of this town.

So what did that make me? In some ways, I felt like I'd made a big mistake by befriending her. I still talked with some of my old friends, but our lifelong relationships had soured because of my decision. I desperately wanted to leave Shepherd's Bay and see what else waited for me out in the world. My mother had once tried to leave this place but, for whatever reason, had dropped out of college and returned home. My father had never left and, quite frankly, had never seen any good reason to leave. He loved this town, like so many others who had grown up here.

I didn't want to go back to my old life, to being the same boring Katie Eaves. The good girl who went to church each Sunday and earned good grades and treated people with kindness and respect. A girl who loved her little brother to death. A girl who never did anything exciting or crazy, and who tried to fit in as best she could.

Truth be told, I was in awe of Willow and happy that she had chosen me, of all the kids in school, to be her bestie. Was there anything she couldn't do? And now her father was making her the star of his reality show, and I would be her sidekick. Ironically, *Shepherd's Bay* could possibly be my ticket out of Shepherd's Bay.

Gil had invited me one day to take a look at some of his footage. It had blown me away. Willow appeared in the majority of the scenes, and she gobbled up the screen with her charisma and beauty. In comparison, I looked plain and unremarkable, as did all the others. I knew it would be impossible for viewers to take their eyes off Willow. It was the first time I truly believed that Gil's show might actually get picked up.

I looked over and watched our musical director approach us, her eyes on Willow, who was still removing her makeup and staring at herself in the mirror. Just then someone brought in a massive bouquet of flowers and asked Willow where to set it down. Willow pointed, as if annoyed, and the kid set the bouquet down on a nearby table. A diva to the core, she didn't thank him, say goodbye, or offer up any kind words. Another kid came in with a single red rose and handed it to me. I felt embarrassed to accept it after what my bestie had just received. I thanked the boy, saw that the rose was from Drew, and then set it down on the table, next to the bouquet. The only other flower I had received was from my mother on opening night.

"You did an amazing job tonight, Willow. There's no doubting your talent," Mrs. Carlson said.

Willow looked up at the woman and flashed her an insincere smile. Then her gaze returned to the mirror.

"Of course, no one can succeed without a strong supporting cast. Now, I know you've had a few creative differences with some of the other performers, but it would be nice if you could reach out and thank them for making you look good onstage."

"Sure thing," Willow said without looking away from the mirror. "Is that all, Mrs. Carlson?"

But she didn't budge. She hesitated a few seconds before saying, "I believe so."

Willow continued to gaze at herself, as if appraising the girl staring back at her.

"I certainly hope you'll audition for a role next year."

"Maybe. If I'm still here."

"Well, I, for one, hope you are." Mrs. Carlson turned and walked away without even looking at me.

I could tell she was exasperated by Willow and, by extension, me. All the squabbling, infighting, and parental bitching had tested her good nature. But the positive reception to the play had made it all worthwhile, especially the money it had brought into the club's coffers. To call it a resounding success would be an understatement. From what I'd heard, there was enough money now to upgrade the sound system in the school's sorry theater. One more year with Willow at the helm and the boosters would be able to replace the lighting, too, especially if they could sell out Ford Theater every night.

Willow turned up the rap music playing on her phone and eyed me knowingly. She had never reciprocated in kind when I told her, after that first performance, what an amazing job she'd done. Longtime theater buffs claimed there'd never been a better Sandy Olsson. So tonight I held my tongue. I shouldn't have expected much praise to come my way; nothing I did onstage warranted much attention, anyway. Sure, an occasional pat on the back would be nice. But the real reward was being on the same stage with Willow as she belted out song after song. Did dance routine after dance routine.

But that was Willow. She would go hot and cold on me, and whenever she paid me a compliment, it made me feel special. Because of that, I found myself craving her attention more than ever.

And yet I was smart enough to know that I was a better person than that. But as my home life began to get crazier, I found myself getting left behind in the chaos. My grandfather had been diagnosed with Alzheimer's, and Raisin, through no fault of his own, had been having a difficult year keeping his glucose levels in check. My father's frequent absences put an additional strain on his already strained marriage, despite my mother's attempts to make it seem like we were a happy and loving family. I just didn't seem to fit in anywhere, which was why I hungered for the attention Willow paid me.

Still, I loved my mother. Had it not been for her, we would have imploded a long time ago. She'd been the glue that held our family together. She was my inspiration and the one who constantly pushed me to be the best person I could be. Still, this didn't prevent our usual mother-daughter flare-ups. Or make me want to live in the manner that she did. Despite my outward appearance as the good girl, the perfect daughter in most ways, I knew the truth. I often vented my frustrations at our shitty home life and at having a well-known father who was more talk than action and who treated my mother like crap. I often wondered why she just didn't leave him. Then I remembered Raisin's chronic medical issues and my grandfather's recent diagnosis and all the bills piling up on the counter. I couldn't lie and tell myself that I wasn't immune to my father's charms and easygoing manner—or to his big promises, which never got fulfilled—even when I knew he was full of it.

I looked up and saw Debbie Lowe and Stacey Swanson standing in our orbit. They gave me a quick glance that told me I was all but invisible to them. These were the two senior girls who'd lost out on the Sandy Olsson role, although Debbie had gotten the coveted Rizzo part. What were they doing here? I had never been accepted into their social sphere and never would, which was fine by me. I glanced over at Willow and noticed that she was ignoring them. And who could blame her, especially after the cold shoulder they'd given her during the show's run?

"We thought you did an amazing job, Willow," Stacey said, as if someone had put her up to the task.

"Thanks," Willow replied, still focused on removing her makeup.

"We're really sorry. We were wrong to treat you that way," Debbie said.

Willow chuckled. "How big of you."

"A bunch of us are having a cast party tonight. We'd love for you to be there," Debbie said.

"What about Katie?"

They turned in unison and looked at me as if I had a contagious disease. "Sure. She can come," Debbie said.

"Hey, Katie Eaves. You want to go to a cast party tonight with these two?" Willow said.

Seeing her discerning eyes flare at me in the mirror, I scrunched my face up in an indeterminate way, not sure how to respond to this question. Gil, I noticed, happened to be standing behind us and filming the entire encounter, an encounter almost as dramatic as the one that took place onstage.

"Sorry, ladies. I think Katie's saying that she'd rather attend my cast party instead," Willie announced.

"Oh, we had no idea you were having a party tonight," Stacey said. "Maybe we could stop by."

"Katie," Willow said, "did you hear me invite these two hyenas?"

I shook my head, embarrassed by her coldness. I actually felt sorry for Debbie and Stacey, even if I didn't like them. Willow's behavior seemed over the top and beyond mean. And yet I smiled to myself, knowing they'd brought it upon themselves. Maybe Willow had been instructed to act this way by her father. To create conflict for his reality show. An act calculated to squeeze maximum drama out of the pettiest of things. I knew from watching all those reality shows that they thrived on this kind of friction, manufactured or not.

"Katie obviously didn't hear me invite you two, either," Willow said.

"Willow, don't be a bitch. We're admitting that we screwed up," Stacey said.

"A little late with the apologies, don't you think?" Willow flashed them a smile so perfectly theatrical that it stunned me. It also made my skin crawl. "Catch you later, bee-yotches." She spun back to her cosmetic mirror and resumed staring at herself.

The girls gave me a sympathetic look as they left, and it pissed me off. Who were they to judge? Weren't they the same girls who'd already made up their minds about Willow and harassed her after she won that part? Refused to speak to her or have anything to do with her? Besides, I knew her better than anyone. To me, she was a loyal friend and a uniquely talented performer. I tried to look past her personality quirks and character flaws and accept her for the person she was. And I believed she treated me the same way.

"That was an amazing performance. You were absolutely wonderful, babe," her father said. He put the camera down and stepped closer to her. But I wondered if he was talking about her performance onstage or backstage.

"Thank you, Daddy."

He leaned down and kissed her on the cheek. "You're going to be an even bigger star one day than you are right now."

"Don't you think I already know that?"

"Isn't that true, Katie? Isn't Willow going to be a huge star someday?"

"She's pretty awesome right now, if you ask me."

"And you were magnificent up there onstage, too, Katie. You've got real potential."

"Thank you," I said, but he had already turned his attention back to his daughter, as if my answer hadn't mattered.

"It was so perfect the way you responded to those two clucks. Keep it up. It'll make great fodder for our reality show," he said.

"Conflict is at the heart of all great drama. Isn't that what you always tell me?" Willow replied.

"See how she always listens to me, Katie? This girl is the best."

I nodded. It felt weird being with the two of them. Was this how families outside of Shepherd's Bay interacted?

"In a few years, all these girls will be watching you on the big screen, while their rug rats are screaming up a storm." He massaged her shoulders.

"I might have a few people over for a cast party tonight."

"Wonderful! Hopefully, I'll be able to get a few good shots."

"No, I want this to be without any cameras around. Just a few close friends."

"Willow, we've talked about this. If we're to do this right, I need to be filming all the time."

"I just need some chill time with my homeys. Please, Daddy?" Willow pouted in such an exaggerated manner that for a second, I thought she might cry.

"I'll tell you what, honey. Let me shoot the first five minutes of your party, and then I'll leave you guys alone."

"Is that cool with you, Katie?" Willow asked.

"That's totally cool with me," I said. Had I missed something? Had she invited me? Should I have presumed to think that I'd been asked to join her and her friends? It excited and scared me at the same time, especially since I was supposed to go to a movie later with Drew.

"Good. Then it's settled," Willow said. "Could you call the caterer and have some food delivered, Daddy?"

"Sure, babe. First, tell me how much you love your daddy."

"I love you more than all the galaxies combined."

"And what do galaxies contain, sugar plum?"

"Why, stars, Daddy." Willow giggled like a little girl.

"And what are you?"

"A star in your galaxy and the best daughter ever."

He kissed her again.

"Will you tell Mom about the party tonight? So she doesn't freak."

"Of course." He picked up his camera and stared down at me as if I was one of her adoring fans. "Bye, Katie. And great job up there onstage."

"Thanks, Mr. Briggs . . . I mean Gil."

He left us alone among the excited chatter to finish cleaning ourselves up.

My mother couldn't believe it when the silver Mercedes pulled up outside our door. I kissed her cheek and ran downstairs with my bag before she could lecture me. I'd told her that Willow and I were planning to relax and watch a movie tonight. But inside my bag I'd packed a change of clothes, along with my pj's and toiletries.

Gil had a driver pick me up. The man in the black suit smiled at me as he opened the back door. No one in Shepherd's Bay ever used a professional driver. Before I made my way inside the car, I looked up and saw my mother peering out the kitchen window. The look on her face made me smile. I suddenly understood the power of money—and I liked the feeling it gave me.

The car took off and headed toward the water. Inside it, I no-

ticed the ornate paneled wood and the stocked bar. The driver informed me that I could help myself to a drink if I wanted, and by
that, I assumed I could take a soda. But when I looked inside the
bar, there were no sodas, only bottles of alcoholic beverages. Did
he know about this? I had not reached the legal drinking age, was
not even close, and I'd never in my life tried alcohol. Was he suggesting that I could have an adult drink? Or maybe he was mistaken about my age.

Beyond excited to attend this party, I bounced nervously in my
seat. I'd never actually been to Willow's house before, although I
knew it was one of the largest ones along the water. All my old
friends' houses were similar to mine, ordinary and unspectacular.
Homes like the one Willow lived in were beyond anything towns-
people like us could ever imagine. Or afford. I felt like Cinderella
attending her first ball.

Who else would be there? Had Willow relented and invited
members of the *Grease* cast? Would I know anyone? Would there be
music and food? Would I get to sleep in a big bedroom with my
own private view of the ocean, like the kind of bedrooms I'd seen
in those reality shows?

I closed the shutter separating driver from passenger and
changed out of my jeans and T-shirt and into my white blouse,
skirt, and heels. Given no dress requirements, I'd erred on the side
of looking my best. When I was done, I opened the shutter. The
driver glimpsed me through the rearview mirror and smiled.

"You look great," he said.

"You think? It's not too much?"

He shrugged. "I have no idea what too much is, but you do look
nice."

"Thank you."

He pulled up in the roundabout in front of the massive home. I
leaned over and peered up at it in awe. It even had a turret, like on
one of those medieval castles. I was reaching to open the door, half
expecting to see a drawbridge or a moat, when it jerked open. I
looked up and saw the driver standing with his hand out, like in the
movies. I grabbed it and stepped onto the pavement with his help.
He took my bag out and handed it to me. The massive front door
opened as I walked toward it. Standing at the threshold and laugh-

ing hysterically was Willow. Was she laughing at me? I turned around and saw nothing behind me. Rap music thumped from inside the house.

I smiled nervously. "What's so funny?"

"You."

"Me?"

"Little Miss Perfect, all dressed to kill."

I looked down sheepishly at my nice skirt, blouse, and heels. "Too much?"

"What do you think you are attending? A ten-year-old's birthday party?" She was dressed in a bleached white T-shirt; acid-washed, pre-ripped jeans; and neon green Converse sneakers. She looked stunning. "Get inside, you. I've got some clothes you can change into upstairs. They might be a little big, but whatever."

"I brought some extra clothes, just in case."

"Did you help yourself to a drink on the way over, like Steve suggested?"

"Steve?" I blushed.

"Steve's our driver. He doesn't care if you drink. I often help myself to a gin and tonic after rehearsal."

"You're joking, right?" I laughed.

"Have you known me to be a big joker, Katie Eaves?"

"No," I said. "Do your parents even know you drink?"

"Sure, and they're okay with it as long as I do it responsibly. My dad used to pour me a glass of wine at dinner when I was ten. They believe we should all be more like the French. Did you know that kids over there are allowed to drink?"

"No, seeing as I've never been to Europe."

"Then you should really go sometime," she said, her body swaying to the rap music. "Might as well change in the first-floor bathroom. Then you can join us in the living room when you're done."

The inside of the house appeared to me like something out of a dream. Before I could fully take it in, she pushed me inside a spare bathroom off the entryway. I marveled at the size of it. It was bigger than my bedroom. Once I emerged, I noticed that the volume of the rap music had been turned up. I walked into the most magnificent room I'd ever seen. A few kids I didn't know lounged on couches, relaxing and talking. They looked tanned and fit, like beautiful rich kids, and nothing like the kids from my end of town. But where was Willow? I stood there, admiring the ocean view and wondering how I would fit in with this crowd. Would these kids accept or even acknowledge someone like me? Finally, Willow emerged from wherever she'd been, with two long-stemmed glasses in hand.

"Have some champagne and join the party," she told me, offering me a glass.

"I've never had champagne before."

"It's expensive stuff. I promise you'll adore it."

"Okay."

"Don't you just love Post Malone?" She danced suggestively.

"Oh yeah, he's one of my favorites."

She laughed. "Don't tell me you've never heard of Post Malone?"

"I haven't," I admitted, embarrassed.

"Come on, nerd. I'll introduce you to the gang."

As I walked around the living room, it felt like the start of something new and exciting—and vaguely dangerous.

ISLA

SHE PULLED UP TO THE MIDDLE SCHOOL, AND THE THREE OF THEM got out of the minivan. She typically dropped Raisin off early in order to meet with the nurse and get his blood tested. She prayed each day that Nurse Feeney had not called in sick, never fully sure that the substitute would know what to do in the event of an emergency.

"I'm not a baby, Mom. You don't have to walk me into school every morning," Raisin told her.

She didn't know what to say.

"Don't worry. I know what to do if something happens," he added. "I have all my Skittles, gummy bears, and juice packs."

"You might not be in the right state of mind, honey."

"But that's why we have Scout. He lets me know way ahead of time if something's wrong."

"Okay."

"I'm not going to be a little kid forever. One of these days you're going to have to learn to trust me."

"I know."

"Go home and take care of Katie."

"Gramma Eaves is watching her today."

"Why can't you stay with her?"

"I have to return to work, remember? We have bills to pay."

Raisin nodded and walked toward the school with Scout by his side. Isla stood numb for a few seconds, thinking about what her son had just said. He was growing up fast and would soon need to take more responsibility for his health. It was true; she wouldn't be around forever. And if, God forbid, something happened to her, she couldn't be 100 percent sure that Ray would keep Raisin safe.

She drove to the salon, knowing it would be a busy day. After canceling her appointments last week, she'd rescheduled them all for this week and next. With her clientele base still growing, she hoped that in the near future she could maybe hire out another chair. Staying busy would bring in much-needed revenue and would keep her mind off the fact that her daughter had been assaulted and her daughter's best friend was still missing.

Willow had to be out there, and yet Isla felt guilty that she couldn't continue to help search for her. With the bills piling up, she couldn't afford to take more time off and potentially lose clientele, clientele that she had built, with a lot of help from Samantha McCallister, over a long period of time. Not only had Samantha been a valued customer, and an overly generous tipper, but she had touted Isla's talents to all her upper-crust friends and acquaintances.

Isla turned into the center of town and parked in the back lot reserved for tenants, next to the big green Dumpster where she emptied the bags of hair at the end of each day. She unlocked the door to the salon and flicked on the lights, happy to be inside her cheerful little shop. In many ways it felt like a sanctuary, welcoming and warm. Working here gave her a respite from all the craziness in her life. Interesting and friendly customers conversed with her, soothing music played over the speakers, and there was plenty of coffee. More importantly, she was finally earning some decent money.

She hadn't planned on cutting hair for a living, but it had turned out to be a good fit. She excelled at it and had discovered she had a talent for dealing with different and diverse people. All those ambitious college plans she'd had as a young woman had given way to the reality of family and financial matters. All in all, she couldn't complain.

She put on her blue smock and glanced in the mirror. She thought she looked more tired and wrinkled than usual. Considering the circumstances, she could have looked worse. Then she powered up the barber pole: red for blood, blue for veins, and white for the towels used to clean up after the bloodletting, from back in the day when barbers did more than cut hair.

Because of Katie's and Willow's disappearance, she expected to receive an avalanche of questions today regarding her daughter's well-being. She decided that when asked, it would be best to address the situation head-on. It would no doubt be the hot topic all week and for weeks to come.

She turned on the television and then unlocked the door. On the screen, a reporter stood in a field, interviewing Gil Briggs and his wife. Gil could barely speak, he was so emotional. He had to look away at one point, he was so overtaken with grief. Isla focused on Felicia, who stood perfectly still next to him, an ice queen, her eyes hidden beneath those patented dark sunglasses. The bell over the door jingled, jarring her out of her trance. Her first customer of the day and she hadn't even checked her appointment book yet.

Brooke Hilton waltzed in as if she'd just come from a society luncheon. It amazed Isla how these women always managed to look their best for any occasion. It had gotten to the point where she could tell the townies from the newcomers at a single glance.

After a hearty *good morning*, delivered with the slightest hint of a Southern drawl, Brooke stood next to her and gazed up at the television. Gil continued to struggle through the interview, begging for whoever had kidnapped Willow to show mercy and set her free. He tearfully admitted that he'd do anything to get his daughter back. Isla was instantly struck by the fact that he used the singular pronoun *I* instead of the plural *we*.

"It's such a shame what happened to that girl," Brooke said, crossing her arms and exposing her manicured French nails. "You must be so happy that your daughter is back home with you."

"Yes, I'm very thankful." Isla felt her eyes start to water.

"Awww! I didn't mean to make you cry, girl."

"I just feel so sorry for the Briggs family."

"No offense, but it's not like they provided that girl with a whole lot of guidance in life. It seemed to me that she did whatever she wanted." She walked to the styling chair and sat down, then swiveled in it so that she could look up at the television. "If I'd acted like that at her age, my father would have opened up a can of whup ass on me." Brooke laughed in a way Isla thought insensitive, considering the circumstances.

She wrapped the cape around Brooke while she eyed the television. The reporter had just finished interviewing Gil when Felicia literally dropped out of the picture. The focus of the camera wavered before the TV screen showed Felicia passed out on the grass. People ran over and tended to her, and the reporter handed off to the local news desk.

"Did she just faint on live TV?" Brooke asked.

"Poor thing."

"Poor?" Brooke laughed. "Have you seen their home? Maybe *poor* isn't the most accurate word to describe Felicia Briggs."

"No, I didn't think so."

"I've been inside that home, and *stunning* doesn't even begin to describe it."

"What's it like?"

"Like nothing you've ever seen before." Brooke turned her wrist and examined her polished nails. "You mean you haven't been?"

"Not to my recollection."

"Well, honey, you're not missing much on the personal end of things. Gil Briggs is an interminable boor, and his wife acts like she's royalty. Thinks she's better than everyone else on the Point. Those two were made for each other."

Isla wanted to tighten the cape and strangle this woman, but she kept her mouth shut and combed the woman's long, lustrous hair. Brooke came in every two weeks for a trim. For that reason alone, she couldn't afford to offend her.

"Still, I hope Felicia manages to survive this crisis. I'll call the girls at the club later, and we'll send her a nice bouquet."

"That's sweet of you," Isla told her.

"It sure is, seeing how the Briggses managed to steal all the good help in town. Consider yourself lucky in that regard."

She understood the subtext of Brooke's statement: she was a poor townie.

"Between you and me, hon, I heard through the grapevine that those kids had a wild party the night Willow and your daughter went missing," Brooke revealed.

"Oh?" This was news to her.

"Now, I don't know that to be a fact. One of the girls at the club told me that, and there's no reason to doubt her." Brooke turned to look her, an annoying habit that she did too often and that forced Isla to stop cutting and wait for her to turn her head back around. "I wouldn't tell you this if your daughter hadn't been found."

"What's said in this shop stays in this shop."

"Like Vegas. I love it."

"If you can't trust your stylist, then who can you trust?"

"Exactly." Brooke glanced briefly at her phone. "Between you and me, I heard that Willow is a hellion on wheels and that her parents can't keep her in line. Sure, she's beautiful and talented and all that, but those are often the most screwed-up kids."

"Katie never mentioned any of that to me."

"You were a teenager once. You really think your daughter would confide in you like that?"

Katie had always been straight up with her . . . until recently. Isla wondered if she'd been naive all this time.

Brooke went on. "I also heard that she was involved with both the James boy and Julian McCallister. Maybe this is all some sort of crazy love triangle gone haywire."

"Do you really think Julian might be involved?"

"Have you seen that boy?"

"I saw him the other day at the search party."

"He's a complete dreamboat, not that I'm looking, mind you. Reminds me of that actor James Dean, if Dean was a hipster rich kid who played in a rock band."

"Now that you mention it, he does slightly resemble him."

"Did you know that Julian got kicked out of his previous school? Some fancy academy in Manhattan that cost a small fortune."

"What for?"

"Rumor has it, he was selling drugs, but nobody knows for sure. And nobody's searching too hard, either. If you land on Samantha's bad side, you can forget about getting invited to all the best parties in town. That woman has a lot of pull around here."

"In all my dealings with her, she's been nothing but kind," Isla said.

"Don't let that friendly exterior fool you. Samantha can be a cold-blooded assassin if you cross her."

"You've seen this?"

"Damn straight I have. She gave the cold shoulder to one of the girls at the club for a simple breach of etiquette."

"What did the woman do?"

"Gossiped about Julian to the wrong people. Poor girl had no idea it would get back to his mother. It took a year and some intense groveling before she started to get back into Samantha's good graces."

"Ouch."

"Ouch is right. Good thing I can trust you." She turned to face Isla. "I *can* trust you, right?"

"I never repeat what's said in this shop."

Brooke patted her hand and smiled. "That's why you're the best, Isla."

"So you think Willow was dating Julian?" Isla realized she needed to be careful about what she said.

"Who knows? Booty calling. Hooking up. Pick your poison with these crazy kids today and all their dating apps. All I know is that Julian is quite the ladies' man."

Brooke took out her phone and engaged in a text conversation with one of her friends. Isla knew it was her cue to shut up and leave the woman alone. She couldn't help peeking over the woman's shoulder and reading what was going on in her life. Yes, she knew she shouldn't be snooping like that, but she'd do anything to find out who had hurt Katie. She glanced down and read that Brooke had a lunch date with Chloe Foster. Then she had to plan a trip to Turks and Caicos for herself and Tucker and their three children. Dinner at the club tonight, right after Tucker played nine holes with Mason Byrd. Also, something about a fundraising event for a friend running for town council.

Isla finished up, spun Brooke around, and showed her what she'd done. She held up the oval mirror so Brooke could see the back. Brooke smiled, pleased at the job she'd done. Isla removed the cape. Then Brooke pulled out her credit card and Isla processed the transaction. Brooke signed the slip and handed it back to Isla with no tip. She thanked her for coming and then watched as her client sauntered out the front door, happy as one of the steamer clams in the mudflats that had escaped the digger's rake.

With broom in hand, Isla walked over to the window facing the street and watched as Brooke got into her BMW. The blowout she had just given the woman would have cost three times the amount in Atlanta, where Brooke had lived before moving to Maine. How could the woman sleep at night, knowing she'd left no tip? It didn't really bother Isla that much, knowing that she'd just pocketed thirty-five bucks. It was a helluva lot better than the seven bucks a cut her grandfather used to charge. She'd heard people say it wasn't customary to tip the owner of a salon, but if she had Brooke's kind of money, she would be generous to a fault.

She swept the hair into a dustbin, readying for her next client. Al Jenkins worked at the auto parts store and had been a longtime customer of her grandfather. It took all of ten minutes to cut his hair, and he was the least fussy man she'd ever worked on. He never even wanted to see himself in the mirror afterward. She charged the locals fifteen bucks, and the seniors got a buck off that price, and yet most every local gave her a twenty and told her to keep it.

The rest of the day went by in a blur, which helped to keep her mind off everything. Because of her absence last week, it was the busiest day she'd had in a while. At five o'clock she put up the CLOSED sign and swept the floor. She had to pick Raisin up from soccer practice. Fortunately, the school had agreed to pay a nurse to sit with Scout during these practices. Once everything was put away, she shut the lights off and headed out the back door. As she was locking up, her cell phone rang. No caller ID. She answered it and was shocked to hear Felicia's wavering voice. Why was she calling her, and why now? She'd been so intent on meeting this intimidating woman face-to-face that to speak to her now felt terrifying.

"I saw what happened to you on the news, Felicia. How are you holding up?"

"Not too well, I'm afraid. The doctor said I fainted from all the stress."

"I'm so sorry."

"Thank you for your concern. He wants me to rest for the next few days and stay in bed."

"Then you should certainly listen to him." She wondered why Felicia was calling her, of all people. Merely to tell her what the doctor had said?

"I saw myself on television this morning and realized just how awful I look. I know that's a terribly selfish thing to say, with my daughter missing and all, but there it is."

"It's not at all a terrible thing to say. Besides, I thought you looked lovely."

"Thank you, but Willow's disappearance has consumed me, to the point where I've let myself go."

"I'm certain they'll find Willow alive, just like they found Katie."

"I really hope you're right." She waited a few seconds. No mention of Katie or how she was doing.

"So how can I help you, Felicia?"

"Everyone tells me what a talented stylist you are. I've been traveling down to Portland every two weeks for a shampoo and cut, but I'm in no condition to drive now."

"You're more than welcome to schedule an appointment with me whenever you're ready. I have some openings next week, if you're interested."

"Well, that's the thing. I really can't leave here. I was hoping you might be able to do a house call."

Isla paused for a few seconds to mull it over. House calls were usually reserved for the elderly and invalids. Besides, the woman's concern for her appearance puzzled her. *Who cares about what they look like when their child goes missing?*

"I'll pay you extra. And it would really be doing me a big favor if you could help me out in this difficult time."

"Sure. I can come over around ten tomorrow," she said, glancing at her appointment book, knowing she'd have to shuffle a few appointments around. Her regular clients would understand, hopefully, and would come back at a later time.

"Thank you. You don't know how much this means to me." Felicia's voice trailed off, and it sounded as if she was crying.

Isla heard the line go dead. Felicia must have been overcome with emotion. She couldn't really blame her. And she did feel for the woman, especially considering that her own daughter had been found alive. It was true that she'd wanted to meet Felicia for some time, but now she wondered how she would approach this visit. Should she converse with her like normal and act hopeful that Willow would be found? Or should she stay quiet and let Felicia do all the talking, assuming she felt up to it? Best to size the woman up once she got there. Small talk was out of the question, as she realized she knew absolutely nothing about Felicia or her background. She figured she might know a lot more about her after the house call tomorrow.

KARL

ANOTHER DAY OF SEARCHING AND THEY'D STILL NOT FOUND A SIGN of Willow Briggs. Karl had a bad feeling about this case, like he had with Dakota James. He couldn't put his finger on why he felt this way. A pall of darkness hung over the town, and his intuition told him that the culprit of these crimes might be right under his nose.

He stopped at the local diner and sat at the counter. The news on the overhead television replayed the interview with Gil and Felicia Briggs and showed the dramatic moment when Felicia fainted. If not for the uniform clinging to his body, he would have ordered a Shepherd's Bay stout with his meal. But he had a lot of work to do and needed his wits about him. Felicia's fainting spell had canceled the interview he was supposed to have with her tonight.

He'd known many locals—good people—who'd gone bad for one reason or another, and it never ceased to surprise him. People who'd turned to drugs or property theft. He recalled the housewife who'd embezzled three thousand dollars from the Little League she'd managed. Come to find out, her husband had lost his job and the family's financial situation had hit rock bottom. Chester Allan had put a pillow over his wife's face when her dementia worsened. Tommy Bigelow had started selling and using meth after his wife left him for his best friend. Karl understood all these destructive acts, even felt compassion for the guilty parties. They were in line with what he knew about this town and its citizens. But now it seemed as if Shepherd's Bay had its first bona fide serial kidnapper—or killer. Finally, he thought, this little Maine town was joining the twenty-first century.

The political signs around town were everywhere, pointing him to a possible answer. The more he viewed these signs, the more he came to believe that a local had committed these crimes. It made perfect sense. It explained the intense animosity toward the affluent who'd settled here, with their big bucks and big attitudes. In his mind, it also explained why Katie Eaves had been allowed to go free. An embittered townie, angry at the changing nature of Shepherd's Bay, would be reluctant to kill one of their own. It would go against everything the person held near and dear. Katie had just happened to be in the wrong place at the wrong time. Or maybe the beating given to her was a warning to all the local kids to stay clear of their affluent peers.

But would killing rich kids change the political climate? Possibly, assuming the affluent decided that Shepherd's Bay was a dangerous place to settle and raise kids. Or if they believed they were being unfairly targeted. Or that the townies resented them and would do everything in their power to drive them out. Shepherd's Bay had always been a safe and welcoming community—until now. Would the threat of a hefty property tax be enough to drive them out? Maybe if the proposed tax passed, it would, but until then, these newcomers would put up a fight.

Politics had never concerned him. In fact, he rarely voted, he hated politics that much. Yes, the schools' infrastructure around town desperately needed upgrades. Teachers and cops needed cost-of-living increases, as well. But the town had benefitted greatly from the wealth of these rich newcomers. They patronized restaurants and cafés and, as a result, attracted higher-end chefs, coffee roasters, and gourmet stores that existed only in big cities like Portland. Last year a heavily tattooed guy from Brooklyn had arrived in town and opened a microbrewery called Shepherd's Bay Brewing Company.

His plate came out piled high with meat loaf, green beans, and mashed potatoes, all smothered in gravy. The waitress refilled his mug of coffee and gave him a begrudging smile. He was one of those lucky few in life who could eat to his heart's content and never put on any weight. Since high school, he'd gained only ten pounds, and that was only because he'd grown another two inches.

Before digging in, he texted Isla and asked if he could come over later and have another word with Katie. Was he interviewing the girl as a way to see Isla? He thought himself a consummate and professional cop. Still, after all those years, he'd expected not to feel anything for her. And then he had sat across from her in her kitchen a few nights ago, and all those feelings had come rushing back.

He remembered being at the hospital and watching with curiosity as Swisher pressed that wad of bills into her palm. Had he been trying to conceal it? Maybe he should follow the guy around town and see what he was up to. He'd heard rumors that Swisher had been seen hanging around with Bugger Walsh, a well-known lowlife and convicted criminal with a considerable rap sheet. He had no idea how someone could harvest and sell seaweed as a health food product. Then again, he hadn't kept up on all the latest fads and food trends. The idea of putting seaweed in his mouth repulsed him.

The two slabs of meat loaf on his plate had to be an inch thick and five inches long and were smothered in dense gravy the color of chocolate sauce. He took a bite with some mashies and felt the swell of comfort warm its way through his body. The food tasted better than his grandmother's, and that was saying a lot. Having skipped lunch this afternoon, he ate without interruption, barely pausing to come up for air.

"Hey, Bjorny," Vicky said from behind the counter.

He nodded at the bleached-blond waitress as he forked gravy onto his next bite. She'd been needling him for years about his bachelor status.

"I can make better meat loaf than that, if you'd ever care to find out."

"It's actually the gravy that makes it."

She watched him eat, one hand on supple hip. "Why you always turning down better offers, fella?"

"Once around the mountain might be enough for me."

"You're going to die an old bachelor if you keep this up."

"At least I'll die with a smile on my face, especially after a meal like this."

"I can think of a better way to put a smile on your face."

"Thanks, but I got two missing kids to find. Looks like my personal life's going to be taking a backseat for a while."

"When you find them, sweetie, make sure you come back and see me."

"With meat loaf this good, Vicky, you're due to see me in here on a regular basis. Just like you have for the past sixteen years." He stood and tossed down a twenty on the counter, frugal in all things except tipping. "We're practically husband and wife, you and me."

"My best work sure ain't in the kitchen." She smiled at him.

"Bet you say that to all the guys."

"That's because most guys want more than just my meat loaf." She winked at him.

He put on his cap, waved good-bye, and left the diner. Once in his car, he checked his cell phone and noticed that Isla had not yet contacted him. He felt like a high school kid all over again, waiting for the pretty girl to return his call.

Isla looked tired when she opened the kitchen door. He took off his cap and nodded politely, clutching his cap over his heart so she wouldn't notice it beating out of his chest. Her father sat at the kitchen table, fiddling with a butter knife in his arthritic hands. Past that, he could see Raisin sprawled on the floor and watching television. Scout was curled up next to Raisin, and he raised his head momentarily to check Karl out before laying it back down on his paws. Katie reclined on the couch with a wet washcloth over her forehead. The lights had been dimmed, due to her sensitivity to light, he guessed.

"Nice to see you. What's the occasion?" Isla's father said.

"Just thought I'd stop by and see how everyone's doing," he said, looking at Isla for guidance. "How are you, Mr. Lee?"

"Been better. My memory's been giving me fits lately."

"Sorry to hear that." Karl sat down next to him.

"No sorrier than I am," he said, turning the knife over in his fingers, as if studying every inch of it. "How's Sven doing these days? Still own that body shop over on Lincoln?"

The mention of Sven brought back mostly happy memories. Karl's father had been dead for seven years now. He remembered the funeral and shaking hands with Isla's father. "He's fine. Thank you."

"Good. Give him my best."

"Will do."

"I see that you're an army man now. When did that happen?"

"I'm a police officer."

"Yup, he's an officer, all right." Isla poured him a cup of coffee and set it down in front of him.

"Well, if you're thinking about taking her out on the town tonight, better think again. She has lots of homework to do tonight."

The comment made Karl blush, and he stared down at his cup of coffee, as if that might help.

"Dad, why don't you go to your room and watch one of your shows?" Isla said.

"That's a good idea. Maybe *Gunsmoke*'s on." He stood from the table and made his way to the doorway. "Take care, army man," he said before disappearing.

"Sorry about that," she said.

"There's nothing to be sorry about. He's very lucky he has a daughter like you to care for him."

"I feel like Nurse Ratched at times." She laughed in a way that softened his mood. "Sometimes it feels like I'm living in an insane asylum."

"You've been through a lot lately."

"I'll say. I'm just lucky Ray's mother comes over from time to time and gives me a few minutes to breathe. She's been an angel through all this."

"Is your father okay to be by himself?"

"For now, but there'll come a day when I won't be able to care for him."

He heard a door open and felt a hand squeezing his shoulder.

"What's shaking, Bjorny? Here to read me my Miranda rights?" Ray said, chuckling as he spun a chair around and sat down.

"How's it going, Ray?" Karl looked away, not wanting to show his intense dislike for the guy.

"What brings you here?"

"I need to speak to Katie for a few minutes."

"Come on now, Bjorny. We just finished eating dinner."

"Her best friend is still missing, Ray," Isla said. "If Karl can get any information out of her, then maybe we stand a chance at finding Willow."

"Everyone knows that the odds of finding a missing person alive after forty-eight hours are slim to none."

"Stop that, Ray," Isla scolded. "How can you say such a terrible thing when your daughter is in the other room?"

"What? It's a well-known fact."

"Okay if I talk to Katie now?" Karl said.

"Knock yourself out," Ray said, getting up and grabbing himself a beer.

Isla walked into the living room and told Raisin to go up to his bedroom for a few minutes. Karl nodded at the boy as he and his service dog passed. Katie opened her eyes when she sensed him standing over her. He dropped to one knee and took out his notebook. As he did this, he turned and saw Ray snuggling Isla in his arms, and he heard her giggling at whatever Ray had whispered in her ear.

"Hi, Katie." He turned back and smiled at her.

"Hi," she said in a weak voice.

"Okay if I ask you a few questions?"

"Have they found Willow yet?"

"No, which is why I need some answers."

She pressed her eyes together. "I really want to help you, Officer, but I just can't remember anything. It's like my mind doesn't want to cooperate."

"Maybe we can jog it."

"Okay."

"Try to think really hard now."

"Don't you think I've been trying my hardest?"

"I do, but now you need to try even harder," he said. "Can you think of anyone who doesn't like Willow?"

"Only half the school."

"Enough to harm her?"

She shrugged.

"Why don't they like her?" he asked.

"Why do you think?"

"I have no idea. That's why I'm asking."

"Because she is beautiful and talented and lives her life to the fullest. But mostly because she is *not* one of us."

"Not from Shepherd's Bay?"

"What else could I mean?"

He didn't expect resistance. "So why do you like her?"

"For the same reasons people hate her. I have just never viewed her as a bad person like the others. They don't know her like I do." She adjusted the washcloth higher over her forehead. "Willow is everything most girls in this town want to be but will never become. And Willow knows this and was flaunting it."

"That seems kind of mean."

"I never said she was perfect."

"So why have you stayed friends with her?"

"I like her, and she likes me. Once I cast my lot with Willow, there was no going back to being friends with the girls I grew up with." Her voice sounded weak.

"Did these kids threaten or tease her?"

"Yes, but she never complained or went to the teachers and ratted them out. Kids can be mean in this town."

"What did they say to her?"

"They called her a spoiled rich bitch, among other things. One of the girls even threatened to beat her up."

"What did she do?"

Katie smiled. "Willow kicked her ass."

"Really? Were there any witnesses to this fight?"

"Wasn't much of a fight. Willow knocked her out."

"Knocked her out?"

"Yes, with some crazy martial arts kick. It happened after school one day. Once word got out what Willow did to that girl—and Tiffany deserved every bit of it—it made things worse. For both of us."

"Can you give me the names of all the girls involved?"

Katie listed them off.

"Maybe it was these girls who committed this crime against you and Willow."

"Maybe, but I doubt it. They kept their distance after that day."

"What about that night after you won the softball championship?"

"I can barely remember the game, except for the bits and pieces that randomly come back to me."

"Your friend is still missing, Katie. You really need to try to remember something."

"What do you think I've been doing all this time?" Tears dripped down her cheeks. "I've been trying to work my way back to that terrible night, trying to remember everything that happened."

"Okay," he said, putting away the notebook. "As soon as you remember something, please let me know. Here's my card."

She took it and squeezed it between her palms, closing her eyes.

"I'll be seeing you soon," he said.

"I'm a good person, Officer Bjornson. I never wanted any of this to happen."

"I'm sure you didn't."

This comment struck him as odd. Why had she said that? Ray still had Isla wrapped in his arms as Karl passed through the kitchen. The sight of them canoodling filled him with sadness, despite the trepidation in Isla's eyes. Could marriage be a form of Stockholm syndrome? He thanked them and showed himself out. For some reason, he visualized gravy being poured over mashed potatoes. He got in his car and thought of that flirty waitress who'd been after him all these years. A nice woman, but totally not his type. Still, why shouldn't he ask her out to dinner and a movie once this case wrapped up? She seemed like a nice person. And if it helped take his mind off of Isla, then all the better.

Of course, he knew he'd never do it.

ISLA

ANOTHER DAY GONE AND STILL NO SIGN OF WILLOW. ISLA DROVE TO-
ward the affluent part of town, where Felicia lived, listening to the
morning news instead of music. She hated to admit that Ray had
been right last night about the poor odds of finding a missing person alive after forty-eight hours but voicing it in such casual manner had seemed in bad taste, especially with Katie recovering in the
other room. She wished that Ray had stayed out in the garage while
Karl questioned Katie, greasing whatever engine he'd been working on.

Karl's reemergence in her life had been unsettling in more ways
than one. She fought to deny the attraction she felt for him. It felt
stupid, for sure, but their shared history deepened whatever feelings she still had, whether she cared to admit it or not. Back when
they were dating, everything had seemed fresh and exciting, and
they'd known nothing about one another, exploring as they went.
Now it felt like she knew everything about Karl Bjornson's life, his
likes and dislikes, as well as his family history.

The magic had faded from her marriage to Ray. She figured it
happened to most couples, even when their romance sporadically
appeared, like it had for her last night, when Ray hugged her in the
kitchen. It surprised her that she looked forward to seeing Karl
whenever he came over. She relished that quiet conversation
they'd had at her kitchen table. It reminded her of old times. He
looked much the same as he had in high school, and he had the
same laid-back temperament, a far cry from Ray and his snake-oil
salesman personality.

She'd rearranged her schedule this morning to accommodate Felicia. Candace Brewer, one of her other socialite clients, had stated her displeasure at having to miss her appointment, and so Isla had managed to squeeze her in, in the afternoon. Home visits were not something she did on a regular basis, especially during the workday, but she did do them on occasion. Typically, she visited a client at night, and only if they were elderly or had a medical condition that prevented them from coming into her shop. Mostly, she did it as a favor. The time and effort were definitely not worth the money. Sometimes she wouldn't even charge an elderly client if they were infirm or lived solely on Social Security.

She pulled up to Felicia's home and parked along the circular driveway. How many times had she cruised around this neighborhood, dying to see how the other half lived—the 1 percent? Standing at the Briggses' door, she grimaced upon seeing her broken-down minivan parked alongside this stately mansion.

She rang the bell and waited. Was Felicia even home? The sound of waves crashing against the shore echoed in her ears. The salty smell of ocean wafted up to her nose and brought back a childhood full of memories.

A voice came over the speaker and instructed her to come inside. The door handle clicked open, and she entered. The scent of lemons and hibiscus petals hit her first. She looked to her left and took in the massive window facing the ocean and filling the house with sunlight. The living room faced the water and flowed naturally into the open kitchen. She walked from the kitchen to the diningroom. The dining-room table consisted of a halved tree, polished and gleaming, and big enough to seat at least twenty people. Weird chandeliers dangled from the vaulted ceiling. The interior was more spectacular than she could have ever imagined. She felt a million miles removed from Shepherd's Bay, despite standing front and center in the town she grew up in.

A woman's voice called down to her. "Hello, Isla."

She looked up and saw Felicia standing on the second-floor landing and wearing a white bathrobe. Stainless-steel cables ran horizontally across the second-floor landing and acted as a railing, allowing Isla a head-to-toe view of the other woman.

"I'll be down in fifteen minutes. I need to take a quick shower before we get started." Her voice sounded theatrical, as if to emphasize every syllable.

Fifteen minutes? Isla needed to get back to the shop for her next appointment. But then she remembered that Willow was still missing, and she bit her tongue.

What would she do with herself for fifteen minutes? She placed her tool bag down on the granite island and stood staring at the waves lapping the shore. She'd grown up near the ocean, but for some reason, it looked different from this vantage. No longer did she see Shepherd's Bay as a gritty fishing town along the water. For the first time, she viewed it as an almost glamorous place.

She waltzed through the kitchen area and took in the stainless-steel refrigerator built into the wall. Spotless, not a smudge on it. She opened it and saw enough food for an army, organized and with everything in its place. Her own refrigerator looked like a terrorist had set a bomb off in it.

She shut the refrigerator door and slipped out of the kitchen. The hallway resembled a bowling alley. She went from room to room, each bigger than the next. Some were bedrooms. One was a study. The third room on the right had no windows and had theater seating. A large screen hung from the ceiling against the far wall. Along the back wall stood an authentic theater popcorn machine. It amazed her that people could afford such luxuries.

She knew almost nothing about film projectors, but she could see that this one was high end and streamed movies as well as played DVDs. She saw an open Blu-ray disc case and examined the front of it. It was a television show from 2000 that she vaguely remembered. Against her better judgment, she flipped the projector's power switch to ON, and the show appeared on-screen.

The picture filled the entire far wall, and she felt like she was standing in a real movie theater. She watched the show with interest, the plot coming back to her with each scene. The show was called *Lost 'n' You*, and the main character was a beautiful young woman struggling to make it through her first year of college but trapped between a lecherous professor and a burgeoning love interest her own age.

She glanced at her watch and saw that she had about seven minutes remaining before Felicia came downstairs. Something about the beautiful girl on-screen piqued her interest, and she moved closer to the screen. Why did she find this show so familiar? Did it remind her of her own painful college experience? No, it was something entirely different. And then it struck her, and she nearly collapsed into one of the theater chairs, in shock. The blond girl on-screen was Felicia Briggs! She was beautiful beyond words. And the resemblance between the younger Felicia and her daughter, Willow, startled Isla. Why hadn't she noticed this before? As she stared longer at the screen, she realized that whereas Willow possessed striking, angular features, the younger Felicia looked softer and her body more rounded.

So why had Felicia dyed her hair black? Did she not want to be recognized in town for her role on that show?

It took a few seconds before she calmed herself down. Her heart raced in her chest as she switched off the projector. On the far end of the projecting table, she saw three photo albums. Her watch told her she had five minutes left before she needed to head back. She walked over to the albums and casually flipped through them. Members of the TV show's cast mugged in silly poses. It looked to her as if all the pictures had been taken on set.

Then she came to one photograph that startled her. Felicia leaned over a handsome man sitting in a director's chair. His black hair was slicked back over his head, and his tanned skin glowed with a healthy vigor. He looked to be fifteen years older than Felicia. Finally, it came to her. The man in the photo was Gil. How had she not seen it right away? It had taken her a few seconds because of the black hair combed back over his scalp. She knew only the Gil Briggs with a bit of a belly, those studded, black-framed glasses, and a full silver mane. He must have been the director or the producer of *Lost 'n' You.*

She lost track of time and then saw that more than fifteen minutes had elapsed. She closed the albums and scurried out of the room before Felicia discovered her snooping around. Thankfully, Felicia had not yet made her way downstairs. This both relieved Isla and pissed her off, as she needed to get back to the salon as soon as possible.

Snooping on Felicia filled her with guilt. She paced back and forth in the open space of the dining room, wondering if she should bring up *Lost 'n' You* to her. She could always say she'd recognized her from the show, but that might be a stretch, seeing that Felicia had starred in it eighteen years ago.

Ten minutes later Felicia waltzed, barefoot, down the stairs in the same bathrobe as before. Or maybe she'd put on a fresh one. A white towel was wrapped around her head, and Isla saw her without those sunglasses wrapped around her eyes. She looked sad. Maybe depressed. How could she not be with her daughter still missing? Oversized silver loop earrings hung from her pink lobes.

Without thinking, Isla reached out and embraced her. But Felicia felt limp and skeletal in her arms and didn't reciprocate with anywhere near the same enthusiasm. After stepping back, Isla noticed that Felicia's eyes had that faraway stare about them, and Isla speculated that she might be on meds.

"Thank you for coming over. I absolutely could not face the world looking like this."

"Stop that. You're a beautiful woman, Felicia. And I'm here for you whenever you need me." She felt excited about working on a bona fide TV star.

"Willow's disappearance has devastated us. She is our only child and means everything to us."

"They'll find her, Felicia. I just know it," Isla said, taking the cape out of her bag and unfolding it.

"Sometimes I wish we had never moved to this godforsaken town." She dragged a dining-room chair under a dangling lamp. "Is there enough light here for you to work?"

"Yes, there should be more than enough."

Felicia sat down and allowed Isla to wrap the cape around her neck.

"Do you know how to do a razor cut?"

"Of course. Would you like me to give you one?" Isla replied.

"If you're able. It's how my Portland girl usually does it." She pulled out her phone. "Here's a picture of her last cut."

"Sure. I can do that."

"Do whatever you think looks best. It can't look any worse than it does right now. I get so frustrated with these frizzies." She lifted up her hair and showed Isla.

Isla unwrapped her tool bag on the kitchen island. Felicia wore her dyed hair shoulder length and jagged, although gray roots had started to show. She combed through her wet hair before removing her three-inch German shears. Then she straightened strands of Felicia's hair between her fingers and snipped off the dead ends.

"Katie really loves Willow. She's absolutely devastated that she's still missing."

"Who's Katie?"

She stopped cutting and gazed at Felicia. "Katie. My *daughter*."

"Oh God, I'm so sorry. Please forgive me . . ."

"Isla."

"Yes, that's it. My mind's been so screwed up since Willow went missing."

Isla picked up the styling razor and opened it. Then she combed Felicia's hair downward and edged the blade against the woman's hair at a forty-five-degree angle. The effect, once dry, would be to shape and create a hip, spiky look that seemed to be all the rage in Hollywood. Isla had attended a weeklong razor-cutting seminar in Boston last year, after a few of her clients had requested the style.

"How did you meet Gil?"

"We met out in LA."

"What were you doing there? Trying to break into show business?" She hoped Felicia might talk about her time on *Lost 'n' You*.

"For God's sakes, my daughter is missing, and all you want to talk about is my past?"

"I'm so . . . so sorry." Felicia's words shocked her. "I didn't mean to . . ."

"Please respect my privacy during this difficult time."

"Of course."

Felicia started to cry. "I'm so sorry for being mean to you. I'm a complete wreck right now and not being appreciative of all you're doing for me."

"No, it's my fault. I should have never pried into your personal life at a time like this."

"You're a good person, Isla. Once Willow is back home, we'll have you and your family over for dinner."

"I'd like that very much."

Isla finished cutting in silence. Razor cutting took extra time and care, and she was eager to prove that she was a better stylist than Felicia's "girl" down in Portland. She whipped out the blow-dryer and ran her fingers through Felicia's damp strands as the hot air created the desired effect. After the final touches, she handed the mirror to Felicia and hoped she liked the haircut. The woman gazed at herself for over a minute, scrutinizing, holding the mirror up at different angles, before sighing.

"Maybe a bit too short on the bangs, but otherwise it looks okay."

Okay? She had put her heart and soul into this cut and knew it looked fantastic. Better than fantastic. Fabulous. And all Felicia could say in response was that it looked *okay?*

She took off the striped cape and folded it up before stashing it back in her bag. All her other tools had been neatly put away.

"God, that haircut wiped me out."

Isla stood there, waiting for her money.

"Would you be a dear and sweep up all that hair for me?" Felicia said. "The broom and dustpan are in the closet."

"Sure." She grabbed them and quickly swept up the hair and discarded it in the trash.

"Do you take cards?" Felicia asked.

"Cards?" How was she supposed to process a credit card here? "I'm not able to do that, Felicia."

"Gil handles all our checks, and it seems I'm completely out of cash."

"Don't worry about it, then," Isla said, biting her tongue. "You can pay me at the salon the next time you come in."

"Oh." Felicia looked confused. "Okay."

Isla thanked her and walked toward the front door. As she opened it, she heard footsteps coming up behind her. She turned and saw Felicia running toward her. Felicia embraced her, rested her newly coiffed head on Isla's shoulder, and sobbed uncontrollably.

"You think I'm a bad person, don't you? I just know you do."

"No, Felicia, I don't at all think that."

"Have you ever loved someone so bad that it physically hurts?"

"Yes."

"Well, that's how this feels to me. It hurts, Isla. Really bad."

"I understand, Felicia. I'm a mother, too."

"I try to be a good wife and mother—and friend. I really do."

"I'm sure you are."

"I'm afraid I can't even live up to my own expectations."

Felicia pushed away from her and then strode back toward the kitchen. With the door half open, Isla watched her with curiosity. She felt sorry for the woman and hoped she'd soon be reunited with her daughter. Maybe they could all be friends someday, when this ordeal had passed and both girls had recovered from their trauma. Was she a bad person to think this way? When the woman's daughter was still missing and possibly dead? She chided herself. And yet she couldn't help thinking that she'd like to become friends with this mysterious woman. An accomplished actor, mother, and wife who'd, for whatever reason, disappeared from the bright lights of stardom and fame and ended up in her little town.

KATIE

*T*HE FIRST NIGHT ALCOHOL TOUCHED MY LIPS, I CRIED. I DON'T KNOW why. Happiness? Hormones? Because of the discovery of my new-found social life? I found myself straddling two different worlds. Added to that, the alcohol had a weird effect on me. It made me sad. And then it made me happy, especially when that cute boy sat next to me on the couch. The fire in the massive stone fireplace blazed brightly and warmed the skin on my forearms.

It felt nice to take a break from school and the daily grind of re-hearsals, as well as the ongoing stress of my home life. There was Raisin's fluctuating blood sugars, the constant lack of money, the continuous tension between my parents, and then dealing with my grandfather's Alzheimer's diagnosis. I discovered that alcohol loos-ened me up and made me less uptight around people. I talked more and didn't feel nervous. I reveled in its powers of escapism, as well as its ability to make me feel like I belonged somewhere, with kids that understood and liked me. I told myself it would be a one-shot deal on account of the upcoming softball season, which would be starting in a few weeks.

It surprised me that I didn't flinch when that cute boy put his arm around me. After all, I had a boyfriend. Drew and I had been together since my freshman year, and he hoped we'd be together for a long time. He would be graduating in the spring and then would begin lobstering full-time. He wasn't book smart or what you would call artistic or intellectual, but he could fix almost any en-gine, whether it be to a snowmobile, a snowblower, or outboard motor. Since Drew was a star football and hockey player, many kids in town looked up to him. Knowing that I wanted to continue my education, he hoped that after graduation I might attend the local community college so I could be closer to him. Little did he know that I wanted more out of life than attending some stupid community college, where kids ended up, rather than choosing to be. No, I wanted to leave Shepherd's Bay and go somewhere else. To a college where I could shed my skin and find the real me.

Everyone at the party laughed and told funny stories about shopping or money. No one seemed to hold it against me that I was a townie—and a poor one at that, as if the two weren't mutually exclusive. Everyone, and I mean everyone, had a drink of some kind in hand. I didn't know any of these kids, but I wanted to know and like them. They seemed interesting and exotic, and they all lived on Harper's Point and attended prestigious Chance Academy.

The boy put his arm around my shoulder and then passed me a bottle. I giggled and pushed it away. I'd tried a sip earlier and found the liquor bitter and off-putting, like liquid licorice. How could people drink such awful stuff? So I had decided to stick to the fruity iced teas and hard lemonades and anything with a "Rita" at the end of its name. At one point he leaned over to kiss me, but I laughed and playfully nudged his face away, even though he smelled like new leather. It was not that I didn't want to kiss him, because I sorta did. What scared me most was what might happen once I gave in to temptation. Where would that lead to? What would I become? And what would Drew think if he ever found out that I'd kissed another boy? Never mind a boy from Harper's Point.

It took me a second to realize that Willow had left the party. Where had she gone? And where were her parents? I had assumed they'd stick around and act as chaperones. Were they staying upstairs while us kids partied like rock stars down on the main floor? Would they be upset if they knew what we were up to?

Someone lit a joint, and the familiar scent hit me right away. I often detected that smell inside my father's truck. It clung to the vinyl seats, the floor mats, and the headliner. I'd even seen him smoking pot on occasion, although he tried to hide it from me as much as possible. When I had asked him once why he smoked pot, he'd said it helped him with his anxiety. I had never known before then that my father suffered from anxiety or thought his life was in any way hard. He seemed happy all the time, seemed like the last person on the planet who might be suffering.

Someone passed the weed to the boy, and he inhaled deeply and passed it over to me. I took the joint and immediately passed it over to the girl sitting to my right, then watched as she laughed drunkenly.

Julian came out of nowhere and stood in the middle of our group, looking delicious in every kind of way. He was like no other boy I'd ever seen in Shepherd's Bay. Whereas the boy next to me was tanned and preppy, Julian looked like a painter or a lead guitarist in a band. He had these narrow, smoky eyes that I couldn't look away from and painted black nails that hinted at some deeper nature. The two boys couldn't have been more different, and yet everyone seemed to get along wonderfully.

A few minutes later Willow appeared out of nowhere, and she hung on to Julian's arm, as if she were a Christmas ornament. She seemed flirty and unusually happy, and I chalked it up to the alcohol. Certainly, she appeared more social with this crowd than with the kids from Shepherd's Bay. It made sense. These were her people. Her clan.

In this part of Maine, people never acted in such a carefree manner. My mother had always claimed that us Mainers were a stoic bunch, and I didn't think she meant that in a good way. This free-spirited attitude opened my eyes to new possibilities as the boy walked over and retrieved another bottle of iced tea for me. I really didn't need another bottle, but I took it, anyway. It felt good to be here, almost too good to be true, and at that point I had no personal knowledge of hangovers or "the agony of kneeling over the porcelain god," as Drew had once described it. Everything felt warm and fuzzy, seemed tinted with glamour, and before long I found myself slow dancing with this boy in the middle of the room. Where had everyone gone? I hadn't noticed when the party came to an end. When had the other kids drifted away? Had they all gone home?

He kissed me, and I turned away from his warm lips. His boozy breath made the skin on my neck tingle. My head spun happily, as cheating on Drew was far back in the sinful recesses of my mind. Maybe in the morning I'd feel bad about it, but certainly not tonight. For once, I decided to be a bad girl and enjoy myself with this boy. Revel in my naughtiness. Besides, I never thought Drew would find out about our kiss. Chance Academy, like Harper's Point, seemed a million miles removed from our high school crowd. It secretly thrilled me that this boy was a much better kisser than Drew. And I rather enjoyed our dance and the way his body pressed up against mine. I took this as a sign that Drew and I weren't meant to be.

The lights dimmed, and he kissed my cheek and breathed hot breaths into my ear. Drake rapped over the speakers.

"You like partying with us?" he whispered.

"I do," I said.

"Everyone thought you were totally cool."

"Really?"

"Would I lie?"

"How would I know? I barely know you."

"I wouldn't lie to you, Katie."

"Okay."

"I like being with you."

"For real, you guys are way better to hang with than the boring kids at my high school."

"Willow says you two are pretty tight."

"Besties, if you really want to know the truth."

"Besties, huh?" He laughed. "Willow's good people."

"She's the best."

"We get together like this every so often. You should party with us again. Everyone's cool."

"Totally." I stumbled and nearly fell, but he caught me under my arms. It felt quite romantic.

"Easy, girl."

"It's all those iced teas you brought me."

"Blaming me now, are we?" he said. "Besides, I know what's better than iced tea."

"What?"

"X."

Were my ears playing tricks on me? "I really think you're nice, but no way am I having sex with you."

"Nice?" He held me at arm's length and smiled. "Are you for real?"

"What?"

He laughed. "You're so wasted."

"Okay, but so are you." I swooned between the intervals of his boozy breaths.

"I said X, Katie, not sex."

"Oh, sorry. What's X?"

"Seriously? You don't know what X is?"

I smiled demurely and bit my fingernail. The house started to spin gently, as if I were standing on a merry-go-round.

"I like you a lot. So does everyone else at the party. But I'd like you a helluva lot more if you could ask around town and score us some X. It'd make Willow happy, too."

"Really?"

"Definitely." He squeezed my hand. "I heard there's some of that floating around in this town. You must know people who deal it."

"I might know a few peeps." Why did I say *peeps*? To sound hip? It ended up sounding dorky, and I hated myself for saying it.

"It's so uncool, living on the Point. Can't get shit around here, especially when you don't know anyone. Consider yourself lucky you don't live among us."

I laughed. "I would so love to live in this neighborhood."

"Needs more Original Gs like you."

"I'll take that as a compliment."

"You should, especially if you can score some for us."

I did know people in town who dealt drugs. Not personally, but everyone knew someone who knew someone. That was because drugs were a major problem in these parts, owing to isolation, hopelessness, and the lack of jobs. I knew this because they constantly drilled "the Horrors of Drug Abuse" into us at school, forcing us to listen to one sober counselor after another lecture us about opioid addiction and the dangers of meth. And I did want to come back here. To hang with these beautiful kids in this beautiful house by the ocean. I'd never felt so liberated in my life.

He kissed me again and reached under my shirt. I quickly moved his hand away, but he tried again. This time I stepped back and re-garded him with suspicion. No way was I letting him go any further than kissing me. He smiled and mumbled something incoherent before stumbling toward the front door. He left me standing alone in this large, empty home. I looked around. Bottles and cans lay everywhere. The entire dining-room table was covered with cups and uneaten food. Where had Willow gone?

I called out her name and heard only the echo of my voice inside the cavernous mansion. For some reason, it now lost its allure. It felt like one of those homes in a horror movie. Where were Willow's parents? Asleep upstairs? I didn't want to wake anyone. The ocean lay dark and hidden just outside. Where would I sleep? I climbed those futuristic stairs, with their razor-gray slate steps pro-truding magically out of the wall. Without a railing, they appeared to have no structural supports. I climbed them carefully, afraid that in my drunken state I might topple over the edge and kill myself. Once upstairs, I tiptoed along the wall until I came to the first bed-room. I opened the door and saw Julian passed out on the bed, dressed only in a muscle T-shirt and cherry-red boxers. After clos-ing the door, I went around to the other rooms, until I heard muf-fled sobs coming from behind a door. I opened it. Darkness enveloped every corner of the room. Despite the fact that the floor was spinning beneath me, I ventured inside the room.

"Who is it? What do you want?" I heard my friend say.

"It's me, Willow. What's wrong?" I whispered. This was a side of Willow I'd never experienced. I didn't think of her as vulnerable and sensitive.

"I don't want to talk about it," she said, slurring.

"But I'm your best friend."

"How's that supposed to help me?"

"Did Julian hurt you? I saw him walk upstairs around the same time as you."

"Go away. This has nothing to do with you. Or Julian."

"We should tell the police."

"Shut up, Katie!" she yelled, startling me. "I said I don't want to talk about it. Besides, I'm just as much to blame."

I sat on the bed, confused and not knowing what to do. In the dark, I could see blood trickling from her nose. What had happened to her? And what had I done? Willow had always seemed strong and assertive, but now I felt as if I was sitting with a very sad and drunk little girl. It made me angry that Julian had taken advantage of her in her condition. I thought back to that boy reaching under my shirt and was now glad that I'd turned him down.

"Just leave me alone, Katie."

"Okay," I said, standing up. "I'll go lie down in the other room."

"No." She reached out and grabbed my arm. "Would you stay with me?"

"Where will I sleep?"

"Right here. Next to me. Please."

"Okay." I lay down next to her and let her cling to me, as if we were tandem parachuters.

"I'm so sorry for being mean to you, Katie."

"It's okay."

"It's totally not okay. You're really a good friend to me. My best friend forever."

"You're my best friend, too."

"You have no idea what I've been through."

"Then tell me."

"I can't. I just need you to be my friend right now. That's all."

But was I really her friend?

I sit up on the couch, bathed in sweat. This new memory frightens me. It's shocking to discover that Julian attacked Willow that night and now she has gone missing. Had she told someone what he did? Had he retaliated against her in a drug-fueled rage? Maybe she rebuffed his advances? I had heard whispers about Julian having a temper. Supposedly, it's the reason why he got kicked out of prep school. Remembering the craziness of that night frightens me. I think about what might happen if Drew gets wind of what I did. Or, God forbid, my mother finds out. Then it hits me: What other bad things will I remember?

That boy had asked me if I could get a drug called X. I'd never heard of such a thing, but I had heard the names of plenty of people in town who would know, thanks to my dad. Had I agreed to go along with this plan? If so, how had I done it? Who had I asked to get this X? These questions frighten me. No, the answers frighten me more. The only person I know personally who deals drugs is Bugger Walsh, and he repulses me. I know him because he some- times does small jobs for my father. I also know that my father buys most of his weed off Bugger, and I had heard rumors that Bugger deals in "other" drugs. But harder drugs?

I lay my head down and close my eyes, trying to put everything out of mind. If only I could go back in time and make better deci- sions. If only I could fall into a deep sleep and make this all go away. Because I now realize I've done things I'll come to regret. Possibly bad things.

I lie here thinking about that boy who'd kissed me. The same boy who'd asked me if I could get him drugs. Why had I gotten my- self involved with Dakota James?

ISLA

She raced back to the salon. By the time she returned, two appointments had come and gone. She felt sorry for Felicia, but she was furious at her at the same time. Not only had Felicia caused her to lose money, and possibly prospective clients, but she'd also neglected to pay for her haircut. A razor cut of a similar style and quality in downtown Portland would probably run Felicia over a hundred dollars. Isla knew she'd never see the money, and to remind Felicia of her debt would only seem in bad taste, considering her tragic circumstance. But damn it, she needed that money way more than Felicia did. And judging by the pricey home Felicia lived in, the Briggses had more than enough money to last a few lifetimes.

She struggled through the afternoon, her mind elsewhere. In hindsight, it seemed a big mistake to let Katie hang around with Willow. She had a bad feeling about Julian McCallister, as well. Something in her gut told her that he had something to do with the disappearance of those two girls.

Her focus waned, and she lost track of her conversations with clients. She cut the bank president's hair too short and left Clair Barnes's bangs too long. Cindy Peters embarked on a soliloquy about her personal life, then stopped ten minutes later to ask for Isla's opinion about something. Only Isla had not heard a word the woman had said, and had to apologize for not paying attention.

This went on all day, and as much as she tried to focus, she simply couldn't. A million thoughts ran through her mind as she snipped and buzzed and trimmed and razored, many of them about what had happened to Katie. And Willow, Julian, and the missing boy, Dakota. What was the connection? She couldn't wait to race home and buy that first and only season of *Lost 'n' You* and binge-watch it in its entirety. What could be derived from watching it, aside from remembering that she loved the show, as well as Felicia's character in it? And she loved the show because she could totally relate to what happened to Felicia's character as a college student harassed by a predatory professor.

It amazed Isla that Felicia had been living in Shepherd's Bay all this time, right under her nose. What had happened to her since the show ended? Had she appeared in other shows? Isla made a mental note to check out Felicia's credits on IMDb. Maybe the birth of Felicia's daughter had put an end to her acting career. She wondered about Gil. She was almost certain he'd not had an acting part in the show. Had he been a cameraman or the director? Maybe a producer?

Closing time approached, and she breathed a sigh of relief. She felt exhausted from standing on her feet all day. Too many mistakes and lapses had been made. Tomorrow she'd need to get back on her game if she was to survive in this business. She grabbed the broom and began to sweep up the hair, wondering how she was going to get answers to her questions. The police didn't seem to be doing a bang-up job of finding out what happened to the girls. Of course, with a force of five, that was rather difficult, especially when their main priority at the moment was finding Willow.

The clock ticked. The big hand kissed the top of the hour. She was reaching for the lock on the door when the bell rang and the door suddenly swung open. Nothing could be worse than seeing a last-minute customer walk through the door. Or turning them down and telling them to come back tomorrow, which she did only when she had an emergency of her own, a rare occurrence.

"I'm so sorry, Isla. My hot yoga class got out a little late," Samantha McCallister said, practically out of breath. "I raced over here as fast as I could. Can you fit me in?"

"Of course," Isla said, trying not to show her disappointment. No way could she afford to turn Samantha McCallister away.

"Thanks so much, Isla. You're such a sweetheart."

"Really, it's no problem at all."

"You're a doll to take me without an appointment like this. What time do you normally close?"

"Five, usually, but it's no prob."

"I'm making you stay late? You must think I'm a real witch."

"As long as you don't cast a spell on me, we're good."

"No spell from this gal." Samantha laughed. "But I will make sure to leave you a nice tip for being so accommodating."

"It's really not necessary, Samantha."

"Stop. I don't want to hear another word," she said, shaking her headful of hair. "Do your magic, girl. You know how I like it."

"Shampoo too?" Which meant extra time.

"The works, please," Samantha said, sitting down in the shampoo station.

"The works" would take an hour, at minimum. Isla sighed and resigned herself to being in the shop until past six. Samantha closed her eyes and seemed to relax. Isla figured that if she was going to stay late, she might as well treat her most valued client in the best possible fashion.

"Can I get you a glass of Chablis before I start?"

"Oh my God. Are you the best stylist in the world or what?"

Isla went back and poured a chilled glass of Chablis. She kept bottles on hand for certain clients, knowing that these women liked to drink. Determined to get answers to her questions, she offered the glass to Samantha.

"This is the highlight of my day," Samantha said, taking the glass. "Thank you so much."

"My pleasure."

"How's Katie doing?" Samantha took a healthy sip.

"She's home, recuperating." Isla wrapped the styling cape around her like a bullfighter, then reclined the chair so that the back of Samantha's head rested against the sink. "The doctor says it might be a while before her memory returns in full."

"Poor thing. Beckett was out volunteering with the search party today. Such a shame about Willow."

"Do you know Willow very well?"

"Not very. The Briggses live next door to us, but we're not particularly close. Julian's told me she's a nice girl, but I often wonder. She certainly doesn't deserve what happened to her."

"No, she doesn't."

"Neither does Katie, for that matter."

"How's Julian doing?" Isla busied herself washing and rinsing Samantha's hair.

"I know Julian doesn't show much emotion, but he's really shaken up about all this."

"That's too bad." She shut off the water and began to towel dry Samantha's hair. When it was sufficiently dried, she directed Samantha to sit in the styling chair.

"We thought that moving here from New York City would be a better fit for us, especially for Julian. Beckett had had enough stress for two lifetimes working on Wall Street, and Julian definitely needed a change."

"Why's that?" Isla pinched a slice of hair between forefinger and middle finger and then snipped off a half an inch.

"The usual bad habits city kids find themselves getting into. Julian absolutely hated that prep school he attended. Told me all the kids there were rich and spoiled, and were backstabbing conformists who stifled his creativity. It's not what Beckett and I wanted for our child. So we thought that by moving here, we could live a slower life and allow him to be whoever he wants to be."

"And how has that worked out?"

"Great, for the most part. Then this happened. Oh, and the disappearance of his classmate Dakota."

"Crimes like this never happened before in sleepy Shepherd's Bay."

"Until us out-of-towners started moving in?" Samantha turned, opened one eye, and gazed at her.

"No, that's not what I meant," Isla said, suddenly fearful she might have offended her.

"Relax, hon." Samantha patted her hand. "I know what you meant. You've been a victim in all this, too."

Isla fingered and snipped, fingered and snipped, afraid to say something else stupid.

"People don't realize how difficult it is to move to an entirely different locale, where no one knows you and you have to start all over from scratch," Samantha commented.

"Must be hard."

"You don't know the half of it. And then there's finding good help. At least in Manhattan we had a network of cleaners and cooks we could call on at our disposal. Granted, most of them were Latinos, but they are wonderful and hardworking people. And there was an abundant supply of them living in the city."

"I see."

"Did you know that Maine is the whitest state in the nation? And the oldest. I just read that somewhere. Isn't that ridiculous? Where's all the diversity?"

By that she meant, Where were all the young minorities to serve them?

Samantha continued. "On one hand, it's so worth living here, if only for the low crime rate and amazing views. And yet try finding a dependable landscaper in this town."

"I know, right?"

"Honestly, I shouldn't complain, especially when you give me the best haircut I've ever had, and at a fraction of the cost of those high-end salons in SoHo."

"The rents there must be exorbitant."

"Sky high. And if this town passes that silly property tax, you can kiss this salon good-bye."

"I can?" Samantha's words alarmed her.

"Beckett bought this building as an investment when we first moved here. That's how I initially found your salon. He's saying that if the council passes that tax on properties over a half a million dollars, he'll need to tear this building down and put up something that will bring in more revenue."

The hairs on the back of Isla's neck stood on end at the idea of losing this shop, especially after all the money she'd borrowed to remodel it. It'd be like she had tossed it all into the ocean. Then there was her grandfather's legacy that needed protecting.

"You should tell all your friends and neighbors what will happen if this stupid proposition passes," Samantha added.

Isla thought about her family finances. She tabulated the costs of

Raisin's medicine, Katie's therapy, and all her daughter's future mental health counseling, as well as the mortgage and other bills that needed to be paid every month.

"Listen, Isla, we're having a fund-raiser tomorrow night at my club for Laura Milton. She's running for that open town council seat and is a vociferous opponent of that hideous tax hike. You should attend."

"Me?" Combed and snipped, snipped and combed.

"Yes, you. It would be wonderful to have you join us, especially since you know this town better than anyone. And you never know, you might pick up a few new clients while you're there."

"Let me think about it," Isla said.

"Considering all that's at stake for you and your family, I wouldn't think too long," Samantha said. "Besides, it'll be a lot of fun. Good food, champagne, and a lovely string quartet."

Samantha closed her eyes and pressed her lips together. Happy for the break, Isla worked in silence. It amazed her that this woman could be so breezy and carefree, considering that her neighbor had gone missing and Isla's own daughter was still in recovery. It only reenforced the notion that life went on for most people. Not for the victims, necessarily, but for everyone else. The victims lived with the ongoing trauma on a daily basis, while everyone else worried about haircuts, gardeners, and dumb property tax hikes.

The invitation to that fund-raiser replayed in her mind. She didn't want to go, if for no other reason than she had nothing decent to wear. Oh, she had some nice clothes, clothes more fitting for church functions and casual get-togethers. Nothing daring or risqué, like she used to wear in her twenties. Certainly nothing for a fancy party on Harper's Point. If she decided to attend, which she knew she would, she'd need to go out and buy a new outfit—an outfit she couldn't really afford.

She felt conflicted about attending this event. It felt inappropriate to appear at a political fund-raiser when a girl from their own part of town, as well as a boy, was still missing. Not to mention Katie and the ordeal she'd gone through. Would people know Katie was her daughter? She knew it would be difficult to be on her game and act all bubbly and happy. It would require focus and concentration, the very skills needed to become a successful hairstylist.

She'd need to act like she had in all those plays she starred in back at Shepherd's Bay High, as well as in the few community theater productions she'd performed in before settling down with a family.

And yet she badly needed the clientele that might come her way if she attended the event. Samantha's invitation felt more like a demand, an implied threat. If she handled herself with grace and aplomb, things might work out in her favor. Samantha had already proved her value to Isla, more than she could ever know. So if Isla attended, and played her part well, it could certainly help bring in new clients.

She was under no illusion about why Samantha had invited her. Since she would be one of few locals in attendance, her appearance might go a long way in convincing other locals to vote against the property tax hike. In effect, she'd be the token townie. More importantly, she had a bully pulpit at the salon, and Samantha knew she could convince others to oppose the tax increase.

Reluctant to admit the truth, Isla knew that self-interest drove her motives. More like self-reliance. There was no doubt the schools needed upgrades. But she couldn't afford to lose her salon because of some vendetta against all these wealthy people moving into town. These people helped her pay her bills and put food on her table. Without them, she might not be able to afford insulin for Raisin. Or pay the mortgage and property taxes. On the face of it, she knew that more tax revenue was needed to rebuild the schools' crumbling infrastructure. She believed it was the responsibility of everyone in town to pitch in. This new tax seemed like retribution for a supposedly changing way of life, a way of life that had gone by the wayside years ago. Was she rationalizing her opposition to this tax hike? Possibly, but for good reason.

As she contemplated the invitation, she found herself falling into the same trap as had the people she'd accused of being insensitive. Willow Briggs was still missing, and all Isla could think about was expanding her business and caring for her family. Was that wrong? It wasn't like she was out searching for Willow Briggs along with the rest of the volunteers. Then again, she couldn't afford to live like the McCallisters, who had nothing but time and money on hand.

She blow-dried Samantha's hair. Then she brushed it out until it looked lustrous under the salon's fluorescent lights. Happy with the job she'd done, Isla swiveled Samantha around so that she faced the mirror. She stood behind her with the handheld and showed her the back.

"You are an artiste, Isla. It looks fabulous."

Isla smiled and removed the cape, grateful that she'd succeeded in pleasing her most important client. Her eye caught something familiar outside as Samantha continued talking. The words coming out of her client's mouth sounded like a foreign language to Isla's ears. The gleaming truck cruised slowly along the downtown street. Behind the steering wheel sat Ray. Had that jerk bought a new pickup?

Samantha grabbed Isla's palm and placed two things in it. Isla glanced up at the clock and noticed that an hour and a half had passed. The woman gave her a quick hug before scurrying out the front door. Isla stared down at the items in her palm. On top sat an ornate card inviting her to Laura Milton's political event tomorrow night. Underneath it lay a crisp one-hundred-dollar bill—a fifty-dollar tip!

KARL

*H*ELICOPTERS ZIPPED OVERHEAD. EVERY DAY THAT PASSED MEANT less enthusiasm, less energy, lower odds that the missing girl would still be found alive. Typically, the number of volunteers fell off gradually from one day to the next in these kinds of searches. He'd seen it happen firsthand while looking for the James kid. That search had taken place in March, when the landscape was still covered in ice and snow, making travel over the terrain more difficult. Still, he'd donned his snowshoes and done the best he could until the snow cleared and the ground thawed.

And then the spring had come and the snow had melted and the search for Dakota James had intensified. At that point, it had been over a month since the James kid had gone missing, and everyone's enthusiasm had waned. Now tragedy had struck again. Two missing kids from the same part of town pointed to something more sinister.

Fowler Woods sat across from a sheltered cove located about a quarter mile from where the newer, pricier homes were being built. A month ago he and fellow officer Olivia Dunn had gone out there to search for Dakota James and had found nothing. Trails meandered throughout the dense woods. Many people strolled through Fowler Woods with their dogs running ahead of them or nipping at their heels. Someone surely would have seen something in all the time that had lapsed. So why did he now have a gut feeling that he'd uncover something in those woods now?

He remembered as a kid hiking the woods of New Sweden with his grandfather and their golden retriever, Klara. That was where he'd developed his love of nature and learned about the various plants and shrubs that flourished in the harsh climes of Maine. Many times he'd seen deer and moose off in the distance. He'd once even seen a black bear too close for comfort. He remembered sprinting ahead, sometimes venturing off trail, while his grandfather had ambled along with the walking stick he'd carved by hand. Cutting through the thick brush had proved difficult, but he'd enjoyed the discoveries he would make along the way and watching Klara run ahead of him, tail wagging. Off trail had seemed far more interesting than on, and a few hours of scurrying about had quickly tired him out.

Fowler Woods bored him. He'd usually trek through it when he needed a quick fix. Mostly, he preferred hiking up the nearby hills and along the densely wooded trails that abounded in the more rural parts of Maine. One thing he liked about Fowler Woods, though, was catching the raw scent of the nearby ocean and then emerging from the woods to that spectacular view. The ocean displayed moods that fluctuated wildly. Sometimes it seemed angry at the world, pounding and crashing against the rocks. Other times it resonated with a calm tranquility, the surface like polished blue marble.

Tiny ripples appeared on the ocean's surface this morning. He glanced one last time at the shimmering cove before moving into the woods. This time he took the least used trail. It circled the perimeter of the woods, adding an extra mile to the loop. When he had gone about half a mile, he noticed that vegetation started to fill in the path. Leaves above provided a canopy that partially blocked out the sun. He stopped on the trail at various intervals, such as when he saw something that piqued his interest.

Sweat poured down his forehead as the temperature began to rise. Bushes and brambles impeded his path, but he managed to trek through and around them. He climbed over downed trees, heard the singsong of birds, observed the muddy vernal pools. Occasionally, he let his mind wander to thoughts of running free with his grandfather and of Klara bolting off into the woods.

Then he remembered taking his daughter hiking for the first time. She was little at the time, maybe six or seven, and headstrong for her age. He'd taken her to Marigold Hill, a short climb of only a thousand feet, thinking she'd enjoy it as much as he did. But he couldn't have been more wrong.

She'd complained almost immediately and wanted to return home. Halfway up the hill, she had collapsed on a boulder, had crossed her little arms in defiance, and had refused to go any farther. Not even when he bribed her with candy had she agreed to move. He recalled how she had taken the chocolate bar out of his hand and tossed it into the woods. Her behavior had puzzled him, and rather than get angry, he had knelt down next to her, with a hurt expression on his face. Why couldn't she share his love for nature?

After a few minutes of coaxing, she still refused to budge. His hurt feelings turned to anger as he started down the trail. But she refused to follow, and he feared leaving her alone, in the event some other hikers happened to be heading down. He scrambled back up the trail and stopped in front of her. Amber refused to look at him, so he scooped her into his arms and carried her against her will. She screamed bloody murder all the way down the trail, even as he passed a pair hiking up. While listening to his daughter scream and shout, he was forced to explain to the two hikers that he was not only a cop—he took out his badge to show them—but also her father. Life went on after that, complicated and messy as life typically was, but he had never forgotten that day. Apart from convincing him never to hike with her again, it foreshadowed their future father-daughter relationship.

He had to stop and take a break. The memories of Amber had caused him to lose his concentration. He looked up past the leaves and noted the blue sky. What the hell was he doing here, in the middle of the woods, searching for a needle in a haystack? He loved being a cop. Keeping order and helping people out. But as much as he enjoyed being out in the woods, he had never envisioned his job would entail searching for missing kids.

A quick chug of water and he took off. He came to a massive boulder and hiked up it. At the top, he could see the bay below, the suspension bridge, and the ocean. He turned one-eighty and surveyed the landscape. On the other side of the boulder, the hillside dropped off dramatically. A significant-sized vernal pool had formed in the depression below. The odds of finding the James boy out here seemed low. At the time of his disappearance, this entire area had been covered in ice and snow. Dragging a body up here would have been nearly impossible while trudging through two feet of snow.

His belly rumbled. He sat on the boulder and took off his backpack, reached inside, and pulled out a sandwich. He wiped the sweat off his forehead and took the sandwich out of its plastic baggie. It reminded him of the first time he'd hiked with Isla. They'd been juniors, and he'd been somewhat of a loner at Shepherd's Bay High. He'd not played sports, nor had he joined any of the student organizations. So it had seemed unlikely that he and Isla would end up as a couple. Being lab partners in chemistry had brought two completely different kids together.

Their first date had been an October hike up one of the local hills. She was not a hiker, but she managed to keep up with him. When they reached the top, they sat on a boulder similar to the one he was sitting on now. He'd packed sodas and Italian sandwiches, and they ate in silence while staring out at the ocean and the explosion of fall foliage around them. It felt natural to be with her, not at all forced. Surprisingly, this was his first date. While other juniors bragged about having sex and partying on weekends, he chose to hike trails and fish streams and nearby lakes.

After lunch, they picked up their wrappers and headed back down. Funny that he remembered how Isla talked nonstop in his father's pickup on their way home. She spoke about all her hopes and dreams, about going off to college and then maybe trying her hand at acting. He said hardly a word the entire time, enjoying the sound of her voice and how excited she got when she spoke. His own family had always been stoic and somber, although no less lov-ing. He chalked it up to his New England and Swedish heritage.

His cell phone chirped, jarring him out of that pleasant mem-ory. He reached in his pocket, pulled out the phone, and answered it. Human remains had been found.

KATIE

MY FATHER CAME AND SAT WITH ME THIS MORNING IN THE LIVING room. Said he cleared his busy schedule in order to keep me company. Lucky me. It makes absolutely no sense that I should like having him here next to me. Ever since I was a little girl, he has always made me feel special. He used to pick me up in his arms and swing me around, calling me his little crabby girl, because I loved collecting crabs in my yellow bucket whenever we went to the beach. He used to give me piggyback rides all the time and took me sledding in the winter. Most of my best childhood memories are of time spent with him.

I curl the blanket under my chin and snuggle my head against the pillow. I do this while he takes out his guitar and strums a few tunes from his repertoire: Elvis, Roy Orbison, Buddy Holly. I love when he sings me these old songs. And he has a really good voice. Most of these songs I know because of him.

Something about him looks different today. From worry? Concern? He typically radiates confidence and charm. I can't ever remember him raising his voice or becoming visibly upset. Despite all the problems in this crazy family and my mother's frequent complaints about him, my father lives each day as if it is his last.

Needless to say, I have a complicated relationship with my father. I love him to death but understand the kind of person he is. He's never been someone we could rely on, and he consistently tries my mother's patience with his frequent absences from home and his inability to provide for us. Deep down, I know all this about him. I know his behavior betrays his good nature. And yet I still love him. I certainly don't absolve him of his many sins, and I can understand why my mother gets so mad at him at times. So I ask myself, Why did she ever marry him? Then I spend time with him and think, Who could *not* fall in love with Ray "Swisher" Eaves?

Maybe this is a character flaw of mine. I consider myself a good person, moderately smart, and hardworking. I'm generally kind and respectful to others. I have volunteered my time down at the nursing home and the local rescue shelter. Some boys even think I'm cute in a nerdy sort of way. So why am I so drawn to exciting, reckless people, like Willow and my father? Do I take after my mother in that regard? Am I hoping that whatever glow they possess rubs off on me? Or am I merely basking in their limelight?

It makes me sad to know that I'm drawn to these types of people, because I don't consider myself a shallow person. I know most of my father's shortcomings, and yet I refuse to take sides against him. My mother, despite her mood swings and temper, is my hero and always has been. Without her, our family would have never survived and stayed together all these years. Raisin might have succumbed to his diabetes or, at the very least, never gotten his service dog.

I didn't befriend Willow to get on a reality show or hang with the cool crowd. I didn't even know her father was planning to shoot that stupid pilot. Or that he wanted Willow to be the star. Willow said the odds of the show getting picked up were extremely low. She wasn't counting on it, and with her talent, she didn't need it. But I knew she dreamed big. Only later in our friendship did I learn that she had the talent to match her oversized ambitions.

"What's wrong, Dad?" I ask after he finishes playing.

"Nothing's wrong. Why you asking?"

"Come on. I know when you're not being honest with me."

"It's just hard seeing you like this, hon." He places the guitar down and stares at me.

"That's not it."

He sighs. "I just don't want to upset you more than you already are."

"Forget about upsetting me. Tell me what's going on so I can remember what happened that night."

His handsome face grimaces. "I got a call today."

"A call about what?" I sit up, my nerves jangling. An intense throbbing consumes my head.

"The police found a body this morning."

"Is it her?"

"I don't know. They haven't said yet."

Just then my grampa walks into the room, dressed in a wrinkled suit and tie. He looks ready for church. He sits down in the armchair and stares at the blank television screen.

"Where you going, Walt?" my father asks.

My grampa turns and regards us oddly. "I don't . . . I'm not . . . sure."

"All dressed up with nowhere to go, huh?" my father replies.

Grampa mumbles incoherently and then turns toward the television.

My father asks, "You want to watch one of your shows?"

My grampa stares straight ahead.

"I'm not sure *Gunsmoke*'s on, Dad, but I'll check." My father turns on the TV and flips through the channels until an old Western comes on.

"*Bonanza*," my grampa utters. "Little Joe."

The irony of this doesn't escape me: two generations of memory-impaired people living under the same roof. I think it strange that my grampa can remember all these old TV shows but not what he had for breakfast. And he could forget his own granddaughter's name. The human brain is a crazy organ. How can I recall things in the past and yet not remember what happened the night I disappeared? Or what happened to Willow?

I lay back on the couch and let the tears flow. A body has been discovered, and I pray it isn't Willow's. Could I live with myself if it's found to be hers? I close my eyes and try not to dwell on the worst. Why had my life been spared? I desperately need to know.

Willow ignored me in school that Monday, even though we were in all the same classes. Was she mad at me? What had I done to piss her off? I'd stayed with her that night after the party and tried to comfort her after what Julian had done. The next morning, with

my head pounding like it had never hurt before, I'd eaten breakfast with Willow and her parents. Her father had talked enthusiasti-
cally about the *Shepherd's Bay* pilot, while her mother had sat quietly
and listened. He had sat next to me with his iPad and had shown
me detailed footage of the show. Whereas before there'd been
scenes with other kids, this footage was almost entirely of Willow.
As stunning as Willow appeared in these scenes, the show seemed
unbalanced and too narrowly focused, but I just had kept nodding
and agreeing with him, determined to keep my mouth shut.

When it was time to go, Willow had given me a quick hug. Then
her father had driven me home. My head had ached during the
ride, and I'd been forced to listen to him drone on about the potential success of *Shepherd's Bay*.

Willow continued to ignore me at school. I tried talking to her,
but she gave me short, clipped answers. No eye contact, either. It
bothered me quite a bit, because I had no idea what I'd done to deserve this cold-shoulder treatment. I'd invested quite a lot in our
friendship. By aligning myself with her, I'd given up all my other
friendships, apart from Drew. I certainly didn't want to spend the
next year and a half isolated and alone, wondering what crime I'd
committed against her. Sure, I had Drew to fall back on, but Drew
alone could not sustain me for that length of time. I wasn't even
sure I wanted to be with Drew, and so stringing him along like that
seemed cruel.

After school, I confronted her as she walked to her car. That's
the thing about me. I can be stubborn when I need to be. She
stopped in front of her car door, looking none too pleased.

"Why did you ignore me all day?" I said.

"You must be tripping, Katie. I did no such thing."

"You most certainly did . . . treating me like I have a disease or
something."

"Get over yourself. Everything's not always about you."

I laughed. "Me? You've *got* to be joking."

"Ummm, do I look like I'm joking?" She opened her car door
and placed a foot inside.

"Everything's about you. This entire show your father's filming is
all about you."

She looked furious. "What's your point?"

"Are you mad at me because of what happened the other night? Because I didn't protect you from Julian?"

"Protect me from Julian? I have no idea what you're talking about."

"I think you do. I found you crying in your room, and so I stayed with you through the night. Remember? You were so drunk, you could barely talk."

"If I'm not mistaken, you were pretty wasted yourself. Maybe you imagined the whole thing."

I hesitated. Had I imagined it? Maybe Julian hadn't hurt her. But it had seemed so real. I remembered the trickle of blood running down her upper lip. And yet . . . I had gotten drunk that night. Maybe my eyes had deceived me and I'd not seen Julian sleeping in that spare bedroom, passed out in his cherry-red boxers. He hadn't breakfasted with us the next morning. Had he slipped out of the house before anyone got up? Because of what he'd done to Willow? Or maybe he had never been there to begin with. I suddenly realized I couldn't trust my memory or what I thought I had seen that night.

"Look, Katie, I'm not mad at you." She got in her car and held the door open. "Want a lift home?"

"Drew's supposed to give me a ride."

"Forget that loser and get in."

"He's not a loser, Willow."

"He's, like, a *major* loser." She made an *L* over her perfectly shaped forehead using thumb and forefinger. "You could do so much better than him."

"Like Julian?" I rolled my eyes, even though I knew I'd crossed a line.

"You don't know Julian like I do," she said. "What if Drew finds out that you were crushing on Dakota that night?"

"You wouldn't." It scared me to think Drew might find out about my casual fling with Dakota.

"Then get in the car, Katie."

Scared, I walked around the hood and let myself in. "Please don't say anything to Drew."

"Chillax." She turned the key, and her Beamer roared to life. "Dakota told me you could get your hands on *some*."

Some what? I turned and stared at her.

"Were you just saying that to impress him, Katie? Because if you were, that's totally not cool. Dakota trusted you."

"No, I was not just saying that to impress him." Was I? Then I remembered the X. "I've got connections in town."

"So you're a regular G now?" She smiled knowingly.

"You know what I mean. I'm just saying I can get some for you."

"Cool, because I'm thinking of having another party soon and inviting Dakota."

My heart somersaulted in my chest. "Do your parents care that we party at your house?"

"Hell no!" She laughed, as if I said something silly. "As long as no one drives or acts stupid, they're totally cool with it."

"Okay."

"So can you?"

"Can I what?"

"Get some X or whatever?"

"Of course I can get some," I said, wondering if I actually could. "I can't promise I'll get everything you want, but make a list and I'll see what I can do."

"You're the best, Katie. I knew I could count on you."

But could I count on myself? I realized there was no turning back now; I was going to be a drug dealer. I had to figure out how to approach Bugger without getting my father involved. Bugger would help me only because I was Swisher's daughter. I couldn't afford to lose my friendship with Willow. She was all I had now that I'd taken sides. I had sworn to my mother that I'd never take drugs, but I hadn't said anything about buying them. I would help Willow this one time. Then, I told myself, I'd never do it again.

ISLA

*T*HE PHONE RANG WHILE SHE HAD SONIA NESS IN THE CHAIR. SHE answered and heard Chip Hicks's voice on the other end of the line. The police had found human remains in a dilapidated boat shed on the north shore. The body had been discovered beneath an overturned wooden boat.

The discovery stung, and she prayed it wasn't Willow's body, but she knew the odds were fifty-fifty that it was. What would she tell Katie if it turned out to be the case? At least if the body turned out to be Dakota James's, she had the relief of knowing that Katie hadn't known the boy.

She returned her attention to Sonia and spun her around in the chair so that she could see the television. On any other day, Isla would have closed the shop and gone down to the sight of the discovery. But she had a full slate of appointments today, thanks to Samantha McCallister's big fund-raiser tonight. Considering the tragic circumstances, would Samantha still hold the event? And if she did, Isla wondered how she would get through the party without breaking down into tears.

"Everything okay?" Sonia asked.

"Not really. It seems the police found a body."

"Oh, dear. Do they know who it is?"

"They haven't said yet, but I'm sure it'll be on the news tonight."

"No one deserves to be treated like that, no matter how much of a handful Willow was."

"What do you mean?"

"You don't know? That girl was trouble with a capital T. Jennifer was over there last summer and saw her canoodling with Dakota and some other boys. I attended a party in late August and spied her kissing Julian while they lounged on the beach. Looked like they were smoking pot, too."

"How could you see them if you were at the Briggses'?"

"The downstairs bathroom was being used, so I went upstairs. It was nighttime, and from that vantage, I had a good view of the McCallisters' property. It looked to me like they were trying to keep it a secret."

"But that doesn't make her a bad person, right?"

"She was a big tease. Rumor has it she got in a lot of trouble at her LA prep school."

"For what?"

Sonia shrugged. "Could be anything, knowing that girl. Did you know that Julian got kicked out of the Dalton School in Manhattan?"

"I've heard some rumors floating around about that." Isla felt like a fool for not knowing about the kids her daughter hung out with. "What was his offense?"

"Again, it's only a rumor, but I heard he was dealing drugs, although no one knows for sure. It's not like that boy is an angel, either." She shook her head, as if disgusted by the whole ordeal. "You can't be too careful in this town. I try to keep my kids grounded at all times, but it's hard."

"That's smart of you."

"Of course, everything we talk about is between us girls, right? I have to socialize with Samantha this evening, and I would *hate* for anything to get back to her."

"I would never say a thing," Isla said, lifting a strand of the woman's dyed hair up between her fingers. "I guess I'll see you at the party, then."

"You're going to be there?" Sonia turned and stared at her.

"Yes. Samantha insisted I attend."

"Then you and your husband must join Jay and me for cocktails."

"Unfortunately, my husband can't make it."

"Look at you, going stag. You'll give me good reason to escape from all those highbrow types. You know, the ones who watch PBS and read the *Wall Street Journal.*" She laughed. "Although you better watch out for Beckett. I hear he's very 'hands on' with his female guests."

"Beckett?"

"Lily Dobbins swore she saw him out with another woman one evening, while they were dining in Portland."

"Really?"

She shrugged. "It's only what I heard."

"What do you know about Felicia?"

"Not much. They moved to Maine from LA. Supposedly, Gil worked in the film industry." Sonia rolled her eyes. "I find this whole reality show idea of his rather silly. This isn't *Laguna Beach* or *Desperate Housewives.*"

"Katie insisted I sign the release form and let her participate in the show. I didn't want to stand in the way of any opportunities she might have, and I figured if it could help defray any college costs, better yet."

"My kids threw a hissy fit. They all want to be reality stars and become rich and famous, although I think Gil was mostly doing it for Willow's benefit."

"And now she's gone."

"I understand she didn't make many friends. With all due respect, my own kids couldn't stand her. They were always saying what a stuck-up snob she was."

"That's funny, because Katie adores Willow. The two girls had grown extremely close after performing in *Grease* together."

"What an amazing performance. We saw that musical three times."

"Willow stole the show as Sandy Olsson," Isla said.

"There's no denying Willow's talent—and Katie's, too." She knew Sonia didn't really believe that Katie had talent, but Isla appreciated the gesture.

"Katie said Willow angered many of the girls when she won the part of Sandy Olsson. Those roles are supposed to go to seniors."

"Not when you have Willow's talent and looks and can sell out every performance at a bigger theater," Sonia observed.

The news came on the television, and Isla held her breath, waiting to hear what the police had found. A reporter stood at the scene, pointing out a dilapidated old boat shed. Isla shuddered upon seeing the faded red lobster painted on the side of the structure. She recognized that shed and had been inside it a long time ago, when it had been in much better condition. Ray's family had once owned it, but they had sold it when Ray's father, a boat repairman, died. Ray had taken her there after three months of dating, and they had made love inside it. That was where Katie was conceived. She remembered it like it was yesterday. He'd brought some wine coolers and beer. Then, while they were sitting in one of the wooden skiffs, he'd leaned over and kissed her.

Who owned the shed now?

A bad feeling settled into her gut. Could Ray somehow be involved in this? She knew Ray to be irresponsible and reckless, but a murderer? Then she remembered how he had doted on Willow whenever she came over to the house. Still, she found it a stretch to think Ray would commit such a vile crime.

Sonia paid for her cut, gave her a hug, and left happy. As soon as she left, Isla called Ray and told him the news and instructed him not to tell Katie until they could project a united front. But he'd already heard about it. Not that it mattered. Telling Ray to do something was as useful as telling her father; he either didn't remember or didn't care.

She had little time to rest, as the next Harper's Point client came in for her trim, and then others followed, each one trying to look better than the next for tonight's fund-raiser. She tried to stay focused and listen to the women unload all their problems, but she couldn't stop thinking about the body found in the Eaveses' old boat shed.

One of her clients politely asked if she'd shut off the television, saying that all this bad news depressed her. Isla put on music instead. All day long her clients complained about one thing or another: the lack of a top-notch restaurant in town, the difficulty of finding good help, a salon that sold high-end fashion, the taxes. Always the taxes. Were any of these rich women happy?

Once the last customer left, Isla locked the door and turned on the news. Nothing more about the body found in the boat shed. She didn't have time to stick around and find out. She had to rush home and get ready for the McCallisters' big fund-raiser. Pick out a nice dress, fix her hair, and put on her best pair of shoes.

She swept up and then counted out the till. Amazing! It was her best day since opening. If business kept up at this pace, the future looked bright.

After locking up the salon, she dashed for her car, thinking about what might happen if Julian was responsible for these crimes. Tonight would be as good a time as any to keep her eyes and ears open. Maybe to ask a few questions and see what she might be able to find out. She'd have to walk a fine line. Because if Samantha believed that Isla was prying into her life, it could mean an end to her livelihood. But this was personal now. Her own flesh and blood had been brutally attacked and left for dead. If that ultimately hurt her business, than so be it. Family came first.

KARL

*T*HREE LOCAL KIDS WALKING THE BEACH HAD DISCOVERED THE BODY. He pulled up and saw two state police cruisers parked at the scene. He understood why: the state police handled most of the murder investigations in the state of Maine. With only five officers, the Shepherd's Bay Police Department could hardly be counted on to solve complicated murder cases, nor did it have the resources to handle the kinds of evidence found at violent crime scenes.

He'd considered becoming a state police officer upon arriving home to Maine. It would have been an easier route to employment in the field of law enforcement had he chosen that path. At the time, a lot of staties had been retiring, and there'd been plenty of job openings. And becoming a statie would have allowed him to work on all kinds of cases. But he had had a wife and a young daughter, and the prospect of working way up in the county, along the Canadian border, those first few years had made him rethink his plans. Nor had he had any desire to work along the Interstate 95 corridor between Portland and the New Hampshire state line, passing out speeding tickets to angry Mass tourists eager to hit the beaches. Then there had been the added hassle of relocating his family every few years. So when the opening had come up in the Shepherd's Bay Police Department, he'd jumped at it.

A perimeter had been set up, and yellow tape surrounded the old boat shed. The shed was a landmark of sorts, with its faded red lobster painted on the side. He knew as soon as he saw it that it had once belonged to Ray's father. Everyone knew George Eaves. Unlike his son, George had been a highly respected businessman in town and well liked. He'd possessed a barrel chest, a huge potbelly, and mutton sideburns. Karl never remembered seeing the man without a half-smoked cigar poking out of his chapped lips. Known around the area for his considerable boat repair skills, George Eaves had built up an impressive business. Too bad he hadn't been able to convince Swisher to follow in his footsteps and learn the trade.

He ducked under the tape and went inside the boat shed. The shed had fallen into serious disrepair since George died from a heart attack at the age of sixty-nine. He had heard it had sold recently, but had no idea who had purchased it. As he looked around, he could see that it would cost quite a few bucks to bring it back to its former glory.

Maine detective Ed Kyle waved him over to where a wooden boat sat against the side of the shed. Kyle had thirty years of service under his belt and had worked alongside the Shepherd's Bay Police Department on the James case. Karl looked down and saw what appeared to be a body covered over with a soiled marine tarp.

"Nice-looking boat, although it needs a little work," Kyle said. "You ever think of owning one, Bjorny?"

"Nope. They say buying one is the second best day of a boat owner's life."

"And what's the first?"

"The day he sells it."

Kyle laughed.

"What have we got here?" Karl asked.

"Badly decomposing male. Looks to be in his late teens."

"Sounds like the James kid."

"You know what kind of boat this is?"

Karl squatted to inspect it. "Off-center skiff, plank-on-frame construction. I'm guessing thirteen feet." He examined it further. "Northern white cedar planks and transom. White oak frame and pine seats. Bronze screw fastenings, oarlocks, and holders. Nice workmanship, although it needs a little TLC."

"For a guy who doesn't own a boat, you sure know what you're talking about."

"Beginner's luck."

"Bullshit."

"My dad owned a few rigs in his day."

"Know who the skiff belongs to?"

"Used to be the old owner, George Eaves's, but he's been dead a few years now. Then again, I heard this shed was sold."

"Care to take a look at the kid?"

"Not really," Karl said, "but I guess if I have no other choice . . ."

Just then Chief Scroggins walked in, huffing and puffing. He was seventy-two, and most people had expected him to retire a few years ago, but for some reason, he hadn't gotten around to it. His jowly face glowed red because of the heat, and everyone in town knew he enjoyed a few stiff drinks every now and then. A high-profile murder like this had never before happened in Shepherd's Bay, and he seemed unprepared for all the media hoopla that followed.

"You want to see him, Harry?" Karl asked.

"Not really, unless you don't want to."

"Sure, I'll take this one," Karl said.

"Just a warning, it's not a pretty sight," Kyle said.

Karl walked over to where the tarp covered the body. The recent rise in temperature had made the heat almost unbearable inside this shed. He squatted down, listening to the waves gently lap the shore. He lifted the edge of the tarp and saw green crabs crawling over the head. March and April had been cold, slowing the rate of decomposition. Then the recent heat wave had quickened the process, providing the crabs with an abundance of food. The clothes on the corpse were definitely those of a male: winter jacket, button-down shirt, and jeans. Having seen enough, he arranged the tarp over the corpse.

"I'm fairly certain it's Dakota James, the kid who went missing in March," he announced. "DNA should confirm it."

"Wonder if he came down here to get high. Maybe it was a drug deal gone wrong," Scroggins said. "Lot of drugs flowing through this town lately."

"It's possible," Karl said. "We'll need to find out if the kid was involved in that kind of stuff."

"Best to keep all avenues open," Scroggins said.

"We should have more information about the cause of death after the medical examiner checks him out," Kyle said.

"Looks like blood splatter on the wall." Karl leaned over and examined the stains. "Someone struck him right where I'm standing. That tells me he must have known the person who killed him."

"What makes you think that?" Scroggins said.

"Did you open the door, Chief? Makes quite a racket when you do. The victim would have certainly heard the killer enter. And you can't take a step in here without one of these boards squeaking."

"True," Scroggins said. "Any sign that a gun was used, Kyle?"

"Can't say for sure, but during my initial look around, I didn't see any bullet holes or spent shells. And the splatter stain on the wall looks nothing like I would expect from a gunshot wound. If I had to say, someone whacked the kid over the head, but it's hard to see with all those crabs swarming over his noggin."

"Dakota James was five-ten and a hundred eighty pounds of muscle. He played football and wrestled for Chance Academy. I doubt most kids, never mind most adults, could have overpowered him," Karl said.

"Unless someone used a bat or a heavy object," Scroggins said.

"There would have been a struggle, had Dakota believed he was about to be attacked. Wrestlers are very good at taking down their opponents." Karl positioned himself near the wall and faced the ocean. "I'm guessing he was not the least bit frightened of the other person in this shed with him. That's why he looked away. He never expected it. Then this person, whoever they were, struck him in the back of the head when he wasn't looking. A crowbar or hammer would have easily done the trick."

"We can stand here all day and theorize about the cause of death, but it's all conjecture at this point. Best for us to get out of here, so we don't contaminate the rest of the evidence," Kyle said.

They exited the shed. Karl stood under the hot sun, staring at his fellow cops. Scroggins immediately lit a cigarette. He looked stressed and unprepared for the intense scrutiny coming his way. He had been coasting in this job for far too long now and finally had to earn his pay.

"I'll leave the rest up to you, Chief, but you might want to wait before you talk to the media," Karl said.

"Wait for what? Didn't we determine that this is the James kid?" Scroggins replied.

"I wouldn't officially comment on that until the medical examiner makes his final determination," Karl said.

"Jesus Christ," Scroggins said, wiping his forehead with his cigarette hand. "I ain't exactly media savvy, and it's not like we have a lot of violent crime here in Shepherd's Bay. Only bodies we ever see around here are the occasional floaters that wash ashore."

"Want me to handle it, Chief?" Karl offered.

"Would you mind, Bjorny? I'm going to head back to the station and start filling out the paperwork."

Karl watched the two men walk away. A few people had gathered near the yellow tape. He looked off in the distance and saw a Mercedes speeding toward him and those who had gathered. It screeched to a halt, and out stepped Gil Briggs. He could tell Briggs had been sobbing. Briggs ran over and almost tackled him to the ground, falling to his knees and wrapping his arms around Karl's legs.

"Please tell me it's not my baby," he wailed.

"Get ahold of yourself, Mr. Briggs. Now, stand up and take a deep breath." Karl lifted the man to his feet.

"Just tell me. Is it her? Is it my Willow?"

"We can't be one hundred percent sure at this stage, but it looks to me like it's not your daughter."

Briggs's eyes widened, and this time he wept with joy, short chortles of hyperventilating breath. Then he practically asphyxiated Karl in a bear hug. Karl stood motionless, allowing the man to empty his tank of emotions. He'd never seen a parent so worked up. It had to pain Gil and Felicia not to know what happened to their daughter. He knew the odds of finding Willow alive decreased with each passing day, but at least this news gave the Briggses a reprieve, hope that their daughter might still be alive.

ISLA

*H*ER WARDROBE LEAVED A LOT TO BE DESIRED, BUT SINCE SHE HAD had no time to shop for anything, she needed to pick out an outfit from her closet. Which dress should she choose? She tried on a few and grimaced at how she looked in them. The majority of her clothes these days came from Target or JCPenney, both stores located seventeen miles outside of town. The five extra pounds she'd put on since last year didn't help, either. Would people be appraising her as soon as she walked in? They weren't her people, after all. Not a one of them could she actually call a friend, despite her clients seemingly friendly attitude toward her. Whenever money passed hands, the fine line between friendship and patronage became more defined.

Did this stupid fund-raiser really matter in the larger scheme of things? Just today a body had been found. Upon learning the news, Katie had barricaded herself in her room and cried herself to sleep. Isla had tried to sit with her, but to no avail. Once Katie felt better, she would begin her intensive therapy, the start of a long road back to wellness.

Isla looked at herself in the mirror and sighed. A hairdresser with bad hair was definitely not a good look. Like a painter with a peeling house. Or a landscaper with a scrubby lawn. She tried putting her hair into different styles before settling on the messy-bun look. A flower tucked into the side added a finishing touch. She had seen this hairstyle once on Jennifer Aniston and loved its breezy sophistication. Then again, most everything looked good on Jennifer Aniston. The actress could get her skull shaved and still look amazing.

The teardrop earrings went surprisingly well with the messy-bun look. She inventoried her tiny closet one last time and settled on a sleeveless beaded blue dress. Simple yet elegant. She tried it on and realized it still fit. Lucky her. It had been three years since she wore it and five years since she purchased it at Macy's for half price while on a shopping spree down in Portland. Simple two-inch black dress heels rounded everything out.

She stared at herself in the full-length mirror. Not bad, considering. Not great, either, but it would have to do. Her face, however, betrayed her attempts at high fashion. She looked tired and more wrinkled than usual. The makeup she'd applied barely hid her worry lines. No surprise there after everything she'd been through.

Dressing up like this suddenly made her sad. It reminded her how starved she was for love and affection. She wanted to feel desired again. She wanted her husband to cherish her and think her the most beautiful and wondrous creature on the planet. Sadly, Ray hadn't looked at her like that in years. Was it her fault? Had she been a bad wife and not made her husband happy? She didn't think so, but now, looking at herself in the mirror, she decided that maybe she should have been more attentive to the way she looked.

A wave of guilt passed through her. Her appearance at this fundraiser seemed so trivial and stupid considering all that had happened lately. But she knew she had to attend. The key was to compartmentalize her emotions and stay focused.

Try to keep everything together, Isla.

She moved to the living room and clicked on the TV, hoping to catch the latest news before she left for the party. The house seemed unusually quiet now, with her father and Katie holed up in their rooms. Raisin had gone over to Tim Simpson's house to hang out. Not only were the Simpsons members of their church, but Gayle was also a registered nurse and could care for Raisin in the event of an emergency. Now all she needed was for Ray's mother to show up. Her close relationship with Esther Eaves seemed the best part of her marriage to Ray.

The news rehashed the discovery of human remains, as well as the painful ordeal of the missing kids. There'd been no definitive ID of the body found in the old boat shed. Standing so as not to wrinkle her dress, she clicked off the flat-screen, which Ray had received in "trade" for some vague business deal. *More like shady,* she thought, although she could never quite prove it. Everyone loved the fifty-inch screen, but she thought it way too big for their small living room.

The doorbell rang, which she thought unusual. Esther typically barged in without notice, making a racket, and then talked non-stop about every little thing she'd done recently. She opened the door and saw a smallish man with an unkempt gray beard and a stack of flyers in hand. He looked familiar, for some reason.

"Hi, Isla," the man said. His eyes looked grim behind round tortoiseshell spectacles, and he appeared uncomfortable in her presence—and in his own skin.

"Can I help you?" She saw a police cruiser coming up the driveway.

"Bob Oden." He handed her a flyer.

"Hi, Bob." Now she recognized him. One of the Odens. The family had suffered a bitter loss when their business property was foreclosed on by the bank a few years ago.

"Hope you'll vote for Don Hansen for town council. He's a strong supporter of Prop Six."

She glanced at the political flyer in her hand.

"You're familiar with Prop Six, right? Ten percent added tax on all properties over five hundred thousand dollars?" Oden said.

"Yeah, I'm familiar with it. I didn't know Don was running for council."

"Well, he is, and we'd be very fortunate to have him representing us. Make these rich folks pay their fair share."

"Gotcha, Bob. Thanks." She started to close the door.

"Can we count on your vote this fall, Isla?"

"Oh, I'll be voting, all right," she said.

"Good, because our schools need all the help they can get. Did you know that our opponents are having a fund-raiser tonight for their candidate? Some Ivy-educated know-it-all. We can't let them screw us."

"Right, Bob. Thanks." She saw Karl get out of the cruiser.

"By the way, I'm sorry to hear about your daughter. How's she doing?"

"Much better now. Thanks for asking." Would this guy ever leave?

"How's Ray doing?"

"Ray's Ray, you know?"

"Great guy. Tell him Bob Oden said hello," Oden said. "You look real nice. Going somewhere special tonight?"

"Meeting some friends."

"Have fun. And please don't forget to vote yes on Prop Six this November."

She watched him wobble down the steps. Oden nodded to the cop as they passed, but Karl's face remained expressionless.

"Hey," he said, making his way up the stairs.

"Hey, you."

"Mind if I come in?"

"Sure, but make it quick. I'm leaving as soon as Ray's mother arrives."

"Good old Esther Eaves. She was my second-grade teacher."

"The woman's a ball of nervous energy, but I love her to death."

"I'll only be a minute."

"The quicker the better." She stepped back inside the house, and he followed her. He immediately took off his police cap.

"Is Ray here?" he asked.

"No."

"That seaweed business of his must really be booming."

"I guess." She looked down at her shoes, having caught the sarcasm in his voice. "He doesn't tell me much about his business dealings."

"And to think we swam in that stuff as kids, not knowing we were swimming in money the entire time."

"Show me the green, right?" she said, feeling vulnerable while standing, dressed to kill, before her old boyfriend. "Are you here to give me some bad news about Willow?"

"Preliminary results are showing the remains to be that of a male teen, but that's between you and me."

"Dakota James?" The shock of this news caused the fine hairs on her arms to stand up. Did he notice?

"Don't take this the wrong way, Isla, but you look amazing. Night out with the girls?"

"Not exactly." She walked over to the coffee table and picked up her black purse.

"I didn't mean to offend you."

"Please, Karl. I'm a little more thick skinned than to take offense at a compliment."

He paused. "What did Bob Oden want?"

"For me to vote for Don Hansen for town council. It seems that both men are fans of Prop Six."

"Oden's been pretty bitter ever since his family's boatyard went into foreclosure after his parents died. A developer from out of town scooped it up for next to nothing and started putting up those McMansions."

"Have they determined how the boy died?"

"No, but he'd been dead for more than a few months. Looks like murder."

"Murder?" She covered her mouth. "Do you think his death is connected to Willow's and Katie's disappearance?"

"Not really sure yet." He shrugged. "Ray taking you out tonight?"

"Ray taking me out? Now, that's the funniest thing I've heard all year. I'm lucky if he brings home a pizza or a few burgers every so often."

Karl didn't respond.

"Okay, if you really must know, then I'll tell you. But I'm begging you not to say anything."

He zippered his lips.

"I've been invited to a fund-raiser this evening at Samantha Mc-Callister's club. It's being thrown to get one of her friends elected to the town council."

He chuckled. "Poor Bob Oden would have flipped his wig had he known about that."

She pointed menacingly at him. "That's between you and me, Karl."

"You won't hear a peep out of this guy. Besides, I'm not sure I approve of taxing one group of people disproportionately because Bob Oden's been holding a grudge all these years."

"I hate to sound selfish, but I know for a fact that Samantha's husband will tear down the building my salon is housed in if this proposition passes."

"That would be terrible. Make it hard to find another space in the downtown area at the right price."

"Exactly. He cuts me a break because my grandfather owned the barbershop there for over fifty years. If that goes, so goes my discount."

"Your grandfather was like a fixture in this town."

"I miss my grandfather so much. He taught me most everything I know about this business."

"I'd come to your shop for a trim, but you charge big-city rates. So I do it myself."

"And believe me, it shows."

"You think?"

"It's uneven and all hacked up. Quite a mess, Karl, if you must know the truth."

"Never really noticed."

"Too bad, because I might take pity on a charity case like you." She craned her neck and checked out his hair. "Judging from the looks of it, you should really come and see me. I could work my magic on you."

"I might take you up on that offer."

"You really should."

"Didn't think it was that bad."

"I doubt you'll win over many hearts in this town looking like that *Dumb and Dumber* guy."

He laughed, and it reminded her of when they were teenagers.

"I'll certainly consider it," he said. "Word of warning, though. You better be careful at that fund-raiser tonight."

"Why's that?"

"Those affluent folks want everyone to know how rich and privileged they are. If you're not careful, you'll end up with your face plastered all over the society pages. People around here might take that the wrong way."

"I never considered that."

"Well, you should," he said. "How's Katie doing?"

She heard a car coming up the driveway and knew her mother-in-law had arrived. "She's moved to her bedroom. Says the light hurts her head."

"Can I swing by and talk to her soon?"

"Please call before you come over," she said, grabbing her sweater off the chair. "I gotta run, Karl. Ray's mother is here."

She glanced at the clock and saw she was running behind schedule. Probably not the worst thing to show up fashionably late. She opened the door for him to leave, and for a brief second, he stopped and gazed into her eyes. She tried not to think of that kiss they once shared while out hiking. Of how she had both admired and felt ambivalent about the kind of boy she was falling for. A quiet boy who preferred to be alone in the woods rather than out with his friends, drinking and acting like a fool. She had thought at the time that she wanted more out of life. A life acting in New York and someday married to a man of wit, sophistication, and charm. Instead, that man had turned out to be Willy Loman from *Death of a Salesman.*

He scampered down the stairs, tipping his cap to Esther as she passed. A look of concern came over her mother-in-law's face as she approached the door. As a former elementary school teacher, Esther Eaves was one of the most upstanding people she knew. That she was also a busybody and inveterate gossip hadn't made Isla think any less of her.

"Why was that police officer here?" Esther asked as she stepped inside the house.

"You didn't hear the news, Ma? They found a body today in George's old boat shed." Isla shut the door.

"Oh my goodness. Was it Katie's friend?"

"They haven't made an official ID yet, but they think it's that boy who disappeared in March."

"What in the world is going on in this town?" Judging from her coiffed gray hair, Isla could tell that she'd sat for a considerable amount of time under the dryer this morning. "So where is everyone?"

"Katie's in her room. Seems the light is giving her headaches. And my father is in his room, too. He'll come out if he needs anything."

"The other day he thought I was his mother."

"He does that on occasion with me, too. One night he thought I was his wife."

"Poor fella." She brought her wrinkled hands together, as if to pray. "Sometimes I get jealous of how George died, quickly and without pain. Other times, I'm mad as hell that he left me without even a good-bye or letting me tell the old jerk how much I loved him."

"Well, Ma, I, for one, am sure glad you're still here." She hugged the squat woman. "I don't know what I'd do without you."

"I'm so sorry, Isla. George and I tried to raise Ray the right way and to be a good man. I don't know where we went wrong."

"It's not your fault. Ray needs to take responsibility for his own actions. You did all you could for him."

"He makes me so sad." She wiped at her tears with a tissue. "Maybe we spoiled him because he was such a wild boy growing up."

"Look at you, Ma. Your hair looks wonderful today," Isla said, changing the subject. "Helen really outdid herself."

"You think?"

"I know it."

"I've been going to Helen for forty years now. I hope you're not upset with me."

"Of course I'm not upset with you. Helen's an awesome hairstylist. Besides, I don't have one of those industrial hair dryers like she has." She lifted her hands and gently pressed them around her mother-in-law's coif, noticing the slightest trace of purple in the coloring. Isla had always thought her mother-in-law could have been the fourth roommate on *The Golden Girls*.

"I'm running late, Ma. I really have to run."

"Where you girls going tonight?"

"Not sure." Isla didn't want to tell her the truth, knowing that as a former second-grade teacher, Esther would most likely be voting for Prop 6.

"Well, you deserve a night out. Have fun, honey."

"I will, Ma."

She opened the door to leave. The last thing she saw was her mother-in-law sitting on the couch with her romance paperback, the red string flowing along the spine, and Lawrence Welk on PBS saying, "And-a-one-anna-a-two-anna . . ."

KATIE

I NEED TO KNOW WHO I AM. I DON'T MEAN BECAUSE OF THE HEAD IN-jury that's affecting my memory. I mean in a more general sense. Am I a townie girl? Or a rich wannabe? Am I meant to stay here for-ever, like my mother? Or am I destined to live elsewhere and build a new identity for myself? Marry Drew? Or to take a chance and look for someone who will try to know who I am and how to com-plete me?

The light doesn't bother my eyes. I just told my mother that so I could escape to my room. I couldn't face her or my brother after coming to the realization that I had arranged to get drugs for Wil-low and her friends. What was I thinking?

That's why I'm in my room, hiding out, praying that all this will magically disappear. Because remembering what happened no longer seems like a good option. I'm afraid—afraid of what else I'll learn about myself and the actions I took leading up to that fateful night. And yet I know I have to push on and try to recall the events that took place. If not for me, then for Willow.

My father said a body had been found. I search my phone and discover that the police haven't made a positive identification yet. I don't know why, but my gut tells me it's not Willow. Should that cause me alarm? Do I know what happened? I'm assuming I would have spoken up if I did. But for some reason, I didn't.

We stood across from each other at the kitchen island. Outside, Dakota was waiting to meet me. Willow couldn't quite believe it when

I told her I'd gotten the drugs. She peered into the manila envelope filled with the twenty-five Mollies. I had no idea what a Molly was or what it did to a person, and I had no desire to find out. It amazed me that Dakota didn't blink when I told him I needed eight hundred dollars up front for the drugs. He claimed that we'd make ten bucks off every pill sold at the party. I told him to keep it, as I didn't want to profit off any drug sales. Then I gave him the name and number of the person who had sold the drugs to me, explaining that I had no intention of ever doing that again.

Willow walked around the kitchen island and hugged me, and just like that we became best friends again. But I felt ashamed and scared about what I'd done in order to fit in with the Harper's Point crowd. I knew I should have run from Willow and never looked back. What if the police found out? Would I go to jail? Facing my mother would be even worse. She'd be devastated to learn that her perfect daughter was nothing more than a party girl and common drug dealer. And yet the sad part was, I knew I didn't want to be Drew's girlfriend anymore. I'd cast my lot with these rich kids and discovered, to my shame, that I rather enjoyed their company. It made me feel shallow and empty to admit this, but it was true.

I ran outside to meet up with Dakota. He quickly kissed me on the lips before I had a chance to say anything. His warm breath cut through the cold March day. I loved his jet-black hair and the way it naturally parted to the side, and how his longish bangs swept over his forehead. He possessed a thin waist that tapered up to broad shoulders, reminding me a bit of that kid in the *Twilight* movie. His eyes were the darkest of browns, like my mother's morning coffee. After taking the envelope from me, he ran out to the street and jumped into his army-green Jeep.

I went back inside Willow's home, my insides swimming with emotions. The party was to start in a few hours. Willow busied herself by helping her mother put away all the food they'd ordered. Her father peered through the camera, filming everything and asking all kinds of questions, orbiting around us like a satellite. It made me feel self-conscious and weird, but I was getting used to seeing him behind the lens. I sensed a layer of tension between mother and daughter, but I couldn't quite put my finger on the cause. They argued a lot, which was probably typical of mother-and-daughter relationships. But their bickering had taken on a darker edge today. Only when Willow's father came between them did the two stop talking.

I sat at the massive kitchen island and quietly observed their family dynamics. I felt invisible around them. Gil's iPad sat on the table, continuously streaming footage of his most recent shoot. They didn't seem to care that I was privy to their dirty laundry. It was like I was one of those servants in my mother's favorite show, *Downton Abbey*, walking through the bedroom and picking up dirty clothes while the owners of the manor lounged about in their pajamas.

Earlier in the day, Willow, the other girls on the softball team, and I gathered in the cafeteria for our first softball meeting. Our school softball teams were never that great to begin with, but we were scrappy and played hard and never embarrassed ourselves on the field. I'd made varsity last year, as a sophomore, although I hadn't got much playing time. But this year, with five seniors having graduated, I expected to start at second base. Coach Hicks wanted me to be a slap hitter and had informed me that I would practice that method every day. That meant that as a left-handed batter, I would try to hit the ball toward third base and use my speed to arrive safely at first.

During our first gathering, Willow's father had circled the room, with the camera pointed toward us. It had felt weird being in that room, next to Willow, knowing we were being filmed during something as insignificant as a softball meeting. I'd seen all the girls sitting up a little taller and posing for the camera, as if they were auditioning for *American Idol*. More than anything, I'd felt silly and insecure. In everything I did, I was the girl behind the scenes, helping to make it all come together. Like I did in the musical and on the softball field, my job was to make those who were more talented than me look good. To be supportive and prop them up.

Willow's mother screamed at her, drawing me out of my thoughts. Tears flowed down the woman's cheeks as she turned to her husband and laid into him. I hadn't heard what they were arguing about, and before I knew it, her mother had fled upstairs.

I didn't want to be there. I felt like a stranger in their midst, an anthropologist out in the jungle, observing a never-before-seen tribe. I watched streaming footage of Willow on the iPad, waiting to see if anybody else would appear with her. Gil turned the camera and briefly filmed me before turning back to Willow, who stood bawling in front of their massive refrigerator. I couldn't believe this. Never in a million years would my mother allow another kid inside our home while she argued with my dad. Everything that happened in our family stayed behind those walls.

Then something happened that stuck with me. Gil put the camera down and hugged his daughter. He wore those signature black glasses with the silver studs adorning the arms. His embrace of her felt odd, seeing it from my perspective, especially after his wife had fled upstairs in tears. Willow clung to him with everything she had, her long nails digging into his gray USC sweatshirt. Willow had told me he'd graduated from there with a degree in film and TV production.

Aside from that night of the first party, I'd never seen my friend so distraught. Was it simply over the brief, volatile argument with her mother? I hadn't heard what they were arguing about, but could it have been that bad? Enough to make Willow sob like that? Enough to cause her mother to scamper upstairs in tears?

Gil whispered something to her, moving her long blond hair away from her ear. I glanced at the iPad and saw footage of Willow dancing onstage in her role as Sandy Olsson. Willow kept nodding, her eyes glued to his shoulder. They whispered conspiratorially for a few minutes. At one point she looked up and gazed at me, as if wondering what I was still doing here. Why was I invading their privacy? Her eyes were red and swollen from crying. Our eyes locked, and I looked away in embarrassment.

The intimacy of a father comforting his daughter was for behind closed doors, not for public consumption, done in private and not in the company of strangers. The emotion they displayed toward each other made me feel like I was violating their personal space. But what was I to do? There was nowhere for me to go in this house. And it would seem awkward if I moved into the living room and completely ignored them.

Finally, they separated. Willow sat calmly on one of the bar chairs lined up along the island. Gil stood behind her, massaging her shoulders. Willow asked her father to pour her a glass of Chablis, and he did so without any reservation, asking if I wanted one, too. Was this the way rich people behaved? Or maybe people from California? My father had always said that people from that state were flakes and screwballs. How he knew this, I didn't know, since he'd never been there. This offer felt so foreign to me that I agreed to a glass of Chablis so as not to make any waves. Besides, I thought a drink might help relax me and calm my nerves.

I drank the wine quickly on account of my uneasiness. Apart from the occasional sip of wine during communion, this was my first real taste of it. The first gulp was not so good, but it grew on me as time passed, so that I didn't hate it as much. Gil refilled my glass, although the wine had already made me light headed, thanks to an empty stomach. I hadn't eaten, and so I slowly sipped from that second glass.

Watching Willow on that iPad was beginning to irk me. As talented as Willow was, I knew she couldn't carry the entire show on her own. Where were the rest of us? She needed drama and friction. Where was her supporting cast?

Loud, aggressive banging on the door jarred me out of my train of thought. This was followed by the sound of the doorbell ringing. Gil took out his phone and fidgeted with it for a few seconds. Then he passed it over to Willow, now composed after her long crying spell.

"Oh, Christ!" she said.

"You know this boy?" her father asked.

"Not as well as Katie does."

"I do?" I said.

"See for yourself," Willow said, stretching out her long arm so I could see who was at the door. Video cell phone surveillance. Was there anything these people didn't have?

"Shit!" I said, covering my mouth. "I'm so sorry for swearing, Mr. Briggs." Father and daughter laughed.

"It's Gil to you, Katie. And believe me, I heard much worse from six-year-olds when I worked at the Disney Channel."

More banging. More doorbell ringing.

"What do you want to do about him, Katie?" Willow said.

"Could you make him go away? Tell him I'm not here."

"With pleasure," Willow said, standing.

"Sit down, bunny. I'll deal with this clown," said Gil.

"No, Daddy, I'll shoo him away. But you should film this encounter. It'll make for good drama."

"Great idea." He picked up his camera and followed her as I trailed after them.

"Why don't you just break up with him, Katie? He's such a loser," Willow said.

"We've been together for two years. I can't just break up with him like that. I'm not even sure I want to break up with him."

"If you stay with him, I promise you'll end up married, with three bratty Drews running around by the time you're twenty-five. Then you'll wished you'd listened to me."

"Don't worry." I laughed. "I know what I'm doing."

Willow walked over and opened the door, and I heard Drew shouting, but Willow didn't back down. I stood behind the door, listening to Drew complain. She told Drew that I wasn't there and to go home. She lied so convincingly that she almost persuaded *me* that I wasn't there. Drew, however, wouldn't take no for an answer. He said he knew for a fact that I'd come to this house, because he'd followed me here. Willow called him crazy and threatened to call the cops if he didn't leave. Drew swore at her and made some threatening remarks. Finally, the door slammed shut. Willow ran over to the window, giggling, and I followed behind, using her body as cover. I peeked over her shoulder and through the shutters and saw Drew hopping into his truck and then speeding off. Tipsy, we both laughed.

"What a dork," Willow said.

"He doesn't own me."

"Forget men. Right, Dad?"

Gil laughed from behind the camera as he filmed us. Willow clasped my hand in her own and swung it up and down. I turned and looked up at her. She had to be seven inches taller than me and ten times more beautiful. Her translucent blue eyes had returned to their natural state, and she looked ravishing. Was it the alcohol? Or had performing in front of the camera changed her mood? In my tipsy state, I laughed at her every silly utterance.

"Fuck all men. Right, Katie?"

"Yeah, fuck all men." I blushed, feeling like a badass for saying the *F* word.

"Not all men, mind you," Gil said from behind the camera.

"All but you, Daddy." Willow pulled me over to where her father stood filming and kissed the camera, leaving pink lipstick on the lens. It felt so ridiculous that it made me giggle.

"We're going to make you a star, bunny," Gil said.

Willow turned to me. "That's what he said when he first held me in his arms. That he was going to make me a star."

"It's true," he said. "I knew as soon as I laid eyes on her that she had star quality."

"Must have been the dramatic way I cried when I came out of the womb."

"And, if I remember correctly, you couldn't get out of there fast enough."

I laughed and grabbed my glass of wine before she pulled me upstairs. We were going to make ourselves beautiful for the party. She would do my makeup and hair, and I would help her with hers. Then we would do our nails. I couldn't pretend to know beauty, despite my mother being a hairstylist. I was a simple girl that boys thought attractive enough. Straight brown hair worn in a plain style, usually a ponytail. Strong white teeth with a subtle overbite. Slender body with small breasts and a boyish butt. Attractive in an average sort of way. The complete and utter opposite of my best friend, Willow.

I don't recall everything that happened at that party. Whether it was because I drank too much or because someone slipped one of those pills into my drink, pills that I had secured.

Bits and pieces come back to me now. I remember sitting next to Dakota, his arm around me. He tried to kiss me, and I let him, but that was as far as I would allow him to go. I remember later that night, while I lay sprawled, semiconscious, on the couch, hearing Julian and Dakota argue about something, their voices echoing throughout the house. I lifted myself up and listened to them and realized that they were going on about Willow. Dakota, drunk and with tears running down his cheeks, turned and saw me sitting up and staring at the two of them. Julian then shoved him and told him to chill out.

"Come with me, Katie. Let's get out of here," Dakota said.

I shook my head and glanced at my watch. It was 5:37 in the morning. As much as I liked Dakota, I didn't want to leave with him. More than anything, I wanted to go home and be with my family. The intensity of his sobbing troubled me. Why was he crying? It made me want to go home and cuddle up in my own bed and wake up and have a hearty breakfast with my mother and brother. No more drama or conflict.

Before I could process everything, Willow's father appeared in his bathrobe and stood between the two boys, his arms keeping them apart. Without his beaded glasses on, he appeared older, more pedestrian and plain looking. His gray hair stood up in every direction. He put his arm around Dakota's shoulder and pulled him off to the side, and the two of them exchanged heated words. I didn't want to know what they were talking about. I fell back on the couch and pretended to be asleep, not wanting them to see me. All I could hear was their muted conversation mixed in with Dakota's unintelligible sobs.

I lay on the couch until nearly seven that morning. Outside, it started to snow. Big spring flakes fell over the churning ocean. A girl staggered toward the door with a set of keys in hand. I remembered seeing her talking to Willow last night. She had ear and nose piercings and a crazy haircut: buzzed on one side and long and pink on the other. I glanced toward the ocean, realizing that I needed to get out of here as soon as possible. I ran up to her before she left.

"Can you please give me a ride home?"

"Where do you live?" the girl asked.

Her eyebrows rose when I told her, but to my relief, she agreed. Concerned that she might leave without me, I followed her outside, not bothering to collect my things. Whatever personal items I'd left in this house, I would either retrieve later or write off as gone. I sat in the passenger seat of her SUV, my arms wrapped around my shivering body until the heat kicked in.

"That was some wild party last night, huh," she said as she drove.

"Yeah," I said, staring mindlessly at the passing landscape.

"That X was crazy."

"I guess."

"You don't go to Chance Academy, do you?"

"No. I'm a friend of Willow's."

"That's cool," she said, her eyes on the road. "Wanna stop somewhere and get breakfast?"

"Thanks, but I really have to get home. My mother's expecting me."

"So is mine, but she drives me so crazy at times that I dread returning home." She drove in silence for a few minutes. "I think it's totally cool that you were at that party. I get so sick and tired of all these spoiled rich kids from Chance. People like you bring a real authenticity to our lives."

Authenticity? People like me? She sounded so patronizing that I wanted to slap her pretty face. But she'd agreed to give me a ride home, so I let it pass, thankful for her kindness.

"Did I talk to you at the party?" she asked.

"Honestly, I'm not sure. I can't remember much about last night."

"I know, right?" She laughed. "That *was* a wild one."

"*Wild* doesn't even begin to describe it."

"My name's Bella." She held her right hand over the seat divide. "Bella Case."

"Katie Eaves."

"Pleasure to meet you, Katie. I'm so glad we met."

"Me too." I felt slightly nauseous and wanted to get out of this car before I threw up.

"You're so down to earth. It's totally refreshing to meet a real Mainer."

"Yup, that's me. Refreshing."

"I'm going to Smith next fall. You should totally come out and visit me some time."

"Thanks. I'll consider it."

She pulled up to the entrance to my driveway. Despite the cold and snow, I told her she could let me off at the edge of the road. I didn't want her to see my crappy house and think any less of me.

"Thanks again," I said while holding the passenger door open.

"I hear you're good friends with Willow."

"Yeah."

"Be careful of that girl. She's totally crazy."

"Duly noted." And yet her words struck a chord with me.

"Hey, we should hang out sometime."

"Sounds like a plan," I said, shivering and eager to leave.

"Doing anything Saturday night?"

"Probably hanging with my boyfriend."

"Oh. Okay."

"Gotta run. It's freezing out here. Thanks again for the ride, Bella."

I sprinted up the driveway and then up the steps, pushed my way inside the house, rushed past my mother, who was sitting at the kitchen table, and collapsed into bed. Tomorrow would bring a fresh start. I'd get back to my routine. Start working out for the softball season. Finish all my homework. Call Drew and apologize for whatever I'd done. I fell asleep with these reassuring thoughts swirling around in my head.

And yet I couldn't get that troubling image of Dakota sobbing out of my mind. Or of him and Julian shouting at each other in the dark and then getting separated by Willow's father. I tossed and turned. My thoughts became agitated and interrupted my sleep. The question remained, What were they all arguing about?

ISLA

*I*SLA STOOD ON THE DECK OF THE SHEPHERD'S BAY COUNTRY CLUB, A drink in hand, admiring the expansive view. Although she had lived here most of her life, she often took the beauty of this landscape for granted. The lush first hole of the club's golf course meandered alongside the rocky coast. Waves crashed against the rocks and created a salty aerosol. Built five years ago to accommodate these wealthy newcomers, the club was on a parcel of land a quarter mile in from the road and possibly the most beautiful property in the area. Of course, the locals rarely if ever got to see this golf course, because of the security gate out front.

Servers dressed in black and white waltzed around, carrying trays of hors d'oeuvres and champagne. Nervous, she grabbed a flute in order to keep her hands busy. It felt odd being part of this affluent crowd. Clearly, she didn't belong here, evident by the other guests' expensively tailored clothes and glitzy jewelry. She should be one of the help instead of a guest. She even knew a few of the servers, and they winked or nodded at her as they passed. At events like this, socializing between staff and guests was strictly prohibited.

Everyone seemed happy and beautiful, conversing easily with one another about subjects far removed from Isla's own life. It made her nervous. She knew hardly anyone save for the few clients she happened to run into. All this happy discourse and lightness of being left her reeling with guilt. Were any of them thinking about Willow's or Katie's well-being? What about the body found in the old boat shed this morning? Hadn't they heard the news? It felt like a cognitive disconnect, standing on this magnificent deck with the great view of the ocean, knowing tragedy had happened in their small town.

Samantha appeared out of the crowd and approached her with arms raised. Everyone turned to look at the two of them as Samantha wrapped her arms around her. Isla could see the surprise on people's faces. A surprise almost bordering on envy. Everywhere she looked, Isla saw couples: husbands and wives, boyfriends and girlfriends, and the occasional gay or lesbian couple. She felt bad for the few LGBT people in town who happened to be out of the closet, and even worse for those who hadn't come out. Maybe with this sophisticated new class of people would come tolerance and acceptance.

"If it isn't my favorite stylist," Samantha announced, champagne in hand. And with one fell swoop, Isla's good mood shifted, and she felt reduced in stature. "I'm so glad you made it."

Beckett appeared beside his wife, and Isla could feel all eyes on her. "Hello, Isla."

"I'm honored to be here. Thanks so much for inviting me."

"Isn't this a lovely spot?" Samantha said, glancing out toward the ocean.

"Stunning, to be honest. I've never been here before, and I grew up in this town."

"The architect did a remarkable job incorporating the golf course into the natural landscape," Beckett said, surveying the manor as if he were king. "Of course, it all might change if this new property tax is passed."

"Let me introduce you to Laura," Samantha said, then led Isla by the hand through the crowd.

Isla smiled at all the faces staring at her as she let herself be pulled along. Clutching her purse and champagne, she waved at a few clients as she passed. They smiled back. Some laughed, which made her wonder if they were laughing with her or at her. They reached the other end of the deck, and all she could think about was the Briggs and James families. Would they have been here under better circumstances?

"Laura, this is Isla Eaves. She's only the best hairstylist in town. Possibly in all of Maine," Samantha announced.

Laura nodded appraisingly. "Is that so? I usually return to Manhattan every month to see my regular girl. I have to go back there on business, anyway."

"Well, save yourself the expense and the hassle. This is the girl you want to see from now on."

"I'll certainly keep that in mind," Laura said. "I'm so glad you're on our side on this tax issue, Isla. It's vital that we convince our citizens how important this is for all our benefit."

"How would you try to convince us local people?" Isla said.

Samantha looked confused. "I would say that the citizens of Shepherd's Bay would lose jobs and revenue if we weren't here. Look at all the economic activity created by this housing boom. Take a look at the money we've put into the town's coffers every year from the taxes we pay—and we don't even place any burden on the school system. A draconian tax on our properties would put a severe halt to development, costing jobs and progress."

"What about the town's crumbling schools? How would you address that issue, when most of your own children attend Chance Academy?"

"Isla! Whose side are you on, anyway?" Samantha said, laughing nervously.

"No, Samantha, these are very good questions that must be addressed," Laura said, assuring Samantha with a pat on her hand. "This is why Isla is such a valuable addition to our team. We need more people with her perspective in order to address these issues on the council."

"Right on, girl. Sly like a fox, then," Samantha said, elbowing Isla playfully.

Laura went into a long, extended spiel about why the tax was a bad idea. She mentioned personal responsibility and equity, fairness and freedom of choice. To Isla's ears, it sounded like a lot of intellectual rubbish. And yet in many ways she understood why this tax might cause a backlash in town that would reverberate for years to come. It was pure envy, retribution by one class against another, and sure to cause bitterness.

Beckett approached the candidate, a sign for Isla to step back. He waved his long arms in the air, and the crowd quieted down. Then he gave the candidate a long and impressive introduction, replete with all the Ivy degrees and high-salaried finance jobs she'd held in her previous life.

The candidate stepped forward, thanking Beckett for that wonderful introduction. She asked for a moment of silence for the families whose children were affected by the recent spate of violence in town. Isla lowered her head, wondering how many of these people knew that her own daughter was one of the victims.

Once the moment of silence passed, Laura began to speak. Isla backed her way through the crowd until she stood near the rear. The sun dappled lightly on her exposed shoulders, and she could feel the champagne going straight to her head. The only thing she'd eaten since lunch was a couple of those fancy scallops wrapped in bacon.

Near the front, she noticed a photographer snapping pictures. Isla stood on her toes and caught a look at him. He was a young guy with short black hair and was wearing a suit jacket with no tie. He had to work for the *Coastal Times*. She made a mental note to stay out of his way so she wouldn't appear in Sunday's society page.

"Can you believe this pretentious windbag? All they care about is fattening their own pockets at our expense," whispered the server standing next to her. She turned and saw Martha Brooks from her church. She had four boys, and she and her husband worked round the clock to make ends meet.

"Oh, hi, Martha," Isla said.

"Such bullshit." She took Isla's half-full glass of champagne and handed her a fresh one. "Here. Make it look like I'm busy. I'm not supposed to be talking to all the fancy guests, like you and Lady Windbag over there."

"I'm still the same person, Martha."

"Looks like you switched sides to me."

"Samantha McCallister invited me to this event, and she refers a lot of clients to my salon."

"It's pathetic, if you ask me. One of their own is found dead, and here they are, drinking champagne and slurping down oysters like they're M&M's." The woman appraised her. "Doesn't being here make you feel dirty?"

"Does it make *you?*"

The woman appeared taken aback. "What's that supposed to mean?"

"You're profiting from this fund-raiser just as much as I am. Two kids are missing, and yet you still show up for work every day in order to provide for your family."

"That's different."

"Really, Martha? Please inform me how it's different."

"This is my job. And those two missing kids are from the rich part of town."

"Kids are kids no matter if they're from the rich neighborhood or poor townies," Isla said. "And don't forget that my Katie went missing, as well."

"None of this surprises me, you taking sides with these beauts. Can't really blame you, either, after seeing Ray driving around town in that brand-new truck of his."

"First off, it's a used truck. And last I checked, people are still allowed to buy new vehicles in this country."

"From running a seaweed business?" She laughed. "Please."

"You should be careful about what you say, Martha."

"Then I'll say this. How much do you know about Chip Hicks?"

"The girls' softball coach?"

"And 'beloved' social studies teacher." She made quotation marks with her fingers.

"What's to know? The girls love Coach Hicks."

"Yeah, that's what I heard. Go ask Emily Benson about how much he loves girls. And haven't you ever wondered why such a good-looking guy like that never married?"

Isla watched the woman storm off with her empty tray of champagne glasses. Who was Emily Benson? Was she from the Benson family who owned the convenience store on the corner of Edwards and Pine?

The candidate running for council ended her speech, and thunderous applause went up. Isla tepidly clapped her wrist, her left hand gripping the glass. She wondered how long she'd have to stay at this function.

Some of her clients came over and thanked her profusely for the great job she did on their hair. Despite their status in life, she could tell they meant it. They complimented her on her outfit, especially the way she'd arranged her hair into that messy-bun style. Would she do that for them sometime? "Of course," she responded. They invited her to sit with them, and she did, and she found herself enjoying all the attention and their company.

Did these women actually like her? Her self-esteem had been so beaten down in the past few years that she found it hard to believe that people might find her interesting and attractive. She blamed Ray for much of that. He'd made her continually question her self-worth. The more she conversed with these people, the more she realized that they shared many of the same problems in life: kids, marriage, friendships. In the greater scheme of things, they weren't all that different from her. Sure, these women had gone to fancy colleges, had careers and money. If not for that predatory college professor, she might have ended up just like them.

And yet she wouldn't trade her life for any of what they had.

Bolstered by the champagne, she regaled them with stories about growing up in this town, and they laughed and egged her on. Should she feel guilty about enjoying herself? She'd get back to her normal routine once she returned home. Would tend to Katie and Raisin. She thought herself a good mother and wife. Ray paid her so little attention that she now reveled in her minor celebrity at this function. She realized that she had so much to offer the world, and possibly someone could love and appreciate her for her real self. All these women looked gorgeous. Maybe they looked at her the same way.

Gina Case stole her away from the crowd and pulled her aside. Isla had styled her hair just a few days ago, and Gina looked lovelier than ever, dressed in a strapless white summer dress. Her long blond hair framed her chiseled cheeks perfectly, accentuating her sea-green eyes.

"Having fun, Isla?"

"More than I care to admit."

"How's your daughter doing?" Gina was the first person at the party to ask about Katie, and it momentarily stunned Isla.

"Better. Thank you for asking."

"Assuming the body found today is not Willow Briggs, I'd say your daughter has some remembering to do."

"She's trying. The doctors said it's caused by her concussion."

Gina shifted her stance. "I've been watching you, Isla. It's a bit embarrassing, to tell you the truth."

"Excuse me?"

"You're like a novelty to these women. A monkey dancing for spare change. Can't you see that they're using you?"

"I appreciate your business, Gina, but I think you're out of line."

"Please, Isla. I really like and respect you. I grew up in a scrappy town like this in West Virginia and know what it's like to struggle. That's why I left."

Isla sipped her champagne for lack of anything else to do.

"Better take it easy on the bubbly, girl. If you have to take a cab home, it might be tough in the morning explaining to security that you left your rusty minivan in the parking lot. Besides, they might tow it away before it even comes to that."

Why was this woman being so mean to her?

Gina went on. "Yeah, I know what you're thinking. That I'm full of it."

"You said it, not me."

"This is all such bullshit, and you know it. Kids are missing—dying, in fact—and schools in this town are going to hell, and here we are drinking champagne and having a grand old time because we want to hold on to our wealth."

"Your wealth, not mine. I don't have much wealth to speak of."

"We all have wealth, Isla, and not all of it is about money."

Isla looked for an escape route, someone to pull her away from this awkward conversation.

"That's all I'm saying. You should be standing up for your community," Gina added.

"I have a business to run, Gina. A family to support. I came to this fund-raiser because Samantha invited me. So if you don't mind, I don't need to stand here and listen to you lecture me about what I'm supposed to do."

"We *should* be paying more, that's all I'm saying. My husband makes good money, and we can afford to pay this tax, especially when we spend all that money to send our kids to Chance Academy. We're privileged."

"Then why are you here?"

Gina looked embarrassed. "My husband begged me to come to this event with him. Because we're both members of the club. But we're both going to vote for someone who supports the tax."

"Good for you, then. I'm so glad you can afford it and not have to worry about your family's finances."

"I'm sorry, Isla. I didn't mean to offend you."

"No, I appreciate your brutal honesty. You've made yourself perfectly clear."

"Please don't say anything to Samantha about our conversation."

"I would never betray your confidence."

Thank you." Gina paused for a few seconds. "You do know that she allows Julian to get away with murder, right?"

"Come again?"

Gina looked to her left and then right. "I have to be very discreet while I'm here."

"You think Julian murdered those kids?"

"It was a figure of speech."

Isla couldn't tell whether she was being sarcastic or not.

"Julian is a spoiled brat who gets whatever he wants. I saw him kissing Willow one afternoon, when we were having dinner over at the McCallisters'."

"Every male in town under the age of eighteen would love to kiss Willow Briggs. Maybe even those over that age, too."

"Julian's different. I can't quite put my finger on it."

"What are you implying?"

Gina crossed her arms and looked around to make sure no one could hear her. "Rumor has it that he got kicked out of his pricey prep school in Manhattan for selling drugs and for assaulting another student."

"So you think Julian might have something to do with my daughter's attack and the disappearance of these two other kids?"

"I understand your daughter is good friends with Willow. Have you heard about the wild parties the Briggses are known to throw? It's why I never let my Bella attend them."

"Katie told me she and Willow had sleepovers . . . watching movies and playing music."

"Sleepovers? Now there's a laugh. Most everyone on Harper's Point knows about the parties, especially the McCallisters. I know you're fond of Samantha, and that she's helped you build your business, but be careful of her. She'll turn on you in a heartbeat if she suspects you're not being loyal to her."

"What about the Briggses?"

"Don't get me going on that crazy couple. Bella put up a big fight when I refused to sign those waiver forms and let her be a part of that reality show. Luckily, she'll be off to college next year and away from all this insanity."

My mood soured at hearing this, and before I could reply, I heard a familiar woman's voice calling out to us. I turned and saw Samantha approaching with a glass of champagne in hand. Did I detect a look of suspicion on her face? It alarmed me. It made me feel guilty for talking behind her back.

"What are you two girls whispering about over here?" she said, a big smile on her face. A string quartet started to play Mozart on the far end of the deck.

"The usual girl stuff," Gina said, smiling stiffly.

"Tell me, tell me. I love gossipy girl stuff."

Gina glanced at Isla with suspicion in her eyes.

"We were just talking about the latest hair trends and what might work on her," Isla said, bailing out Gina. She took a few strands of Gina's hair between her fingers. "I was thinking something more spiked and jangly, with sharp lines and an edgy look. Maybe a razor cut."

"Ooh, that sounds amazing," Samantha said, clapping excitedly. "Maybe I'll try something like that next time."

Gina was about to say something when Isla heard banging and a loud commotion coming from the opposite end of the deck. The quartet stopped playing as heads turned to see what was happening. A woman screamed and swung her arms to keep people away. Isla pushed through the crowd. By the time she reached the third row of the chairs that had just been set up for listeners, she could see the woman responsible for the ruckus: Jessica James.

"Don't put your filthy hands on me," she shouted at the security guard assigned to escort her out. She scanned the crowd, her eyes glossy from crying. "Look at you all. You people make me sick. The police just discovered my baby's body in a shed, and all you can think to do is have a big party and drink champagne and congratulate yourselves on how incredibly fortunate you are."

She went on. "Is some stupid tax proposal really worth it?" The security kid tried to grab her elbow, but she snapped at him. "He was my only child, and now he's gone. Lost too soon. And now Willow Briggs is missing, too, and all you people can do is stand around and tell yourselves how wonderful life is. Well, my beautiful baby's dead, so I think you all suck to the high heavens." The security kid reached for her arm again, but this time she turned and left of her own accord.

The crowd buzzed, and the mood changed almost instantly. Samantha waltzed around the deck, trying to bring back the cheer, but the appearance of Jessica James had soured everyone's mood. She ordered the quartet to resume playing, only when they did, their music sounded like a sad dirge to Isla's ears. After the woman's outburst, Isla felt sick to her stomach and wanted to leave this party as soon as possible. But judging by the look on Samantha's face, she knew she couldn't leave just yet. She'd have to stay and bide her time until the end. Not a second sooner if she hoped to keep her salon open and profitable. She thought of Raisin and Katie, and it helped her put on a happy face, despite the tragedy of Dakota James and Willow Briggs. And, more importantly, Katie.

She wanted to cry because of all that had happened. Gina's words echoed in her ears, as did the words of Jessica James: *Lost too soon.*

KARL

An emergency check at town hall had revealed to him that the boat shed was owned by Beckett and Samantha McCallister. Now, that was an interesting development. Did it mean anything? Had the location of Dakota James's body been merely random?

It was a Sunday morning, and he needed to work. Sunday mornings had been the worst time for him since he'd become a bachelor again, although with time they'd become more bearable. He remembered the Sundays when he could lounge in bed, his arm draped over his wife's soft body. Then coffee, pancakes, and eggs, all of which he would whip up for his little family. His daughter would be in her pajamas, watching cartoons and giggling. Winters were the best time, when the fireplace roared while snow accumulated on the ground, the temperature hovering in the single digits. He loved many aspects of his old life and missed it more than he knew. Would he ever find anything resembling that tranquility again? Maybe his old life looked better in hindsight. Had he forgotten all the turmoil and bitterness that had led to his wife leaving him?

Right now he needed answers. He pressed the McCallisters' doorbell and waited for someone to come to the door. Someone had to be home. All three cars sat parked in the garage. Suddenly the door opened, and a stylish-looking woman appeared before him, dressed in an expensive silk bathrobe.

"Can I help you, Officer? There's nothing wrong, is there?"

"Morning, ma'am." Something wrong? Had she been living with her head in the sand? Her house sat next door to the Briggses' home. The woman's obliviousness to everything going on in town nearly made him laugh. "You must have heard that we found a body yesterday."

"Yes, unfortunately, I did hear that. Someone at the club last night said they found the body of Dakota James. Such a tragedy."

"You were at the club when you heard this news last night?"

"Yes, one of the members told me while we were holding a fund-raiser for Laura Milton. She's running for town council."

"Excuse me for asking, Mrs. McCallister, but we didn't release the victim's name to the public. How could someone at your club have known about that?"

She reached back and began to massage her neck. Her robe opened slightly, giving him a peekaboo view of her cleavage. It looked to him as if she'd gone through enhancement surgery. He guessed her age to be midforties, but he wouldn't have been surprised if she was over fifty. Women today took much better care of themselves than when he was growing up, especially these women with lots of money to burn. He remembered the days when fifty-year-old women in this town looked old and haggard, life being much harder back then.

"Mrs. McCallister?"

"Oh, right. It was very uncomfortable, Officer. Not the time or place."

"Not the time or place for what?"

"Jessica James made an appearance at our fund-raiser last night. She was visibly upset and looked like she'd been drinking. It was all we could do to escort the poor woman off the premises."

"Why was she there?"

"Really, I feel terrible for her, I do. But she had no right to chastise us for holding a fund-raiser, especially at our own club. This event had been planned many months ago."

"I still don't understand why she was there."

"She said she couldn't understand how we could be enjoying ourselves, drinking and socializing, after her son's body was discovered. But it wasn't like that at all. We were there for a specific reason. A good reason."

"To prevent that proposed tax hike from happening?"

"No, to help get Laura Milton elected to the town council."

"So that she'd vote against the proposed tax hike?"

"Well, that and other things. Laura went to Harvard and worked as a corporate CFO in Manhattan. She's more than qualified to be a town councillor, and she's certainly not a one-issue candidate." She placed her hand to her sternum. "Our hearts were broken over the discovery of Dakota James. We even observed a moment of silence for those kids. Just because we threw a fund-raiser for Laura doesn't make us uncaring monsters."

"I never said you were."

"And this was an inclusive event, open to all citizens and not just the ones from Harper's Point. Do you know Isla Eaves? She was there last night. She's one of the locals, like you."

"Yes, I know her."

"She's an amazing person and a very talented hairstylist."

"The reason I came here is to ask you about the boat shed you own on the northern side of the cove. We found Dakota James's body inside it."

"I don't know what to tell you, Officer. To be honest, I didn't even know we owned it. Beckett purchased a number of investment properties when we first moved here, with the idea to renovate them."

"He didn't mention that to you?"

"No, I didn't," Beckett said, appearing behind her, "because I didn't even know it myself. There's a lot of those old boat sheds along the north shore, and I bought up more than a few of them."

"Is it normal not to lock it?"

"There's nothing of any real worth in that old shed. Besides, I haven't been in it in over a year, so I wouldn't really know."

"Are you two close to Jessica James?"

"She is a divorcée and frequents the club on occasion, but otherwise we rarely socialize with her," Samantha said.

"Was your son friendly with Dakota?"

Samantha looked up at her husband before returning her gaze to Karl.

"The two boys were not close, despite hanging out in the same circles," Beckett said.

"If you're implying that Julian had anything to do with his murder, then you're way off base," Samantha said.

"I wasn't implying anything like that, Mrs. McCallister," Karl lied. "What about Willow Briggs? I heard a rumor that the two boys were romantically involved with her."

"It's true, they had an argument over Willow," said Beckett. "This is what teenage boys do. Not like we never fought over a girl when we were that age."

I wish I'd fought harder over one in particular. "And yet only Julian is still here." Karl regretted saying that as soon as it left his lips.

"I think we're done with this interview," Beckett said. "Please refer all other questions to our attorney."

The door slammed in his face. At least he had more answers than when he'd shown up. He had to get Katie to tell him what she knew. For whatever reason, he didn't completely believe this story of hers that she couldn't remember anything from her ordeal. It seemed too convenient. He needed to press her. Make her aware of the serious consequences of not telling the truth.

He drove over to the Eaveses' house to ask for permission to speak to Katie. Isla answered the door. She looked much different than she had last night, when she'd been all made up and dressed to kill. He liked her much better this way, natural and true to form, rather than the way she looked when she was trying to imitate all the gussied-up women on the other side of town, most of whom were desperately trying to look younger.

Standing in front of him, she seemed to know almost instinctively that he'd come here to see Katie. He asked for permission but really didn't need to. With a simple nod of her head, she led him down to Katie's room. Raisin waved to him from the couch as he passed.

"Remember, she's sensitive to light," Isla whispered.

"No problem. I can work in the dark. How was the party last night?" he asked.

"Fund-raiser, you mean."

"Maybe not so much fun?"

She looked at him. "You heard what happened?"

"I did. Must have been quite uncomfortable."

"More than you know."

"Do you think you and I can have coffee soon and talk about some things?"

"Not sure that's a good idea, Karl."

"It's about the case."

"I don't know what else I have to offer."

"I think you have a lot to offer. You seem to be the most popular woman in Shepherd's Bay these days." He allowed the subtlest of smiles to cross his lips. "Why else would you be invited to the biggest fund-raiser in town?"

"Okay, I'll contact you."

"Sooner than later, I hope."

"Yes, soon."

She opened the door to her daughter's room and he made his way inside. Katie lay smothered in blankets, facing the opposite wall. Her body rose and fell with her breathing. He moved to the side of the bed and knelt next to the mattress so that her back faced him. Something told him that the girl was not asleep, but wide awake and avoiding his inquiry. He glanced up at Isla, who stood in the lit doorway with her arms crossed. Gently tapping Katie's shoulder, he called out her name. After no response, he did it again.

"Leave me alone."

"Come on, Katie. I know you're in there."

"Go away."

"I'm not going anywhere until you talk to me."

She turned so that her blanket-covered face appeared to him.

"Attagirl. I know you can do it."

"Can you be quick? I don't feel so well."

"Of course."

"Can you ask my mom to leave the room?"

He turned to Isla. "Would you mind? It should only take a few minutes."

Isla stood unmoving for a few seconds, her face tight and her body conveying unease. Then she stepped back and shut the door, and the room fell into darkness. He waited for his eyes to adjust before speaking.

"You must know by now that it was Dakota's body they found."

She nodded and, in doing so, caused a tear to fall down her cheek.

"Do you know what happened to him?"

"No."

"How well did you know him?"

"He hung out in the same circles as Willow."

"Were they dating?"

"Don't know."

"Don't know or don't remember?"

She shrugged ever so subtly.

"You need to be truthful with me, Katie."

"I'm trying. Honest."

"You need to try harder, or else we can do this down at the station."

"Nooo."

"Then don't force my hand."

"I'm doing my best. What more can I tell you?"

He paused to let the moment linger. "I'm getting irritated. I really don't think you are doing your best."

"You don't know that."

"I think I do," he said. "How about you and Dakota?"

"What about us?"

"Were you seeing him?"

She stayed silent for a moment. "We kissed once."

"He kissed you?"

"Does it matter who kissed who?"

"Did you tell your parents about the kiss or the wild parties you attended?"

"What do you think?" She wiped her eyes. "Please, don't say anything to my mother or Drew about it. I'm begging you."

"I'll take that as a no."

"How did you find out about those parties?"

"It's my job. Besides, your mom is going to find out about them eventually."

"Please don't tell her just yet."

"I'm assuming alcohol was involved, but were there drugs?"

"Willow's parents wanted to make sure everyone stayed on the grounds if they drank. That's the only way they would allow her to host those parties."

"But were there drugs?"

"I don't know. I think. Maybe." She sniffed back her tears.

"What do you mean, you think? Either there was or there wasn't."

"I can't remember for sure. It's possible."

He sighed long and loud so she could hear his displeasure. "Where did they come from?"

"I just told you, I don't know. I'm no drug user."

"Was Julian at these parties? And if so, was Willow romantically involved with him?"

"Maybe. I don't know. Every boy wanted to be with Willow. How would I know about all this?"

"You are her best friend."

"Only at our school. She has all those Chance Academy friends, too."

"We read some of your texts. In them, you call her your BFF more than once."

"Yes, but she didn't tell me everything that happened in her life. I could tell she hid a lot of things from me."

"You're not being very cooperative, Katie, considering that your friend might still be out there and alive."

"Could you please go now? My head is killing me."

She turned defiantly in the opposite direction. He could hear her crying softly as he stood to leave. There was no doubt in his mind that she knew more than she was letting on, and that she'd been using her concussion diagnosis as a convenient excuse. But what did she know? He now felt certain that those kids had procured and used drugs. The question was, Who had supplied them? And had Katie used them, as well?

KATIE

*I*T'S OBVIOUS THAT THIS POLICE OFFICER KNOWS THAT I'M EVADING HIS questions. Of course he doesn't know everything that happened, or he wouldn't keep badgering me. I can't claim a head injury forever, despite not knowing what happened to Willow. It's like my mind doesn't want me to know. Maybe my mind has been blocking my memory for a reason. Does that mean she's dead?

The cop knows a lot more than he's letting on. Like that we held wild parties and that drugs were involved. I couldn't tell him that I'd set up the purchase of those Mollies. What would my mother think if she knew this? It would freak her out. As for the parties, she'll be shocked when she finds out her good little girl lied to her. What will Drew think when he learns that I kissed Dakota James, the missing boy? The *dead* boy.

I don't want to see or speak to anyone. I feel nauseous and irritable all the time. Drew came by this morning, but I told my mother not to let him in. Coach Hicks came by, as well, and I also refused to see him. I cannot deal with anyone in my fragile state. It's bad enough that I have to talk to that stupid cop, who so obviously has eyes for my mother. He thinks I don't see it. He doesn't really care about me. He comes over here to see *her*. Besides, I have to retrace my steps and remember what happened to Willow. And what happened that night. I know it's somewhere in my memory.

Five days had passed, and I'd put that disastrous party in the rearview mirror. I'd rededicated myself to school, softball, and being with Drew. In June he would graduate and start lobster fishing for a living. I felt safe and at ease with him, if not totally convinced that we should be together till death do us part.

Willow acted like nothing had happened. She chatted with me nonstop and walked alongside me between classes. I couldn't avoid her even if I tried, and believe me, I tried. But the thing about Willow was she sucked you in. She was the kind of girl who made you feel like the most important person in the world when she focused all her attention on you. And she was funny in the most irreverent and wicked sort of way. She made me laugh even when I tried not to. She made me want to be her friend even as I tried mightily to resist her charms.

Other girls tried to curry favor with her, only to be ignored or ridiculed. Then she would loop her arm through mine as we walked to the cafeteria and gossiped relentlessly. Other girls stared enviously at me. Boys openly drooled at Willow without embarrassment, and I imagined I garnered some looks simply by my association with her. I felt like a queen. No, I felt like the queen's personal assistant, carrying her dress as she passed down the aisle.

It pissed Drew off when he saw me with Willow. So I excused myself from her company at times to be with him. I knew she despised Drew. She told me many times that I could do so much better than him. That I was a special person who deserved someone who treated me with decency and respect. She never believed me when I told her that Drew was a good guy, if a bit simple. "You don't want to end up with that small-town loser, Katie," she kept warning me.

"How many times do I have to tell you, Katie? Willow's bad news," Drew repeated for the thousandth time as we stood in the hallway in between classes one day.

"You don't know her, Drew. She's really a good person."

"She's a stuck-up bitch. Besides, I barely get to see you these days."

"It's a busy time for me right now, with school and softball."

"But I'll be graduating soon. I want to spend more time with you."

"There'll be plenty of time to hang out this summer. You need to give me my space."

"She's crazy, I'm telling you. Don't get sucked in by her, or you'll end up regretting it."

"I need to get to class now," I said, walking away from him. "I'll see you later, Drew."

His utter and constant disdain for Willow made me see Drew in a new light. It bothered me that he would try to dictate who I could and could not be friends with. Despite Willow's many issues, his attitude toward her made me want to openly defy him. He didn't own me. I wanted to tell him to mind his own business. I never dictated who he could or could not be friends with, and many of his own friends were way worse than Willow: drunks, losers, potheads, and low-life grease monkeys who spent half their lives under a hood. Drew's domineering manner drew me closer to Willow, even though in my gut something was telling me that I should keep my distance from her, and that Drew was right in his assessment of her character.

But listening to one's gut and orbiting her planetary system seemed like two entirely different things. Her personality felt like the weaker gravity on the moon. Everything came easy to her. Or at least it seemed that way to me. She could sing and dance and play piano effortlessly. Her grades weren't the best, but then again, she never bothered to study. And although she ignored and privately mocked most of the other kids at our school, a few even continued to suck up to her, to try to be her friend.

I headed to my next class. Five days since that disastrous party, and I wanted desperately to try to put that night behind me. I had vowed not to drink or buy drugs for others. A wave of guilt hung over me and refused to lessen its grip.

I thought I could distance myself from Willow. But then softball practice started and everything changed and all the lines got redrawn. The start of softball season was typically a happy occasion for us Shepherd's Bay players. It signaled the start of spring. It meant sunshine and grass, although the reality of a Maine spring was quite the opposite. The first four weeks of practice usually got held in the gym because of the messy fields and the accumulation of ice and snow.

Shepherd's Bay High had never been a powerhouse in the sport. We muddled along, usually in the middle of the pack, but we had fun. Coach Hicks worked us hard and got the most out of our scrappy teams. Until that first day we all caught sight of Willow in the gym. I stood in disbelief as I watched her warm up. We all did. The way she zipped the ball underhanded through the air drew gasps from the girls standing nearby. It sounded like a gun going off every time the ball exploded in the catcher's mitt. Then during drills she goofed off, and Coach Hicks blew his whistle and called her out on it. He did this time after time that week. Willow would scowl during the water breaks and call him all kinds of terrible names as sweat dripped down her face. She threatened to quit the team because of Coach Hicks, and it was up to me to calm her down and convince her to tough it out.

"Don't worry. I won't quit," she told me during one practice.

"He's only doing it to make us a better team," I replied.

"I don't need to be abused to be a better player. Besides, I hate softball."

"Then why do you play?" I asked.

"To be with you, Katie."

It soon became obvious that the other girls on the team resented Willow for her bad work habits, and yet she couldn't care less what the others thought of her. Nor did she notice that they were giving her the cold shoulder and, in turn, giving it to me, as well. I hadn't chosen this. In fact, I'd always had good relations with my teammates. But not this year. All that changed when she befriended me. Willow barely left my side during these practices, and thus my fate became sealed.

But no one could deny Willow's athletic talent. She crushed every ball into the net as the sound of ball hitting aluminum echoed in the gym. Ball after ball she struck with a ferocity that frightened me. I wondered if she might kill an opposing pitcher with those vicious line drives. Then she'd take the mound and proceed to strike out every batter she faced. Blazing fastballs that whirred past like a ghost pitch. Curveballs that turned girls' knees into jelly. She smiled devilishly when I stepped up to the plate during one practice. Then she proceeded to fire three fastballs past me. I swung at them all, a complete guessing game, each swing occurring well after the ball had reached the catcher's mitt.

I couldn't believe she hated softball. I loved it. If only I had half her talent.

It soon became obvious that our team had a real chance of winning states this year with Willow powering us. I knew the other girls didn't like her and, in fact, resented her for taking the starting pitching job away from senior Emma Jeffries. But Coach Hicks always said he planned on playing the best, and Willow by far was our best player. As much as they resented her, the girls also recognized her talent and so were of two minds about Willow. They disliked her, but they would also ride on her coattails if it meant winning a state championship. Then again, they had no other choice if they planned on remaining on the team.

"What are you doing this weekend?" Willow asked after our Friday practice.

"Drew and I are going to a movie tonight."

"Oh." She seemed disappointed.

"What about you?"

"Probably hanging out with Dakota."

Was she purposely trying to piss me off by mentioning Dakota's name? It worked, because the sound of his name made me slightly jealous. But why should it when I had Drew?

"Maybe we could hang out this weekend," she said, sounding like a sad, lonely kid.

"I have tons of homework to catch up on."

"I really don't want to be by myself all weekend."

"I also might have to babysit my little brother."

"I still can't get over that dog that follows him around. I wish I could go over there and hug the snot out of him."

"My mother loses it when people come up and try to pet Scout. She reads them the riot act every time."

"Because your brother could die if he doesn't get his medicine?"

"Yes, but only if Scout alerts us that his glucose levels are off."

"That really sucks for your poor brother."

"It's all he's ever known," I said. "And he's very fortunate that the people in our community donated all that money to buy him a service dog. I'm not sure how we would have gotten Scout without them."

"Please call me if you get any free time, Katie." She walked toward her car. "I could really use a friend."

"I'll see how things turn out," I said. "You be sure and take care of that big arm of yours."

She turned and shot me a smile that could have landed her on *Glamour* magazine. Then she curved her right arm into a muscle and kissed it.

My father comes in and sits next to me on the bed. Although I'm facing away from him, I can always sense my father's presence in a room. His odor is as unmistakable as it is pleasurable. As a young girl, I loved that particular smell, and before long my father and his scent became interchangeable.

"How you doing, hon?"

"I'm okay." I wasn't, but I knew he didn't like to hear bad news, so I never gave it to him.

"How's the noggin?"

I lift my hand out of the blanket and make a so-so gesture.

"Can I do anything for you?"

"Can you sit with me for a bit? You don't have to say anything."

"Sure thing, kiddo."

His smell comforts me. It took me years to put two and two together and figure out what that scent was from. It came from the oils that he used to paint his portraits and landscapes. It clung to his skin and became a part of his being, even when he didn't paint every day. Oftentimes I'd see him in that art studio, moving paints around or combining them together, sometimes dipping a stained finger in a paint to gauge the color.

I looked past my father's many transgressions because I believed he possessed an artistic temperament. He was born a free spirit and couldn't be reined in or put into a box. It seemed ironic because I was nothing like him. More like my mother in that regard. An old soul, she jokingly called me. But in Shepherd's Bay, a grown man pursuing art was not looked upon kindly, especially if he couldn't support his family. That didn't mean I forgave him for the way he treated my mother. Because he should have never gotten married or had kids in the first place, not that it mattered now.

Despite the lock on his outdoor studio, I still managed to sneak in there from time to time and witness the startling graphic nudes he painted. As a young girl, I'd often wander out there on a cold winter's night and peer through one of the studio windows. He couldn't see me, because of the dark. Only on occasion would I actually see him putting paint to canvas. Most of the time he'd be sitting there, drinking beer or smoking pot, while the wood stove glowed in the corner.

Once, when I was fourteen, my friend's mother dropped us off downtown one Saturday afternoon so we could window-shop and then see a movie. We were walking around when I saw my father stumble drunkenly out of a fishermen's bar with a woman by his side. He put his long arm around her, and the two of them staggered down a side street, laughing, with not a care in the world. Thankfully, he didn't see me. Nor did my friend see my father, which would have totally humiliated me, because the two of us went to the same church.

I want the best for my parents. They shouldn't be married, but I know why they stay together. I've heard it said that it's better to be from a broken family than in one. Not entirely sure about that. Love, in my view, is rarely a monolith, something unto itself. It feels like it's built onto other things, so much so that to pull one block out of the tower to which it belongs could make everything come crashing down. It's the only reason my mother stays with him.

These are the things I think about as I fall asleep with his scent filling my nostrils. Not about Willow or Dakota James or the fact that I am the one who purchased drugs and drank alcohol to fit in. I don't think about my poor, overworked mother. Or about my glucose-challenged brother or my brain-injured grandfather. I think only of my reckless, irresponsible father, whom I can never stop loving, no matter how bad he treats us.

My phone dings, telling me I have a text message.

I raise my head up in that darkened room and notice that my dad is not there. What time is it? I don't even know what day it is. A subtle throbbing loops in my brain, as if someone is playing bongo drums on the right and left hemispheres.

Someone has sent me a text message. I open it and read what it says.

Katie, it's me, Willow. Please, I really need your help! But whatever you do, Do. Not. Call. The. Cops! Or I'll end up dead! It's too dangerous for you to contact me right now. I'll get in touch with you when the time is right.

Wait to hear from me.

Luv,

Willow

ISLA

MYRNA BENSON SLAMMED THE TRAILER DOOR IN HER FACE AFTER their brief, terse discussion. No, Emily would not care to speak to her, even if Myrna did happen to know where Emily was, which she didn't. Isla didn't push the matter. Instead, she sped away from the trailer park and headed home.

She drove toward the water, to where the well-to-do lived. Pine trees and pastures passed her on both sides. Driving tended to clear her mind and allow her to think about everything going on in her life. Myrna Benson's angry demeanor lent credibility to Martha's claim that Coach Hicks had possibly done something inappropriate to Emily.

She now remembered Emily. She'd been a senior when Katie had first started as a freshman. Both girls had been involved in the school's musical productions. Although pretty, Emily had always looked frail and vulnerable, as if something bad had happened to her that caused her much anguish. Isla understood that look, because it had once belonged to her. At one time, she had gazed at that same anguished face every day in her bathroom mirror.

The large homes suddenly appeared, and she slowed down as she made her way into the neighborhood. The nearer she got to the water, the bigger the houses became. Unlike her own neighborhood, all the lawns burst with vivid greenery, the landscaping was manicured, and the shrubs were all perfectly trimmed. Sealed driveways had regulation basketball hoops made of the clearest Plexiglas. Every house had luxury cars sitting in the driveway. Then she turned onto the street where the Briggses and the McCallisters lived, and everything appeared even larger and more impressive. Harper's Point at its finest.

A wedge of ocean appeared between the massive homes. She cruised at low speed while taking everything in. Down a ways, she could see the Briggses' residence, the biggest one on the block. She passed the McCallisters' place, close enough to get a peek at the Briggses' private beach. She slowed down to get a better look.

What she hadn't noticed at first glance, to her chagrin, was the Briggses standing in their driveway. Were they arguing? Felicia turned, and their eyes briefly met, and Isla felt something resembling shame course through her veins. Did they believe she was spying on them? She had no valid reason to be driving through Harper's Point. Should she speed off or acknowledge them? Gil looked horrible, as if he'd aged a decade in the past few weeks. Like a fool, she raced away, eager to get out of there.

Just as she arrived home, an anonymous email appeared on her phone. She didn't recognize the address but bristled at the subject line: *Information about Chip Hicks*. Had Martha Brooks sent this? She made her way inside and sat at the kitchen table. Then she opened the attached file.

Someone had sent her confidential documents about the accusation of sexual misconduct against Chip Hicks. The student's name had been blacked out, but she deduced from all that she knew that Emily Benson was the accuser. She read the documents and learned that the charges, while serious, had never been substantiated and had therefore been dropped. The teachers' union had gotten involved and had defended Hicks. Hicks and his union rep had requested a private meeting with the superintendent, and it appeared that the charges had been dismissed soon after. That didn't mean the sexual misconduct hadn't happened. It simply meant that the school department hadn't had enough evidence to file charges and release Hicks from his contract. What had he said in that meeting? Had he proclaimed his innocence? Had he threatened to sue the school district?

Had he been inappropriate with Emily Benson?

The secret charges against Hicks alarmed her, especially now that one boy was dead and Willow was missing and her own daughter was still in recovery. But if Hicks had been involved in these crimes, what was his connection to Dakota James? She knew that both Willow and Katie sat in his advanced US history class, and both of them played on his softball team. It alarmed her to think that Katie would be enrolled in his class next year and would also be playing on his softball team. Of course, neither of those would happen now that she had caught wind of this accusation. Although he was presumed innocent, she needed to put her daughter's safety first.

Maybe that was why Hicks had never married: he preferred young girls.

Her mother-in-law joined her at the kitchen table, and so she put her phone away. Her father, who sat quietly in the living room, got up out of his chair and joined them. Sometimes he sat so quietly that she forgot he was even there, and that made her sad. She patted his wrinkled hand, and he smiled at her, looking not at all sick. But she knew this was wishful thinking. His brain was so ravaged from the disease that she knew he'd never be his same old self.

"Can I make coffee for everyone?" Isla asked.

"A cup of coffee would be nice," her father said.

"Maybe a small cup for me," her mother-in-law said. "I saw Ray today. He stopped by the house earlier in the day."

"Is that right? Just to say hello?"

She laughed. "You know my Raymond. He doesn't ever call on me unless he needs something—until today."

"Oh?"

"He actually paid me back the money I lent him."

"Is that so? I had no idea he even borrowed money from you."

"Said it had something to do with this new business he's getting off the ground. Says he wants to do better by you and the kids. Maybe he really means it this time and is changing his ways."

"Selling seaweed, Ma?"

"I've heard of crazier businesses. How about that guy who invented those little sticky notes?"

"True."

"Noticed he bought himself a new truck, too. Saw him driving around town with that lowlife Bugger Walsh." She pronounced it "Buggah," like everyone else in town.

"Bugger Walsh? I don't like the sound of that."

"His father was a no-good bum, too. Served time in prison for writing bad checks."

"Lucky Walsh," her father blurted out. "I remember he got arrested for running cigarettes down from Canada. Used to sell them around town out of the back of his truck."

"You remember that, Dad?"

"Like it was yesterday," he said. "You think I'm a pea brain, Nora?"

Isla heard her cell phone go off. She glanced at the caller ID and saw that it was Felicia Briggs. Was she calling to pay for the haircut?

"Can you come over tonight?" Felicia sobbed when Isla picked up.

"But I just gave you a cut, Felicia."

"I really could use a wash and blow-dry. I'd be forever grateful."

"I'll try, but I can't guarantee anything. I'll need to get a babysitter."

"Please, Isla. I'm in so much pain right now that it's killing me."

"Okay. I'll see what I can do."

After pouring coffee for her father and mother-in-law, Isla excused herself and went to her room with laptop in hand. She Googled the show *Lost 'n' You* and clicked on the cast. Felicia's maiden name came back as Hastings, and her filmography listed only twelve episodes of *Lost 'n' You*. Nothing else.

She typed in the show's name to find out why it had been canceled after one year. If memory served her, the show had been quite popular, and the ratings good. She had watched it with her friends, and they had almost always discussed the episode the following day. The similarities between the main female character's abuse and her own were too much to bear, and so she'd eventually stopped adding her two cents' worth to the discussion, claiming she had too much homework.

It didn't take her long to find the real reason why it had been canceled. The character who played Felicia's college boyfriend died of a drug overdose after the first season. She read that the network decided not to continue on without him. Further on in the article, it said that Felicia and her costar, Dean Wells, had been linked romantically, but that the two had broken up shortly before Wells killed himself. Or overdosed. Gossip rags speculated that he was so distraught over the breakup with Felicia that he went on a self-destructive drinking and drug binge.

She clicked on the images of Felicia and scanned her photos. She was quite beautiful back then and wore her hair in a curly blond style. Perfect white teeth and radiant smile. Looking at Felicia's old photos, Isla found it almost difficult to believe that this was the same woman she knew. Age and grief had utterly transformed Felicia into a different person. Darker and more mysterious. Or maybe marriage and motherhood had caused this. She scrolled down farther and discovered a photo of Felicia with Gil at some awards show. Soon after breaking up with Wells, it seemed, she'd taken up with Gil.

Did any of this really matter? It intrigued her but meant nothing in the bigger scheme of things. She knew she should be more concerned about Chip Hicks, Bugger Walsh, and Julian McCallister than the grieving mother of a missing girl. And about helping Katie recover, so she could remember who had done this to her. She feared now that Willow Briggs hadn't survived her ordeal. Someone out there had killed those two prominent Harper's Point kids. But for what reason?

KARL

*H*E STOOD IN THE SMALL CONFERENCE ROOM AT THE POLICE STATION and stared at the chart on the wall, scribbled with arrows and lines. What connected everything together? A possible love connection between Dakota, Willow, and Julian? Now that he knew drugs and alcohol were involved at these parties, it made the idea of violence more predictable. He suspected that Julian was involved in one or more of the crimes. The kid's arrogance and entitled attitude made him the number one suspect. But what about Bob Oden? Any number of people in town could have done this.

His phone rang, and he saw Isla's number pop up. Why was she calling him? Had Katie remembered something?

"I've learned a few things you should know," she said when he answered.

"Good. I could use any help I can get." He wondered if he should tell her about Katie, the parties, and the drug use.

"Did you know Chip Hicks had been accused of inappropriate behavior with a female student?"

"Do you really think Chip Hicks has anything to do with this?"

"I don't know what to believe anymore, especially when my mother-in-law tells me she's seen Bugger Walsh riding around with Ray—in his new truck."

The name Bugger Walsh set off alarms in his head, and he hastily scribbled his name down on the whiteboard, for no other reason than Bugger was a well-known lowlife with a considerable rap sheet.

"Are you there, Karl?"

"Yeah, I'm here."

"How much do you know about Julian McCallister?"

"Not much."

"A friend of Samantha's claims that he got kicked out of his private school in Manhattan for fighting and selling drugs."

"It's amazing what people in that salon tell you. You should have been a cop."

"A lot of times it's things I have no desire to know. Clients tend to open up to me after spending twenty minutes in my chair."

"How do you do it?"

"I shut my mouth and try not to interrupt them," she said. "There's something else I should tell you, but I'm not sure it means anything."

"In a case like this, everything can mean something."

"Felicia Briggs used to be a TV star many years ago. Her name was Felicia Hastings back then."

"Really? What show was she on?" He didn't know why he was asking, since he rarely watched TV.

"It was called *Lost 'n' You*. I used to watch it religiously when I was in college."

"Never heard of it. But why would that matter to the case?"

"The show was canceled after one of the lead actors died from a drug overdose. He'd been romantically involved with Felicia but went off the deep end after she broke up with him."

"Interesting, but I'm failing to see the connection."

"Gil Briggs produced and directed the show. It appears that she dumped this young actor to take up with Gil."

"Okay."

"Maybe it's something you might want to look into."

"I'm not entirely sure how that helps me. Unless you think they have something to do with Dakota's death and Willow's presumed abduction."

"I don't know anything. Best to throw everything up against the wall and see what sticks."

"Spoken like a true amateur detective," he said, weighing if he should say his piece. "I have something to tell you, Isla, and you might not like it."

"Oh?"

"When I interviewed your daughter, she admitted some things."

"Like what?"

"She didn't go to Willow's house just to hang out and watch movies. There were parties."

She paused before answering. "I was afraid of that."

"I'm sorry to have to tell you this."

"I heard as much but never suspected that Katie had been involved in that kind of thing. She's a good kid. She'd never do any of that crazy stuff."

"Are you forgetting that you were once a kid?"

"But Katie's always been so . . . responsible. So good."

"I hate to be the bearer of bad news, but it wasn't just alcohol those kids were using."

"I can't accept what you're about to tell me."

"Don't be like those parents with their head in the sand," Karl said.

"What proof do you have?"

"She all but admitted it to me. She's deathly afraid that you'll find out and think the worst of her."

"Trust me, being deathly afraid will be the least of her worries if it's true."

"I know it's not up to me, but I'm hoping you'll not say anything to her. Not now, anyway. It might cause her to shut down and stop talking to me, and that's the last thing we need at this stage in the investigation. Best to wait until she's fully recovered from her injuries before you talk to her."

"So you want me to keep quiet and pretend that nothing happened?"

"Yes."

Silence on the other end of the line.

"Isla? Are you still there?"

"I should have never let her go over there. What the hell was I thinking?"

"You can't second-guess yourself. This is a time in kids' lives when they screw up and do stupid things. Let's just hope she learned from her mistakes."

"You never did any of that when you were her age."

"My only drug was hiking and enjoying nature. Of course, that's why I was such a nerd back in high school." He laughed, although it was tinged with regret.

"You weren't a total nerd. If I remember correctly, there was one cool girl who thought you were pretty special."

"And she was a little crazy herself, if I recall."

"Maybe she wasn't so crazy, after all. Or maybe she was crazy for another reason."

What did that mean? His pulse ticked a little faster. *Crazy in love? Crazy to have left town for college, only to end up with Ray? Goddamned Ray!*

"So you'll check on that accusation leveled against Coach Hicks?"

"I don't think that'll be necessary, Isla."

"Why not? I thought you were supposed to check out every lead and be thorough."

He hesitated, wondering if he should say anything.

"Karl? Are you still there?"

"Yeah, I'm here."

"So are you going to do it?"

"Don't think there's a reason to."

"Why not?"

"Can you keep a secret? I mean, you cannot tell a soul."

"Of course."

"Chip Hicks is gay."

"Gay? Chip? Not possible!"

"It's true, although I can't tell you how I know."

"Are you sure about that?"

"Positive. This is a small town, Isla, which is why he stays in the closet. Not exactly the friendliest place for a gay man to live."

"Chip Hicks? Really? I mean, Chip was a star baseball player."

Karl laughed, as if being a star baseball player would disqualify someone from being gay. "That's why they exonerated him so quickly."

"Okay, then I guess that explains it. I won't say a word."

The line went dead, and yet he clutched the phone to his ear, longing, wanting to hear more of her voice. Now *he* felt like the crazy one—crazy after all these years to still be in love with a married woman with two kids.

He had things to do. He needed to find out if Bugger had been hanging out with Ray and behaving badly. It hadn't escaped his notice that Ray had purchased a newer truck: a 2014 Chevy Silverado. Ray had claimed it was for his burgeoning seaweed business. Odds were that he had paid for it in cash. Karl wanted to see for himself if Ray was harvesting this so-called seaweed, and learn if this was a viable business or not. He needed to call Julian's Manhattan school and find out if the rumors about him were true. And what about the Briggses? Couldn't hurt to give it all a good looking-into and see where the pieces fell.

He grabbed his cap and mug of coffee and headed out.

KATIE

Willow is alive! I can't quite believe it. Part of me wants to call the police and help her get to safety. But she specifically asked me not to. She said she will end up dead if I call the cops. Is she being held captive? Being beaten or tortured? The thought of this puts a huge damper on my initial enthusiasm. But at least she's alive. At least there's hope. I know it because she texted me from her phone. Me, of all people. Her bestie.

I put the light on in my room and lock the bedroom door. I don't want my lie exposed, the lie that I'm sensitive to light. But it's true about my memory. When I stand, my head feels like one of those plastic buckets street musicians use to drum on for spare change. It aches and pulses, telling me that I'm not quite ready to learn the truth. And why do I feel so nauseous all the time? Another symptom of this head injury?

The old Katie doesn't exist anymore. This is the new Katie now. The Katie who cheated on her boyfriend and drank alcohol. Who purchased drugs. The Katie whose memory is supposedly impaired and who constantly lies about her sensitivity to light. Who lies to her mother about what she really knows. Who refuses to go to the police with evidence that her bestie is still alive.

I've thought a lot about who could be responsible for what happened to us. I've made a running list in my head. The most surprising name on that list is Katie Eaves. Could I have done it? It scares me because I know I became insanely jealous of Willow's relationship with Dakota. And then Julian. Her shifting moods and random bouts of meanness had made me feel trapped in a psychotic friendship, from which I couldn't escape. It seems crazy to think that I might have hurt Willow. Then again, I had never thought I'd drink alcohol or take drugs. But I had. Does that also mean I killed Dakota? For cheating on me with Willow after I helped him get those Mollies?

I remember the night that Dakota took me back to his house and we chilled for a while. He lived in a beautiful home, cute and tastefully decorated. I remember thinking, *Why can't I live in a home like this?* Smaller than Willow's, Dakota's home sat back from the ocean, but for some reason, it seemed comfier and more relaxed than Willow's.

We listened to music and talked about our lives and our hopes and our dreams. I couldn't take my eyes off him. He was definitely one of the hottest guys I'd ever laid eyes on, with his olive skin and jet-black hair. His muscles bulged out of his T-shirt, but not in the bulky sort of way that Drew's did. His were more defined, as if a surgeon had strategically padded him in all the right places. He told me he worked out every day in order to become a champion wrestler. Supposedly, Chance Academy had one of the best wrestling teams in all of New England, and Dakota had his eyes set on winning the New England Prep Championship.

He said he wanted to go to Brown and wrestle and study literature and write poetry. I thought that was so cool—and incredibly sexy, especially when he read me some of his poems. I thought of my future with Drew, who wanted nothing more out of life than to own his own fishing boat, bury himself in engines and grease, and have a large family to come home to. I imagined a household filled with tiny, screaming Drews, and the inside of our home forever reeking of lobster and herring bait, and it was all I could do not to cry. Because I didn't want that life. I didn't want to end up like my mother, married to a charismatic townie who'd lost interest in her years ago.

The snow started to fall. His mother had gone out for the night. After reading his last poem, Dakota added some logs to the fireplace and got a blaze going. From it, he lit a joint. Then he sat down next to me so that our shoulders and thighs touched. I got goose bumps from his proximity to me. It took three tries before he convinced me to try some pot. I didn't want to do more drugs after that wild party, but he said that pot wasn't really a drug. Pot was an herb, he said, and was legal in most states. Something God had put on earth for people to use for their benefit. I had no idea whether pot was legal or not and didn't really care. I took a few tokes to please him. Then I relaxed.

To my surprise, being high felt wonderful, far better than I had ever expected. And it was strong weed. Everything seemed better when high. After we smoked it, Dakota leaned over and kissed me on the lips, and this unleashed something sensual and animalistic in me, although outwardly I resisted him. As he unfurled the condom, I squirmed and tried to talk him out of it. I didn't actually say no, and I didn't put up much of a fight, either. I felt trapped.

He drove me home soon after.

In my bed that night, I cried myself to sleep because of what had happened. I blamed myself. My virginity had slipped away from me, virginity being something I'd held near and dear because of my religious upbringing. Even Drew had agreed to wait until I was ready to have sex with him. Dakota and I were both to blame for it happening—or at least that's what I convinced myself. I didn't want to think of myself as a victim.

Three days later Dakota disappeared. A day before he vanished, however, I walked out of the school's front doors and saw Willow jumping in his Jeep. Maybe he was giving her a ride back to the neighborhood, but that's not what I suspected. I suspected the worst. And it pissed me off that both of them would betray me like that.

And that's what worries me.

It soon became apparent that we were a very good softball team. Or, I should say, we were an okay team with one star player. Game after game, Willow stymied teams with her dominant fastball, knee-buckling curveball, and mesmerizing changeup. When I asked her where she had learned to pitch like that, she told me her parents had sent her to a softball sleepover camp every summer. Her parents, she said, liked to keep her super busy with activities. No girl in

Shepherd's Bay had ever gone to a softball sleepover camp. When spring came, we just picked up our bats and gloves and played ball.

Reporters showed up and interviewed her after every game. College scouts started to show up in the stands and take note of her performances, and the rest of us prayed we might also get noticed. Willow pitched one perfect game and two no-hitters. The only hits she ever gave up were singles or bunts down the line.

And could she ever hit. During an away game, she hit one so far over the fence that even the fans on the opposing side stood up and cheered.

But the abuse she suffered during most of these games was enough to make me cry. Fans and players alike called her all kinds of terrible names in order to ruffle her feathers. It never worked. In fact, it usually had the opposite effect. It steeled her and made her more determined than ever to win at any cost. I hardly ever saw her break down or let the name-calling bother her. Her face settled like granite, her nerves were unfazed, and she remained that way throughout the game. Her icy ferocity awed me.

It awed me because I knew she hated the sport. Her father, Gil, roamed freely around the field and the players' benches. He shot footage of the opposing team's reaction to her and recorded the nasty words the fans in the stands shouted. All the controversy and drama made him extremely happy, despite the emotional toll it had to be taking on his daughter. He captured the beefy red faces of the opposing parents shouting at her. He filmed Willow flipping the fans off after striking out the side. I often wondered if these parents were mugging for the camera or were merely upset that their children were being thoroughly embarrassed by this wealthy, skinny beauty queen with the ice-blue eyes.

Gil let me watch a lot of his footage, even though I had no desire to see it. It was all Willow all the time and not much else. A huge letdown. He went against his own advice and deleted most of the drama in favor of more scenes with Willow, and in my opinion, he was turning it into a boring spectacle.

But as I watched the opposing fans from my position at second base, I could see the hate in their eyes, and it always saddened me that adults would behave this way. Word around all these small, hardscrabble Maine towns must have gotten out that Willow lived in a massive home on Harper's Point. Not all the adults acted this way, but enough of them did that their antics stayed with me. I felt for her. It wasn't her fault she came from wealth and hadn't grown up in Maine. Softball seemed like a stupid game, anyway, and one that most of us would never play after high school. I would have quit then and there had it not been so much fun watching the opposing teams suffer defeat after defeat. Then watching as the other teams' players were forced to line up in humiliation and shake Willow's hand. One team even refused to shake hands with us afterward, protesting that Willow was not a legal Maine resident.

We were a team in name only. Or a team splintered into three parts and playing under the umbrella of Shepherd's Bay High School. There was Willow, and there was the rest of us. Then there was Willow and me pitted against the rest of the team. Bad enough that the opposing teams talked smack about Willow, but to hear her own teammates say nasty things about her made me furious. It brought me even closer to her and cemented our friendship. It felt like us against them—our own teammates, as well as the opposing teams.

And yet I kept a psychic distance from her so as to preserve my sanity. She knew how to push my buttons. It was the only thing that kept me from worshipping at her feet. I never forgot watching her get into Dakota's Jeep that day. Whether I was right or wrong about their intentions, perception fueled my reality. The more I got to know Willow, the more I came to realize that she used people for the things she wanted. Coach Hicks, for example, despite his harsh discipline, appeared enamored with her after those first few practices. His infatuation didn't bother me, because for whatever reason, it didn't strike me as creepy. I think he felt the way I did: fortunate just to be in her orbit. As far as coaching went, I overheard him tell a parent one day that a player like Willow came around only once in a lifetime.

His partiality didn't bother me, obvious as it was. In most of her classes, she earned average grades, although everyone knew she could earn all As if she applied herself. We all knew that Willow was smart and articulate and would go on to do great things in life. To get into an argument with her on any subject was an invitation to be humiliated. I wouldn't deem it bullying, but I wouldn't *not* call it that, either.

The spring went by in a blur, especially after Dakota went missing. Thinking back, I can't quite remember my state of mind when I heard about it. Maybe I was so busy with school and softball, and trying to appease Drew, that it never fully registered. Maybe I really didn't believe he was gone, or maybe I thought that he would soon return home. I never once believed that someone had killed Dakota. Dakota wrestled and played football; he was clearly a boy who could take care of himself. He constantly talked to me about moving away and seemed eager for the day to come. He couldn't wait to get away from this town and his overbearing mother.

Wherever we went as a team, Gil followed. He interviewed team members separately and together and filmed them when they didn't realize they were being filmed. Some girls played up to the camera, while others ignored it. I guess I leaned toward ignoring it most of the time. I didn't mug or act any different when he pointed that weapon at me. I tried to blend into the background, similar to how I went about things in my everyday life. Besides, I knew that we wouldn't play prominently in the show and that most of the juicy scenes would be cut.

That's because Gil loved filming his daughter the most. On the field, dressed in her full uniform, she resembled a goddess. Her long legs stretched out of those red shorts. Off the field, she laughed and posed and teemed with personality. I knew the camera loved her as much as she loved it. Gil showed me more footage one day after practice, and her star power blew me away. Her beauty and strength powered through the lens, and her smile was so brilliant that it crowded everything and everyone else out. Still, she couldn't carry the show by herself.

She pitched every inning of every game, seeming never to tire. She wanted the ball as much as she wanted to hit when the game was on the line. My mother came to every home game, and on occasion my father was there. As was the case with Willow, everyone seemed to be drawn to Ray "Swisher" Eaves, a legendary hoop player back in his day. In one of his yearbook photos, he's smiling and holding a basketball under his arm, his long black hair flowing down his neck, like that of a warrior prince.

We blitzed through the play-offs, and I had a great couple of games, making some nifty plays on the field. I slapped at the ball and beat out my share of dribblers, which allowed Willow to drive me home time and time again.

All that time, the police continued to search for Dakota. Did we talk about him? We must have. I'm almost certain that we did. I think that Willow and I thought alike on the matter: that Dakota had run off somewhere and wouldn't be returning. But I'm merely guessing at this. Neither of us really believed that something bad could happen to a kid like Dakota. The common view was that he was too beautiful, too strong and proud, and was blessed with so many positive attributes. A boy like that didn't just die. None of us thought we would ever die. We were young and had our entire lives in front of us.

Of course, I knew the real Dakota and hated him for what he'd done to me. Personally, I was glad he was gone, even though I'd convinced myself that I was equally to blame for what had happened that night.

The state championship game arrived. Of all the teams to face, it stunned me to go up against Chance Academy. All the girls appeared excited as we warmed up along the foul lines. The unspoken truth was that it was the rich kids versus the poor townies—except for Willow. Before the game started, Willow spent more time socializing with the opposing team than with the team she played for, although that didn't really surprise me. She had gone to school with many of those kids and lived in the same neighborhood.

As I played catch with Lisa Powers, I looked up in the stands and saw practically my entire hometown sitting there. My mom, included. But where was my dad? I should have expected he wouldn't show up. Gil roamed the field during warm-ups, videotaping everything. Drew stood with his friends in the back row, and they were whooping and whistling and punching each other's arms. Wads of tobacco protruded from their lips. When I looked over at Willow, I saw Coach Hicks standing with her on the practice mound, whispering in her ear, his arm around her shoulder. It struck me as odd. Was he giving her a last-minute pep talk? Then I saw Julian standing by the right-field fence, on the Shepherd's Bay side. He wore a gray wool cap and inhaled vape smoke. He looked so alone that for a moment it made me sad for him. Didn't he have any of his own friends at that school?

I don't recall much of the game. It went by in a blur, and the next thing I remember, we were dancing on the pitcher's mound and celebrating our championship. Gil circled around us like a vulture, filming it all. The crowd thundered with applause. I heard Drew shouting out my name and whistling through his oil-stained fingers. It momentarily made me feel guilty for cheating on him. A scary thought hit me as I turned to look at him. Could he have found out about my and Dakota's night together and killed Dakota? He hunted deer and moose and had lots of guns in his house, and he shot most weekends in a gravel pit outside of town. And although he had a long fuse, he had a very bad temper.

The only person in the stands who wasn't cheering was Willow's mom. She stood impassively, with her hands in her jacket, those hideous sunglasses covering half of her skeletal face. It felt like she was staring directly at me, and so I looked away and tried to act happy, but for some reason, I felt nothing but dread. With the softball season now over, I had to face all my issues.

For the first time since Dakota had gone missing, a shroud of darkness dropped over me.

I now know that Willow is somewhere out there and alive, waiting for me to save her. Knowing this, I realize I can't stay in this dark room much longer and pretend to act all scared and confused. I need to know what happened that night. I simply can't lie here and wait for my memory to spit out answers. But what to do? She said she'd message me when the time was right. I have no option but to wait. But I don't want to wait. I want to go to her. To save her. When she calls for me, I will be ready. I will help my friend out of this mess, whatever this mess happens to be.

I only hope that my mother will forgive me to the extent that God will. Because I was taught to believe that God forgives all people who ask for His forgiveness.

ISLA

*T*HE DOOR TO THE BRIGGSES' HOUSE OPENED, AND ISLA SAW GIL standing before her in a blue sweat suit and pointing a camera in her face. What the hell was this? She made her way inside the dimly lit mansion, embarrassed and feeling self-conscious at being filmed. After a few moments, Gil went into the kitchen and placed the camera down on the granite island and began to sob into his hands. She followed him in stunned silence, unsure of what to say or do.

"I'm sorry. I don't know what else to do but get behind the camera and film everything around me. If Willow were here right now, it's what she'd want me to do."

"It's okay, Gil."

"I can't believe she's gone. I'm so devastated. She means everything to me, the best daughter a father could ever have."

Did Gil also realize he had a grieving wife upstairs?

"She would want me to keep filming and making art."

Art?

He went on. "I truly believe she's out there and waiting for me. Waiting to come home and be the star everyone knows she'll one day become."

"They'll find her. I'm sure of it."

"Yes, I believe you're right. I have to believe that, or else I'll have no reason to live." He wiped his eyes. "I'm sorry. I'll go get Felicia for you."

She placed her bag down on the kitchen island and circled the living room. She hadn't before noticed the abstract art hanging on the wall or the colorful giant glass sculptures hanging from one section of the ceiling. There was so much to take in. One piece of glass sat on a side table. Blue inside and with speckled brown streaks in the outer layer, it looked like an exotic clamshell from outer space. She gently lifted it up and saw the word *Chihuly* etched in the bottom.

Footsteps came up behind her. She turned and saw Gil pushing a wheelchair out of the hallway. Felicia sat slumped in the chair, her slender hands resting on her knees. She looked old and worn down. Despite the dimness of the room, she still wore those hideous sunglasses. Gil kissed the top of her head and announced that he was retiring for the night, then headed upstairs.

"Thank you for coming over," Felicia said.

"It's my pleasure. However, I'm afraid I won't be able to wash your hair while you're in that chair."

"I'm weak but not an invalid." She pushed herself off the wheelchair, headed into the kitchen, Isla on her heels, and walked over to the massive stainless-steel sink. "Will this do?"

"Yes. Thank you. I moved a dining room chair next to the kitchen island so I can access the outlet."

"That should work," Felicia said, as if she was doing Isla a big favor.

"How are you holding up?"

"Dreadful." She removed her sunglasses, and Isla instantly recognized fragments of that beautiful girl from *Lost 'n' You.* "Do you want me to just lower my head into the sink?"

"Yes, and then I'll shampoo your hair and add conditioner before blowing it out." Isla grabbed her phone and secretly clicked on the recording app. For what reason, she didn't know.

"Very well."

After removing shampoo, conditioner, and a towel from the bag she'd left on the island, she scrubbed the woman's hair, thinking about what she would say to her afterward. Felicia's hair, despite being black, still looked gorgeous after all these years, and for a brief moment, Isla felt thrilled to be working on a bona fide celebrity, although one whose stardom had long ago dimmed.

She guided the woman's head out of the sink and wrapped a towel around it. A particular episode of *Lost 'n' You* came to mind: the one where the college professor placed his hand on her bare thigh while they were sitting in his office. Isla remembered the shocking scene vividly because it had happened to her in almost the same fashion, and it had eventually caused her to drop out of school and return home to Shepherd's Bay.

After Isla towel dried her hair, Felicia sat down in the dining-room chair. Isla turned up the lights so she could see better. It took a few seconds for Felicia's eyes to adjust to the brightness. After removing the hair dryer and a brush from her bag, Isla plugged in the hair dryer and waited a second before turning it on.

"I hope you don't think I'm out of line, Felicia, considering the circumstances and all, but I loved that show you starred in."

Felicia turned and gazed at her as if she was angry. "How do you know about that?"

"I put two and two together. Besides, I was a big fan of *Lost 'n' You.*"

"That was nearly twenty years ago."

"It's too bad about your costar. I was hoping there'd be a second season."

"So was I. Then Dean had to go and screw everything up by killing himself," she said, her voice cold and callous.

"Why wouldn't they continue the show without him?"

"Those empty suits decided it wasn't worth it. It's all about demographics and ratings with these networks. They believed women wouldn't watch the show without the main heartthrob."

"Speaking for myself, I watched because of the situation your character got herself into with that sleazy professor. I think most of the college girls I knew at the time could relate to that kind of inappropriate relationship," Isla said.

"Did a professor abuse you?"

"Yes, but I was too young and impressionable at the time to resist, although I eventually dropped out."

"You slept with him?"

"I didn't want to. I know it's no excuse, but I felt helpless to stop him once he started grooming me. In my mind, I convinced myself that I was a willing partner, when the truth was quite the opposite. I didn't realize that he'd victimized me until later."

"Goddamned men. They're such dogs."

"It affected me for a long time. It caused me to question myself and my future relationships."

"What happened?"

"I had a breakdown. I didn't label it that at the time, but that's what I believe happened."

Felicia laughed haughtily. "That's how Hollywood operates, despite all this Me Too bullshit. You take your turn on the casting couch and then screw your way to the top. Anyone who says otherwise either doesn't know the truth about show business or is a fool. Don't let all those holier-than-thou actresses convince you that they didn't sleep their way to stardom."

Did she dare ask Felicia if that was how she'd landed her role on the show? No, best not to.

"Is that why you left the business?" Isla turned on the dryer and began to brush out Felicia's hair.

"Who said I left?"

"I read that you and Dean were in a relationship."

"Wow. It's like you've been keeping tabs on me."

"I scoured all the tabloids at the time, and I remember the rumors circulating about the two of you."

"I was a whole lot prettier than than I am now." She crossed her arms. "Dean became infatuated with me. Yes, we dated for a little while, but he was too crazy and immature for any long-term relationship. People thought I liked to party, but Dean put most people to shame."

"They said he died of an overdose."

"Either an overdose or a broken heart. Pick your poison," Felicia said. "I don't want to be rude, Isla, but my thoughts are elsewhere today."

"Totally understood," Isla said, aiming the hot air at the bristles brushing through her hair. "What do you know about Julian?"

"My husband despises that boy. He's so rude and disrespectful. Must be bad parenting."

"I heard he got kicked out of his previous school in Manhattan for dealing drugs and fighting."

"I don't doubt it. Samantha once told me that Julian had a drug habit, as well as anger issues."

"Do you think Julian could have harmed our daughters? And possibly Dakota?"

"Between you and me, I've always thought that boy was capable of violence. I told that police officer about him and let it go at that. I think Gil would strangle Julian if he suspected him of hurting Willow."

"There are rumors that you held parties here and that drugs and alcohol were involved."

Felicia shot out of her chair and glared at Isla. "Who told you that? Because that's a bald-faced lie. We never allowed drugs and alcohol into our home when there were kids here. Now, if some of those kids drank or took drugs before coming over, well, that was out of our control. We always instructed them to return home if we suspected that they were intoxicated."

"I'm sorry for mentioning it."

Felicia fell back in the chair. "That's the problem with living in such a small town. Everyone's always in your goddamned business."

"I'm just trying to help find your daughter."

"Please, Isla, just stick to doing hair and let the police do their job." She covered her eyes and started sobbing, and Isla shut down the dryer.

"I'm sorry for prying into your life, Felicia."

"No, I'm sorry if you think I'm being mean to you. You've been nothing but kind to me, and I've treated you so rudely. I'm the one that should be asking you for forgiveness."

"It's okay. I understand the immense stress you're under."

"You can't even begin to understand. No one can. Your daughter came back to you. So why can't mine?"

"She will."

"My husband is practically suicidal over Willow's disappearance. How do you think that makes me feel? That my husband loves his daughter more than his own wife."

"I don't believe that's true. It's just that parents love their children differently than they love their spouse."

"I love Willow, too, but I want to live my life to the fullest no matter what happens. Gil and I need each other if we're to have a future together."

Felicia's words confused her. They didn't seem to fit the narrative of a daughter gone missing. But people reacted in strange ways during crises, and Isla knew not to judge. Maybe Felicia's mind was not where it should be with all the antidepressants and other medications she'd been taking. And yet she couldn't get the woman's troubling words out of her head.

She finished brushing out her hair. Then she showed Felicia what she'd done. A subtle nod was all she got for her efforts.

"That exhausted me. I need to go to my room and lie down now," Felicia said as she stood up from her seat and then sat down in the wheelchair.

"Would you like me to push you there?"

"If you wouldn't mind."

Isla guided her wheelchair down the hallway until Felicia pointed to a room. It appeared that she and Gil were now sleeping in separate bedrooms. Isla pushed her inside. "All set?"

"Yes. Thank you so much. Can you see yourself out?"

"Sure," Isla said, steeling herself for what she was about to ask. "I hate to trouble you, Felicia, but I've not received payment for my services." Saying this made her cringe.

"Gil never paid you?"

"No."

"Well, he was supposed to. And he's already turned in for the night." She wheeled over to the dresser and opened it, then pulled something out. "Will a check suffice?"

"A check will work just fine. It's just that . . ."

"I'm sorry if it's a little light. Gil's supposed to transfer funds to my account any day now." She scribbled on the check, ripped it out of the checkbook, and brusquely handed it to her.

"Whatever's fine. You can always pay me the rest later when you stop in the shop," Isla said, stuffing the check in her pocket. "I'll show myself out."

"If you wouldn't mind."

Once in the car, Isla sat fuming. How could that woman be light on money with all the opulence surrounding her? She turned the ignition, and before shifting into drive, she removed the crumpled check from her pocket. It took her a few seconds to read it in the dark. Had Felicia made a mistake? Isla clicked on the overhead light and saw that indeed she'd made the check out for two hundred dollars. *Two hundred dollars.*

She sat for five minutes in the car, not quite believing the sum of money that had just been paid to her. Should she go back and ask Felicia if she'd made a mistake? No, she'd watched the woman write out the sum. Felicia had made no mistake.

ISLA

SHE TOOK THE SUSPENSION BRIDGE, THE QUICKEST WAY BACK TO THE mainland, despite being afraid of heights. She gripped the steering wheel at ten and two, trying hard not to look down at the glistening bay below. Not a car passed her, and so she strayed over the yellow line to keep as far away from the railing as possible. She rarely drove over this bridge, hardly needing to travel this way. But it was the quickest route home from Harper's Point.

A Volvo wagon sped past her on the right, the driver beeping loudly and giving her the middle finger. She steered nervously back into the right-hand lane, thinking about all that Felicia had said. Understandably, the woman seemed unhinged. It made Isla realize that dysfunction happened to both rich and poor families alike, and in this case, it had created the perfect circumstance for Willow's disappearance. Unfortunately, Katie had been caught in the same crosshairs of dysfunction and was now paying the price.

The end of the bridge appeared, and Isla breathed easier as she guided the car onto the terra firma. She took a right onto Bayview Road. It wound up and along the coast, and she could see the lights twinkling from across the bay. In the rearview mirror, she could also make out the illuminated suspension bridge rising up majestically behind her.

Her eyes returned to the road as she ascended a hill. Since she was lost in thought, it took a few seconds before she realized that a vehicle was on her tail. To her left, the granite wall rose fifty feet or more. To her right, the steep cliff appeared beyond the guardrail. Afraid to take her eyes off the road, she gripped the steering wheel with both hands and hoped the vehicle would quickly pass her. But a quick glance in the rearview made her skin crawl. The vehicle had its headlights off and was inches from her bumper.

She slowed and felt a bump. Did the driver just ram her? Then the driver did it again, only this time with more force. Someone was trying to force her off the road. Frightened, she sped up. But the vehicle—an SUV or truck, she guessed—kept pace with her. She knew she had to make it to the top of the hill. If she went over the cliff, she would crash in spectacular fashion on the rocks below—and surely die.

Her foot stomped on the gas, and the vehicle behind her flashed its high beams off and on, making it impossible for her to see who was behind the wheel. She could barely look into the rearview mirror without temporarily blinding herself. Her heart raced in her chest at the thought of leaving Katie and Raisin without a mother.

She turned the wheel so that her car veered into the middle of the road, hoping that the vehicle behind her did not sideswipe her minivan and send it into the bay. The steepness of the hill caused her van to sputter. Another collision jarred her. The vehicle then locked bumpers with hers and began to push her toward the guardrail.

The bay's dark waters appeared below. Beyond that she could see the lights of Harper's Point, and beyond that, the cold, dark Atlantic Ocean. She remembered her father's rules for driving in snow. Why she was remembering this now? Route 25 appeared up ahead. If only she could reach it and turn left, she'd be all right. Her van veered closer to the guardrail. Another twenty feet and it would sail over the edge.

With her father's words echoing in her ears, she pumped the brakes and turned the wheel to her left. Her intermittent braking caused the vehicle behind her to back off momentarily. The vehicle then sped up and crashed hard into her left rear wheel well, causing Isla's car to spin a full 180 degrees, so that she was facing the suspension bridge. The minivan skidded along the road until the passenger side bounced up against the granite wall. It came to an abrupt stop as water from the wall dripped onto her roof. Steam hissed out of the front end.

Isla, breathing hard, glanced in her rearview mirror and saw the vehicle stop up ahead. Would it come back and finish her off? After idling for thirty seconds in the dark, it sped up and turned left onto Route 25, then disappeared from sight. She pulled out her phone and called the police. Then she got out and flagged down the vehicle that was coming up the hill. Thank God for this driver. Had this other vehicle not arrived on the scene, her attacker might have spun around and pushed her over the cliff. Blood dripped from her head and onto the pavement. Dizzy, she reached up and felt a cut on her forehead.

A convertible BMW roadster pulled over to the guardrail and stopped. To her surprise, Julian jumped out from behind the wheel. Her head now pounded, and she felt nauseous. She brought her hand up to her forehead again. Upon bringing it back down, she noticed that her palm was covered in blood. The lights from the suspension bridge began to blur, and she fell to her knees.

"Jesus! Are you okay, Mrs. Eaves?" Julian's voice called out.

"Someone tried to run me off the road." She could see the kid's blurry silhouette running toward her.

"Dude! Someone was trying to off you?"

She held out her hand. "I'm bleeding."

"Here. Take my shirt."

Julian removed his T-shirt and pressed it against her head. He scooped her up in his arms and carried her over to his parked car. She felt close to passing out as he lifted her over the door and sat her upright in the passenger seat. He fastened her seat belt before jumping in next to her. Then he sped off, passing the minivan's steaming pile of twisted metal. She held the shirt to her forehead before losing consciousness.

When she woke up, she saw a clock and a curtain. She recognized the hospital's emergency room because she'd spent so many hours in it caring for Raisin.

"You okay, Isla?" Karl Bjornson said. "That was quite a crash."

"Someone tried to run me off the road."

"Did you get a good look at them?"

She shook her head, which pounded with pain. She wanted nothing more than to reach out and caress his smooth cheek.

"You're lucky Julian McCallister arrived when he did and drove you to the emergency room."

"Yes, lucky indeed." She now felt guilty for talking bad about Julian.

"What were you doing over at Harper's Point?"

"Giving Felicia Briggs a wash and blow-dry."

"Someone had to be waiting for you to leave Harper's Point, Isla. They must be worried because you've been digging into things that have happened in this town."

"It was a truck or an SUV that rammed me. Something big."

"And you didn't see the driver?"

"They put their high beams on before attempting to run me off the road."

"How did you manage to escape?"

"My dad taught me never to lock the brakes in a snowstorm. Always pump them and keep the wheel straight. Only this time I turned it."

"Your dad's a wise man. Doing that helped you spin around instead of going over the edge."

"My dad is a wise man, even if he doesn't quite know it anymore."

KARL

*I*T MADE HIM SO MAD TO SHOW UP AT THE HOSPITAL AND SEE ISLA LYING there by herself. Where the hell was Ray? He should have been the first one here to comfort his wife. Was he working on his so-called seaweed business? After speaking with her and not getting any solid leads, Karl made his way into the waiting room and saw Julian sitting there and staring into space.

His head swam with conspiracies as he thought about all those intersecting lines on his whiteboard. He wanted to like Julian, not because the boy had helped Isla in her time of need, but because he genuinely wanted to like most people, even if in reality he didn't. His inclination was to be alone, trekking in the woods or climbing a hill, and far away from others. But that didn't mean he universally disliked people; they usually did something first to make him not like them.

Julian didn't look at him when he sat down. The two sat in silence for a few minutes, while a mother and her sick kid walked in. The kid coughed nonstop, as if trying to expel a lung. Karl's suspicion of Julian seemed unwarranted after the kid's role as Good Samaritan. But what were the odds that Julian would arrive so soon after the crash? Was it a mere coincidence? Or had he been following the other vehicle in order to insure that Isla went over the edge of the cliff? Had he set the whole thing up?

The kid looked pathetic to him, with his long, greasy hair and his hipster jacket barely covering his shirtless torso. Then he remembered that Julian had given Isla the shirt off his back to staunch the bleeding. Black nail polish covered his fingernails. What was that about? He recalled watching an interview with the rock star Steven Tyler and seeing that he, too, wore black nail polish. Maybe it was a musician thing.

"How you doing, Julian?"

"Been better, dude."

"That was quite a heroic thing you did, helping Isla Eaves like that."

"I didn't do nothin' except drive her to the ER."

"I think it was pretty brave of you."

"Whatever." Julian laughed.

Karl leaned over and examined the boy's eyes. "Are you high?"

"I smoked a little weed to take the edge off. You gonna bust me for that?"

"No, I'm not going to bust you."

"Everything's so messed up in this town. Makes New York City seem tame in comparison."

"What were you doing out there? Where were you going?"

"I like to get away from my crazy parents and clear my head. Driving around tends to chill me out."

"Your parents are crazy?"

"They're always at each other's throats. Why are they still together if they like to argue so much?"

"I don't know. What were they fighting about?"

"How much time you got?" He laughed. "One day I overheard my mother saying that I'm the cause of all their problems and the reason we moved out of New York City. But that's bullshit, because it was my dad who wanted to move up here. Said when the shit hits the fan, we'll be safer here in Maine. You know, zombie invasion and aliens coming down to earth."

"Sounds like he's been watching too many episodes of *The Walking Dead*."

Julian held his arms out and started to moan like a zombie. Then he laughed. "I like how they call them walkers on that show instead of zombies. It's as if by calling them that, it'll make the situation less dire."

"You a fan of the show?"

"Big-time. You?"

"Don't watch much TV. One of my coworkers is always going on about it."

"You should check it out. It's a cool show."

"Did you know that your next-door neighbor was once on a TV show?"

"Willow?" He turned to face Karl. "Dude, I thought her father was shooting some reality pilot or some shit."

"He is, I guess. But I'm not talking about Willow. I'm talking about her mother."

"Mrs. Briggs? For real?"

"Yeah, before you were born. The show lasted one year and then got canceled."

"Wow! That's one totally messed-up lady. I try to stay away from her whenever possible."

"Messed up in what way?"

"I don't know. She kinda creeps me out." He made claws out of his hands and pretended to attack Karl. "Cougar, you know. Sometimes I thought she wanted to get it on with some of us younger dudes."

"She came on to you?"

"Not exactly. I don't know. I'd get a vibe from her at times. Like the way she looked at us when we were chilling on the beach. Very weird."

"So it was just a vibe?"

"Yeah, I guess you could call it that. I remember Dakota was drunk one night and being obnoxious, as usual. Started bragging about all the bitches he'd nailed and how he'd seduced them with his poems, although he didn't really write them. Got them out of some book and memorized them. Then he mentioned something about how he could have both Willow and her mother if he wanted."

"He said that?"

"I thought he was just being a dick, but then he started going on about how he dug older women. Bragged about how Willow's mom wanted to get it on with him. I thought he was just smack-talking."

"And you never thought to tell anyone about this?"

"Why would I? That's just Dakota being Dakota, is all. Still, I got a vibe from Willow's mom, so it didn't really surprise me." Julian stood. "I gotta get the car back before the dragon lady freaks. We good, yo?"

"Yeah, we're good." For a kid who attended pricey prep schools, he talked like a gangster wannabe.

"Tell Katie's mom I hope she feels better."

"Will do."

"She seems like a nice lady."

Karl watched Julian swagger out the ER's doors, hoping that the kid arrived home safely. As Julian exited, Ray walked through the sliding glass doors and looked around the ER. Karl caught his eye and pointed in the direction of the room where Ray's wife lay recuperating.

"What the hell happened, Bjorny?"

"Someone tried to run her off the road."

"How's the van?"

Karl wanted to flatten the bastard for asking about the van before his wife's health. "Totaled, from what I hear."

"The nurse said something about a bad cut."

"She's a little shaken but all right."

"You catch the bastard?"

Karl shook his head.

"Whoever did this better hope you catch him before I do." Ray turned and, with righteous indignation he didn't deserve, headed toward the room to visit his wife.

The entire right side of the minivan had caved in. Good thing Isla hadn't been transporting a passenger. Flares had been set up around the vehicle for cars to pass with caution. Olivia stood nearby, directing what little traffic approached the wreck. Karl stared down at the illuminated bridge. The bay flowed beneath it in murky silence. Across the water he could see Harper's Point. It was late, and most of the lights were off.

"Where's Walt Sebold?" Karl said.

"His tow's out of commission for a few days, so I called Dicky Fox."

"Guy's such an asshole."

"Tell me about it, but that asshole is the only tow available to-night."

"What's his ETA?"

"Dicky's rig is twenty miles out of town."

"Gonna be a little wait, then," he said. "I don't mind staying if you wanna take off, Olivia."

"You sure? I was about to get off shift when this happened."

"Go. You've got a family waiting for you at home."

"For real, Karl? I don't mind staying."

"Get out of here."

"Thanks so much. I owe you big-time."

She jumped in her cruiser and sped away, leaving him standing alone in silence. From where he stood on the hill, he could see the bridge and the yellow traffic line bisecting the two lanes. Upon pointing his flashlight down, he noticed tire tracks greasing the road. He went over and examined them. The vehicle that had crashed into Isla's car had skidded to a stop moments after hitting her. Then had sped up while driving away. Thick, new rubber. Most likely from a truck or an SUV. That didn't help much, considering that half the population in Shepherd's Bay drove either an SUV or a pickup truck.

He returned to the van and peeked inside. Isla had left a bag on the passenger seat. He opened the passenger door and snatched the bag. It contained all her styling tools. But her phone also sat in there. He grabbed hold of it and debated whether or not to take a peek inside, assuming she hadn't locked it. There was no one around to see him. He turned on the phone, and it opened to a recording app. Had Isla recorded her conversation with Felicia Briggs? Was that the real reason she'd visited Harper's Point and cut Felicia Briggs's hair?

Headlights came toward him. He stashed the phone in his pocket and waved the Escalade away from the flares. Once it had safely passed by, he returned to the minivan and pulled the phone out of his pocket. He pressed on the app and listened to Isla and Felicia's conversation.

Afterward, he stood quietly, absorbing Isla's words. Although she hadn't come right out and said it, Isla had hinted at being raped in college. Or, at the very least, feeling pressured to have sex with a sleazy college professor. The revelation enraged him. Had she told Ray about this? Probably not, as Ray had been the temporary solution to her feelings of shame and guilt. He felt his hands forming into fists. *Best to forget it.* If someone ever told him the name of that professor, he'd seriously consider driving over to that campus and having a man-to-man talk with the guy. It made him glad he had never gone to college.

Next, he searched her browsing history and discovered two sites dedicated to the show Felicia had starred in. One detailed the overdose death of Felicia's costar, Dean Wells. The other mentioned Felicia's new beau, Gil Briggs, the producer of her show. His ears perked up whenever the word *death* came up. As a cop, he knew that death followed certain people around the way a dog might follow someone gifted with animals.

Intrigued, he wondered if any other crew or cast members had died. So he Googled it on her phone, expecting nothing but always hoping. Wild stabs often led to unexpected discoveries—or so he read in all the police procedural books he perused in his spare time. Not like he had a lot of experience investigating murder cases in Shepherd's Bay.

Nothing came up. He tried a few different iterations. He put in the names Gil and Felicia Briggs, as well as Felicia's maiden name. He put in Willow's name. He typed "murders in LA" and saw the futility of that needle-in-a-haystack search. LA was to murder what peanut butter was to jelly. A car came up the road, and he watched it safely pass. Then he tried a few more searches, all of which came back without a hit. Finally, he tried Willow's old LA school, Canyon Prep, which he had to fish out of his notebook. A name came up. Was this a strange coincidence, luck, or something more meaningful?

Jalen Stark. The boy's photo appeared on-screen. He was a handsome kid, tall and athletic looking. He had been found dead inside his home, the victim of an apparent overdose. He was a senior when Willow Briggs was just starting out as a freshman. Karl looked up Canyon Prep and saw that it enrolled eleven hundred kids. What a strange coincidence.

He shrugged off this discovery. Probably a lot of kids took drugs to excess in LA. That the overdose had happened to a kid who went to the same school Willow Briggs attended meant nothing except another coincidence. Back to square one. Now he also had to find out who had tried to run Isla off the road. If he located that person, he had no doubt he'd find the person who was responsible for Dakota's death, Willow's disappearance, and Katie's injuries.

The tow truck barreled down the hill and stopped in front of the misshapen minivan. Dicky Fox climbed down, cigar in his fat mouth, looking all of his sixty-plus years. Karl erased the browsing history and then stashed the phone back inside Isla's floral knitted workbag before hooking the bag over his shoulder. He had no desire to speak to this miserable bastard.

"Love the new purse," Dicky said. "Exploring your feminine side?"

"You're quite the comedian."

"Looks like somebody knocked back a few too many milk shakes tonight."

"Tow it back to the yard, will you?"

"Righto, Captain." Dicky puffed on his cigar, obviously in no hurry. "It's a good thing whoever was driving this piece of crap didn't go in the drink."

Karl stood and watched the man hook the van up to the tow. After shifting the minivan into neutral, Dicky tipped his cap to Karl and stopped for a second to enjoy his cigar. Smoke whirled around his jowly, unshaven face.

"There's one thing you and I have in common, Bjorny."

"I doubt you and I have anything in common, Dicky."

"Oh, my friend, but we do. It's called job security."

"Get that rig outta here."

"Toodle-oo, cupcake." Dicky climbed up into his rig and then drove off with Isla's minivan following behind him.

KATIE

*R*AISIN COMES INTO MY ROOM AND ASKS IF I'LL PLAY CARDS WITH HIM. I don't want to play cards, but I realize that I've spent very little time with my brother lately. Once I go away to college, I'll hardly ever see him, and that makes me sad. Maybe playing cards will take my mind off the fact that Willow is out there and waiting for the right time to contact me with her whereabouts. Besides, there's nothing I can do until she calls.

My mind races. It's possible that I'm a good person who's done some very bad things. Or maybe a bad person who has pretended to be someone else all these years. The inescapable fact is that I've been involved with drugs, alcohol, and parties. A boy has been found dead, a boy I once liked and had a brief relationship with. A boy who used me and then discarded me, like I was garbage, and whom I now hate.

Why wasn't I upset over Dakota's death? I should have been. Was it because I still didn't believe a boy like that could die? Was there a disconnect between reality and what I perceived to be true? Or maybe it's the fact that he convinced me to sleep with him before I was ready. Oh, and that I later discovered that the stupid poems he read aloud to me were not his, but some old classics he'd lifted from one of his literature books.

We play Uno. I exchange cards with Raisin and allow for a playful war of words between us. He seems happy and totally into the game. I care not about winning but about making Raisin happy. I keep glancing at my phone to see if there's anything from Willow, but nothing has appeared.

Scout raises his head every now and then and appraises me. I have always wanted to like Scout but at times have found it difficult. And I should be thankful to him for all he's done for my brother. Scout has dedicated his life to Raisin and has lost out on an easy life of taking long walks and restful naps and getting lots of pets and scratchies. I've always wanted a dog I could love and snuggle with in my bed, a dog who would come running over to me when I came home from school after a bad day. A dog who would lick my cheeks and knock me over with his wagging tail. A dog who would give me the love and attention I felt I was not getting at home. But Scout is *definitely* not that dog. His life is dedicated to one thing: saving Raisin. Play and companionship no longer matter to him, but they might have if he hadn't been chosen to serve.

But the real reason I haven't warmed up to Scout is this: he seems to judge me with those appraising eyes. Am I nuts to think this way? Apart from alerting us about Raisin's glucose levels, Scout, I've come to believe, can see right through me. Like he has a bullshit meter and knows whenever I am not being truthful. He seems to sense that I am not only a phony person but also a bad girl. That's why I look away from him whenever he stares at me. And he seems to be staring at me a lot during this card game.

"You don't have to play cards with me if you don't want to," Raisin says.

"Of course I want to play cards with you. What makes you think that?"

"You look like you want to be somewhere else."

"That's silly. Why would you say that?"

"Because you've been different this past year, Katie."

"Trust me, Raisin, I'm the exact same person I've always been. I'm just trying to get healthy again."

"You'll be leaving next year and going away to college."

I don't know how to respond to this.

Raisin continues. "Everything's so messed up now. Dad's rarely home anymore, and Grampa can barely remember his own name. And Mom worries all the time about us."

"It'll get better."

"No it won't. What'll happen to us if something happens to Mom?"

"Don't worry. Nothing's going to happen to Mom. She'll live to be a hundred."

He looks as if he's about to cry. His reaction alarms me. Raisin rarely, if ever, cries, despite all the health issues and medical emergencies he's been forced to deal with growing up.

"What's the matter?" I say.

"I'm not supposed to tell you."

"Tell me what?"

"No. I'll get in big trouble if I say anything."

I lean over and grab him by the shirt and pull his face close to mine. Scout sits up and looks nervously at me.

"It's Mom. Something's happened to her."

"What do you mean, something happened to her?" Panic fills me.

"Gramma told me not to tell you. Someone tried to run her off the road. She's in the hospital now."

"What?" I release my brother's shirt, and he falls back. "Is she okay?"

"Gramma says she's fine, just bruised and scared. She drove over to the ER to bring Mom home."

"Do they know who did this?"

Raisin shrugs and shuffles the cards.

"Where's Dad?" I ask.

He shrugs again, sniveling.

Knowing my mother, she was sticking her nose into things she probably shouldn't have been. My mother is fiercely protective of us, to the point where I can envision her searching for answers in all the wrong places.

Once again, my dad has failed us when we most need him. I want to stay mad at him but know that I won't. Or can't. Because I have failed everyone, too. Still, that doesn't stop me from hating his guts right now. I hate him now more than ever, and possibly always will hate him.

Raisin puts his hands up to his face and starts to cry. I've been so lost in thought that I haven't even considered trying to make him feel better. Our mother has always been there for us, and as much as her injuries alarm me, I can't imagine how scared Raisin is. Or how we would ever go on as a family without her.

"Don't worry, buddy. She'll be okay."

"How do you know that?" he snaps. "Don't you get it, Katie? Someone tried to kill her. Probably because of what happened to you. What if they succeed the next time?"

"They won't. Besides, if anything ever happened to her, I'm here for you."

"Great! That makes me feel so much better."

"I didn't mean it that way. What I meant to say is that I'm here for you and always will be."

"No you won't. You've barely been around these past two years because of that stupid boyfriend of yours. Then, after you met Willow, you changed even more."

"I did not change."

"Yes you did change. Even Mom noticed it. I heard her complaining about you to Gramma."

"I'm sorry if you feel that way, Raisin, but you're wrong. I swear that I'll make everything up to you."

"You lie, Katie, and you never used to lie. No way you'll make it up to me once you go away to college. Then you'll forget about all of us." He throws down the cards and runs up to his room. Scout follows after him.

I glance down at my phone. Still no message from Willow. The sad fact is, I have let Raisin and my family down. I feel like I've let the entire town down, too. But now's not the time to dwell on that. I have lots of remembering to do before Willow calls back. Before I can even begin to mend my family's many wounds.

After the group photo, the players separated and wandered around the field, snapping pictures with their cell phones and talking to loved ones. Willow grabbed my hand and led me around like a pony while Gil followed us with his camera. Willow was the star of the show, and everyone wanted a piece of her after the amazing feat she'd accomplished by pitching a no-hitter.

It felt incredible being the object of everyone's attention. Sure, I'd been a key member of the team, but it was Willow who'd brought us this championship. Without her, we would have barely made the play-offs. She held my hand as we stood in front of the news cameras and answered the reporters' questions. Most of the questions were directed to her, but my mere proximity to Willow put me in the crosshairs of stardom, and I happily provided answers and smiled for the cameras.

I turned and saw Coach Hicks hugging Becky Higgins. A girl went around and announced that the Nelsons planned on having a celebratory cookout at their home later in the day. I wanted badly to go and rekindle some old friendships, forever cemented by our amazing championship run, but I knew Willow would not even consider attending their party. The Nelsons' cookout would be safe and fun, and I wouldn't need to worry about drinking, drugs, boys, or getting into trouble.

"Forget their stupid cookout, Katie. We'll throw our own party, and it'll be awesome," Willow said.

"Don't you think it would be more fun to celebrate as a team?"

"As a team? I was the one who batted in the two runs. I was the one who pitched the no-hitter—and I can't even stand playing softball."

"Still, we all had your back."

"Maybe you had my back, but the others certainly didn't. They can't stand me." She pulled out her phone and started to walk away. "Go if you like, Katie, but that's not where I want to be."

"Wait," I said, catching up to her, knowing I couldn't go to that party alone.

Was I weak? Socially messed up? The only way I could show up at the Nelsons' party was with Willow by my side. Those girls wouldn't give me the time of day if I showed up there without her. I pictured myself standing off in the corner, ignored and alone, nervously shoveling potato salad into my mouth. I understood the corner I'd backed myself into: it was a corner that I could never pull myself out of until the day I finally left this town.

She drove me home so I could get a change of clothes and my swimsuit; then we went back to her house. We sat on the beach, reclined on lounge chairs, dressed in our swimsuits. Mine was a conservative one-piece, while Willow had donned a revealing string bikini that left little to the imagination. Between us sat a small cooler filled with cold drinks. I opened a bottle of pear cider and nursed it for as long as I could, telling myself that I'd not get drunk this time.

Willow's father came out a short while later, dressed in baggy swim trunks, and asked if we'd like to go in the water with him. I had no desire to swim, the ocean still being cold in June. But Willow leapt up, grabbed his hand, and pulled him along with her. I watched as they jogged side by side down to the water's edge. It felt weird observing their father-daughter relationship. Was I jealous because of the crappy relationship I had with my own father? I couldn't quite put my finger on my uneasiness.

The late afternoon sun shone down on us as the tide rolled in. Gentle blue waves rippled ashore. I couldn't believe we had this whole beach to ourselves. Off to the left stood a full-size volleyball net. Behind me, the patio extended far out onto the sand and was crowded with smokers, grills, refrigerators, and something called a Big Green Egg, which actually was this weird outdoor cooker that resembled an oversized avocado.

I'd taken only a few sips before the cider started to kick in. Then I began to forget all my worries. The sun felt nice on my face and arms, and I felt content to bask in the admirable glow of our championship season. I tried hard to erase everything bad from my mind, and the alcohol sure helped.

Someone called out my name. I sat up and saw Julian standing on his family's side of the beach, wearing only surf shorts and sunglasses. The shorts hung down over his shins, and his hair was twisted up in one of those man buns. I tried not to stare at Julian, and yet I couldn't take my eyes off him. He looked exotic and gorgeous, so totally different than Dakota, who I'd all but forgotten. He smiled at me in that goofy manner of his. I giggled and waved him over. He seemed to think about it for a few seconds before jogging over to me. He knelt down, grabbed a bottle of Corona out of the cooler, and let his long fingers twist it open. His nails were painted red and black. Then he slugged a good part of the beer down in one gulp.

"What's up, gorgeous?" he said.

"Just chilling after our big win."

"Congrats on that." He gave me a fist bump, and his knuckles touching mine made my skin tingle. "You must be so psyched."

"Big-time."

"You going to stay for the getty tonight?"

"The getty?"

"That's what they call parties in South Beach. I spent two weeks there on winter break, and it's insane."

"Yeah, I'm going to stay."

"Cool." He guzzled down the rest of his beer and tossed the empty in the cooler.

"Are you?"

"Girl, I was put on this earth to party."

I heard shouting down by the water and sat up straighter to see what was going on. Willow and her father had started play fighting in the surf and were splashing water at each other. He picked her up and tossed her into a wave. When she came up, he moved behind her and wrapped his arms around her stomach. It struck me as odd, but then again, what did I know about normal father-daughter relationships? The people in my part of town rarely, if ever, showed any public affection. I guessed it was a Maine thing.

"Asshole," Julian said.

"You don't like him?" I asked.

"Hell no, and it's totally mutual."

"How could anyone not like you, Julian?" I smiled flirtatiously, but he didn't see it.

"It's pathetic how he hovers over her like that. He thinks he's going to make Willow into a big movie star and then cash in."

"You doubt she'll be a star?"

"Nah, she'll be a star, all right. Willow's got serious game. I just don't think that loser father of hers is gonna be the one to do it."

"She obviously believes in him."

"And that's what I don't get. It's such a fucked-up relationship."

"I think it's nice to see a father love his child as much as he does. I only wish I had half the relationship with my own father."

"Me, too, Katie Cutie." He caressed my cheek.

I looked over at him. "You think Dakota's okay?"

"Of course he's okay. I'm just jealous the dude managed to get out of here and start his life over."

"Have you heard from him?"

"Nah. You?"

"No." I stared up at the blue sky. "You don't think anything bad happened to him, do you?"

"Dakota? No way." He laughed, as if I was crazy. "Why you stressing? You miss him?"

"No, not at all. Just curious."

"Don't worry that pretty head over him. Trust me, that dude's living large right now." Another fist pump. "I see you tonight. A'ight?"

"A'ight," I replied, slightly embarrassed by my faux gangsta slang. I tried not to stare at his long, lean body as he strutted over to his side of the beach. I lifted the cold bottle to my lips and drank the rest of my cider. It went straight to my head.

This is where things get dicey. I remember sitting on that chaise lounge and watching with curiosity as Willow and her father wrestled in the surf. I reached for another cold drink and this time pulled out a chilled bottle of raspberry margarita. I remember drinking it while basking in the late afternoon sun.

My memory gets worse after that. Kids started to appear along the beach. I suspect someone slipped something in my drink during that get-together, but I can't say for sure.

Bits and pieces return. Like dancing with Julian on the sand while Drake rapped over the loudspeakers. Kids playing volleyball. Others drinking and vaping. My head a whirring blur. Talking to that girl Bella. I remember that at one point I hadn't seen Willow for quite some time. She had a habit of disappearing during these parties and then reappearing out of thin air.

I remember a gentle breeze blowing in off the ocean. Then lying with Julian on that chaise lounge. Him kissing me while tucking strands of hair behind my ear. Willow appearing out of nowhere, begging Julian to take off with her somewhere. Me angry but not saying anything as she pulled him by the hand and dragged him away. Julian looking back with an innocent smile on his face.

After that, my memory fails me. I close my eyes. I am trying to remember something else when my phone pings. Another message.

Katie, it's me again. Willow. Please help. I'm in BIG trouble and need you now more than ever!!!!

But where should I go? What can I do? *I want to help you, Willow. Just give me a clue as to your whereabouts.*

No sooner had I received this message than I hear a loud crashing noise in the kitchen. I run in and see a brick lying on the floor, with a note attached to it. A car door slams outside. I run to the kitchen window and see a vehicle speeding out of our driveway. It's so dark out that I can't see anything else.

I pick up the brick, pull off the note attached to it, and read it.

Everyone in town knows you went to that rich bitch's fund-raiser. Mind your own damn p's and q's, Isla. Stay out of this, or you'll get hurt much worse the next time. Stop snooping around, or you'll lose your grandfather's shop.

I throw down the brick as if it's hot charcoal and wonder what I've done. Have I caused this? Did my mother get run off the road because of me? I've caused enough damage with my actions, whatever they are. The least I can do is save Willow from the trouble she's in. She just needs to tell me where to go.

I realize I have no way to get to her—until I hear the loud sound of my dad's truck as it rumbles up the driveway and he parks next to the house. The keys! I realize now what I have to do: lift the keys out of his pocket and take off in his truck. I've always been the good girl, the one who never does anything wrong or gets into trouble. He'll trust me. It'll be too late before he realizes that I've taken off in his new pickup.

"What was that noise?" Raisin asks, running into the room, with Scout by his side.

I'm lost for words. Raisin's gaze goes from me to the broken window to the brick sitting on the floor. There's no hiding the note. He runs over and grabs it from me as I stand by. I have to avert my eyes from Scout's withering gaze. Tears pool up in Raisin's eyes as soon as he reads the note.

"This is your fault, Katie!" he shouts, pointing at me.

"I have to go, Raisin, before Gramma and Mom come home."

"Where are you going? You don't have a car."

"I will soon. Dad just pulled up."

"Why are you leaving?"

"I can't tell you right now, but the place I'm going will help me remember what happened and possibly save Willow's life."

"You should never have hung out with that girl. I could tell she was a bad person the first time I met her."

"She isn't a bad person. She just never knew any other way." Why did I just say that?

"Mom raised us right, Katie. What's your excuse?"

I realize I have none.

My father staggers up the stairs, and I think about all the grief he's given my mother. Wonderful role model, driving in that condition. The smell he gives off hits me right away—the not-so-subtle fragrance of pot smoke and stale beer. He sports a winning smile as he staggers into the kitchen. Has he any idea what happened to his wife?

"There's my big girl," he says, arms wide.

I rush over and wrap my arms around his waist, and my hands search for the keys in his pocket. Raisin sees what I'm doing and runs upstairs. Despite the fact that I'm angry at my dad, it still feels good to be enveloped in his arms. I smell the familiar scent of oil paint, and it momentarily comforts me. Will I ever get over this stupid, crazy love for him?

It brings back memories of Willow horsing around with her father in the surf. The easy way he picked her up and wrestled with her. It reminds me of being a little girl and having a huge crush on my dad, telling everyone how I was going to one day marry him.

My phone pings. The scent of alcohol on his body practically suffocates me. I peek around his waist and glance at my phone. It's Willow, and she's messaging me her location.

I guide Dad into the living room and down onto the couch. He's more intoxicated than I thought. I turn on the TV. Grab him a cold beer. Then stash it back in the fridge because Dad's passed out, and because I remember that Raisin is still home. Raisin! What will happen if his sugar levels change? Should I chance leaving him here alone with my passed-out dad?

"Raisin!" I shout until he comes downstairs. "You have to take care of yourself if something happens."

"I can just wake Dad up. He'll take care of me."

"No, it's time to be a big boy. You know how to test yourself and what to take. I've seen you do it."

"Dad knows what to do."

"You have to face reality, Raisin. We're not Dad's main priority anymore. Maybe we never were. He'd rather smoke pot and drink beer than care for us."

"Don't say those bad things about him."

"It's true, and you know it."

"I saw you take Dad's keys. Where are you going?" he says.

I don't answer, because I'm already bolting upstairs to grab the gun out of my mother's safe. She doesn't think I know the combination, but I do. When I return downstairs, I notice that Raisin is gone. Where did he go? It doesn't much matter now, because I need to go and find Willow.

"Katie?" Dad opens his eyes and wakes up.

"What, Dad?"

"I hate to tell you this," he slurs, "but your mother's been in an accident."

"I know."

"Don't worry, though. She's all right."

"Why didn't you go to the hospital and drive her home?"

"Your grandmother said she'd do it."

"So where did you go afterward?"

"I stopped at Sully's for a quick beer." He closes his eyes.

"Jerk," I mutter under my breath.

Then I leave the house and get inside his truck. Stick the keys in the ignition and drive away.

PART THREE

KARL

*T*HE NAME STAYED WITH HIM AS HE DROVE BACK TO THE STATION. HE felt wired, uneasy, irritable. His intuition sensed that something big was about to break. No sooner had he parked in the station's lot than a call came in. Years ago, Shepherd's Bay had switched to a regional dispatch to save money, so now 911 calls went straight there. The regional dispatchers had no clue about the crazy street patterns of Shepherd's Bay.

A disturbance at the McCallister home. He headed back the same way he'd just come. Now what could be happening? He switched on the lights and siren and raced to the disturbance. Upon arriving at the residence, he noticed a group of people standing in the street and watching whatever seemed to be happening. Karl got out of the vehicle and pushed his way through the crowd. There he saw Beckett standing, with a baseball bat, next to a bloodied and battered Julian. About ten feet away stood Drew, also battered and bruised. A large gash on his head oozed blood, and he appeared unsteady on his feet while shouting at father and son. He had recklessly parked his old pickup on the McCallisters' property and, in doing so, had made deep trenches in the near-perfect lawn.

"Why'd you assholes have to move here and ruin everything?" Drew slurred. "Even worse, you hurt Katie."

Karl walked over to Drew and tried to calm him down, but the boy pushed him away. Left with no other choice, Karl shoved him to the lawn and cuffed him. Drew put up no resistance. Beneath him, Karl could hear the kid sobbing. He smelled like a brewery.

"How much did you drink, Drew?"

"What does it matter now?"

"You shouldn't have been driving."

"I don't care. I don't give a shit about anything anymore."

He stood the kid up, trying not to get blood on his uniform. Drew lunged for Julian, but Karl managed to hold on to him long enough to guide him into the backseat of the cruiser. Once inside, Drew fell sideways onto the seat and continued to sob. After closing the door, Karl approached father and son.

"What happened?"

"He came over here and assaulted us. I want to press charges against that boy," Beckett said.

"Any reason why he attacked your son?" He looked at Julian's bloody face.

"He's drunk and pissed off that his girlfriend chose to hang out with me instead of him," Julian said. "We were tight."

"Tight?"

"For real."

"My son has done nothing wrong, Officer," Beckett said.

"Seriously, I would have kicked his ass if my pops hadn't come out swinging."

"Look what he's done," Beckett said, pointing toward his ripped-up lawn. "He even threw a rock through our window. That kid was drunk and out of his mind. It's a good thing he didn't kill anyone while driving over here."

"I'm going to take him down to the station. Do you need medical attention, Julian?"

"A little ice on that bruise and he'll be fine," Beckett said.

"With all due respect, sir, I was asking your son."

Beckett turned and looked at Julian with a glare, which Karl interpreted as threatening. Something told him that the McCallister family dynamics were a lot more complicated than anyone believed.

"Nah, I'm good," Julian said, eyeing his father warily.

"I'll be in touch, then," Karl said.

"I fully expect charges to be brought. And I want this piece of shit towed off my lawn as soon as possible," Beckett muttered.

"I'll call the tow company, but it may be a while before anyone gets here. I'll take a statement from you later," Karl told him.

With Drew lying silent in the backseat, he headed back to the station. What the hell was going on in this town?

After processing Drew and locking him up, he called the boy's parents. They informed him that Drew could stay in jail for the night. That would teach the kid a lesson. Typical fisherman hard-ass family. Then again, Karl knew his own parents would have done the same thing had he done what Drew had.

He went to the computer and typed in the name Jalen Stark and "Los Angeles" and was surprised to see a number of listings. Jalen Stark's father was African American and had played seven years of professional football before retiring. His mother had been a Playboy centerfold and a wannabe reality star. The first ten entries were about his death. He clicked on one and read quotes from his parents, all of which expressed their profound sadness at Jalen's passing. They claimed not to have known that their son was a hard-drug user. The detective on the case, Tilly Cruz, was quoted as saying that it appeared to be an overdose, but that they were still looking into the boy's death.

On a whim, Karl called the LA Police Department, explained his situation, and asked to speak to Detective Cruz. He was expecting a callback, but he heard a Latino woman's voice answer almost immediately.

"Yeah, I remember that case," Cruz said. "It was ruled a heroin overdose for lack of any other evidence."

"Did you suspect otherwise?"

"It was weird. The kid had no history of hard-drug use, according to his parents. No track marks on his arm. No evidence he used anything stronger than weed. Then again, it was well known that he liked to have a good time."

"So you assumed that he tried heroin once and accidentally overdosed?"

"That's pretty much all we could conclude from the evidence."

"Any indication that he knew or was friends with a Willow Briggs?"

"Let me access the file on my computer." A few minutes of Cruz humming passed. "Here it is. Seems this boy had a lot of girlfriends. And yes, one of them was named Willow Briggs, but we didn't question her. No reason to. His mother said he went over to her house from time to time."

"She was a freshman then."

"Yes, and he was a senior."

He thanked the detective and hung up. His hand shook because of the overwhelming feeling that he was getting closer to the truth—and that the truth would lead him back to Willow Briggs. He speculated that she had to be alive. There was only one person now who could tell him what had happened to Willow, and that was Katie Eaves.

He grabbed his cap and headed over to the Eaveses' house. Dealing with that stubborn girl was starting to get tiresome. He vowed to get answers this time.

ISLA

*T*HE RINGING IN HER EARS STARTED SOON AFTER RAY'S MOTHER AR-
rived at the hospital to drive her home. Thankfully, Ray had come
and gone. Her entire head now seemed to vibrate with a high-
pitched shrill. She wanted badly to be surrounded by her family,
satisfied that everyone was safe and sound. If only the doctor would
return and clear her to go home, she could get on with her life. At
least Katie was home. In the event something happened to Raisin,
Katie knew how to care for her brother.

Who had tried to run her off the road? And why? Was it because
she had attended that stupid fund-raiser? She had grown up in
Shepherd's Bay and knew practically everyone in town. Had the
lines been so desperately drawn that to take sides meant you were a
traitor to your own people? Had things gotten that bad?

The doctor returned and wrote her a prescription for the pain,
which she knew she wouldn't take. Too many addicts in town had
started on prescription meds and then had found it hard to stop.
All she could think about was how much this visit to the emergency
room would cost. A thousand bucks, which she didn't have? Maybe
more. She had yet to meet her deductible in a year's span. Raisin,
on the other hand, exceeded it every year.

Apart from the loud ringing in her ears, she felt surprisingly
good, considering all that had happened. Thank God for her mother-
in-law. How Ray had been spawned of such an amazing woman,
she'd never know.

"I can't thank you enough for everything, Ma," she said as her mother-in-law drove her home.

"It's the least I could do, knowing how useless that son of mine is. I smelled alcohol on his breath the second he opened his mouth."

"Typical Ray."

"What about Raisin?"

"Katie's home with him right now. She knows what to do in the event something happens."

"I can stay at the house for a while if you'd like. Keep an eye on Raisin."

"You really don't have to, Ma. I'm feeling a lot better now."

"I beg to differ, sweetie. Doctor said you got shook up pretty bad in that accident."

"It was no accident," Isla said. "And if it wasn't for this cut on my head, I'd be perfectly fine."

"Maybe I'll stay for a little while, just to make sure you're okay."

Aside from the ringing in her ears and the throbbing in her skull, she felt okay. Good enough to return to work tomorrow and cut hair. Even with a concussion, she'd return to the salon. She had no other choice. With her family's finances in dire straits, she didn't have many options. Not working meant no money coming in—and the bills were piling up.

Her mother turned into the driveway and pulled up to the house. Almost instantly, Isla felt a sinking sensation in her gut. Where was Ray? His truck was not parked out front. She looked up at her kitchen window and noticed something odd. The curtain was flapping in the wind. It took her another few seconds before she saw the shattered window.

She jumped out of the vehicle and bounded up the stairs, feeling the aftershocks in her brain. She pushed open the unlocked door, and she saw the brick sitting on the kitchen table. Next to it was a crumpled sheet of paper with writing on it. A wave of nausea swept over her as she picked it up and read it. Once she had done that, she glanced over and saw Ray passed out on the couch. He leaned to one side, with his feet up on the cushion. The staccato sound of his heavy snoring filled the room. She went over to him with the note in hand and shook his shoulder.

"Wake up, Ray!" His breath reeked of pot smoke and beer. *The bastard!*

He opened his eyes and stared up, as if surprised to see her.

"Wake the hell up, Ray."

"I'm awake, I'm awake," he said, rubbing his eyes.

"Where's Katie and Raisin?" She then ran from room to room, calling out their names.

"They should be here," he said once she returned. "Or at least they were here when I came home."

"Well, they're not here now, and your truck is gone." She pointed toward the brick on the table. "See that brick, Ray? Someone tossed it through our window. What kind of father are you, anyway?"

"What the hell are you talking about?" He stood groggily and stumbled into the kitchen, and stared in disbelief at the shattered window and the brick resting on the table. Isla followed behind him. "Raisin was in his room when I arrived, and Katie gave me a big hug as soon as I walked in."

Just then Ray's mother walked in.

Isla pointed toward the broken window. "Someone took your truck, Ray. Did they take the kids, too?"

"Jesus!" He ran over to the kitchen window and noticed his missing truck.

"And you slept right through it. Better yet, you were so drunk, you passed out."

"Shit!"

"Oh, Ray," his mother groaned. "How could you be so irresponsible?"

Isla picked up the phone, in a panic. She had started to punch in numbers when she heard the sound of a car coming up the driveway. She ran outside and saw only Karl stepping out of his polce cruiser. Panicked, she started shouting at him hysterically.

"Calm down," Karl said to her as he made his way up the stairs. "Take a deep breath and tell me what's wrong."

"Katie and Raisin are gone."

"Gone? Where?"

"That's what I was going to ask you. They weren't here when I came home. Someone threw a brick through our window while I was in the ER. There was a message attached to it." She pointed at the shattered kitchen window; the remaining shards resembled an inverted star.

"Do you think whoever did this kidnapped them?"

"I don't know. Ray's truck is gone, too."

"If someone took them, why would they take Ray's truck?"

"Jesus, Karl, I don't know. All I know is that they're missing. Just do your job and find them."

"Let me take a look inside first." He pushed his way past Ray, who stood in the kitchen doorway, looking paralyzed with fear.

Isla trailed behind him. "I've already looked for them inside, and they're not here."

"What does the note say?"

"Basically, someone is warning me not to help Laura Milton and to stop looking into the disappearances of these kids."

Karl went upstairs and into Raisin's room and turned on the light.

"I told you, he's not here."

"No, but his bottom drawer is open, as if he was in a desperate rush to get something."

"That's where he keeps Scout's Day-Glo vest." She ran over and noticed it missing. "He took the Day-Glo one with him and left the other one here. But why?"

"I don't know why. Maybe in case he planned to be away from the house all night." Karl turned and exited the room, and she followed anxiously behind.

"It makes no sense. Why would someone kidnap Raisin and let him grab Scout's vest?" she said.

"You're assuming it's an abduction. How about we consider another theory?"

"Why in the world *wouldn't* I assume it's an abduction when three kids in this town have already gone missing and one of them is dead?"

She followed Karl downstairs and watched as he nearly knocked over her father, who stood mumbling in the hallway, looking lost and confused. The cop held the old man in his arms to prevent him from falling. Her father cussed at Karl to get away from him, and so Isla intervened by taking her father's elbow and steering him in the direction of his bedroom. She didn't get far. A sour stench punched her nose, and she stopped in her tracks, realizing that he'd wet his pants.

"But I'm hungry," he complained. She looked over and saw Ray staring at her.

"We'll get you some food, Dad, and a new change of clothes, too." She nodded, and Ray came over and grabbed the old man. "Take care of him."

"I'm real sorry, Isla. I never meant for any of this to happen," Ray said.

"Any of what?"

"You know. *This.*"

"You and I are going to have a serious talk soon."

"I swear to you, everything I've been doing has been for the good of this family."

"Please don't make me laugh."

"Here. This is for you." He pulled out a thick wad of bills and handed it to her, but she slapped it away.

"There's more to being a family than just money, Ray."

She looked past him and noticed that Karl had gone back upstairs. She scrambled up the steps to see what else she'd overlooked. Footsteps told her that he was in her bedroom. Why would he go in there? It felt like a violation of her privacy. But now that her two children had gone missing she didn't care about any of that. She entered her bedroom. Squatting, Karl glanced back at her so she could see what he was seeing. The door to her gun safe lay open, and her Glock was nowhere in sight.

"God no."

"I don't think they were kidnapped, Isla. I think Katie took Ray's keys and your gun and went somewhere."

"But where would they go? And how does Katie know the combination to my safe?"

"I have no idea," he said, dialing the chief, "but I think I might know why."

She watched as he called in Ray's pickup and license plate number. Once he'd provided all the information, he ended the call, sat down on the bed, and explained what he'd learned from the Internet. He theorized that Willow might still be alive and that she called Katie for help.

"So why did she take the gun?" Isla asked.

"I'm guessing that Willow must have persuaded her that she was in trouble and needed help."

"But why would she help Willow if Willow committed these murders?"

"I'm not certain she did commit them, but I bet she knows who did."

"And who do you think that is?"

"I have no idea. Maybe Willow convinced your daughter that she, Willow, killed Dakota in self-defense. Or maybe Katie really can't remember what happened, and that's why she agreed to take Raisin with her. So she could look after him, since your husband couldn't."

"God, Karl, I'm scared. We need to find them before . . ."

"We'll find them, Isla. I promise."

KATIE

I RACE ACROSS TOWN IN MY FATHER'S NEW TRUCK. HE TAUGHT ME HOW to drive when I was fifteen, and so I feel confident behind the wheel of this rig. On the passenger-side floor mat sit three empty beer cans, like a trio of little orphans all named Bud. No sense obeying the speed limit, because I know everyone's out looking for me, anyway. Five police officers for an entire town seems a bit paltry, but tonight that might work in my favor.

My mother is probably frantic with worry. At least Raisin will be safe once she's home, meaning I can save Willow.

I turn on the high beams because of the lack of streetlights outside of the downtown area. The road twists and turns through the dense grove of trees. It seems I'm the only one out tonight. On the seat next to me rests my mom's loaded Glock. The only time I've ever seen her use it was when a black bear started rooting around in our trash bin. One shot above its head and it took off into the woods, never to be seen again. I was ten at the time and remember being impressed with my mother's bravery.

What I've done will have consequences. I've come to terms with that, however misguided my actions may be. I left my father asleep on the couch, with the window shattered and that threatening note sitting on the kitchen table. It will look bad for him when my mother shows up and sees him in that condition. Then, when she notices that I've borrowed his truck and taken her gun, she'll be beyond worried. I only pray that Raisin's numbers stay normal until my mother arrives home.

There'll be a reckoning after all of this plays out. How it will affect me, I'm not quite sure, but everyone will know where they stand in this family. There'll be no more deception and lies, and maybe that will end up being a good thing.

Or not.

It could end up being bad. Because I'm not all the way back to feeling normal. It's this memory of mine that's still giving me fits. My head feels perfectly fine at the moment, which tells me that something else is at play. It tells me that my brain is resisting my heart's many questions. But for what reason? Because the truth will be too traumatic? It's my biggest fear, that the reality of what I've done is so horrible that my mind refuses to cough up the truth.

I'm on my way to save Willow. Or it could be myself I'm trying to save. Or the self I'm meant to one day become. My mind feels numb as I drive through town. The road comes to me like I'm playing in one of Raisin's video games.

For the first time in a while, I feel answers are close at hand.

I keep thinking about how Willow grabbed Julian's hand and stole him away from me, laughing the entire time. Was she laughing at me? I remember becoming angry. She was supposed to be my friend and not a backstabbing bitch. It took me a few minutes lounging in that chair to build up my resentment toward her. She had done this to me before, with Dakota, and look how that had turned out. I downed the contents of the bottle in my hand and stood uneasily to my feet, nearly falling over. I'd already drunk too much—four bottles—and felt light-headed and dizzy. No way I was going to let myself get pushed around by her anymore.

It was time to take a stand.

I saw two kids passed out on the beach. I saw the moon high above, glimmering over the ocean's glossy surface. There were no other kids inside the house, judging from where I stood as I looked in. A lone light shone in the kitchen. I glanced at my phone and noticed that it was 2:47 a.m. After letting myself inside the large house, I staggered drunkenly around it, muttering incoherently to myself, looking for any sign of Willow. I didn't find her on the first floor, and so I climbed those futuristic stairs, wishing there was a bannister I could hold on to, deathly afraid that I might fall through the cracks in those steps.

At the top of the stairs, I took a deep breath and sternly lectured myself not to back down. *Don't be a punching bag, Katie. Face Willow head-on and tell her what's on your mind. You're better than this. You can do it.*

Down the hallway I shuffled, checking room after room, switching the light on and then off when I didn't discover the two of them together, which I half expected to do. I pictured their naked bodies intertwined, and it angered me, especially after the way Julian had hurt her that one night. Why wouldn't Willow admit to me what Julian had done to her? That he had struck her and caused her nose to bleed? Was she in love with him? And if she was, why wouldn't she tell me, so I could back off? Because maybe I was a little in love with him, too, although I was reluctant to admit it.

Muttering curses under my breath, I realized that I loved Willow like a sister. "Hoes B4 Bros," she had once scribbled in her chemistry notebook before showing it to me. Thinking about it now made me laugh. I knew I would love her until one day, for whatever reason, I didn't, whenever that day came. I also knew I could forgive her for stealing Julian away from me. To me, Julian was merely a stupid, expendable boy that I had a crush on. An indulgence that would soon grow wearisome. Or maybe that was what I told myself at the time so as not to have hurt feelings.

I remember that as I tiptoed down the hallway, I saw a set of golf clubs leaning against the wall. I randomly pulled one out of the bag and rested it over my shoulder. It was a putter, like the kind we used at the miniature golf course over in Old Orchard Beach the few times our family vacationed down there. I gripped it in my hands like a weapon. Something inside me wanted to inflict much pain on Julian. "Grip it and rip it," Drew had once said to me at the driving range, while teaching me how to golf.

Two rooms left to search. I opened the last door to the left and was surprised to hear someone sobbing inside the room.

"Are you all right?" I asked.

"Go away," answered a voice that was *definitely* not Willow's.

Who was that? I gently closed the door and moved toward the

room on the right, which was located at the far end of the hallway. Sweat poured down my forehead, and I felt dizzy from the combination of alcohol and adrenaline. Oddly, my anger had dissipated, and all I wanted now was to find a soft place to land. Then to sleep like Rumplestiltskin and wake only to discover that half my life had passed me by.

Why should I be so mad at Willow? Or Julian? It seemed silly, the more I thought about it. I had a boyfriend who cared about me. A good family that provided me with love and support, despite the fact that I felt neglected and ignored most of the time. I envisioned a decent future for myself, one in which I was enrolled at a prestigious college far removed from Shepherd's Bay.

I figured that since I'd gone this far, I might as well come to grips with Willow stealing Julian from me. After all, he wasn't my type. He was rich and artsy and from the other side of town, and I was an old soul. Willow seemed far better suited for him than did I. Sometimes things just weren't meant to be.

Behind the door on the right, I heard two people whispering as they engaged in a heated discussion. What were they arguing about this late at night? I cupped my ear to the door and stood on wobbly legs. Heard muted words that shocked me—words such as *pregnant, fetus,* and *abortion*—and something about how *this* didn't feel right.

Goddamned Julian! He'd gotten Willow pregnant. Tears spilled from my eyes. No wonder she'd dragged him away from me. She was carrying his baby. Was Julian trying to force her to abort it? It had to be the reason she'd been so upset that night.

Why did I care? It wasn't my problem. And why was I always playing second fiddle to others and helping them with their problems? I had my own problems to deal with, and yet I was always coming in second to all the kids in school who were smarter, better looking, and more talented than I. Always second to Raisin, whom my parents doted on because of his illness. Even in my relationship with Drew, it felt as if I'd settled for less than I deserved.

But what did I deserve? Other than earning good grades, I hadn't done anything in my life deserving of much attention. Who was I? Katie Eaves: a completely average girl who deserved shit. I'd never done anything special to cause good things to come my way. So why should I care now?

Furious at my shortcomings—and at myself—I lifted the putter off my shoulder and opened the door, fully prepared to inflict pain. I flicked on the switch and stepped back from the jarring sensation of light. My anger came rushing back in one fell swoop. I saw his surprised face turn toward me. My stomach rumbled, and for a second, I thought I might puke. Willow screamed as I staggered forward, bile in my throat, the putter held over my head. She pulled the sheet up to cover herself. Rage filled me, and I swung wildly at the blanket, which he held up to protect them. I heard shouts and shrieks as I swung the club again and again before dropping it and taking off, in tears, down the hallway.

My phone's GPS leads me to a dirt road off the main artery. Then it stops. I never knew this dirt lane existed. Then again, I have hardly ever come this way. This long winding road, taken to its conclusion, ends at Harper's Point.

I turn onto the narrow dirt lane and cruise down it, glad that my dad purchased a truck with four-wheel drive. There's barely enough room for this pickup to navigate. Bushes and tree branches swipe against the side of the truck. Mice and bats are outlined in the high-beam lights. How far must I travel before I reach my destination? I know I should be scared, but I'm not.

The lane finally opens up to a clearing. A pickup truck bigger than my dad's sits parked in front of a simple log cabin. I perform a U-turn so that I'm facing the way I came in, in the event I need to make a quick getaway.

A light is on inside the cabin. My mood brightens at the prospect of seeing my best friend again. Why she's at this location, I have no idea. Is someone holding her captive? Is she hiding from someone? I tell myself to let bygones be bygones. Julian means nothing to me now. I remember Willow's pregnancy, wondering what decision she'll make about the life in her belly. After our senior year, we'll both be off to college and on our divergent paths. Surviving my last year of high school will be my only goal in life, with or without Willow, but hopefully with her. All my other friendships have been burned, never to be rebuilt. It will be either enjoying a fun senior year with Willow or enduring high school alone.

I grab the Glock, stick it in my jacket, climb out of the pickup, and head toward the front door. It's a nice cabin, and in far better condition than I initially believed it to be. It's not the roughing-it kind of summer home with no electricity or running water. Just the right size, too. Cute and homey. Crickets chirp in my ears. The light of a pockmarked moon reflects off the pond below. An owl hoots as I walk up the three steps and knock on the door. No answer. It's unlocked, so I step inside, gripping the gun in my pocket.

Upstairs, I hear the stream of a shower. It's her. I can just feel it. I call out her name and hear a muffled reply that echoes off the lacquered log walls. Something to the effect that she'll be right down. The shiny logs appear everywhere in this dimly lit cabin. It's small, tidy, and comfy looking. I walk around happily and peek my head into the kitchen.

Another shout from the second floor. I tiptoe halfway up the stairs and try to make out her words. She wants a towel from the linen closet. My nerves buzz excitedly at the prospect of seeing her again and hearing all about what happened to her. I head to the top of the stairs, reach inside the linen closet, take out a fresh towel, and walk over to the bathroom. The sound of the running shower streams into my ears. I knock on the door, realizing I have a huge grin on my face. A handle squeaks from being turned, and the shower stops. Everything goes quiet. I'm so happy that I forget all about her betrayal of me over that stupid boy. Two stupid boys, actually. *Hoes before bros*, I tell myself. I shout out to her that I have her towel and that I'm super excited to see her.

The door opens, and I lift the towel toward the crack. Steam pours out. At the last second I see a purple aluminum club arcing toward my head. It's Willow's lucky softball bat. I duck, but the bat makes contact along the base of my shoulder. I scream in agony as I fall to the floor, just in time to feel the second blow glance against my skull. The gun falls out of my pocket and onto the floor. A constellation of stars rotates in my blurred vision. I lay there on my side, unable to move, feeling nauseous and numb. Am I paralyzed? She steps over me and takes off down the stairs. The pain of Willow's betrayal hurts more than the blows she just delivered. Why did she attack me? Is it because I caught her in bed that night? With him? Is it because I know she's pregnant? I close my eyes and fall into a black spiral. Down and down I plummet.

I'm not sure what I saw that night in that bedroom. Did I see Willow and Julian in bed? Did I hear them arguing about her pregnancy? All I remember is swinging that golf club and hitting the blanket he held up to ward off the blows.

I hear footsteps coming back up the stairs. This is bad. I suddenly realize I don't want to die in this log cabin.

KARL

*H*E SPED DOWN THE DARK ROAD, FOLLOWED THE TWISTY TURNS, AND prayed for a miracle. Isla sat next to him, staring quietly out the passenger window. He wanted to assure her that he'd find Katie and Raisin and that everything would be all right. Of course he didn't know how all of this would end. And the way things were playing out, he wasn't too optimistic. A queasy feeling settled into his gut.

More than anything, he wanted Isla to see Ray for the man he really was: a selfish bastard who cared only about himself. Was it bad of him to think this way? Yes, and he knew it.

They passed the spot where Isla's car had nearly gotten forced over the guardrail. The car had long been towed away. Debris littered the area where the car had settled. Tomorrow a road crew would arrive and sweep it all up before hosing the road down. Below lay the suspension bridge, lit up and devoid of traffic. He sped down the hill and turned onto the bridge for the thousand-foot drive over to Harper's Point. Waves below crashed against each other in an unorganized, random pattern.

He turned on the blue lights and raced across the bridge and didn't stop until he reached the Briggses' home. A light was on upstairs, in one of the bedrooms. Was it Willow's room? He jumped out of the cruiser, resting his hand on his gun. The passenger door opened and slammed shut, reminding him that Isla had come along with him. His vision turned myopic; his mission, single-minded. Was it too late to order Isla back in the car? She wouldn't listen, anyway, and so he decided not to say anything. He made his way to the Briggses' front door, determined to get answers. After ringing the doorbell, he waited for someone to answer.

Something gnawed at him. Was he second-guessing himself? The small police department in Shepherd's Bay didn't have enough officers for backup, and time was of the essence. What if Willow was armed? Or had seen them coming and had scrambled out the back?

The door started to open. Karl stepped back with hand on gun. When the door opened a few more inches, he was surprised to see Felicia standing there in a white robe and shower cap. Dark bags sagged under her eyes. He could only assume that she'd been crying.

"Where's your daughter, Mrs. Briggs?" Karl asked.

"What is this? Are you purposely trying to upset me, Officer?"

"Is Willow inside?"

"Do you actually think I'd be in this sorry condition if my daughter was home?"

"Can you answer the question, please?"

"You're a disgrace and should be ashamed of yourself. You probably don't even have kids, which means you have no idea what it's like to have a child go missing." She turned to Isla. "Tell him what it's like."

"I'm sorry, Felicia. Officer Bjornson believes that Willow is alive and has made contact with Katie."

"Willow's alive? Is it true? Where? How?"

"We don't know yet. That's why we came here. To ask you if you knew anything about it," Isla said.

"I don't know anything about that. I just want my daughter back home with us." Felicia waved them inside the house.

"Where's your husband?" Karl asked as he and Isla entered the house.

"I have no idea." Felicia walked back toward the kitchen. "He went out a while ago."

"And you have no idea where he went?" Karl asked. He and Isla trailed behind Felicia.

"No." Felicia turned toward them once she reached the island, then sat down. "Willow's disappearance has put a strain on our marriage."

Karl glanced around nervously, hand still on his revolver.

"Not that it's any of your damn business, but he's been unfaithful to me. Several times, in fact."

"May I look around?"

She turned and laughed bitterly. "Knock yourself out, but I'm telling you she's not here."

After taking out his gun, he went from room to room, searching for Willow. A bad feeling came over him when he had searched half the rooms and found them empty. Had he made a mistake by coming here? His job was now on the line, and he felt like he was failing badly. He continued to check the rooms, the pit in his stomach growing. A door on the first floor led down to the basement. He flicked on the lights and went downstairs, but quickly ran back up after seeing nothing.

"Happy now?" Felicia called from the kitchen.

He stood uneasily, feeling like a fool, as he stared down the dark stairs. Had he done a thorough enough search? He returned to the kitchen.

"You'll certainly be sorry when I report your ugly behavior to your superiors," Felicia snapped. "I'm amazed that you even have the moxie to barge into my home like this and harass a grieving mother, especially when your number one priority should be finding Willow."

"I'm very sorry to bother you." He turned and nodded to Isla, and together they walked toward the front door.

Isla stopped in her tracks and turned around. "Honestly, Felicia, we didn't mean to trouble you," Isla called. "It's just that Katie left the house with a gun, and we think she went to help Willow, wherever Willow might be."

Felicia left the kitchen and headed toward them. "So am I supposed to jump up and down and get all worked up now that *your* daughter is missing?"

Karl watched Isla turn and walk out the door.

"Go to hell, the both of you!" Felicia shouted as Karl made his way outside. "I can't believe you two have nothing better to do than barge in on a depressed mother."

The door slammed shut. Karl stopped for a second and glanced at Isla. Staring at her face, he couldn't quite read her expression. For the first time in a long while, he was at a loss for words and in need of direction. But he was a cop. People looked to *him* for answers. Only this time he'd run out of ideas, and it frustrated him.

Where had Katie gone? More importantly, where was Willow? If he found Willow, he'd locate Katie. Or vice versa. Had he been mistaken about all this?

Isla stared up at him, in need of answers. "What do we do now, Karl?"

"I . . . I don't know."

"Katie has my gun. And what happens if Raisin's numbers go off the rails?"

"If only Ray had been more attentive."

She turned away from him, and he wondered if he'd crossed a line by blaming her husband. Lamenting Ray's uselessness did nothing to help the situation. Now he wished he'd never said it.

"I'm sorry for blaming Ray. I should have never said that about him."

"No, you're spot on about Ray," she said. "But now is not the time for blame. I'm concerned only for my kids' safety."

They climbed back in the car.

"In the meantime, I think we should drive around town and see if we can spot his pickup."

"I suppose that's our only hope of finding them."

"It's not the best idea, I know, but it's the only thing I can think to do at the moment."

"Thank you, Karl. I know you're doing your best."

Ray didn't deserve such a good woman. Then again, she was the one to marry the lazy bastard. Granted, it was many years ago, after her college career had fizzled. And she'd been the recipient of unwanted sexual advances by that sleazy college professor. Was that why she had returned home and fallen for Ray's bullshit charms? It really didn't matter now how things had turned out. It was time to deal with reality.

He turned on the ignition and sped down the road. If only they could catch a break.

KATIE

W HEN I WAKE UP, MY SHOULDER THROBS AS MUCH AS MY HEAD. I'M sure it's broken. Someone lifts me up and guides me down the stairs. I grit my teeth to counter the pain, only to realize that my eyes and mouth have been covered over, and my wrists secured behind my back. A door opens, and I'm led outside and into a vehicle. The engine roars, and soon we're moving.

After about ten minutes, we stop. The front door opens and closes, and I'm escorted out of the vehicle. I can feel the barrel of a gun pressed against my back. Whoever has kidnapped me does not say a word. I'm led down a set of stairs and into a room. The restraints on my wrists are released, and my hands are freed. I'm shoved into a sitting position on the floor. A restraint is used to secure my hand to something above my head. Then the door closes.

I settle back against the concrete wall. It's obvious I'm not going anywhere. Whoever has done this has a reason for kidnapping and blindfolding me.

Did Willow direct me to that cabin? But why? Is it because I burst in on her that night in a drunken rage? My shoulder aches so bad that I want to scream. I want to remember more about that night. Like seeing his face and then swinging that putter against the raised blanket. Or registering his surprised expression when I caught the two of them in bed together.

Did I misjudge Willow? I knew she had emotional issues that caused her to act out in unpredictable ways. But I never thought she, of all people, would turn on me. I'd seen her punish Tiffany with that head kick, and so I knew she was capable of violence. But is she capable of murder? Did she kill Dakota because he was interested in me? That couldn't be true, because he dumped me soon after he'd coerced me into having sex with him. Or did she kill him because of *her* interest in me? Because she wanted me—her bestie—all to herself?

I remember delivering three hard blows to that blanket. Then I remember dropping the putter and staggering drunkenly down those crazy stairs.

What happened next?

I suddenly remember something else. I started running in my bare feet across the tile floor. The contents of my stomach tickled in the back of my throat. As I opened the front door, I heard him call out my name. He told me to come back and talk this matter through. To sit down with the two of them and figure out how to deal with everything that had just happened. He tried to convince me that it wasn't what it looked like and that I was drunk and seeing things.

But I knew what I saw. And what I heard.

I ran outside, into the black of night, and the sound of waves lulled me into a false sense of security. The gentle breeze licked at my tears as I considered which way to turn.

The beach offered me a dimly lit path, and so I took it. With the waves cascading to my right, I dug my heels into the soft, cool sand and took off. I breathed in short rasps, my lungs searing. I heard voices behind me, calling out my name. I passed the McCallisters' home to my left. The beam of a lighthouse swept over the landscape like one of those laser lights at the roller-skating rink we regularly visited. I turned to see if anyone was following me and, in the process, tripped over a drift log that had washed ashore.

"I'm so sorry, Katie," Willow sobbed, suddenly standing over me. Where had she come from?

I didn't say anything. I just lay there on my back, staring up at the two moons while trying to catch my breath, praying for this nightmare to end.

"I didn't mean for you to see us like that."

I held my tongue.

"I know it's wrong what I did, but it's over now. I swear to you. I'm never going back to him. Hoes before bros, remember?"

"How long has this been going on?" I asked.

Her sobs grew louder. "Too long."

I felt sick to my stomach and wished I could be anywhere but here.

"Do you hate me? I know I would if I were you."

I lifted myself up to my knees, wanting to wretch but unable to. "No, I don't hate you. I thought you hated me."

"I could never hate you, Katie."

"I can't believe this is happening."

"I know, and I'm going to end it, I promise. Then it'll be like old times again."

I watched as a shadowy figure approached us. Was it him? I hated everyone and everything in this town, especially *him*. I hated myself, as well. And Harper's Point. I even hated that scumbag Dakota and was happy he was gone from my life. If only I could graduate from high school and get the hell out of Shepherd's Bay, I knew I'd be better off.

"Willow, don't do this," said the person in the shadows.

"I'm totally done with you," Willow said.

"You know that's not true. You know you love me."

"Yes, I love you, but I hate you more for what you've done to me."

I thought of the life growing in her stomach and wondered if she'd keep it. Would I keep it if it were me?

"I love you so much, Willow. You can't just walk away from what we have." He grabbed her arm.

"I can and I will. You ruined me when you got me pregnant."

"We can get a doctor to take care of it. Then everything will be good again."

"No, I'm going to keep the baby. Then I'm going to tell everyone in town what you did to me. And they'll know what a jerk you truly are."

"I can't let you do that." He squeezed her arm. "You'll destroy everything."

"I hate you!"

He slapped her.

"I don't care what you do to me. Did you kill Dakota, too? Because you knew he liked me? Because you were jealous of him?"

"Shut up! You know that's a lie." He shoved her, and she collapsed in my arms. "I'm so sorry, Willow. Will you please forgive me?"

"I'll never forgive you. You used me, and now I'm going to make you pay."

"I'm begging you to reconsider. I'll change. I'll be better and treat you right."

"I'm done with you. I'm leaving this town, and you can't stop me."

I cradled her head in my arms as she sobbed. His face came into full view, lit by the hanging moon. He took a step forward. Would he come over and manhandle me, too? Like he'd done to Willow? Like he'd done that night when he gave her a bloody nose? I thought of all the time I had spent with him, and it made me want to throw up.

"You two stay right here until I come back." Then he turned and took off toward the house.

"Please don't think worse of me." Willow looked up into my eyes.

"I don't," I said, burying my chin in her hair. She was my best friend in the world, and I finally knew the truth.

"You know what the saddest thing about all this is?"

I didn't want to know. Tears streamed down my face. I felt so sorry for her and what she was going through—and the terrible decision she would be forced to make. I felt sorry for myself, as well, for getting involved in this mess.

"I know it sounds weird, but I still love him."

"I don't understand. How can you love that jerk after everything he's done to you?"

"Because that jerk is still my father—and he's promised to make me a star."

Why now? Why has this sick memory just come back to me while I'm being held here against my will? I want to run out and tell the world what Gil Briggs did to his daughter. He baited me to come to that cabin by impersonating Willow and sending me those fake messages. Did he kill Willow because she threatened to tell everyone what he did? That he killed Dakota and impregnated his own daughter? What a disgusting person! He created Willow and raised her for his own sick benefit.

I'd read about girls who'd been groomed by powerful men. But groomed by her own father? Gil must have started in on Willow when she was a young girl, promising to make her a huge TV star, twisting her young mind like a French braid until she didn't understand the boundaries of love. It makes sense now: she couldn't understand right from wrong, because he'd warped her mind. She never tried to steal Dakota or Julian from me. No, she was merely struggling to come to terms with everything, to grasp what a normal relationship was and what it was not.

The restraint does not budge as I try to pull it off of whatever it's secured to. Numbness sets into my hand from the lack of blood flow, and my shoulder aches. I can't scream. I can't move or see anything or tell anyone where I am. Why did Gil leave me here? Will he return later to take care of me?

Gil Briggs now represents all that is evil to me. It makes complete sense. He killed Dakota because Dakota, like me, found out about Willow's sick relationship with him. Because of that, Willow made sure to keep Julian and me out of harm's way. Only she never thought I'd go to the lengths I did to discover their disgusting secret.

I try again to free myself, but it's futile. Sadly, I'm not going anywhere. Though I'm being held prisoner, I'm surprisingly calm. Everything is out of my hands now. At least I have the satisfaction of knowing who committed these crimes and who attacked me that night. I just need to stay calm and figure a way out of here. If only I could remove this blindfold, as well as the tape over my mouth, which is restricting my breathing.

ISLA

HE PAST THIRTY MINUTES OF DRIVING AROUND TOWN HAD PROVED fruitless. There had to be a better way than this. She had seen no sign of Ray's truck around town. No sign of Katie and Raisin. It felt like her personal hell was beginning all over again, only this time she'd lost Raisin, too. They had to be somewhere in this god-forsaken town. But where? If only they had a clue as to where Katie had gone.

She watched Karl drive now and remembered him as a young man, when they'd hiked some of the nearby hills. He had possessed a quiet confidence even back then, although she hadn't recognized it for what it was—a strength that emanated from deep within his core. Back then, she had just thought he was a shy, quiet kid. He was so totally different from Ray, whose bright luster had faded the more she got to know him.

Karl's finger tapped nervously against the wheel. What was he thinking? She watched the landscape fly past. Nothing in all this added up. Why would Katie take the gun out of her safe? And why would she take Raisin with her, knowing the danger the two of them faced? Could she have been worried that Drew might attack her? Isla had seen a side of Katie's boyfriend she'd never before experienced. She didn't believe he'd ever been abusive to Katie, but who knew? How about Coach Hicks, who, according to Karl, was living in the closet because of the small-town attitudes in Shepherd's Bay? Or Julian? That boy allegedly had a history of drugs and violence. What about Bob Oden, who was still bitter about losing his family's boatyard? Then there was Bugger Walsh and his long criminal history.

"I think we should turn back," Karl said.

"Back to where?"

"To Harper's Point. My gut is trying to tell me something."

"What is it telling you?"

He tapped his finger on the wheel and stared at the illuminated road ahead.

"Come on, Karl. Spit it out."

"I don't know if it means anything, but I dug into the Briggses' past. Did you know that a boy Willow once dated passed away from a heroin overdose? They moved to Maine soon after he died."

"Are you saying that Willow had something to do with the boy's death?"

"I don't know. It just seems odd that two boys she might have dated ended up dying."

"You said it was an overdose."

"That's what they ruled the boy's death, but the detective in charge of the case told me there was no indication the boy had ever used heroin before. He didn't have any track marks on his arm or any history of ever using the drug. But there was no evidence to prove murder, either."

"Willow is a high-maintenance girl, but do you see her committing murder?"

"I'm so confused right now, I don't know what to believe. All I know is what my gut is telling me. Whoever did this is somewhere on Harper's Point."

"So what are you going to do? Go house to house, searching for that person?"

"I don't know. I haven't thought that far ahead."

"I've been considering this crazy theory I have. Probably too crazy to even consider."

"Nothing's out of the realm of possibility. Let's hear what you've got."

"What if Gil set all this up to make his show more dramatic?"

"Okay." He seemed to think it over. "But kidnapping and murder? Seems a bit over the top."

"Maybe Dakota James's death was an accident."

"An accident?"

"See, I told you the idea was nutty."

"It's not nutty at all. Continue."

"Then he stages Willow's and Katie's disappearance, only something goes wrong. Very wrong and Katie gets hurt. But Willow hides out until it all blows over. Then she calls Katie and tells her she needs her help."

"That's not a crazy theory at all. If only we could locate Gil and find out the truth for sure."

"Maybe you should get a search warrant for the Briggses' home and take a look at his most recent film footage. It's possible that will lead us in the right direction."

"That's actually a great idea. And I didn't fully check out all the rooms in the Briggses' basement." He pulled the police cruiser over and took out his phone, then called the local judge and told him what he needed. He impressed upon the judge the necessity of approving the search warrant as soon as possible, as the lives of three kids were involved.

Karl came running out of the judge's home, waving the search warrant in his hand. He jumped in the car, handed Isla the warrant, and sped off toward Harper's Point, lights flashing and siren blaring.

She prayed to God that her kids were not in harm's way. She felt horrible for not having fully vetted her daughter's friendship with Willow.

Karl pulled up to the Briggses' house and parked in the circular driveway. He jumped out and sprinted over to the front door. Isla struggled to keep pace with him, but he was too fast. He rang the doorbell and waited as she pulled up next to him. She tried to catch her breath, regretting that she had let herself get so out of shape.

"You better wait in the car, Isla."

"I will most certainly not wait in the car, Karl Bjornson. My kids might be inside, and I'll be damned if I don't do everything in my power to save them."

"Isla, this search warrant is for law enforcement personnel only. You don't want to jeopardize the prosecutor's case if we discover something incriminating, do you?"

"The hell with your prosecution. I only want to find my kids, and you can't stop me."

He nodded, understanding that he couldn't prevent her from entering the house. Anxious to get inside, she reached out and rang the doorbell. It seemed that no one was inside. Or maybe Felicia refused to answer the door this late at night. Isla stepped back and surveyed the home. Not a light was on in the house. What would they do next? Karl reached out and turned the handle, and to their surprise, the door opened.

"Let's go," Karl said.

She followed him inside, her nerves sizzling. Karl flicked on the lights, and the cavernous interior came into view. He made straight for the door in the middle of the first-floor hallway. She followed him down a steep set of stairs, and together they opened every door they came across. There was still no sign of Katie or Raisin. Isla approached the last door and tried to pull it open but discovered it was locked.

"Help me with this one, Karl."

He ran over and tried to pull the door open, but it didn't budge.

"Shoot out the lock," she ordered.

"Jesus, Isla, I could lose my job for this."

"You'll lose more than your job if my kids are inside this room."

"Stand back." He took out his revolver, aimed it at the lock, and fired two shots, until it shredded.

Isla pushed the door open and flicked on the lights. On a table sat a keyboard and a huge computer screen. Gil's camera sat on a side table. On the other side of the room, she saw a twin bed. Maybe that was where Gil slept after he edited his film footage on the desktop computer. Felicia did say they were having marital problems.

Karl turned on the computer, and an image appeared and remained frozen on-screen. She recognized it as Willow. He pressed PLAY, and Willow came to life. She sat on a chair, gnawing seductively on her lustrous blond hair. Behind her the ocean sparkled through the floor-to-ceiling window. She wore a short denim skirt, and one of her tanned legs lay crossed over the other, bouncing nervously up and down. From behind the camera, Gil asked her a series of innocuous questions. Isla felt her stomach churning as she watched.

"What kind of music do you like, Willow?" Gil asked.

"All kinds, but mostly rap. I love Drake and Rihanna," Willow replied, strands of hair dangling from her rouged lips. "Depends on what kind of mood I'm in."

"What's your favorite mood for listening to music?"

"When I'm with someone I like."

"Have you found anyone yet?"

"Maybe." She giggled, and Isla realized she was high.

"How about singing? You have a beautiful voice."

"Thank you," she said a bit too sweetly.

"Could you sing something for me?"

"What do you want me to sing?"

"I'm sure whatever you choose will be good. Maybe you could show us some of your dance moves while you're at it."

"For real?"

"I think people would love to see your talent on display."

"Didn't they see it when I played Sandy Olsson onstage?"

"Sure, but that was a musical. I think people would like to hear you sing something a bit more contemporary."

"Why?"

"To hear your amazing vocal range."

"Oh, okay." She seemed to think about it. "How about if I sing 'I Will Always Love You,' by Whitney Houston?"

"Perfect. I love that song."

Willow stood and sang an amazing rendition, hitting all the right notes. When she was done, she sat back down on the chair and crossed her bare legs, refusing to look into the lens.

"What's the matter?" Gil asked.

"It's just hard to sing without an audience."

"Think of the camera as your audience."

"You know what I mean. I like performing in front of people and then hearing them applaud me afterward."

Gil clapped his hands together. "You were very good."

She glanced up and smiled briefly into the camera before looking back down again.

"You're so beautiful, Willow."

She swiped her hair over her studded ear.

"Would you put your hair up for me?"

She reached back and held her hair up in a bun.

"Perfect. Now dance a little for the camera. Close your eyes and let your body move on its own." Soft music started to play.

"How's this?" Willow asked.

"Great. You're doing wonderful."

"I love dancing for the camera."

"You want to be a star really bad, don't you?"

"More than anything in the world."

"Would you like to slip into something more comfortable?"

"What would you like me to wear?"

"You know what I like."

Isla turned away from the screen. "Shut it off, Karl. I can't watch any more of this filth."

He shut off the computer, and the screen went dead.

She felt sick to her stomach after watching this disgusting video. She looked over at Karl and saw him staring down at his shoes, as if he couldn't bear to be in her presence after what they both had witnessed.

"The sick bastard has been abusing his daughter." Bile formed in her throat.

"Maybe it wasn't Willow who killed those kids, after all."

"Gil got jealous when she started dating those boys."

"I can understand Dakota James, but how did he kill the kid out in LA? He had to get inside the house and administer a fatal dose."

"Gil worked in film. Maybe he promised to make the kid a star and then used that as an excuse to gain access to his home."

"It's possible. I read in the kid's file that his mother hoped to be a reality star."

"All this is secondary to finding my kids. Where the hell are they?"

"I'm really sorry, Isla. I honestly thought we might find them here."

"It's not your fault."

"Felicia must have left the house. I wonder where she went?"

"I don't care about her. I only want to find Katie and Raisin right now."

She started to tear up, and to her surprise, he came over and held her. She didn't resist. It felt good for once to be embraced. She needed someone to comfort her and tell her that everything would be all right. Her kids were in trouble, and there was nothing she could do to help them. What if Raisin experienced an episode? Would Katie be able to help him? Would he be able to help himself, assuming Scout was still by his side? Would whoever had kidnapped her children try to kill them? She didn't know how she'd go on living if something bad happened to Katie and Raisin.

KATIE

THE DOOR OPENS, AND I PREPARE FOR THE WORST. HAS GIL RETURNED to finish me off? I hear footsteps approaching.

The person removes the blindfold. It takes a second for my eyes to adjust. To my shock, I see that it's Raisin. I'm so happy to see him that I can barely contain myself. I look over, and to my surprise, I see Willow sitting many feet away from me, her eyes and mouth covered. I'm relieved it wasn't she who'd hit me with that bat. But where's Scout? What will happen to Raisin if his glucose goes haywire? He could die before help arrives. I mumble something, but the duct tape over my mouth prevents me from speaking coherently. My nose is clotted with mucous and nasty phlegm, and it's all I can do to get air into my lungs. Raisin's hand reaches down and gently peels the tape away from my lips. I open my mouth and gulp in air. Then he hugs me.

"Oh my God! Raisin! What are you doing here?"

"I snuck into the back of Dad's truck when you went upstairs."

"But why?"

"Because I knew you were up to something, Katie, and I didn't want to lose you again."

Tears of gratitude form in my eyes.

"I stayed in the back and waited for you to come out of that cabin. Finally, I saw someone escort you into the backseat of that truck that was parked there when we first arrived. When they went back inside the cabin, I snuck into the truck bed."

"Did you recognize who it was?"

"No, it was too dark."

"Why didn't you take Scout into the truck with you?"

"I couldn't risk him alerting the driver if something happened to me. Besides, I couldn't have gotten him up into that bed. He's heavy, and it was too high off the ground. So I told him to stay down."

"I'm scared, Raisin, but I'm so glad you followed me here."

"We need to get you and your friend out of this place," he says, pointing to Willow. "She's in pretty bad shape."

"Willow is unconscious. She really needs medical attention."

"What should we do?"

"Whoever did this handcuffed us to these pipes," I say, pulling my wrist in futility. "The only way out of here is to cut us free or find the key."

"Then what can I do? Tell me, Katie."

"I can't risk putting you in harm's way, Raisin."

"I know, but there must be some way I can help you."

"There is. I just don't know how right now."

"I can't stay here, or the bad person might do the same thing to me. Then I'll be no good to either of you." Raisin appears to consider his options. "I'll go upstairs and try to find a phone, and then I'll call Mom. She'll know what to do."

"But we don't even know where we are."

"I'm smart. I'll figure something out." He kisses my cheek and turns to leave.

"Wait!"

He turns to face me.

"You have to put the tape back over my mouth. And pull the blindfold down over my eyes, or else they'll know you were here."

"Right." He picks up the strip of duct tape and presses it against my mouth. Then he pulls the blindfold down until my eyes are covered.

"I love you, Katie," he says before scampering out of the room.

We lay together on the beach. I held Willow in my arms and allowed her to cry. I stared at the stars and listened to the tide coming in, thinking how much I wanted my old life back. The soft sand cushioned me, although the clamshells and dried seaweed straws pressed sharply into my skin. Willow rested her head on my lap and wrapped her long arm around me. I looked down and noticed that her eyes had started to swell. All of this combined to lull me to sleep. A disturbing sleep, but sleep nonetheless.

Sometime later I awoke to the sound of a thumping noise. Willow screamed, and I opened my eyes. Almost immediately I felt a blow to my head. I could barely see, the pain was so bad, and I assumed that Gil had returned to reclaim Willow. If she breathed a word of what he'd done, he knew he'd be going away to prison for a long time.

I stood dizzily and heard Willow's high-pitched screams. I rushed over to her and tried to fend off the blows. Blood dripped from my forehead and into my eyes. My vision became blurred. Something hard smashed into my face and knocked me to the sand. It surprised me more than anything else. I should have been unconscious from the blow, but for whatever reason, I wasn't.

My eyelids began to form into slits, and I felt disoriented and lost. Blood poured from cuts on my face. Willow screamed again, pleading for her life. Would we die out here on this beach? My ribs ached, as if broken. The only emotion coursing through me was fear, fight or flight. Willow shouted for me to run. She told me to forget about her and save myself. Since I had no fight left in me, I ran.

Through slitted eyes, I grasped shadows and forms. Every inch of my body trembled with pain. Blood flowed out of my nose and into my mouth, making it hard to breathe. The sound of the waves began to recede in the distance, informing me that I was running away from the shore.

I heard footsteps behind me.

I ran, bloodied, through the streets. Blurry images of affluence passed me on either side. Pebbles and sharp objects stabbed into my bare feet. I heard a shrill voice call out my name and realized that my attacker was on my tail. I had no desire to stop at someone's doorstep and ring their doorbell and beg for help. I knew they wouldn't help me in my condition. Stopping would only give my pursuer time to catch up and drag me away. Then, because of what I already knew, Gil would find a way to get rid of me. I pictured my head being forcibly held down in the ocean, seaweed filling my mouth and my eyes bulging, until I stopped breathing. He would make it look like I had gotten drunk and had accidentally waded out into the ocean and drowned.

I ran until all the expensive homes receded behind me. I made my way into the woods, and then deeper, pushing branches out of my way and stepping over sticks and thick brush. My blistered bare feet cried out for relief. Was someone still on my trail? Or was my mind playing tricks on me? No sense taking any chances. All I could think about was drowning and then my body drifting far offshore until it sank to the bottom of the ocean floor and became lobster bait.

My head felt as if it might explode, the pain had become so immense. Never in my life had I experienced a headache so agonizing. And yet I kept moving deeper into the woods, constantly looking behind me to see if Gil was still on my heels.

Streaks of light began to fill the sky. Although my vision remained blurry, I caught sight of a run-down hunting camp. The door was opened. I staggered inside, then tripped over a soiled mattress. I could barely see anything in front of me. Exhausted, I knew I could no longer run. Whatever happened to me now, so be it. I collapsed on top of that disgusting mattress and wept, clutching my head and feeling the scrapes and bruises on the soles of my feet. I had finally given up. I simply couldn't run any longer.

I prayed to God to watch over me. To bring an end to all this.

My arm hurts from being in the same position, and I can barely move my injured shoulder. I drift off for a short time and experience terrible dreams. When I come to, I vow not to fall asleep again, but to stay awake and alert.

I glance over at Willow, despite not being able to see her. But I can sense her presence in the room. When Raisin removed my blindfold, I noticed that her face was bruised and bloodied. I have so many questions to ask her.

Raisin! I pray that Gil doesn't get his hands on my little brother. I have no doubt that he'll try to hurt Raisin if he catches him snooping around in this house. Why hasn't he already killed us? He probably intends to. Maybe he's trying to figure out a way to get rid of us, so that none of this will point to him. Otherwise, there's no good reason why I'm still alive.

I was beginning to lose hope, until Raisin arrived. I don't want him here, but there's nothing I could have done to convince him to leave. Without Scout to watch over him, I worry more about his diabetes killing him than him getting found out by Gil. Hopefully, he'll be able to find a phone and call for help.

ISLA

INSTINCT TOOK OVER, AND SHE RAN UPSTAIRS AND DOWN THE HALL until she came to what she believed was Willow's room. Posters hung on the walls. Clothes lay strewn over the dresser and over the unmade bed. She searched around, not quite sure what to look for. Possibly a clue as to Raisin's and Katie's whereabouts.

She dumped the trash can over the desk, placed the can back on the floor, then hovered over the messy desk and rummaged through the trash, hoping to find something that might point her in the right direction.

"What are you doing?" Karl stood at the door.

"You have a search warrant, don't you?"

"That doesn't give us the right to trash the place."

"I'm sure they have enough money to hire a maid." She shuffled things around over the desk.

"Wouldn't our time be better served searching for Katie and Raisin?"

"You were the one with the gut feeling."

"Yes, but this?"

"It's pitch black outside, and we have no clue as to where they are. Do you really think driving around town will get us any closer to finding them?" She pulled open the desk drawer.

"Better than staying here."

She froze momentarily. "Oh my God!"

"What?"

"This." She held up a pregnancy test. "Two lines."

"What is it?"

"Willow is pregnant." She opened the laptop on the girl's desk, turned it on, and then opened a file. Hundreds of photos were saved in the file. She began to scan through them.

"Looks like she has had lots of suitors," Karl said, standing shoulder to shoulder with her.

"Julian and Dakota and some other boys I don't recognize."

"I really can't look at these." Karl walked away in disgust.

"She must be pretty insecure to have sent nude selfies of herself."

"Maybe one of these boys is the baby's father. Dakota? Julian?"

"It's possible, but after the video we just watched, the truth may be more awful than we think."

"That's too sick to even consider."

"Here's a photo of her and some boy standing on the Hollywood Walk of Fame."

"Can I see that?" Karl approached the desk again and gazed over her shoulder. "That's him."

"Who?"

"Jalen Stark. The LA boy who was found dead in his own home of a heroin overdose."

"Maybe Willow is the one who killed him."

"I don't know what to believe anymore."

Isla ran out of the room and into another bedroom. It was tidy, with the bed made to perfection, hospital corners and not a wrinkle to be seen. The bedroom was the size of the main floor of her home. She searched around, looking for any clues that might help them.

Karl stepped into the room. "What are you looking for now?"

"Felicia's laptop. These Briggses appear to be a photogenic bunch." She opened a desk drawer. "Aha!" She pulled out a MacBook. "Maybe we can find out more."

"What can it tell us?"

"I don't know. Let's find out." She turned on the computer and began searching.

"I can't believe these people don't use passwords," he said, standing next to her.

"No one ever uses a password on their home computer. Do you?"

"I don't even have a computer."

"You don't own a computer?" She found a bunch of photos.

"No need for one. I use the department's whenever I have the need."

"Felicia sure has a lot of pictures stored on here." She clicked on photo after photo.

"Every single one of them is from when she was younger. Same guy appears in most of them, too," Karl noted.

"You know who that guy is, right?"

He leaned in and studied the photo of Felicia kissing a man's cheek. "Well, I'll be damned. Gil."

"These were taken years ago, when she starred on that TV show."

"It's the slicked black hair that threw me. He looked like a movie star back in his younger days."

"Every single photo in this file is of that time in her life, when she starred on *Lost 'n' You*."

"Weird. Seems like she's been living her life in the past."

"Like a famous basketball player in town I know."

Karl started to say something but stopped himself.

"You'd think she'd have some pictures of her daughter on here. That's all I have on my computer, photos of Katie and Raisin growing up," Isla said.

"What do you think it means?"

"I think it means she badly misses her old life."

"Must be pretty sad to live in the past."

Her phone bleated. She pulled it out, hoping the caller was Katie or Raisin. But the caller ID was blocked. She answered the phone and, to her surprise, heard Raisin's voice.

"Raisin! Where are you?"

"I don't know, but I found Katie and Willow," he whispered. "Someone grabbed them and put them downstairs, in a basement. I snuck upstairs and found this phone and decided to call you."

"Why did you sneak off with Katie?"

"She had no idea that I hid inside Dad's truck. She wouldn't have let me come with her if she knew."

"Do you know why this person took Katie and Willow?"

"I don't know anything, Mom. I just want them rescued."

"Do you know who did this to them?"

"I don't know that, either."

"You need to be careful, Raisin. If the person knows you're in their house, they might try to grab you, too."

"Think I don't know that? It's why I'm whispering."

"Do you know where you're at?"

"I can't tell. It's too dark outside."

"Can you find out and tell me your whereabouts?"

"You're going to be really mad at me, Mom."

"It's okay, honey. I promise you I won't."

"I really want to find out where I am, but there's one problem."

"What is it?"

"I'm feeling really dizzy."

Her worst fear was becoming reality. "Is Scout with you?"

"I had to leave Scout behind in order to stay with Katie."

"Okay, honey, stay calm and relax. We'll find you, no matter what it takes."

"Oh crap."

"What is it, Raisin?"

She heard another voice in the background. Then she heard Raisin shouting at someone to leave him alone. Suddenly the line went dead. Isla felt all the blood drain from her face.

"What, Isla? Is he okay?"

"No, he's not okay. Whoever took Katie and Willow has just found my son."

"Oh no! I'm so sorry."

"It's worse than that. He's having a diabetic reaction and has no medicine." She turned to him. "He could die, Karl."

"Then we need to find him as soon as possible."

KARL

*T*HEY FACED THE WORST POSSIBLE SITUATION. HE COULDN'T IMAGINE how he would feel were it his own child in jeopardy. Double jeopardy, as it was, and not in the legal way. Raisin faced his mortality both from external and internal forces, now that his blood sugars had flared up at the worst possible time.

Once again, Karl had no answers. Their only hope had been if Raisin somehow managed to tell them his location. But he couldn't even do that. Not knowing where the kid was ate away at him. As a cop, he needed to be assertive and have a strategy always at hand. But now he had no idea what to do, and it made him feel powerless.

Isla paced back and forth in the room, thumbnail wedged between her teeth. He thought it incredible that she was able to keep herself together for the sake of her kids. Most women would have collapsed in a pool of their own tears. But not Isla Eaves. It was one of the reasons he so admired her.

He convinced her to get into the cruiser, telling her that the state police had brought in police dogs to help locate Raisin. They just needed to get a piece of his clothing in order to track his scent—and fast. She rocked in her seat as he drove to her home, and he knew that every second mattered.

He had sped off the bridge and was turning right onto Bay Road when he saw something at the top of the hill. Two glowing eyes approached his vehicle. Whatever it was, it was running straight downhill and toward them. There were lots of deer in town. And moose, too. Was this a coyote or a lynx? He slowed the cruiser, knowing that if he struck a moose out here, it would total the cruiser and put an end to their search. Or worse, the moose might crash through their windshield and kill them both. He'd responded to a few moose-car collisions in his lifetime, and the outcome was never pretty.

Isla shrieked and pointed a finger at the animal running toward them. Karl hit the brakes and stopped to watch it pass. When he saw it, he couldn't quite believe his eyes.

"It's Scout! He's alerted on Raisin," Isla said.

"No way he can smell Raisin from out here."

"Don't doubt that dog, Karl. Scout's our medical miracle."

"But where's he going?"

"Who cares? Just turn around and follow him. Go!"

Karl cut the wheel and started down Bay Road, then slowed to keep pace behind Scout. This dog amazed him. Could he really detect Raisin from so far away? Scout bolted onto the bridge and sprinted down the center line. Karl maintained his speed, careful to watch for any oncoming traffic. But it was late, and there were no cars out this time of night. The bridge's lights reflected off Scout's Day-Glo vest as he ran, giving him an almost supernatural glow.

It was one of the most amazing things he'd ever seen. Isla shouted out the window and encouraged Scout to run. If only Scout could go faster. But he knew the dog was running as fast as he possibly could. How far had he run already? His lungs and legs must be ready to burst by now, but nothing except death would stop this animal from reaching Raisin.

He bounded off the bridge and sprinted onto Harper's Point. Karl switched his high beams on to keep the dog in sight. Scout sped through the dark streets, heading straight to the place from which they had come. He turned the corner and saw the Briggses' home up ahead.

Isla turned and stared at him, in shock. Had Raisin been under their noses the entire time? In the Briggses' home? But how could that be? They'd scoured every inch of it. Was there a secret room in the Briggses' home, buried below the basement? But Karl knew that couldn't be the case. He knew a little about the geology in this part of town. Engineers could dig only so far down on Harper's Point before hitting the water table.

The dog continued running, not seeming to tire or slow. He headed down the middle of the street and toward the Briggses' home. Upon reaching it, Scout banked left and made straight for the McCallisters' residence. What the hell was going on?

Karl hit the brakes between the two homes and skidded to a stop. He and Isla jumped out. He didn't see Scout until he rounded the corner and observed the dog frantically jumping up and down, and shaking his body next to the French door located at the back of the house. The sound of waves gently lapped the shore.

Isla sprinted toward Scout, but the dog was so frantic to find Raisin that he leaped up and nipped her nose.

"Karl, take out your gun!" Isla shouted, rubbing her nose with the palm of her hand. "We need to go inside."

He'd been so mesmerized by all this that he had forgotten momentarily why he even came here. He took out his revolver and smashed it through the French door. Shards of glass fell all over the tiled patio under his feet. He reached inside the broken glass, opened the door, and watched as Scout disappeared inside the house.

Scout ran too fast, and so they followed the sound of his footsteps. Karl felt confused and unsure of himself, but the adrenaline coursing through his veins kept him moving. Down the stairs they scampered, and they kept going until they reached a locked door. Scout stood on his hind legs and started scratching frantically at the wood.

"Stand back," Karl said.

"Be careful. They might be near the door." Isla grabbed Scout by the collar and, with all her might, held him back.

He stood on his toes and off to the side, pulled out his revolver, and blasted the lock until the door swung open. Isla released Scout's collar and he sprinted inside, and then he and Isla followed behind the Lab.

He saw a home movie theater with six rows of plush seating and an aisle running down the middle. A film played on a large screen near the back. Two faces in the front row turned toward him, and instinctively, he raised his gun. He realized it was Gil and Julian and lowered his weapon. Scout disappeared down a row to his left, and the room suddenly filled with the voices of the actors speaking on-screen.

"Don't move, or I'll shoot the boy," said a voice from the shadows.

"Felicia?" Isla said.

"How did you find me?" Felicia emerged from behind the curtains along the left side of the theater.

"Actually, Scout found him. My son's suffering a life-threatening diabetic reaction and is in desperate need of my assistance. Please, there's not much time."

"Don't move! Either of you." The woman turned to Karl. "And I suggest you drop that gun on the floor, cop, if you don't want the boy to die."

"Okay. Take it easy. I'm putting it down now."

Realizing he had no other choice, he placed his gun down on the tiled floor and then stood up straight and held his arms up for her to see. He could barely make out the woman's face because of the shadow enveloping her.

"Felicia, please let me attend to my son before it's too late," Isla pleaded. "I'm begging you."

"If you try anything, I'll shoot the both of you," Felicia said.

"I promise you that I'll do whatever you say if you let me give him his dose. He's sick and could possibly die if he doesn't get it."

"You're ruining my show." Felicia pointed toward the screen.

"Please."

"Hurry up, then."

"I'll need the lights on." Isla ran to the left middle row in order to tend to Raisin.

"Fine. But I want the cop to keep his arms up and to sit down in one of the seats in the back row. And slowly."

Karl gently toed the revolver under a seat in the last row, then sat in that very seat. He dragged his foot back as far as he could to locate the weapon but struggled to find it. He looked up and watched as the woman moved behind him and switched on the lights. Isla lowered her head behind the theater seat to get a reading on Raisin's blood sugar. He sensed Felicia standing behind him with gun in hand, pointing it at his head.

Feeling helpless, he aimed his gaze toward the drama unfolding on-screen. It took a few seconds before he realized that he was watching a younger version of Felicia Briggs, back in the day when she starred on that TV show. He hadn't seen *Lost 'n' You* until now. What struck him was how beautiful and glamorous Felicia was back then. She very much resembled her daughter, only softer and less angular, and with curly blond hair.

"Thank you, Felicia," Isla said, breathing a sigh of relief. "He was low, but he should be okay now. I'll need to test him again in fifteen minutes."

"I suggest you do as you're told if you want your son to stay alive," Felicia said.

"Of course. Anything you want," Isla said.

Felicia directed her attention to the drama on-screen. "Look at me up there on-screen. So beautiful and young. Gil said he would make a big star out of me."

"But you already were a big star."

She laughed. "Not big enough. Gil promised that I would be in movies and win Academy Awards and become a household name. For years, he claimed to be writing a screenplay with me in mind. Of course it never materialized, because of *her* and that stupid reality show."

Karl kept his gaze on Gil and Julian, both of whom were still sitting in the front row, although on opposites sides of the aisle. Their head movements seemed unnatural, and Karl wondered if Felicia had drugged them.

"Why are you doing this, Felicia? You have a wonderful husband and an extremely talented daughter. You don't need to be a star again to validate your life," Isla said.

"A wonderful husband? Ha!" Felicia switched off the lights, and only the glow of the screen cast light upon them. "That piece of shit forgot all about me as soon as I had *her*." Her voice dripped with hatred.

"I don't understand," Isla said.

"Everything I did was for Gil. So my husband would love me like he once did and make good on his promise to turn me into a star again. We were madly in love and had the most wonderful times together when we first started dating. It was why I broke up with that moron Dean. Then *she* came along and ruined everything—my career, my marriage, and my beautiful body."

"Where are Katie and Willow, Felicia?"

"They're alive, for now, so don't worry your head about those two."

"I need to see Katie," Isla said.

"Willow told me all about that daughter of yours. She said Katie's father is a useless jerk who is never around for her. Katie told Willow how neglected she feels and how you give all your attention to your sick son and demented father. Do you have any idea how alone your daughter has been? It's no wonder she fell under Willow's spell."

Karl knew Felicia was saying this in order to push Isla's buttons. Everyone knew Isla to be a dedicated and loving mother.

"How could you possibly love your husband when you couldn't even love your own daughter?" Isla said.

"You really think I wanted to raise a snot-nosed, bratty kid?" Felicia scoffed. "Gil begged me to have a child with him. He said it would be good for my public image, and that after *it* was born, he'd do everything in his power to get me another starring role. Wouldn't you know, he lied. But that's men, right?"

"And yet you continued to love him, even though he ended up loving your daughter more than he loved you?"

"I tried over and over to prove how much I loved him. It seemed the more I demonstrated my love for Gil, the more he pushed me away, until I had nothing left to give. I lost myself in him, my identity and my sense of self-worth. He became so obsessed with Willow that it seemed like nothing else mattered in his life, including me."

"Is that why he killed Dakota James? To keep him away from her?"

"What do you think?"

"Don't listen to her!" Gil shouted from the first row. His voice sounded strained.

"Shut up, Gil. You've relinquished your right to speak," Felicia said, charging down the aisle so that she stood directly in front of him. She lifted the gun and pointed it at his head. "Don't make me do this."

Karl shoved his right foot under the seat and moved it around until he located the revolver. He carefully nudged it forward. After slouching down in the seat, he placed his toe against the trigger and slowly dragged the revolver out from under the seat. Then he waited for the right moment to reach down and snatch it.

"Who killed Dakota James?" Isla asked.

"Gil killed him so he wouldn't reveal Gil's dirty little secret. That he likes his own daughter better than his wife."

"She's lying," Gil said. "She seduced and then killed that kid because she didn't want me going to jail. He was going to tell the cops and ruin me." He stopped to cough violently. "All those years and you thought I was writing a screenplay for you. You were such a fool, Felicia."

"You lied about the screenplay?" Felicia said.

"Yes, to keep you off my back."

"I killed those kids for you, Gil. To keep you out of jail. And because I loved you and thought you would turn me into a star again."

"Who are you kidding? You only loved yourself, Felicia," Gil said, turning to face them. "She hoped to win back my love by murdering those boys, but I wanted nothing to do with her. And if you don't believe me, ask Julian."

Felicia laughed. "Guess the cat's out of the bag now, sweetheart. Why would you admit to being such a lying pig?"

"Because I'm dying, Felicia. You shot me in the belly, remember?"

"So I did. I guess *true love* is finally letting go of the ones you love." She lifted the gun, took aim, and fired a bullet into his skull. Gil slumped over, and blood dripped down the back of his seat. "Finally, I'm free from your cruel version of love, dear. Thanks for nothing. Now I'll be forced to take care of the rest of this mess myself."

Karl was shocked that Felicia had just killed her husband in cold blood. Would she now try to kill the rest of them?

"I might as well tell you everything, since I have nothing left to lose." Felicia walked halfway up the aisle and stopped. "I may not have been the cat's meow in Gil's eye, but I can still turn a head or two, especially with these horny young boys hanging around all the time and drooling over *her*."

"You seduced Dakota?" Isla said.

"I suppose you could say that. I lured him to that boat shed with a seductive promise." She laughed. "All it took was a special drink to relax him. Then I hit him over the head with Willow's bat, and down he went."

"What about Jalen Stark?" Karl said.

"So Shepherd's Bay's finest speaks." Felicia walked over to him with the gun pointed at his head. "You found out about that boy, did you?"

"It was no accidental overdose, was it?"

"Hardly. And yet the police had no evidence to prove otherwise. Jalen called Gil that evening and told him he was planning to go to the cops and tell them what he saw Gil and Willow doing after a party one night."

"He barged in on them?"

"I don't know all the sleazy details," she said. "But I despised Willow for coming between us, even when she was a little girl. Gil said she reminded him of a younger version of me. He said I changed after the pregnancy and became a different person. Well, I changed for him by having that little brat. I gained weight, added wrinkles, and suffered from postpartum depression. I loved him so much that I couldn't bear to see him go away to prison, especially when he claimed to be writing a screenplay with me in mind. So I took care of the situation with Jalen the way I took care of my costar seventeen years ago."

"You killed Dean, too? Why?" Karl said.

"He was a major pain in the ass on and off set, high maintenance and never on time. Stupid jerk could never remember his lines and was always hungover. Sure, I liked him in the beginning. He was harmless fun. Then Gil came into my world, although I tried to resist his charms. I told him I was involved with Dean, but he kept wooing me with flowers and gifts and saying he could make me into a big star. Give the man credit. He was persistent. He finally convinced me that if Dean was out of the picture, I'd be the sole star of the show and have tons of leverage. Then go on to act in block-busters and win awards. He said that with his help, I would become America's sweetheart."

"So you decided to kill Dean?" Isla asked.

"Not at first. But Gil said they couldn't fire Dean, because the ratings were too good, and Dean was under contract for season two. There was only one way out, and the way he phrased it made it sound like it was an idea that only I could pull off. It took only one injection to do the trick, and knowing Dean's troubled history with drugs, no one had any reason to believe otherwise. Dean even let me shoot him up."

Julian began to cry in the front row. Karl had forgotten about him. Had he also been shot? Was he here because this was his house or because he, too, had witnessed Gil and Willow's debauchery?

Felicia became irritated as Julian continued to wail. She shuffled down the aisle, keeping the gun aimed at him. Julian cried out in agony, saying his parents were upstairs and had been shot by Felicia and left for dead. Felicia ordered him to shut up. Rather than stop, Julian pressed his head into the barrel of the gun and begged her to end his misery.

Felicia's finger tickled the trigger as she looked over at Isla. "You're just lucky this idiot kid came along when he did, or you would have ended up in the bay."

"So it was you who tried to run me off the road," Isla said.

"Of course it was me. Why do you think I called you to come over? I was the one who followed you after that wash and blow-dry." She turned her attention back to Julian. "Okay, lover. Time to say good-bye."

Karl reached down and snatched the gun off the toe of his shoe. Then he jumped up and fired the weapon until he emptied it. Blood spattered against the screen behind Felicia. She staggered back, in shock, eyes open, until she collapsed against the screen, which showed her younger self on that fictional college campus, kissing her handsome costar, Dean Wells. Music played as the cred-its started to roll.

Isla clutched Raisin to her bosom and turned back toward Karl. Whether her expression was one of horror or gratitude, Karl didn't quite know. Or care. This long nightmare was finally over. Or would soon be over, once they found Katie and Willow.

He called the police station for support and then sprinted out of the room to search for the two girls. His best guess was that they were somewhere inside the bowels of this house.

KATIE

I'M BACK AT THE HOSPITAL, WITH MY FAMILY ALL AROUND ME. MY ARM'S in a sling, my shoulder having been dislocated and broken in two places. Raisin lies in the bed next to me and must stay the night for tests and observation. Sitting next to the bed is Scout. Normally, the nurse told my mother, dogs weren't allowed in the hospital for sanitary reasons, but because he was a service dog, an exception would be made.

Scout saved my brother's life. He saved my life, too. We always knew that he was our miracle dog. We just never knew how truly *special* he was. The police found my father's truck three miles from the McCallisters' home, at that cabin next to Dexter's Pond. The Briggses owned the cabin, and it was where we were held prisoner before we were relocated to the McCallisters' basement. Raisin left Scout at that log cabin so he could follow me. No one knows exactly how that dog did it. Did he really scent Raisin's glucose level from three miles away? And then have the smarts to follow that scent all the way to the McCallisters' home? I could hardly believe it myself—and yet it happened.

Willow's resting in the room next to mine. I hear she's in rough shape. The nurses are not allowing anyone inside the room. I feel sorry for her now that she's all alone in the world. Relieved too. I wonder if she knows that her parents are dead. Or that Felicia shot her father in the head. Or that Officer Bjornson killed her mother before she had the chance to shoot Julian. Would she care? She couldn't have been born with worse role models. It amazes me that she made it this far in life with those two sickos.

She'll survive. She's talented beyond words. I must admit that those two at least gave her that. She turns eighteen in the fall and can make her own decisions. Will she stay in Maine or go else-where? I need to find out what her plans are for the future, now that she's been liberated from those two monsters. We need clo-sure. A time to say our good-byes.

Visiting hours are nearly over. I'm thankful for that. I'm worn out. My entire body hurts. My head, too, although I'm glad that at least I have my full memory back. It's hard to be nice to everyone when all you want to do is run screaming from this small town. And yet I feel deeply, intimately connected to Shepherd's Bay and will be sad to one day leave.

But leave I will.

My mother hugs me. My father goes next, followed by all my friends and relatives. They love me, and I love them, but I can't wait for them to leave. I need peace and quiet right now. I need time alone with Raisin. Scout still stares at me with that appraising look, and yet how can I be upset with him? Not after the way he saved our lives in such a dramatic fashion. I'm thankful for what he's done, and yet on the other hand, it's pretty sad knowing that I'll never be as courageous as that dog.

I close my eyes and try to forget all that's happened. It's a far cry from trying to remember all the bad things. Sometime later that night, I slip out of bed and, wearing nothing other than my nightdress, make my way to the door. I open it, peek out, and no-tice that the hallway is empty. Looking both ways, I see that the coast is clear. I scoot out of my room and slip into the room next door. It's dark inside this room, and I can't turn on the lights, for fear of being seen. I tiptoe to the bed and take her in. Despite her battered and bruised face, her plump, blistered lips, she still looks beautiful.

"Willow," I whisper, gently shaking her shoulder.

Her eyes slowly open, and she smiles at me.

"It's me. Katie."

"Katie Eaves," she says in a raspy voice. She reaches out and clasps my hand.

"How are you holding up?"

"I'm alive. What more can I ask?"

"Do you know what happened?"

She nods.

"So you know that your parents are dead?" I ask.

The hint of a smile comes over her face, and I can't say I blame her.

"They can't hurt you anymore," I tell her.

"My mother hated me from the day I was born. She resented all the attention my father showered on me."

"You're free from them now."

"As crazy as it sounds, I'll miss my father. At least he cared about me and wanted to make me into a star."

Her words stun me. How could she still love that monster after the way he abused her?

She goes on. "Not exactly the way I planned my life. At least I'm free to be whoever I want to be now."

"What about your pregnancy?"

"I lost it the night my mother attacked us. I wouldn't have kept it, anyway."

"I'm so sorry."

"Thanks. Probably for the best. Bad parenting runs in my genes." She pauses to stare out the window. "I never thought it would be my mother who'd turn on me. Mothers are supposed to love and protect their daughters, not hate them. I couldn't help being born, but I couldn't risk bringing a child into *that* crazy life."

"I couldn't imagine having a baby at our age." Nor a baby fathered by my own father.

"Perfect little Katie Eaves. I never wanted you to get involved. You were the only true friend I ever had. You were someone I could trust."

"What will you do now?"

"I'll most likely move back to LA and try my hand at acting. You should think about joining me."

"Thanks, but I'm going away to college."

"Who wants college when you can be a star?"

"Stardom is not in the cards for me, like it is for you."

"You can get character parts. Walk-on roles. Besides, there's lots of good colleges out in LA. I can pay your tuition once I get my inheritance. We can even be roomies. Hoes before bros, remember?"

The offer sounds enticing, but I know that I'll never go anywhere with her, especially after everything that has happened. I realize I don't know who the real Willow Briggs is. I need normalcy and routine in my life. I never want to live that insane lifestyle again.

"I'm going to be a big star, Katie. You could, too, if you really wanted."

I laugh a sad laugh. "No thanks."

"That's the only life I have ever wanted, and I have done everything in my power to get it," she says, releasing my hand. "Didn't you see me on TV? *TMZ* and *Extra* covered this whole ordeal. The only surviving child of the once famous *Lost 'n' You* actress, Felicia Briggs, and noted television producer Gil Briggs. I'm even getting movie offers for my story."

"I have to get back to my room now."

"How's Raisin?"

"Okay, I guess. They're keeping him overnight for observation."

"Tell him I said hey."

"Will do."

"And that amazing dog of his . . . Someone should make a movie about Scout and how he saved everyone's lives."

"Yeah, that'd be pretty cool," I say. "I gotta get going now. G'bye, Willow."

"Later, Katie Eaves."

I tiptoe out of her room and return to mine. I slip back into bed, crawl under the sheets, and close my eyes. I can't wait for Willow to get better and move out to LA. I can't wait to have my old life back.

I lay in that hunting camp that horrible night, on that soiled mattress, in the middle of the woods, worried that Gil was still coming for me. Worried that he might kill me, like he had killed

Dakota. Only I didn't realize that it was Felicia who was chasing me and not Gil. She was doing it for him. So he wouldn't disappear from her life and go to prison. So he would make her a star once again. My head hurt so bad that I couldn't lift it off that mattress without screaming in agony.

Maybe I was delusional and in the throes of concussion-like symptoms. I hid out in that dilapidated hunting camp, reflecting on what had happened, although time lost all meaning in my paranoid state.

I knew that Drew loved me in a way I could never reciprocate. If I stayed with him, I'd end up like my mother: stuck in a bad relationship, with nowhere to turn. Then I'd never leave Shepherd's Bay. So no, I decided I would break up with him as soon as I got out of that hunting camp—if I ever got out. Life was too short to have a boyfriend you didn't love.

My senior year would be defined by what happened to me, as well as by my relationship with Willow. I needed to get through this ordeal and then escape from Shepherd's Bay and leave all this nastiness behind me. Attend college and get a good education. Land the kind of job that would allow me to be self-sufficient and happy. No way I wanted to be dependent on a pathetic man like my father. And a useless and unreliable man at that.

I promised myself that I would finally confront my father about his "seaweed business." To tell him that I knew it was a cover for selling drugs to all the rich kids in town, using Bugger Walsh as the go-between. That was how I was able to buy those drugs in the first place, with Dakota promising me full acceptance into that high society if I came through for him. I'd become a drug seller and user. For that reason, I promised myself I would no longer be a daddy's girl and allow my father to skate by on his good looks and charm. He needed to be held accountable for the way he treated us, especially my mother.

At the time, I had no idea how much time passed in that hunting camp in the woods. Later, it was explained to me that I'd gone missing for two whole days. I remember listening to my stomach growl. Then an overwhelming thirst came over me. My mouth felt dry and parched; my tongue, crusted over like burnt toast. I forced myself to sit up on that mattress and allow the pain and nausea to pass. I knew I would die if I stayed there any longer. Then, mustering all my energy, I staggered out of that dump and wandered until I stumbled onto a road. A car pulled over. A woman who knew my father got out and helped me. She called my father, then an ambulance, and I ended up in the hospital with that traumatic head injury.

My nightmare was finally over.

But my new nightmare had just begun.

The next day brings more of the same. Smiles, hugs, and kisses. Cookies and cakes. A doctor comes in and says how lucky I am to be alive. He announces that both Raisin and I can go home that afternoon but that he needs to talk to me before I leave.

My father leans over the bed and hugs me. I can practically smell the booze on his breath.

"I know about your *seaweed* business," I whisper in his ear.

He freezes, his whiskered cheek pressing up against mine.

"Do you really have to sell drugs?"

"I did it only to help your mom pay all those bills."

I don't know why I'm so mad, considering that I too am guilty of helping spread drugs in Shepherd's Bay.

"I swear to you, Katie, it was only temporary. I'm all done with that now."

"Because of what happened to your kids? Is that what it took?"

"I swear I'll make it up to you."

"How about making it up to Mom instead? Your loving wife, remember?"

I decide not to sound off about everything. About his drinking and pot smoking. His graphic paintings. About how I know he's been cheating on Mom all these years. I don't say it, because I know he'll never change. He's Ray "Swisher" Eaves.

Instead, I reach up and hug my father. Tears drip down my cheeks as his familiar scent fills my nostrils. I squeeze him as hard as I can because I love him, and because I'm very thankful he's here with me, and that he is not a monster like Willow's father. Despite all his faults, I realize that I need him in my life, and maybe always will.

I really don't want to go home and deal with all the sickness, poverty, and deceit that will once again engulf this family. But I will. Despite everything that's happened, I love them. My senior year is coming, and I've promised to make the most of it. To spend quality time with my mom and hang out with Raisin. To be as good a friend and a student as I can possibly be. And to try not to let Scout's constant withering scrutiny bring me down.

That's all I want before I leave town and head off to college. I don't think that's asking too much.

"Katie, can I speak to you for a minute?" the doctor says, closing the door behind him.

"Sure," I say as I'm gathering up my things. "What's up?"

"Please, sit down."

I sit on the bed and watch as he pulls up a chair and plops down.

"How are you feeling?" he asks.

"Okay, except for my shoulder."

"I'm afraid I have something to tell you."

Do I have cancer? Or some other serious disease? His tone scares me, and I tense up.

"The blood tests we took indicate that you're three months pregnant."

"Pregnant?" The word sounds foreign coming out of my mouth. It makes no sense. "No, that can't be."

"I'm afraid the test doesn't lie. You're young, and you've been victimized. If you want, you can terminate the pregnancy."

"Terminate?"

He coughs. "Abort it."

"Have an abortion, you mean?"

"Yes, and it's totally your decision. You don't even have to tell your parents if you don't want to."

This conversation feels surreal. Then I suddenly remember that night with Dakota, after he read his fake poems to me. He unrolled the condom and then peeled it off after a few minutes, telling me not to worry, that he would be very careful. I was high and scared and stupid. It was my first time having sex. This is the last memory to come back to me, that painful night when I lost my virginity.

I thank the doctor and then walk out of the room in a daze.

KARL

*T*HINGS WENT BACK TO NORMAL. HE RECEIVED A COMMENDATION FOR his brave actions and quick thinking in that home theater. He went back to his regular day shift, cruising the streets and pulling over the occasional speeder. Showing up at domestics and taking drunk, abusive husbands to jail. Chief Scroggins finally retired, and he applied for the job. Everyone said he'd be the perfect candidate after the way things had played out. The other officers liked and respected him, and the money would be better. *Why not?* he figured.

He hiked all that summer, on his days off. It cleared his mind and helped him fight the intense feelings of loneliness he often experienced. His daughter visited for a few awkward days, and the visit proved to be a baby step forward in their relationship. He noticed that the Briggses' house went up for sale. What had become of Julian, he didn't know. The bitterness and evil of the past few months had left a sour taste in his mouth.

At least a few times a week, he drove by Isla's little shop. Business seemed good, as she was always working on a client whenever he cruised past. They hadn't talked much since it all went down, and that was probably a good thing. It seemed like nothing had changed in her life. Ray was still in the picture, although Karl couldn't for the life of him understand why. Was she waiting for when the kids graduated from high school? Would she leave him then? Or maybe— and this was something he couldn't even begin to fathom—she still loved him. It seemed incomprehensible. But there it was.

Today the sun shone with a late summer intensity. He put on his hiking gear and made his way up the mountain he and Isla once climbed together back in high school. He remembered when they reached the top, then held hands and kissed. As he recalled that day, he pulled out the sandwich he'd packed and began to unravel the wax paper. He could see Shepherd's Bay down below. And Harper's Point, the suspension bridge, as well as the rugged Atlantic Ocean. A cool breeze refreshed his face as he gazed down at the town he had sworn to serve and protect.

Life could be worse.

ISLA

Already November and a light snow had started to fall. Katie sat next to her on the couch, and Raisin lay sprawled on the carpet, with Scout curled by his side. A fire crackled in the wood stove. Raisin was putting together a Lego starship, and it appeared nearly done.

She glanced at Katie while waiting for their favorite show to come back from commercial break. Her belly bulged, as she was due to give birth in a few weeks. Understandably, her daughter had changed during the ordeal, and Isla detected a noticeable coolness in her demeanor, as if she'd decided to keep a psychic distance from everyone. It was a subtle observation that only a mother could make. Then again, Katie was a senior in high school and eager to graduate. She had endured that terrible ordeal, only to come out the other end carrying a dead boy's baby.

Isla couldn't believe she was going to be a grandmother.

Drew had not taken the news well when Katie broke up with him. He had come to her and cried, had begged and pleaded for her to take him back, saying he would raise the baby as if it was his own. But Katie had refused and had told him it was over between them. Isla was glad that they were no longer together. No way did she want her daughter to end up like her, stuck in an unhappy and unfulfilling marriage. Sure, her life could be worse. At least she had Katie and Raisin—for the time being. And Ray being away from home all the time wasn't the worst thing in the world. She realized that she could survive and prosper without him.

She thought of Karl when lonely, which happened on more occasions than she cared to admit. Okay, she thought about him a lot, which was why she hadn't had any contact with him. She always noticed when he cruised past the shop, but she wasn't leaving Ray anytime soon. A vow was a vow, no matter that Ray had broken his own vow so many times now that no one would blame her if she left him.

Of course, things could change. She told herself that she reserved the right to kick him out once the kids graduated from high school. He was the one who had broken their marriage contract, not her.

Everything seemed fine at the moment. Her shop had grown, and she was busier than ever. Raisin's blood sugars seemed to be stabilizing as of late. Katie's grades were stellar, and she was planning to enroll at the community college come fall. All Katie's plans had changed when she learned of her pregnancy. It had been the same way for Isla all those years ago, after that lecherous professor had put his filthy hands on her and ruined her college experience. Then Ray had gotten her pregnant, forcing them to marry.

Leaving this town would have helped Katie escape the horrors she suffered. But the decision to keep the baby had been all Katie's. At least she had her family to assist her through these tough times, as well as a supportive community willing to help her raise the child.

Beckett had died from his gunshot wound, but Samantha had managed to live. One day she and Julian had vanished from town without a trace. Isla had no idea where they'd moved to, but she felt sorry for them. The Briggses' home had sold quickly, to no one's surprise, and rumor had it that Willow was set to inherit everything once she turned eighteen. But then Willow had also disappeared from Shepherd's Bay, and no one had heard from her or seen her since. Not even Katie had heard from her. Had a relative whisked her away? Where had she gone?

But maybe that was a good thing. No, that was most definitely a good thing. Through no fault of her own, Willow had become a bad influence on her daughter. Isla didn't blame Willow for what had happened to her while she was growing up. Gil and Felicia had messed her up so bad that she had no sense of right and wrong. This was why she had gravitated to such a nice girl like Katie. Isla couldn't believe that parents could treat their own child so horribly. She wished her the best in life, but she was also glad that Willow no longer lived in Shepherd's Bay.

The sound of Katie shrieking brought Isla back to reality. What was wrong? Had her water broken? Was she ready to give birth? Their favorite TV show, a sitcom, had returned from commercial break just before Katie sounded off. The three of them loved this show. It was about a blue-collar family struggling to make a life for themselves. It was a clean family show they could all relate to. The two teen daughters were hilarious and were total opposites, and the older son, Jake, was the kind of boy all the girls dreamed of dating.

Katie shrieked again. Isla turned and noticed that she was pointing at something. Raisin shot up, as did Scout. Had Scout scented her son? It took Isla a split second before she saw what Katie was pointing at. She gazed at the drama on-screen and couldn't believe her eyes.

The girl Jake had brought home to meet his parents was none other than Willow Briggs.

ACKNOWLEDGMENTS

I need to thank the many people who helped with the writing and publication of this book, starting with my amazing agent, Evan Marshall, whose encouragement and advice helped make this novel the best that it could be. A big thanks also goes to my fantastic editor, John Scognamiglio, for his spot-on editing and guidance. I was totally amazed by Rosemary Silva's eagle-eyed proofreading skills, so big thanks to her. Thanks to the publicity and marketing team at Kensington for all your efforts.

I'd also like to thank my good friend, Tim Queeney, whose input contributed greatly to this manuscript. Also, Julie Kingsley, who advised me how to handle the character of the teenage girl in this novel. And thanks to all my friends and fellow authors who helped me along the way.

My biggest gratitude is to a fellow author, Fiona Quinn, who generously gave of her time and taught me all about service dogs and childhood diabetes. I am indebted to her and hope, in some small way, this book helps to educate the public about these amazing dogs.

Last, but not least, I'd like to thank my family for their patience and love. Without Marleigh, Allie, and Danny, I would never have been able to write this novel.